ONEIROS

A NOVEL

SIR CHARLES SHULTS III

authorHOUSE®

AuthorHouse™
1663 Liberty Drive
Bloomington, IN 47403
www.authorhouse.com
Phone: 833-262-8899

Published by AuthorHouse 09/28/2022

ISBN: 978-1-6655-7062-6 (sc)
ISBN: 978-1-6655-7061-9 (e)

For Patricia Dixon and James Calvert

Oneiros – (ō-nī'-rōs)

In Greek mythology, *Oneiroi* were the crafters of dreams. The dreams of man were said to come from two gates; one made of horn from which true dreams came, and one made of ivory from which false dreams came. The people, animals, objects, and settings of each dream had to be made by these beings and this was the origin of all our dreams and their contents. *Oneiros* is the personification of dreams. According to Homer, *Oneiros* dwell on the dark shores of the western Oceanus.

"And there the children of dark Night have their dwellings, Sleep and Death, awful gods. The glowing Sun never looks upon them with his beams, neither as he goes up into heaven, nor as he comes down from heaven. And the former of them roams peacefully over the earth and the sea's broad back and is kindly to men; but the other has a heart of iron, and his spirit within him is pitiless as bronze: whomsoever of men he has once seized he holds fast: and he is hateful even to the deathless gods."

– Homer

TABLE OF CONTENTS

CHAPTER 1

H e was just sitting on a park bench tossing a few crumbs of something to the birds. I was eating a half a sandwich and watching a blue balloon drifting in the late summer afternoon. Distantly, faintly, I heard some child cry out about something and failed to connect the cry with the errant scrap of rubber and helium.

"Somewhere in the universe" a mellow and slightly hoarse-sounding voice intoned gravely, "there is a world that has precisely our motion through space, our distance from a sun quite like our own, and it is spinning through its night just as we spin through our day." I looked slightly to one side, saw a little more of his long, somewhat moth-eaten brown all-weather coat.

"Probably" was the only answer I had. "Big universe, could be anything out there."

"Surely there is. Surely." He was silent for a bit, then idly scratched and dug at his left wrist with his right thumb. I hoped for silence. He sighed lightly. "But most things have no bearing on it of course. It is only those that are precisely as we are, those are the bridges and templates."

Templates? I lost the tiny thread of whatever thought was in my head. This loon was odd enough that I considered running for a moment. Well, walking rapidly at least. "Templates you say." I knew better than to speak. I really shouldn't lead people on or fall into their fantasies. "In what sense?"

I looked in his direction. His watery eyes drifted slightly behind round lensed wire frame glasses. "Oh, general of course. It's all about compartmentalization. In an unlimited universe there are only so many possible configurations." He tossed a few more crumbs. The birds seemed to cluster right under his feet. "Therefore, duplication will happen. Just so many planets, just so many stars."

1

I thought about it. Well, possibly. But the universe is really, really huge. I have no idea how huge. Just pretty darn huge. "Well, aren't there literally millions of sizes of planets? And millions of sizes of stars? And what would the odds be… of two being just the same?"

He seemed to smile faintly. "Oh, odds, well. Nothing to do with it really. I mean, if there were a limited size to things and then you would say that odds were the answer. But if there is an unlimited size to things then there are no odds at all. It is dictated that all things that are, will be. All things will be and be. Copies will happen and that is because in an infinite universe, there cannot be any unique thing."

That sounded outrageous. Impossible! "I can't see how that can be. I mean, in an infinite universe, one of everything should be enough. But I thought the universe was finite. Something I heard on TV or something. A hundred billion light years across or something."

"True. So how big does a universe have to be?" He nodded as if that were a sage statement. Then he rummaged through a couple of pockets and pulled out a small wooden tray that had compartments on it. Odd thing to have in a pocket, I thought. He blew on it and a bit of gray lint twirled softly away into the light breeze.

Admittedly I was hooked. He probably wasn't a serial killer or a mugger. He seemed relaxed and comfortable feeding birds and chatting about the size of the universe. I was thinking about getting back to business and not sitting on a bench all day. But a few more minutes wouldn't hurt.

I looked at the wooden tray. It was only a few centimeters square and had about twenty five little boxes on its surface. It was like a little jewelry tray or something of that sort. A centimeter thick perhaps, well made. It had a dark finish and looked hand crafted. "Hold this please." I took it automatically.

He dug some more and found a small leather pouch with a drawstring. "Ah, here we are." He opened it and poured a few small beads into his hand. "Now, let us say that we have three different types of object to deal with. These are red, blue, and silver. In each compartment we can place only three objects. How many ways can we fill the compartments before we have duplication?"

I thought about it. "Well, we could have an empty compartment, so that's one. Then we could have one of each bead in each compartment, that's three more." He nimbly sorted out three beads and dropped one of each into three compartments.

"Now we could also have a red and a silver, a red and a blue, and a blue and a silver. That's three more for seven. And one could have all three." He obediently placed the beads in other compartments.

He said quietly "Eight different ways. Any more?"

"Oh. Of course." I saw that you could have duplicated beads and so I went through the two-bead combinations. That made three more. Then I went through the other three-bead combinations. That added nine more. "Twenty I think."

"Yes, quite good. Now, no matter what you do, the next cell you fill must be a duplicate. There is no way to make that cell have a new and unique combination of beads. True?"

I went through each pattern quickly and saw no flaw in the logic. "True. This little universe can only have twenty unique cells. After that you have copies of previous cells." He smiled now.

"Yes. That is the point. No matter how large the universe is, at some point you are going to get duplicates." He carefully lifted the little tray from my hand and poured the beads into his drawstring bag. The tray and the bag disappeared into his pockets.

"Okay, very informative. You have a valid point. But three beads in a tray and billions of atoms are completely different. You can have all sorts of combinations of atoms and they can be very different from each other." I felt a sort of rightness to this argument.

He laughed lightly. "Yes, yes. But ask yourself just how different they can really be. Suppose I had two identical spheres of iron, like two cannonballs. They are precisely manufactured to be the same, polished and weighed and balanced. In the end they are so identical that you cannot tell them apart. Does it matter that one will have a few more aluminum atoms or copper atoms than the other? Close enough counts."

I gave it some thought. He went on. "You have two tuning forks. You tap one and the other rings in harmony. How close to identical must they be for this to happen? Not too terribly, I should think. The resonance is the key you know." He tossed a few more crumbs or bits. The birds gobbled them quickly. I wondered.

"So you're saying that close enough counts. We aren't talking about two worlds with the same people and the same names, but one has a cigarette burn on a coffee table and the other doesn't."

"Oh, no. Far too improbable. Just close enough. Same mass within a fraction of a percent, same sun within a fraction of a percent, just happens to be in the same place in the orbit right now. That sort of thing." He leaned back a bit and seemed to stretch slightly. "There are something like two times ten to the twenty fourth stars if I am not mistaken, so we only need to be close enough. There are maybe a dozen or so worlds that are close enough. Would that be enough for you?"

What a strange question. "I suppose it would. And I can see your logic. There probably are a dozen Earths floating around out there." I looked away at the park entrance, saw a passing city bus. It was getting late. I didn't even know his name.

I turned back to ask him. The bench was empty. The birds were still there, picking over tiny bits that were scattered on the dirty concrete pad. Time for me to go.

* * *

I sat at the desk and idly twiddled my pencil. General business noises floated around me, one fluorescent was buzzing fitfully and faintly. I looked up at it and spotted the little orange tag that said "saving energy". One lamp was missing and so the other had a hard time working properly. Was there really a savings there? Or did a lamp burn out and somebody forget to order them?

Beads and pockets. Odd thoughts floated through my head but when I aimed my attention at them they would scatter like leaves and I had no idea what exactly I was thinking so industriously a moment before. Like a stranger looking inside somebody else's window at the goings-on inside and not understanding what was happening, but this was in my own skull. There are no windows in this office.

There, that had nothing to do with anything. It was futile; I could not focus on a single coherent thought. Madness. I thought of sage sounding old men in tattered brown longcoats feeding pigeons and finches and then, strangely, vanishing without disturbing the birds. That was madness in spades.

Maybe I had imagined it all. There was no watery-eyed fellow with thick, round glasses, just my feeble mind making something out of nothing. But the birds had been eating something. No name, no sound. That softly burring voice spelling out sureties of cosmology with no more than beads and logic. He was right, of course. There had to be all manner of things in the dark, and the universe, so large as it is, would only allow so many ways to make something like a world.

Or a sun or a solar system. Twenty combinations of beads. Maybe twenty trillion solar systems. No, many more. Twenty quadrillion. Twenty… something I had no name for. An unimaginably huge number. And some, some of them absolutely had to be so Earthlike, so identical, that some sort of resonance was present. Was that what he had said?

What would it be? How would we know? Madness. The pencil, tired of being twirled, scuttled under the desk with a clattering noise. "Mike, done with that form yet?"

I nearly jumped. "Uh, yeah, a minute more. You have the roster for tomorrow?"

The sandy yellow haired fellow with the slight gap in his teeth (all of them) dug into a small clutch of papers and produced a bad copy. What in the world, doesn't everyone have a printer? Why do people even use copiers any more? He had a sharky sort of look, a little too built up and flabby at once, eyes that seemed to look in too many directions at the same time. He handed the paper to me and it seemed to need to be peeled from his fingertips.

"Thanks." I rolled my chair back, snagging the bum wheel on the flat carpeting. Time to retrieve the pencil. "I'll send this form your way in a few."

"Yeah, need it. Thanks." He was gone in a whirl of barely smelled bad aftershave. I found a couple of paperclips on the floor under the desk and started fishing with my fingertips. That felt like it, yes. I stuffed the pencil in my pocket and rolled forward slightly, unwilling to immerse in the insipid glow of the screen. Beads and madness. I typed rapidly for maybe thirty seconds and clicked the "okay" button.

I was way behind, guilty-feeling behind in the work. This day felt like a wash and so did I. No compass, no direction, head feeling like wool and distraction. I could walk in front of a bus and not know what was happening. I resonated with nothing. No, that wasn't right. I was like a rock in the sun, or a piece of wood on a beach. Content to be nothing. Even analyzing it made me feel like I had invested too much energy.

Engineering had been my choice, but somehow I ended up analyzing risk and then underwriting technical projects. Automation tasks, security tasks, bridge building tasks; everything technical carries a risk. This was not at all what I wanted from my life. The only plus was that it paid the bills and was simple enough work. Stupid work.

I halfway tried to get a few more forms done. Something caught more by instinct than anything else and soon I was in a wonderful nothingness of automatic work and unaware of the passing minutes. My mind was swaddled in pattern and completion and I felt like I was getting something done when the red and silver beads came back to my mind.

It was nearly the end of the day, time to open the center desk drawer and sweep everything into it, leaving the desk clean and orderly. Riffle and collate the papers in the in box, same for the out. Logging off, shutting down, hearing the slight rise in chatter from cubicle to cubicle. I wondered if I should walk through the park on the way out. Just curious.

I walked slowly in that cottony distracted feeling. The office was just three stories at the edge of town, near the park. There was a sandwich shop and a coffee shop below, a clothing store on the left, nothing really outstanding. I wondered idly how anyone makes any money running a shop in the area.

I smelled pastry and coffee, bus exhaust and a little perfume. What would another world be like? Other places had to have jobs. There would be farming and history and music lessons. Fried stuff to eat. Gambling and poverty probably. It would be very much like this maybe, so much so that if you stepped into it you might walk a while before the strangeness hit you.

When the two worlds match up, resonate, you might be walking down a street and make a strange turn that leads somewhere different. It might be that you are taking a slightly different route than the one you know so you wouldn't catch on at first. Things were strange on this route because you had never walked it before. Then when you came to your senses it might be that you couldn't quite retrace your steps or it would be like one of those funhouses where the walls move and you can't go back the way you came.

The thought gave me a chill. I thought of people who wander off in the foggy night and were never heard from again. Maybe they were *over there* down a road that can't be followed. Worlds that match up were both attractive and faintly scary all at once. What if more than one matched at the same time? Chaos, you could be lost in some weird place forever, and you would have to wait for another world to line up.

That was the thought that clicked into place. If worlds can align, they can also fall out of alignment. You might be stuck forever looking for the next alignment, trying to get back to something a little less alien, maybe stuck elsewhere and never quite… what?

How often do worlds line up? How would I know? Surely if there were anything to this, there had to be a way to see when worlds were coming together or were in place, wasn't there?

I slowly rose from this thought into reality and realized I was standing at the park entrance. Just standing. I definitely needed to get home, not a long walk from here. The advantage of a small town was that you were never far from anything. I turned with some reluctance from the gluey attraction of the park and willed myself to walk, careful step at a time toward the small house that I rented just five blocks from here.

Dinner was cheap macaroni and cheese followed by a ham sandwich and a beer. The television was a few dozen channels of junk. I idly flipped around in TV-space and found something that didn't kill too many brain cells. I looked through my black-sock-clad feet that were propped a little too high on the foot stool with two pillows on it. I found an episode of Sagan's Cosmos and listened to his nasal chat about billions of something. Every so often a word like "universe" or "statistics" would poke through the gauzy listless feeling and drag a corner of my attention back but I really wasn't into it at all.

There was a period of mild dozing and the smell of fried chicken wafted through, probably from the woman next door. It was there that I felt a connection like a thin thread, something like an anvil held by a cobweb. I let it come and it slowly stabilized into something a bit more tangible, soft and misty but definite.

There are two tuning forks, and when you strike one, no matter how softly, an answer from the other is heard. Sympathetic resonance was the thing. Two worlds, and when you affect one, the other will answer. I was getting that sense of certainty that comes in a dream, that something is *right* and I tried gently to grasp it and I hoped it would be there when I woke up.

What is the resonant frequency of a world? A soft, slightly hoarse voice said "tap it lightly and see." I swam upward from a dimness toward the conscious world. Tap a world and hear it ring. My legs were tingling and my eyes gummy. I stretched and yawned, looked at the TV and a program about crushing old bottles and making windows out of them was running. Hideous looking things, the glass was also used as divider panels in kitchens.

I got up slowly and let the sensation return to my legs. Instinctively I shoved my hands into my pockets and yawned once I was standing stably. My right fingertip encountered something small and hard and round, smooth and polished. I fished a bit and caught the little thing, pulled it out to inspect it.

It was a tiny bluish stone or bead about half a centimeter across. Just the size of a pea and a clearish watery blue color, the stone had a slight starlike pattern in it. It might have been a small sapphire, but it had a lighter color that I expected. Celestine? I had seen a piece of the stuff before, paler blue and crystalline. But this had the star look from fine fibers or crystals and I had never heard of star celestine before. Where had this come from?

I could only imagine one place; that the fellow in the park had somehow slipped it into my pocket. He had the look of a seedy magician or stage conjurer, come to think of it. Somebody who had loads of pockets with God knows what in them. I found that I was thinking of him, unconsciously, as the magician and not "some old fogy in a rain coat."

But this stone looked rather... not cheap. Why would he have given this to me? This was one little mystery that was not going to be solved tonight. I held the stone up to the light and looked through its slightly cloudy interior. I needed something to compare it to. I had a small sapphire ring from a girlfriend of years before. I was going to give it to her but things didn't work out and I had already paid for it. I thought about selling it but

I had just kept it. It stayed in my tie tack box all these years, and what the heck. Jewelry rarely decreases in value. I told myself it was an investment.

I thought I might compare the two and get an idea of what the differences might be. I could always take the stone to a jeweler and get an idea of what it is, maybe how much it might be worth. The case was on the dresser and it took only a couple of moments to pull out the ring and hold it next to the mystery stone.

It was odd; there was a faint pulling sensation like a magnet might exert on a small piece of metal. The two stones seemed to draw toward each other and a gentle light was present. Or was it illusion? I turned off the room light and yes, there was a barely seen glow. Spooky.

I pulled the two stones apart slowly and watched the glow fade out and the pull drop to nothing. Something very odd was here in two small bits of mineral. It deserved investigation. I brought the two up and slowly let them approach each other. I felt the slight tug at the same time that the glow started to build. It grew to a small level and then remained there, regardless of how much closer the stones got. The pull grew to some level and also stayed there, neither growing or weakening.

Stones are not supposed to do that. At least, I had never heard of stones doing it. Magnets could pull bits of metal or other magnetite, and hematite could be magnetized also. But the glow was completely different. On top of that, I had never heard of a transparent or translucent magnet before. I turned the room light back on.

Where did this odd stone come from and what was it? Surely I would remember picking it up so the only explanation was that I had not. That magician would have done this. I thought back carefully to what he spoke about, what he said.

Of all the universe, there was certain to be a world just like this one. Sometimes when things are just right, two worlds will resonate. Tap one and the other will resonate. Resonance is the key.

Odd enough, I actually felt that this small stone might be a piece of some other world. One of those resonating places that must exist and must at this moment be in just the right configuration to... do something. So now what?

The ring was growing warm. Would it get hotter still? I pulled the two apart and put each on the dresser. For good measure I put the ring back in the ring case after a moment of consideration. It wouldn't do to have the pair snap together in the night and burn the house down. I was wide awake and unable to consider sleep.

If this actually wasn't a trick of some sort, it was going to be tough to resolve it with grace. It raised a whole set of questions. Did he seek me out or was I a random find? And purpose was another issue. Surely if this was something he was pursuing he would find me again.

One phrase came to my mind repeatedly- down the rabbit hole. Nothing but questions and that phrase. I couldn't think of any other day that I had had so many strange and unanswered questions. I wanted to experiment with the stone and couldn't think of anything to try. I knew nothing of experimenting or how to do it.

I spent a few minutes thinking about the response to a simple sapphire. What about something else? It wasn't unthinkable that some other material would respond in some way. What did I have that I could try with it? I stood up quickly and opened the tie tack case and looked through it. There was a small tie tack with a little ruby in it. And here was a pair of cheap cuff links that had little cubic zirconia crystals in the faces of fairly low-cost gold plated settings.

I held the stone next to the ruby. It was barely more than a pinhead but it seemed to tug slightly. It might have been wishful thinking. The zirconia did nothing. Ah, I did have a small diamond pin in the case somewhere. There it was, a fresh candidate. I put it next to the stone.

That was odd, it felt like it was slightly repelled. I laid the pale blue bead on the dresser top and let it stop rolling around. Then I brought the diamond slowly toward it. Yes, it did roll away when the diamond was a few millimeters from touching the stone. I tried the same trick with the ruby and it did pull the stone forward a bit. What had I learned?

The zirconia did nothing. The sapphire reacted strongly and was attracted to the stone. The ruby attracted it weakly but it did attract it. The diamond repelled it. Now I was enthused. It was like a game, trying to see what would happen. I turned the light off and tried the ruby and got a faint little pink light from it. The diamond remained dark.

I flipped the light back on again, thought about things to try in the kitchen. An ice cube did nothing, a few foods I tried did nothing. A scrap of sandpaper from the drawer, surprisingly, drew towards the stone. I turned off the light and saw in amazement a faint yellow-green radiance from the black crystals of grit glued to the paper. There was something in common in the sapphire, the ruby and the sandpaper. I pocketed the stone and turned on the computer.

The internet yielded a few hits about aluminum oxides and that was clearly the connection. Diamond was carbon, it got repelled and would not glow. Sapphire was aluminum oxide with some titanium or other things in it, ruby had chromium in it. I wondered what salt crystals would do, if anything.

Back in the kitchen I tried salt and got no response. Sugar seemed to slightly repel but if so it was very faint. I wondered about sand. It took a few minutes to gather a small amount of sand from the side of the building, and while there I spotted a small pile of white builder's sand used for a recent sidewalk repair. I placed it in a small cup, wondering if the neighbors were looking. Suddenly self-conscious, I carefully made my way back to the sidewalk and casually picked up a handful of the dry soil.

Back inside I placed a pinch of the soil in a plastic lid from a margarine tub. I ran the stone beneath it like a magnet. The soil seemed to follow it a little, but not much. I then tried it with the builder's sand. It seemed to move out of the way a bit. I took a glass and put a little water in it, then put in a pinch of the builder's sand. The bead was moved beneath the glass and lo, the sand parted in the middle. Slowly, not very energetically, but it did it. I put a pinch of the darker soil in and it moved toward the stone.

With a little laugh, I stirred the glass up, mixing the sand. Then I ran the stone under it and watched as the lighter sand moved to the edges and the darker sand covered the place where the stone was beneath. It looked like a bulls-eye. Wow.

This was something new. Something that had not been seen before or documented. Nobody had ever seen a magnet for aluminum oxide. Or one that repelled diamond. This was truly incredible. I could think of a hundred applications. This was indeed some bit of mystery, but was it from another world? I couldn't imagine what else it could be.

It still made me wonder why it had to work at all. Weren't all the atoms in the universe the same? Why would this little bead somehow do things that other normal beads would not, and that was a good question. I had to find the magician again and see what he would say, ask him some things.

I cleaned the kitchen slowly and put everything away. The soil was tossed out the back door on the grass along with the muddy water. Enough for one night, I was tired. Still, after putting things as they should be, I was drawn back to the computer to do some searching and find some answers. It was well after 2 when I was thinking about how I would regret having to get up for work.

***

"You've been practicing your wizardry I see."

The voice stunned me. I fought the urge to jump and turn. I must have started a bit. "What makes you say that?"

"It appears that you have made a rather handsome resonance detector there." I looked at the same face, the graying hair and the rather beaten looking hat. "Nice bit of work for a starter. Well done."

I was sitting on the same bench, holding a small piece of clear plastic tubing. I had spent a few dollars on the largest cheapest diamond I could find in a pawn shop. It was still a tiny scrap but worth it. I also had a small sapphire that I had found in a junk store as costume jewelry. I used the stone over the whole box of junk and found one that responded eagerly. It was a steal for three dollars.

The sapphire was glued in the top of the clear tube, the stone in the middle, freely moving, and the diamond at the bottom. The stone hovered mysteriously in the center of the thing, repelled by the diamond below and drawn by the sapphire above. A small pin through the tube kept it from clicking into the sapphire.

"You have caused me many a sleepless night now. I wondered if you would be back or if this was just a sort of joke." I held the little tube up and watched as the stone seemed to dip slightly, then rise again.

"I will first formally introduce myself, and yes, I was coming back. Things commanded my attention for a while." He turned and faced me full on from his side of the bench. He extended a slim and scarred hand. "I am Anlyt Vood". The name rhymed with wood or hood.

"Anlyt. I'm Michael Winston." We shook. His hand had the strength of steel wires under leather and felt reassuring. I noticed a number of white scars along his wrist under the brown coat. "Call me Mike, please."

"Surely. You may call me Lyt if you like." He gave a creased but genuine smile and settled backward on the bench. "I hope that the parts for the detector didn't cost you too much. I'm sure you learned a few things on the journey."

A journey it was. I had figured out a few things but it raised more questions that I would ever have had otherwise. "Not much. I can afford it. So this really is a piece of another... planet." I peered at the floating stone in the tube.

"Mmm. Everything has to be from somewhere. But yes, from some place perhaps halfway across the universe. It is useful to have a collection of bits and pieces as you travel since you never quite know where you will be or what will work there. I make a few stops and collect a few things, then move on."

I breathed deeply and slowly. This was real. "You travel the universe. Many places? I imagine you see a lot of very unusual things."

He laughed briefly. "I travel the universe, yes. Not always of choice. But I have seen many strange things. Mostly things are quite normal however. Worlds are predictable in a sense, cultures as well. Some places are very dangerous, others are quite nice. The greatest danger is in people however. Not places."

I looked at the grass and the sky, watched the swell of a cloud and the dive of a bird. "How long have you traveled, Lyt?"

At that he seemed to pause. "Too long, friend. Too long. This is one of perhaps a hundred worlds I have seen. I am here for a short while, like many of the other places. But think of my stop as a shopping trip." He smiled once more. "There are things here that will be helpful. Would you have some time to spend directing me about?"

My heart thundered a moment. "Er, shopping. Of course. What are you looking for?" I thought of the things a universal traveler might need. Clean water kits? Camp gear? Maybe.

The magician, no- the traveler looked off as if listening to a distant voice. "I will have to spend a little time deciding the details. My first need here would be quarters. I need to exchange for some local currency and to establish a place to work. It should take perhaps a month at most."

That was longer than I had expected but it was also an opportunity as well. I could see things were changing now, the quiet life of office work was going to be shaken like a dusty, empty box turned over and made ready for new use. "I would be very happy to help. Let's see what we need to do. I live just a short while from here. Have you eaten?"

"Not for some... hours. What do you feel is appropriate?"

Something came to me. "Can you eat local food? Is your digestive system different or do you have special needs?" Then something else snuck into my thoughts.

"You probably aren't uh, human. Right?"

"No. Not at all, just a very, very similar form. We are far less related than you are to that tree over there. Many of the chemistries are similar enough though. And you touch on a very good point about travel to other worlds. We can share information on this at our leisure as we work together." He stood slowly. "We should start then. While there is no great haste, we also do have strict limits. Worlds move, and things change."

I stood as well, shook imaginary dust from my pants and put the little detector in my pocket. That was what I had made, a detector. One for seeing when a world was in alignment with my own. How amazing is that!

"So, do you know what pizza is? It has meat and cheese on a bread crust." I was looking for the franchise store that promised a five dollar pizza. One of those would be worthwhile and I hadn't had pizza in a couple of weeks.

"It sounds good enough. No diet restrictions for me, really. I can eat most anything and I do, I must say. Sometimes I look back on some of the things I have eaten and wonder why. So pizza it is." He smiled, a common thing it appeared. "Where do we exchange currency and what do you think we should use?" He produced three small drawstring bags and seemed to weigh them against each other.

"Oh, precious metals, gems, I don't know what is best. Say, if you sell precious metals they aren't going to start sticking to other metals or floating or something, are they?"

He rubbed his chin with the free hand, the three bags hanging by their strings in the other. "I would think not. Metals are not usually so disposed for some reason. My understanding of the effect is not great. It appears to be some quantum effect related to angular momentum or entanglement. But I am no scientist really." We walked along and I noticed that his coat was an odd cut. I couldn't quite place what was different about it.

The shoes too had something strange. It took a moment to see what it was. His soles and heels were split in the middle from front to back and left footprints with a cleft in them. That seemed unsettling for some reason.

We walked along and chatted about small things. The sky was a bit too violet from his perspective. There were no holograms. Why did nobody grow vegetables here? It was a talk spiced with the bits of perspective from completely outside.

We entered the pizza shop, ordered and took a table. He spoke about the bags. The gems were probably not a good idea since some might have odd reactions to the local stones. The metals were common and would not do anything unusual.

We decided that metals were the best thing to sell. He had some fair amount of something called iridium and some platinum in small discs and cubes. The discs were pretty normal coin-like things with no details or inscriptions. He showed me bare discs of metal with a raised lip, each about three centimeters across and with no adornment on one face. The other had a triangle and a depression like a test tube or a long U.

The cubes were like dice but larger. The edges were rounded and the faces stamped inward slightly so that you could see the raised edge all around. One face had a triangle again but no depressed U shape. The opposite face had an oval with raised dots around it.

I was impressed by the great density of the cubes and discs. I don't think I had ever picked up anything so small that weighed so much. Worse than fishing weights, the bits of metal were far more dense than lead from the feel of them.

"We'll have to get these appraised. I have no idea what that iridium is worth but the platinum is very expensive. You could live for a long time on that." He nodded. The coins and cubes went back into the bag and all disappeared into his voluminous pockets.

That third bag was something else. He showed me what appeared to be tiny capsules of glassy black material. They looked like sand grains with tiny iridescent color sparkles on them. I once saw a piece of something called silicon carbide and it looked sort of like that.

He opened one of the capsules and poured the granules on the table. They spilled out and lined up like soldiers at attention. I stared shamelessly. "What the hell." The granules formed perfect lines and fell into the shape of a hexagon. Hundreds of tiny black grains filled the hexagon in moments like a fluid filling a container. I watched as they all shifted somehow and simultaneously reflected the light, almost like they had borne arms or lifted tiny shields.

"What is it? Or what are they?"

"Long life. Immunity. Cures. They are each granules containing uncounted numbers of tiny mechanisms that fix things. These are a valuable commodity in many places where medicine is poor or lacking." He placed the empty capsule on the table and the grains filed inside it, filling it like they were being packed into a tight mass. He replaced the other half of the capsule and put it in the drawstring bag.

"The display they performed is the guarantee that they are real and active. Like a sales advertisement. You can see if the cure is potent or capable and not be fooled into taking something that will not work. If the granules do not perform, you have a fake."

"Wonders and signs. I think those would bring untold wealth here but trying to sell them would be very tricky. It would probably get you killed or locked up. Let's keep those hidden." He gave a knowing nod.

"Of course."

The pizza arrived and sat there for a moment in the center of the table. I pulled a slice free and slid it onto the plate. He did likewise. He closed his eyes for a moment and dipped his head forward. I followed suit.

"Careful, the cheese tends to keep the heat in." He was already lifting the tip of the cheese lightly and blowing beneath it to cool it. He had it figured out from the start. Why hadn't I thought of that?

His first bite was slow and appraising. "Very basic, very good. This is something not too different from…" He said something I could not catch. "Yes. This is a good choice. My thanks." He ate carefully and clearly enjoyed it.

We chatted lightly as we ate, letting the situation develop itself in our minds. At least that was what I did. I was winding down and decided what to do.

"So my place is the best for now. Do you have somewhere to stay for the night? It is getting a little late in the day for business and the jewelers and coin stores will be closing very shortly. We need a solid plan and I have a friend who is a numismatist. A coin dealer. He can probably get the best deal for the metals."

Lyt took the next to last slice of pizza. "I will trust your judgment on this matter. I have a place that I can stay if I must but I would prefer not to. Things are not good there right now." He made a curious side to side movement of his head.

"Not a problem. I have a spare bed and pillows. Everything is clean. Say, how many languages do you know? You must hear a lot of them on your travels." This brought a real laugh to him.

"Well, in truth I know few. Perhaps half a dozen for the places I have spent the most time. But there is some very good translation software so I can get along quite well. Greater exposure increases the chance I will say the proper things." He was finished with his final slice and wiped his fingers carefully with the napkin. He then produced a small thing like a bottle cap and tapped it gently. When he set it on the table, a tiny yellow flame appeared above it. He said a few quiet words, almost like an invocation. His eyes were closed again and his head tilted forward.

I thought I heard "thought, time, culture" or something like that but I could have been mistaken. He raised his head and made a sprinkling motion with his fingertips. The flame extinguished. He made the cap vanish into his hands. I could only think of the mages of old. He spoke.

"Very well, let us hasten to your abode."

The sun was setting and the air was cooling a little. We walked along and chatted lightly of traveling between worlds with little more than the contents of one's pockets.

CHAPTER 2

Lyt took the couch which folded out into a bed. He slept without sound and apparently had no trouble sleeping through the night. I woke many times, and often just laid in the bed thinking of the strangest of strangers whom I had befriended and who slept just bare meters away in the living room.

What suns had he walked beneath? What air did he breathe? He had seen sights and wonders and probably been places unlike any that I could imagine. My mind roiled with possibilities. He had things in that coat that might well topple worlds and end economies. A chill thought passed through my mind. Was he armed? If so, with what?

I figured I really didn't want to know. It was his business. Don't piss off the wizard; that is a good general survival rule. I slept poorly but not from fear. It was excitement- good, clean fun coming to my life for the first time since I could remember.

I thought of fun things I had done as a kid. The most exciting things. Staying up really, really late for the first time and seeing the sun coming up. The first time sledding down that really steep hill. Jumping off a really high rope into the lake. My first car. This was better than any of it. It was Christmas and Easter and the first of everything. This was magic.

When I did sleep it was with that barely restrained sense of wonder and the dreams were confused and happy but I woke so tired that I felt I had barely gotten any rest at all. Lyt was sitting at the kitchen table and had a small tablet and stylus. He was making rapid little triangular markings and swirly lines. What caught my attention was not the cursory similarity to Arabic but that when he reached the end of a line, he would sometimes hold his stylus there and drag it somewhere else. The line of text would obediently slide over the paper and move to his whim.

Once he raised his fingertips and waved them carelessly in midair and a line of glowing fiery script seemed to linger there like a magical spell. Something changed on the pad and the paper got a funny glassy look. I can't really describe it. It made me think of sorcery and computers and graphical user interface stuff. It was probably some sort of computer device that we had never thought of.

"Breaks the day and so my greetings. Well rested you are not, I see." He barely glanced up as he continued scribing fire in the air and moving screwy Arabic on a yellow pad. Something chimed faintly and he smiled. The script faded from over the tabletop and the pad darkened marginally. "Done and done."

"Morning Lyt. Coffee?"

"Barely would I know. Surely will I try. Thank you Mike." He stood and stretched like an aged but lithe cat. "I slept very well in your home. This is one of the more comfortable places in the universe I must say. No worms or parasites, no hungry amphibians. And the radio bands. So much to hear and learn."

"You hear radio?" I should be used to surprises.

"Of a sort. I have tools. But I was very tired as well and took this opportunity to rest and so I am quite well. The days here are longer than some worlds and that means a good rest at night. Of course they are almost exactly the same length as the last world or the resonance would not work well. Or at all." He had a slim blazer sort of thing on. This was the first time I had seen him without his coat.

Even the blazer had lots of pockets. They had flaps with something like velcro but it was noiseless. His tablet and stylus went into one of them.

"Okay, cinnamon rolls and coffee. I'll get that going right away. Then while the rolls are cooking I'll call my friend the coin dealer." I washed hands, pulled out a flat cookie sheet and got a can of rolls from the refrigerator. Lyt watched carefully as I opened the can (with a minor concussive pop) and doled out the flabby bits of pastry dough.

The oven was warming and had that slightly burnt oil smell. The pan slid in with a rattle of the rack and I was stuffing a coffee filter into the machine. I figured there would be time for a fast shower once done and breakfast would be done. The coffee was in the machine and the water was just starting to percolate through. Lyt got a funny look.

"Is that coffee? No no, that's rather disturbing. I will have to drink something else. It has a most foul odor. I cannot describe it truly." It had my stomach rumbling with that long-conditioned urge for breakfast. His was doing flip flops at the smell. Oh yeah, alien tastes and metabolism.

"Would it be poisonous or something?"

"Not at all. I have enzymes in place for most anything, even many reversed molecules. But that smell is revolting, I am unhappy to say." He had the first unhappy look I had seen on his face. "It puts me in mind of burning spoiled sea life."

"Ah. Got it. Okay, I'll have my coffee outside and the windows will be opened to get rid of the smell. I hadn't thought of it. There are things that we will disagree on as a matter of biology or chemistry or something. I hope you like cinnamon rolls."

I opened the windows and turned on the vent fan. Lyt went into the living room and sat on the couch. I needed that shower.

After a few rapid minutes of scrubbing and hair washing I was ready to check the rolls and make that phone call. I wondered what iridium was worth.

The rolls were done, the frosting was applied and these were quite acceptable to Lyt. He had some orange juice and said it was very good.

We chatted about flavors and smells and I discovered that peppermint and caraway were the same molecule but simply mirrored from each other. How could that be?

It drove the point home that somehow what we taste or smell can be radically different even if the chemistry is identical. The geometry of the molecule can be left or right handed and our senses can then perceive them in entirely different ways. So coffee had some molecules in it that were produced in putrefaction on his world. This was a really odd development for me.

After a few minutes on the telephone I told Lyt the news. "Platinum is at a pretty strong point in the market. You won't have any problem selling it. Iridium… that stuff is absolutely incredibly expensive. He can buy it but he wants to check a sample of it first. Can you spare a cube for a few days?"

"Of a certainty. I shall provide three coins and three cubes." He withdrew the heavy drawstring bag from his coat and handed me the metals. "I should likely stay here to prevent too much exposure. It would not be good to call more attention that is warranted here. This world seems a bit controlled. Authoritarian." He caught on quickly, but good sense on your feet was always a survival skill for a traveler.

I grabbed a light windbreaker. "Good enough. I will return as quickly as possible. Don't answer the phone. Let the machine do it." He nodded as if it were the most natural thing in the world. I left and locked the front door.

Walking back to the so-called downtown area was uneventful but the dolorous weight in my pocket made me a little apprehensive. I had only a fair idea of how much money it might represent. Let's see, five grams is almost exactly the mass of a nickel. I added up the number of nickels it would take to equal just one coin in weight. Ridiculous.

That had to be wrong. There were about twenty eight grams in an ounce, right? The price was quoted by the ounce and it would be more than five nickels to equal an ounce. More like six. Those coins were a couple of ounces it seemed. Maybe a little less. Three times… I couldn't see it. And the iridium. Those *cubes*. I was carrying a lot of money.

The coin shop was a quiet place, not like the ones of my boyhood. The old glass racks in the wooden cases were gone. This was like a vault. The displays were still glass cases but all in chrome and behind thick plexiglass panels. Morris, my friend the coin dealer, was cordial. He was always smiling. I knew him so it didn't bother me but I could well imagine that a lot of people got a little suspicious of such a happy guy.

"Mikey. So you've come into some metals. Let's have a look and see what we can do. Unusual too. I don't get iridium at all. Rare stuff really." He always spoke like that, in little sentence fragments. Still, he was a very personable guy. His clothing was neat, nice shoes, something nondescript about him. Money dealers always looked like regular people, almost never did anything loud or outstanding. But the shoes and the watches were pretty clear signs of wealth.

We went into a small office with a plain desk and a passthrough on the wall next to it. A copy machine and computer were on a long table on the wall behind the desk. He closed a rather solid metal door and it clunked like a bolt had dropped. Secure, of course. He indicated a pricey chair and I sat. I took out the handkerchief and unrolled the discs and cubes. His eyebrows rose greatly.

"Huh. Okay." He opened a drawer and took out a small scale. Placing it carefully on the desk, he then removed a wooden box and set it next to the scale. It hinged open to a red felt lined interior. He pushed a button on the scale and the display lit and a tiny beep sounded. He rotated it slightly so I could see the display.

Morris removed a small shiny weight from the wooden box and placed it on the scale, read the display. He changed to a smaller weight and read it again. Satisfied, he placed the weights in the box and moved it to one side. "Calibration is good. Let's see one of your coins."

I lifted the top disc and placed it in his palm. He felt it and hefted it, then placed an eye loupe over his left eye and looked it over. He rotated it slowly and examined the edges, looked at the triangle and U depression. He made little tuneless humming noises as he looked it over.

"Peculiar." The scale was next. It read 2.671 ounces. He removed it and placed each of the other coins in it, reading that all read 2.671 and not a whit more or less. "Odd weight. Were these some sort of commemorative or decoration?" I shrugged.

"Quick check here." He opened another drawer and took out a caliper. He measured the thickness of a disc and its diameter. He took a small calculator out as well and punched in some numbers. "Density is good." He rapped on the passthrough with a knuckle.

"Josie, standard." He passed all three coins to a hand that appeared in the now open little passthrough door. The door closed and clicked.

"We have a pretty good EDAX system and a Mossbäuer for this sort of stuff. You wouldn't know it but I have one of the best precious metals ID labs in the state. I won't need to send it out after all. Head of my group back there assures me she can do it."

I was impressed. "Business must be good."

"Yes, and I have to keep it that way. The money spent is the best protection we have. Some goofball was plating fake coins made of depleted uranium and he'd figured out a balancing system that matched it up nicely with gold. I can't understand why he put so much effort into it. We busted him pretty fast. The coins had the right density all right but x-ray showed the little plugs that he had used to match the balance up.

"In the end he was busted not for fraud but for dealing with nuclear materials. The stuff wasn't radioactive enough to be dangerous at all but it was a technicality the feds used to get him."

I was fidgeting in the chair. "Where did he get the uranium?"

Morris shrugged. "Probably Russian weapons. A lot of the stuff was broken down and sold as pretty harmless material. Some is nasty with chemicals and some is clean. But he really went a long way for nothing. It's tough to machine uranium. That stuff catches fire and before you know it you have nothing but the oxide. He clearly had the right equipment so why didn't he just do something legit?" He shook his head.

The passthrough clicked. Morris turned and accepted the discs, now in a small cup. A small stack of papers came with it.

"Ah. Well, it's the real deal. Pure stuff too. I don't think I've seen it with this low an impurity count more than once. Odd. But it's genuine. I can offer you…"

He poked at the calculator again, squinted at it. "Here." Figured were written on a small pad. He tore the sheet free and handed it to me. Wow. I accepted and he knocked once more on the passthrough. The cup and the discs disappeared inside.

"Now, the iridium. I don't see this stuff ever except in some really special cases. This is more a strategic metal than a precious metal but the market for it is solid. Those cubes I assume are it." I smiled wanly and pushed the handkerchief his way. He lifted one of the cubes carefully and measured it with the caliper. More calculator abuse followed and then he scribbled a number on his pad.

He measured the depth of the stamped in faces, the various features and calculated some more. This was a mixture of boring and worrying. I felt an odd sense of panic as he weighed the cube and compared it to his notes. He seemed satisfied. The passthough got knocked on again and the cubes vanished into the maw. He looked at me pointedly.

"Where in the hell did you get this stuff? This is really strange. I mean, as a friend I can preserve your confidentiality but I am really curious."

I slumped into the seat a bit. "Old friend, he travels a lot. He just got into town and wants to settle in for some quiet. He is used to living comfortably and has no regular currency on him yet. He's been telling me a few of his travel stories. Fascinating stuff but just between friends. And I'm just helping him relax for a while."

Morris made the "and?" face.

I shrugged. "Not much to tell but he is a quiet guy who gets things done. He trades and deals with people from all over the… world and seems to do pretty well." The answer seemed to only make him more curious. "I'd bring him by to meet you but he's sort of private." The passthrough knocked and the door opened. Morris accepted the small tray with the cup and papers.

"Very good. Thanks." He peered at the report. His head shook slowly from side to side. "This is pure. Never seen so much of it before. Not even at the shows. You have any idea what this is worth? The purity is the key. This stuff is better than the Malinkrodt stuff. Really laboratory grade." He hummed and abused the calculator some more. Then he wrote and handed me the paper. I felt faint.

"Let me advise you. If I cut you a check for this all at once, you are going to be red flagged for an audit or something. I think we should do this in three draws. As a friend I want you to be aware."

"Sure. You've been good with advice in the past." He nodded and put everything away and then opened a locked drawer on the right side of the desk. A cashbox appeared and a checkbook. "I will give you five thousand in cash now plus a check. In one week I will give you another check, and in another week the final check." The box contained a small ledger which he wrote rapidly and neatly in.

"Here." He peeled off hundreds and counted them out. One stack, two stacks, three… he then wrote a check and passed it over to me. I carefully folded the bills into two stacks; the larger went into my shirt pocket and the smaller into my pants pocket.

"Thanks Morris. I had no idea that this was so much. Thanks for the advice."

"There's more. This is a receipt for the remainder, don't lose it. If I'm not here you wouldn't be able to get the next two checks easily. I'll need a copy of your license of course." I removed my wallet and handed the license to him and placed the check and receipt in the bill side. I realized that I was sweating in the cool office. Money of this sort made me nervous.

Morris ran the copy and handed my license back to me. "There you go. And I would be fascinated to meet your friend some time. But professionally I won't say that, just between us. Good stories are hard to come by."

At that I actually smiled. "If we have any more business I'll call on you." He stood and extended a hand. We shook and the bolt to the metal door clunked back. I was happy to get out of there.

━◆━

I spent a couple of hours online with Lyt looking at buildings and rental properties. We settled on a brief list of places that were not too far away and would give him some room to work. I ran the printer and made some sandwiches. A couple of bottles of water and a soda for me and it was time to dust off the car.

During the work week I didn't drive anywhere. It was too easy to just walk and only during rainy weather did I really take the car to work. But out of the area it was the way to go. We spent little time talking about the money but I made clear that it was a large amount and he would be able to afford most anything.

Driving through low hills and valleys we passed scrubby dry areas that had once been project housing but had been bulldozed. The trees were just greening back up from a mild winter. We found a metal building that was surrounded by trees and little more.

It was clean and neat, had a couple of grape arbors next to it. There was a small but useful gravel parking lot. A realtor met us at the door with key in hand.

"We only need a place to do a short project. Perhaps a month or two. I see that the owner is willing to do short term rental."

She was short and thick and red haired. Her yellow blazer was almost obnoxious in the early afternoon sun. Too much smiling, too red lipstick. "Oh, he's traveling for three months and anything he can get will be good. This is so far out that few people want to rent it for anything." She must be new, I thought. Never give so much information about a client.

"That's fine. Let's see how much room there is inside." She went through a search for the alarm code on her aluminum clipboard and then opened the place up. The lights came on and we saw an empty shell. Lyt looked about, touched the walls and looked at the high windows.

We walked about in the bare space and saw a small loft and an office. The concrete floor was painted light gray and a bright red set of pipes in the overhead said that there was a working sprinkler system in it. I watched as the realtor went on about the electrical power and the access to the local airport. She talked about water mains and light traffic. I nodded and went "uh huh" a couple of times. Lyt was sizing it up in his own way.

"I must see the building from outside." He was out in a moment and left nothing but the dusty shaft of sunlight in the door. The realtor felt she had a signature in hand.

She looked at me as I spoke. "He's eccentric but very smart. He's figuring out if it's what we need." She lapsed into silence for a few seconds. Relief, my ears thought. I decided to follow him out and see what he was looking for. I didn't see him anywhere. He was probably behind the building.

Something curious happened. A tiny *click* sounded in my pocket. I remembered the little detector and pulled it out. The bead was suspended as always in the center of the tube, just floating above the diamond. I watched it for a few seconds, waiting to see what it might do. Then it dipped. And clicked at the top as it jumped.

Lyt walked around the back of the building. I pocketed the detector as he smiled as if with a secret. "This is workable." Good.

It took very little time to sign things and make the deposit. We did have to go to the reality office and do paperwork but that was no problem. Keys were handed over and alarm codes given. Lyt was fascinated by the oddest things. "We will need some tools and parts. Is there a store for electrical items?" I looked around.

"Probably. I'll check." I pulled into a gas station and asked the cashier inside. "Radio parts and electronic surplus. Two miles that way in the big ugly building. Can't miss it."

We drove and I mentioned the detector. "There was a click and then another, you appeared from around the building. What's up?"

"Up?" He considered it carefully. "Most things when compared to us." He dug into a pocket and removed a vial of tablets. They were a faint greenish sickly color. He took one out and swallowed it without chewing. I caught a smell that made me gag slightly. He took a draw of water from one of the chilled bottles in the cooler.

"No no, I mean, the detector clicked a couple of times. Is there a reason for that?"

He understood. "I had to make certain that the adjoining land was clear for travel. I went through to the resonant world and verified that the building is in a good place."

Ah, so traveling through to some other place affected a detector. That was good to know. "How do you travel from world to world? Is there a special device or what?"

"There is. It can be done without it under just the proper conditions but the device makes it much easier. Far more repeatable and helpful. In part this is why I am here. I need to make new tools and gather resources. Are you capable with your hands?" He took another drink of water and watched the passing landscape with open curiosity.

"Each world has a flavor that is its own. Here there is a quiet energy to things. It smells good and it is appealing to the eye." He inhaled slowly and deeply and seemed to relax a little.

I considered the travel aspects. "You can step through easily and get back just as easily. Are there some places that might be... oh, I don't know. Like what if something is where you are trying to step through. A solid object."

"There is a *tension* to occupied areas. It would be like walking up a slippery hill. You cannot force your way there." He adjusted his thick glasses a little and surveyed ground, air, and roadway.

"Okay. So what about land level? Could you step through and fall into a hole or something? Like off a cliff?"

He nodded. "That is one hazard. Some places have different air or you will find an ocean of predators. Sometimes it is raining or you end up in the middle of a crowd of people. Or worse." He sighed deeply. "There are many things that can go wrong and you try to prepare in advance as fully as you can. You heed signs and warnings as well as possible."

It could ruin your day to step into a landslide or fall into a deep hole. "Are there any ways to see in advance what you will run into? Some sort of spy probe or gadget that can look around for you?" He smiled broadly.

"I have thought of this. Again, I am to… regroup I believe the term is. I have many ideas that will help me finish this pathway. You are quick. It will be to our advantage and much can be done now."

We arrived at the electronics surplus place. A large, gaudy fluorescent orange building with badly faded paint and a large black sign painted on it announced "Surplus and unusual goods". The parking lot was well enough cared for, but there were a few potholes that bore attending to.

Inside it was cooler and much brighter than I expected. There were large skylights and the overhead was mostly iron trusses made of thick rebar bent back and forth in a zigzag pattern. A parachute was suspended near the ceiling and spread out like a canopy. Lyt was looking at rows of cardboard and plastic bins, sheets of metal and phenolic. He was enrapt. "Oh my. Oh yes indeed. The very thing." He turned to me and looked positively childlike and happy. "Wonderful," he breathed.

I located a clerk and asked if he had a shopping cart. He shook his head and handed me a basket. "Ain't a grocery store but we can get a dolly if you need." He bulged belly-first in his blue polo shirt and nodded to the left. I saw a line of roll around carts that were a little too flat and low. I grabbed another basket and placed two on the cart and followed after Lyt. It would do.

"Soldering iron," he hummed. "Circuit board material. Resistors. Ah. Strain gauges. Yes, yes. Many times wonderful." He located a small niche with paper bags and pencils. He was happily counting out small parts and placing them in the bags. "A moment please Mike? Your assistance."

I had to write out the labels and quantities. He didn't dare pull out his tablet or computer or whatever here. I did the writing and adding up. We soon had both little baskets full of small parts and odd gizmos.

"Tools of course. We will also need a worktable or perhaps two." I made fast notes on one of the empty paper bags. Tables. Work lights. Hand tools. Sanity check.

We spent a couple of hours just gathering bits and pieces. Batteries and battery holders, power supplies, metal tubing. I had no idea what some of the stuff was. Lyt was in heaven and spent about three thousand dollars on parts and stuff. We were going to need a trailer if we did this again.

It took a while to stuff everything in the vehicle. I was glad to have a large trunk. The tubing hung out an open back window. The clerk improvised a red flag for us and tied it to the end of the tubing. We were off to the metal building and then to a building supply store.

I was eating some chips and driving and Lyt was playing with his tablet and stylus. "Melios. Sando. Yes." Quick scribbling and a few moments staring into space, and he was smiling again. "I have a real hope of getting this done properly now. I am quite glad to have found this world. Do you like to travel, Mike?"

I was waiting for that question. "Love it. I don't do much any more but I enjoyed a lot of it years ago." We were getting close to the building. The landscape was greener and more inviting here than near the town. Sturdy oaks and a few elms flashed past as I drove. Lyt hummed a little tune with a foreign air to it. The scale was not quite right but somehow it sounded good. There were lots of odd turns to the melody. Catchy.

Gravel crunched under wheels and we pulled next to the door of the place. Lyt was ready to go, had the door open and the alarm code in with no trouble. I started unpacking bags and boxes. We moved all the random stuff into an area along one wall. Lyt had the small bag of tools located and carried them into the office. I knew that we were going to be hauling more than my vehicle could hold.

"Lyt, we need to rent a larger vehicle. A truck. Then we can haul everything without messing up my car." He assented. His hands flew over tools and bits, sorting and taking stock. He had conscripted a desk and was plugging in the soldering iron.

"All is very good. Yes, we will need building supplies and more tools.

Let us get food, you look hungry and tired. Then we will have that truck and get the rest of the materials I will need."

The afternoon was nearly gone but there was a truck rental still open in town. That was our next stop.

We spent the whole weekend moving and making. I have to break it into each day due to the many things that happened. He was an expert with a table saw and we had decent work benches and tables in a couple of hours. I found myself on a ladder dropping power cords from the ceiling for long fluorescent work lights. Lyt removed his eternal long coat and moved things and arranged until he was content. It was actually looking like a nice work place. A truck arrived out front with a set of cabinets and more boxes of things. We jockeyed and moved until we were both really tired.

"Well, time for me to get back home. What do we do now?" Lyt settled into a heap of packing material and sighed. "We must share information now. I would want to stay here and work but there are things it will be helpful for you to know."

"Well, there's no food or refrigerator or anything. What will you do?"

"Oh, I have resources. Let us see some things and then you will most likely go." He dug into the coat which lay beside him. A brass circular object was extracted and held up for me to see. It was slightly larger than his palm.

"First, I will explain some of the rules of travel. Laws actually. Worlds of similar mass, orbit, and star can come into resonance when they match each other's positions and movements just so. Sometimes the resonance is for moments, and those can be traps to the unwary traveler. Usually the resonance is for days or weeks. Almost never is a world in resonance longer than a few months. There are other factors but these are the most important ones."

I decided to take a seat and listen.

"When you travel, there is some resonance between worlds that are close in mass and orbit but that guarantees little. A world can be off a little bit in mass and its sun can as well, but overall things will be quite similar.

You can travel to worlds that are successively more varied but they must be closely in resonance and the real factor seems to be your potential energy."

I was trying to understand. "So you will probably find a yellow sun and an Earth-sized planet with an orbit much like this one but sometimes it will be a little off."

"Yes. For example, the mass of this star is going to be very close but the other star might be somewhat larger or smaller, as long as the mass is right. Stars can be in difference stages of their lives, or might be a little more iron rich or different in other ways. But your potential energy here and your speed of orbit must be very close for resonance to work.

"Some worlds will be primitive or pastoral. Some will be advanced or empty. Some worlds are only good as stepping stones to other worlds. But most worlds do not have intelligence or people. They are mostly animals and plants, sunsets and seashores."

His attention turned to the brass object. It had a spring clasp and looked hand made, although of nice workmanship. He clicked the latch and it opened easily.

Inside was a circle of set stones. Each was like a turquoise or an amethyst. Each was mounted on a tongue of metal that extended like the petals of a flower from a central hub. Two of the tongues were empty. Lyt lifted the circle of stones and a second one was beneath it. "Here you see why it is wise to collect a crystal or a stone from each world you visit." He replaced the wheel and spun it idly.

As I watched the wheel began to slow, back up. Two of the stones aligned and started to glow softly. "These stones are aligned and so are their worlds. If I were on either I could travel to the other. This is a simple device that I made some years ago but it has been very useful." The ever-present drawstring bags made an appearance. He drew a stone from one and placed it in one of the empty slots. The wheel was spun lightly.

The stone did not align or light up. He removed it and tried another from the bag. It took three tries before he found one that worked. "Ah, there. This world is aligned and could be reached from this one." He pointed out faint curls and triangles. "I could step from here to there, thence to this world. But when some fall out of alignment, sometimes others will be present in their stead. Other times, you cannot reach a world easily or perhaps at all. It depends on how many stones you have showing your alignments and how well your resonator is tuned."

He reached and dug, found another device. "This is the heart of things." He opened a small rectangular box. It looked almost like a manufactured thing, as large as a wallet and made of some ceramic or plastic. He pried it open gently.

"While travel is possible without this, it can be difficult." The interior showed a three pronged metal thing like a mutant tuning fork with copper windings positioned around it. A small circuit card and a bundle that might have been batteries was also crammed into the case. "This is a resonator. It synchronizes with the resonant frequencies of worlds and shifts you from here to there."

He closed the case and touched a switch on the surface. A small light came on. "This is what makes a low level electromagnetic field that is matched to the resonant frequency of a world. Each world has one, each is a little different, and when they match up properly you can make the change from one to another. Think about moving vehicles with platforms on them. You can step from one platform to the other when the vehicles are next to each other and moving at the proper speed. This chooses the platforms."

That was it. Some stones and a coil, some batteries. It was too simple to believe. "So you can move from this world to another, and from it to another. Stepping stones. How do you find new worlds?"

He moved a control on the resonator, little more than a small knob. "This will cause the resonator to sweep its signal up and down until it finds something like a notch. When the resonator makes a weak signal and shifts its frequency slowly, it can show if a dip or change in its level is present. This usually indicates that another world is present and that we could travel to it. Then a quick trip and grab any stone or crystal you can.

"After you return you can fabricate an indicator that tells when the two worlds are in resonance. As you have done." I self-consciously touched the little tube in my pocket.

After a moment I had a thought. "It seems to me that you could use some sort of electronic method to tell when the stones are aligned. Right?" He looked curiously at me. "I mean, they repel or attract, they glow. Surely there are parts that can detect that sort of thing. You get a crystal from each of a dozen worlds and you get a dozen crystals from Earth that match them, and then you… well, that would be a lot of crystals. I think."

Lyt pointed to a box on the desk top. "That is a very good plan and the answer is yes, there would be many, many crystals. But if you could make each very small, then you would have something well worth making. And that is what I plan. Your friend, the coin dealer. Does he deal in jewelry and the equipment for cutting and polishing stones?"

"Morris? No, just coins and metals. But he's sure to know somebody that is. Come to think of it, that's a really good idea. I had no way of explaining why you needed to have so much cash on hand. If he though you were planning to make some jewelry then it might explain a lot. Sort of remove some scrutiny. I'll make sure I ask him."

"Ah, the conjurers' first and most powerful tool- misdirection. Indeed, ask him." Lyt stood and replaced all his gadgets. "I think we should take a brief trip and get you acquainted with the ways of wizards." I was immediately paralyzed. Trip?

Lyt consulted something in a pocket and indicated that I should stand. "Here, my friend. Let us see something new for you." I slowly, reluctantly made my way upright.

"I have a question. If Earth resonates with some very similar world, and it resonates with a similar world, isn't there a good chance that Earth will also resonate with that third world at some point? Like if A is similar to B and B is similar to C, then isn't it usually true that A is similar to C also? There should be a dozen like Earth and most of those will be like each other, right?"

"So many questions. Yes, it is true. And of nine that match out of the dozen, those may have two or three others that do not directly match but could be reached in two steps rather than one. I have been mapping some of them and have good predictive tables for when most should be reachable. But not all of my stones are in my possession. Part of my task is to recover them, to save many years of work without having to retrace my travels.

"Alas, some would be nearly impossible or truly impossible now. It would be a great service to find and acquire my lost stones. They are in a bag such as this." At that he held up one of the drawstring bags. "I have most labeled and others I know well. I was somewhat circumspect with the data. Others will not easily puzzle them out."

He was putting that coat on and preparing himself.

I was as ready as I could be. "Well, let's see this other world." He walked close and grasped the resonator in a sort of pistol grip hold and set something easily with two fingers. With his other hand he gripped my wrist tightly. "Brace your senses. Look at your feet."

I watched my shoes and felt a breeze that carried salt and straw smells. My ears felt tight as if they should pop. And the light faded up like a cloud lifting, a yellower sort of light than I expected. I exhaled rapidly and a sense of mild vertigo took me. I looked up as Lyt released my arm and realized that I was outside in a field of yellow grass.

We were on a flat stony patch of bare ground and all around was a mostly flat hillside covered with waving fields of yellow grass in all directions. I caught my breath and looked up at the sky. The sun was just a funnier yellow shade than I remembered but otherwise the same. The air smelled good, clean. That strange straw smell was the grass, and the soil was a brownish color.

This could have been anywhere on Earth, it was so familiar and simple. Lyt walked forward a few steps and the grass swished over the coat. I reached down and grasped a few of the long, wheat-like blades and pulled a couple free. I sniffed them and crushed them between my fingers, rolling them lightly to free up some essential oil or juice. Another sniff.

Yes, straw smell. But the juice that stained my fingers was yellowish also, not at all like the green of any normal grass. This was not dead and dry, it was living and moist. Lyt pointed to a tree some distance off. "The plants here are mostly yellow in color. Some are green and some are violet. Yellow dominates."

I started to taste the grass. Lyt warned me. "Ah-ah. I would warn against that. You have no idea what may be in that plant. It could be harmless, it could be toxic. Maybe a hallucinogen or a stimulant. Chemistry is one thing to be very mindful of."

I dropped the blades and wiped my fingers on my pants. Lyt led us along a thinning in the grass and pointed out something in the distance. Something white and glistening.

"Now what do you suppose that might be?" I looked at the distant thing and thought "glacier". Lyt pulled a small pair of binoculars from a pocket and handed them to me. I placed them over my eyes and peered at the white thing.

It was like shields or panels of something. They sometimes fluttered a bit but kept together and made the shape of a long hill. What the hell? I watched carefully for a moment and saw one flake off and fall to the ground. It righted itself and *crawled back up* where it took its place. It had long, jointed legs and appeared almost like a crab or large insect.

"Whoa. That's a big bug! What are they doing, nesting?"

"Climate control. They like it much cooler. When enough colonies are present, they actually lower the temperature of the planet and can start an ice age. They are reflecting sunlight back into the sky. Even their excretions are white. They leave the group to defecate and then return to keep the group cool.

"This world has no higher intelligence. It would be ready to colonize from the viewpoint of many people. There are some apelike creatures but they are a long way from being dominant in any realistic manner. Oh, and they are not mammals. More closely related to birds from what I have seen."

I thought of my little detector. "Is this the world that my detector is tuned for?"

"Yes. The stone came from here, quite a distance off." He consulted something and mumbled.

"Okay, that raises another question. How do you travel around here? No trains or bus service I would think." That earned me a broad grin.

"You are observant. No, I have a train system that I can use. It goes most anywhere." He twiddled the resonator and grasped my wrist again. I looked at the white scars on his arm as the light shifted and the grass smell went away. "It was time for me to look at this anyway." This time my ears required that I swallow a few times. Smells like oil and dampness filled this dim place. There was an overcast look to the sky. And then I saw the buildings. Very tall, very dense, like downtown Dallas or something.

"This was a technical world but the people apparently died. Some of the systems still work and one is a very serviceable transportation system. I believe that the machines are repairing things constantly but there is nobody here to take advantage of that."

Lyt pulled out the tablet and waved fiery letters into being. A map of some sort appeared in midair like a strange projection. It broke into sections, zoomed, broke again. A red-orange line grew and the tiles of map fell into place on it. A blue circle faded on and seemed to say "you are here".

"It would be a challenge of a walk for now. In theory we could get to nearly any place on your world, as long as the resonance is good, in about twelve hours. We enter the system, ride to the main hub, then travel to a point that would correspond to where you want to be on Earth. Then we step back two worlds and we are there. Unfortunately, this world will not be available in about three days, and it will be nearly six months before you could get to it again. Then, however, it will be in resonance with Earth itself."

I took a quick look around. There were buildings, rather odd looking but sort of futuristic. Mostly it was a city of metal and glass with long, empty planter boxes here and there. No streets, just broad walkways and plazas. Between some of the buildings were walkways at varying heights. Violet and orange graphics floated in front of a small nook that held something like a mailbox. Dead plants were in the planter boxes. A few small green vines twined upward in the scaled trunks of something like dead palm trees.

Lyt looked at a low wall that seemed to be made of dark glass. A rubber handrail topped it. "Ah, we could use this instead." I trod over to the wall and found a moving sidewalk strip behind it.

The blue-gray light of the place was slightly depressing but the buildings and walkways were intriguing. I wanted to run and explore and try things. "Mike, we want to stay close to our entry point. Otherwise we will emerge somewhere that requires a long walk back to the building on Earth."

"Right. Okay. Ah, is it okay to look around a little?"

"Harmless enough. We can spare a few moments." I saw what appeared to be a large store. The floating image of graphics was violet and green. Small off-white dots moved through the air toward the doors. The doors silently opened as I approached. A musty dry smell wafted out. The inner doors parted, Lyt not far behind me. I smelled machines, concrete and dry rot.

Inside were rows of displays and merchandise. The mannequins were almost people-like, but had smooth, hairless heads. The noses were mere tiny nostril holes, the eyes large and dark with horizontal pupils. I saw hands with four large identical digits that tapered like cones. On the bare arms you could see something like a dew claw above the wrist. Or second wrist. Wild. Alien mannequins. I wanted to take one home.

Lyt was quiet, walked lightly. I became wary. "Something wrong?"

He sighed. "No, I have seen too many worlds that were empty or abandoned. Technology often enough seems to be the death of a race. Or a world. This one is so nearly perfect that it could not have been long ago."

"Could it have been a disease? A virus?" I was suddenly terrified. Would I carry it back home?

"Never worry about viral infections. The genetic codes are different. A virus from this world would be completely harmless on Earth."

"What a relief." I spotted a jewelry case. "Ah, here we are." It was simple to open the latch from the back and extract a few cases. "In the name of science you know." I picked through a couple of things that looked like diamonds and rubies. Large ones.

"I just realized. I can't take large ones. It would be too hard to explain. Small will have to do." And then another thought. "Damn. Not too many. Same reason. Oh well."

Lyt was blasé. "Wise. Just what you need. I always try to leave things as neat as I found them. Destruction and waste are stupid." I chose a total of three stones; one diamond, one ruby, one topaz. The settings were either earrings or something else small. Did these aliens have ears? The metal was either white gold or platinum. I saw beautiful workmanship, but I am no connoisseur of trinkets. The tiny boxes were clear plastic, not like the velvet boxes I traditionally associated with such things.

"Okay, I can build a new detector now. And we have stuff for others if we need."

"I have samples of course. But you did properly. Fast learning is commendable."

I followed him out. I expect that we had been gone fifteen minutes. My watch said otherwise. "An hour already? That's crazy." Lyt found our point and grasped the wrist tightly, did something to the resonator. We were in yellow grass. My ears complained again and I breathed a little fresh air. The light was welcoming buttery yellow and made the blue-gray light of before a wan nuisance. I saw the distant white mass of crab insects bent on dominating the climate. Lyt led me to the small stand of rocks.

"This has been really… I don't know the words. Great. Wonderful." The tight grip on my arm and the shift in light and air pressure, and I was standing outside of the building. "Oh? I thought we would be back inside."

"The worlds are moving, the alignment is shifting. You must keep track of each planet and its sun and how it is moving. Alignment can be predicted by the relative velocities and alignments in a computer. They are detected as you know by the reactions of the stones.

"Longer trips accrue larger errors. Trips near the end of a resonance or alignment accrue rapidly growing errors. Best to keep them brief and have the least distance to travel." He placed the resonator back in a pocket and led us the last dozen steps to the building.

"Mike, I will stay here and work. There are things I must become familiar with. I have to practice wizardry and become proficient with the tools of your world. You, consider purchasing a garment with many pockets. Or have one made by hiring a tailor. The funding is available."

I nodded slowly. "Okay. Thanks. That's a really good idea. Oh, is your coat bullet-proof?"

"I have some armoring. Is it available here?"

"Maybe. I'll check."

Lyt turned to the building and walked carefully. He appeared to be deep in thought. I got in the vehicle, almost reluctant to leave. I had some phone calls to make and a few things to get planned for the next day. Sunday.

CHAPTER 3

It was a little overcast and the wind spit little droplets every so often. A strange chill was in the air. I ate breakfast, called Morris at home, and started asking about lapidary equipment.

"My friend wants to make some jewelry. He's sort of artistic and that was why he needed to cash in so much of his metals. I've seen some of the things he has made and they're unique."

Morris sounded relieved. "Ah, that explains a lot. You can burn through a lot of money doing jewelry. I'll call a couple of people and see what I can find. He needs lapidary saws and a casting furnace, hmm? I'll have some sort of answer by oh, Tuesday I think."

"Thanks Morris. Talk with you then."

I called the office and told them I had a family emergency and needed a few days off. They operated all week due to the nature of the business. I had until Friday before I had to worry about that.

The place seemed very empty. I was ready to see new worlds and do some exploring. I had the three stones on the counter in the kitchen and was looking at them with wonder. They were probably not cheap. I had already dug out my diamond tie pin and checked it against the diamond from the alien world. It did nothing. That's fine, I thought, it will soon. The little ruby was also nonresponsive but… I had the materials to make three new detectors.

The real issue was that if you had three worlds, you would need three detectors. If you had four worlds, you needed more. How many? I scribbled on a pad, trying to work it out. If you had world A, it could test for B, C, and D. That was three. Then B could test for C and D. And C could test for D. Total of six detectors for four worlds.

What about five worlds? That should be ten detectors, and I could see a pattern emerging. For any number of worlds, I would multiply it by one less. Then I should divide by two. Let's try it. Five worlds times four is twenty, and over two I get ten. Perfect.

What about four? Multiply by three and divide by two, I get six. Right on the mark! So for a hundred worlds I would have ninety nine hundred over two, or four thousand, nine hundred fifty detectors. That would be a serious mass of detectors.

How small could they be? And really, in some cases there would never be a resonance with some worlds and crystals. Maybe a dozen of each would work so let's call it a good working number. So for a hundred worlds, each having only a dozen resonant worlds, you end up with about three hundred really.

That would still be a serious number of detectors. If only they could be as small as a grain of rice, I would have something. Perhaps so. What if I cut the crystals into small pieces and placed them next to each other, small as millet seeds. They could be a millimeter or so and some sort of light detector placed in the mix.

Are there force detectors? I wondered if there were. Surely there had to be some sort of devices that could feel an attractive or repulsive force. If they were small enough, he could have a real detector literally as small as a rice grain. Lyt would appreciate that in his work.

I had to drive out to see Lyt and get a feel for what he was doing. But there was a knock at the door and there he was, surprising me somewhat. I let him in.

"How did you get here? Subway? It seems strange to cross the universe to get to the other side of town you know." He waved the thought away.

"Really, it is second nature to a traveler. I gathered a meal so I have eaten. You may enjoy your rancid coffee in peace." I had to laugh at that. "What brings you here? I was preparing to go out and meet you."

"I have been working most of the night. I wanted to discuss the devices we will be needing and share my plan with you. And I think you might enjoy a little hunting and gathering." I liked the sound of it.

"I had a few thoughts too. I was thinking about detectors. We could cut tiny bits of crystal and put them together with light sensors or force sensors. Make tiny dedicated sensors for each pair of worlds. What do you think?"

"A natural wizard you are. Tell me, is this what you had in your vision?" He showed me a small piece of circuit board with four capsules about a centimeter long each. There was a dark sleeve on each one and five little wires leading away.

Each capsule had an indicator next to it and all the wires ran to a microchip of some sort. A connector at the bottom was next to the batteries. "This will sense each resonance of four world conjunctions. When all four are true, the final indicator tells me that a path that leads across those four worlds is valid."

He had the same idea, but clearly it was obvious. The capsules were each sealed and safe, nothing to get lost. There was a lot of epoxy or heat glue holding it together but the concept was perfect.

"Do you sense the light or the attraction force?"

"Both. Attraction force can be masked by impacts or sudden movements. It can foggy... muddy the signal. The light output is steady and can be sensed very easily."

I assented. "Yes, I thought of cutting tiny pieces and sealing them into little sensors that would be very tiny."

"Indeed, the very thing. That is why I need the lapidary equipment. We will be able to create very tiny sensors and place many of them in a small space." He turned a little switch on to activate the sensor. Two of the LEDs lit up. He shook it slightly and I saw the other LEDs flutter slightly. "These are known as strain gauges. They can measure a tiny force and tell if it is pushing or pulling. When I combine the information with the light output I can get a very reliable signal."

"Lyt, it seems to me that we would want to arrange the crystals so that we can pack them densely. Put the most we can in a small space. If we do it right, we might get all hundred worlds on a tiny circuit board." I could see putting five or six crystals in a line with the light sensors maybe... behind them. On the back of the board, where they would be out of the way. Why, if you stacked things up, you might be able to get a couple of hundred worlds in a pocket sized device.

"Interaction of course. We cannot place detectors next to each other if they might interact. So we will have to sort them out and make certain that non-resonant worlds are in the same sensor. Then only the proper crystals will react." I could see a computer being given the data and working out a non-interfering pattern of tiny sensor crystals.

"Great. Hey, if we are making a lot of these sensors, why can't we hire a company to make the things, like a thousand of them? It would be cheaper and faster. We could have your strain gauges and the light sensors all packed into tiny tubes or slots and... well, we could have them made empty, and we just drop the crystals in with some glue or something to hold them in place."

He smiled at that. "Wonderful. We can make the first models and test them. Then we have the others bulk produced."

"Mass produced. Yes."

"Well then. Have you hired a tailor? You are going to need traveling clothes." He stopped. "Better still, let us go on that hunting and gathering trip. We may find something very suitable that way. Bring something to eat and drink, I would recommend." I hurried to the kitchen and made some sandwiches and put bottled water and soda in a knapsack. I had an old backpack from years ago, college. It was dusty but useful. I never got around to getting rid of it. Now I was glad to have it.

Lyt consulted his tablet. "Let us stand over here." He moved by the television, almost into the hallway. "This is suitable." I moved close and he grabbed my wrist with that wiry grip. The air pressure changed.

There was a dampness and a cool, chill breeze. A low morning (or was it evening?) sun was too orange in the thin yellow grass. Lyt adjusted something and we transited again. Now the air pressure was a little higher and a faint oily smell was present. Blue gray sky and overcast, we were on an open road near a small kiosk. To the left about a kilometer off was a solid wall of varying skyscrapers. To the rear was another. Right was a long rocky wall with a soaring bridge that led off over bare ocean. The salt smell was just detectable. Before us was a park of some sort.

We were on the alien world. I had to think of a better name for it. "Lyt? Does this place have a name?"

"Boro, as close as I can tell. I think of it as the gray tech world. Let us find stores and do some searching. We need a new computer and you need a coat." He sat at the kiosk and waited. I felt a little surprise. "Come, come, the vehicle will arrive soon." I pulled out a water bottle and handed it to him.

"Thank you." He pulled out one of those gag-inducing greenish tablets and swallowed one. I watched as he took a deep pull on the water. "Rather good, to say. Most appreciative of your kindness." He made the bottle vanish into another of those pockets. And soon a small and silent bus-thing arrived and slowed to a stop.

I watched as it hovered silently and dropped wheels to the ground. As it was in motion the wheels were retracted but when it slowed the wheels came down and rolled it to a stop. Very cool. The doors slid back without a hiss and we boarded. There were large and well padded seats. They looked like leather or some sort of vinyl. Everything looked like new.

Lyt chose a window seat and started humming. I sat near the front and watched from the vantage point that gave the best city view. After a few seconds of waiting, the doors closed and a purplish light came on near the front. A sound of a voice with odd trills and clucks thrown in started running. Probably said to keep your hands in the windows and not spit out your gum.

There was a soft click and a fine whining hum at low volume, barely noticeable. The bus started moving forward and with a slick clunk noise I assumed that the wheels were retracting. It was smooth, quiet, and very neat. I thought of some sort of airport tramway.

Why was everything predominantly blue? Violet seems to be the favorite color here and bright orange. Tacky but it somehow matched the mood of the place. The sky continued to be overcast. I watched, fascinated as the city approached.

"Lyt, there seems to be plenty of plant life. Are all the animals dead here?"

His eyebrows raised a little. "The only species that died out was the people. I think. But the machines tend the city and so there are very few wild creatures that make it here. I don't know about the farms or any agriculture. There are too many worlds to explore to search for details sometimes. And data can be sparse." He laughed. "They did not leave an owner's manual for the planet."

For some reason this was insanely funny. I could barely stop laughing. The city was nearly around us, and I was laughing like a maniac. Lyt seemed amused as laughter, even across species, must be infectious. He began to chuckle as we slowed at a terminal in a broad, very attractive plaza.

We stepped from the vehicle and I was awed by the massive hexagons that stood before us. The plaza was a pentagon in shape and was ringed by a hexagon on each side that stood on edge. A water fountain was in the center and above it was an encircling ring of water nozzles aimed down.

As I approached it I watched the nozzles open and close, dropping precise bursts of water that clearly were creating graphics. Walls of water dropped geometry and what might have been text. The noise was not as bad as I expected; the water fell into deep slots and was captured below the plaza so the splashing was not overly loud. Leaping bursts of water seemed to sprout from the pond in the center and jump into other small ponds around it.

I passed my fingers through the water and felt that it was nearly icy. The sight of the dancing water gave me a sense of peace but the excitement was ever-present. I felt like something might walk out of a doorway at any time and confront us. Lyt was in no hurry; he seemed completely at ease. I tore myself from the sight of the fountain and walked back to the general area of the bus stop.

He led the way. We entered a long, glassed-over area that led from the fountain plaza and looked at the buildings. Some showed glowing signs or projections and others were rather anonymous. I picked one. "This looks about right."

It had storefront window displays along either side of the broad doorway. It just *felt* like a store. We sauntered in and started looking for merchandise. This was rather nice with lots of lattice work and display cases. Many of the things in the cases were fairly obvious. Some looked like maybe cosmetics, pens, small devices. We continued toward the back.

This place had little more than trinkets and gadgets. It was all very nice but I saw little that would be practical. Lyt seemed to think otherwise. "Here. This could be what I need." He pointed to a case full of remote control looking thingies. I shrugged.

He stepped around to the back of the case and found a latch. In a moment he had selected a small device and what might have been a battery pack. He slipped the pack into a small cavity and squinted at the many buttons. After some consideration he touched one.

A floating display appeared in front of the device. He dragged his fingertip through the orange and violet cloud of icons and shapes. Then he retrieved his tablet and held it next to the device. After a few seconds the tablet showed screwy Arabic and a progress bar (does every planet have progress bars? Something to think about.) In a few seconds the new gadget showed screwy Arabic and Lyt seemed quite pleased.

"Yes, this will do nicely. We will take a little time to get the fine points worked out but it will do." He found a set of boxes in the bottom of the case, then selected an identical one to the model he held. Wrappings came off, batteries went in, and Lyt repeated the procedure from his tablet.

"You will want this one. I am setting it up for your language." He repeated the tablet interactive thing and then started fiddling with the keyboard. I came closer to see what he was doing. As I watched, the patterns of dashes and squiggles on the buttons shifted and melted. New markings grew right in the rubbery button tops. English letters appeared. "For you." He gave me the alien device. "You can start keeping notes on where we go, what we do, and learning how to work with me. Now let us find a proper garment, if possible."

I took the thing and felt the heft of it, the rubbery grip of it. The display was sluggish but in a good way. When you jogged the device the display didn't wiggle around. It sedately followed like one of those Steady-cam devices. I could spend weeks playing with this just to get used to it. The hologram or whatever it was had only a hint of granular nature to it. Its only irritating aspect was the orange and violet color. I would have to find the desktop or wallpaper settings and do something about that.

Lyt was nearly to the door and I, laggard that I am, had to hurry to catch him. I had to think that Lyt himself must be from a pretty high-tech world in order to have this sort of easy familiarity with odd technical things. But a computer is a computer and no matter who made it or where you find it, there will always be some sort of common ground with the things you know, true? Well, maybe.

We were back in the plaza and I was looking for mannequins and clothing. Two small machines not much larger than bread boxes scooted along, patrolling for litter perhaps. They had a rounded look to them, smooth like an old fashioned refrigerator. Both were a light metallic blue color and seemed to fit right into the scene. Lyt ignored them and they ignored us. Ahead was a long stretch of windows that did contain alien clothing displays.

"This may be acceptable." I followed him into the store.

This was much more "high end". There was some indefinable air of class to it that seemed to ooze from the air itself. We wandered and looked, touched garments on various displays and racks. I saw a thing that looked rather like a long coat, but it had strange cut out sections in the sides and back. I had no idea what that was about.

Lyt walked casually, taking in details. I pulled out a sandwich and started to munch. The lighting above us had the same bluish quality that the light outdoors had, and my sandwich looked a little unappetizing for some reason in that light. I ignored and bit and chewed, enjoying a little salami and cheese. Then I got a surprise.

A hologram or projection appeared in front of me. It was an alien in some sort of neat outfit that appeared to be telling me something. I stopped and watched it. The speech was fairly normal although foreign and with a few trills and clucking noises. Lyt stopped and looked back.

"Turn on your computer. Find the translate function." I did a little poking and found something that looked like it might be it. The voice repeated from a tiny speaker.

"Consuming premises within do no more. Express comply please now." I was a bit slow.

"Oh. My sandwich. No eating in the store. Got it." I folded the sandwich into its wrapper and put it in the backpack. "If the computers are smart enough to recognize eating then they are smart enough to do other things. We might want to be really careful in some places." As usual Lyt simply nodded.

The hologram faded out and I had no more trouble. It was clear that I would have to behave as I did in any nice department store on Earth, dead civilization or not. I wasn't really that hungry anyway. "Lyt, should we be looking for hunting or traveling supplies?" He made a very normal shrug. "If we asked the computer for that sort of information, it might be able to direct us."

"I have been mildly reluctant to engage the systems to any great degree. What is your sense of this?"

"Don't know. Nobody is buying anything, nobody lives anywhere, nothing is being consumed or used. What does the system think of it? Is it smart enough to know that something is terribly wrong? I can't figure that out without asking it."

Could I talk to the computer or whatever was running things? Perhaps.

The translate function was still active on my computer. I spoke to the device. "I need some assistance please." There was a pause, then the computer spoke a set of chirps and words. I waited.

The hologram appeared once more. "Provide shall I help." It actually looked attentive.

"I need clothing for hunting and traveling. Long coats with many pockets."

The computer spat out the nonsense noises. The hologram spoke again.

"Which region to travel and beasts desired you for."

I didn't think about that. I had no idea what regions or areas or even animals there were. "Uh, general. Maximum utility."

Lyt was paying attention closely. "Good, that may work." He aimed his tablet at the developing scene. The hologram turned halfway and beckoned.

"Direction orient self to follow." I oriented self to follow as prescribed while chuckling inside. The lighting which had been at a dim standard in the rear of the store began to grow much brighter. We walked behind the hologram and gawked at things on the way.

It stopped in front of a large display of clothing and what appeared to be weapons. I recognized two styles of crossbow and rows of arrows and darts. Farther down was what appeared to be camping supplies. "Thank you for helping me. I will look around now." The hologram made a sort of bowing movement and vanished. Lyt applauded subtly.

"Well done. You have saved us time and effort."

"The English is rotten on this thing. I'm going to need to train it a little. Geez, I'm using alien computers and chatting with holograms and shopping in a department store billions of light years from home. Totally weird."

I looked at clothing and camp tents and weapons. It was really very homey. "Lyt, we should find a library and take full advantage of this place.

I mean, you say it will be unavailable soon, but surely we could download a ton of material and study it later at our leisure. Whenever that will be."

"The very idea. I agree that this would be wise. I have become somewhat more cautious of late. And truly, we have an escape route should things go wrong. My concerns were of taking an action that would be irrevocable. Turning the systems against us as it were. I would not want to lose this place as a resource you know."

"Well, I would like to ask some pointed questions and perhaps we could learn a lot of things. Knowledge is power." I felt the thin fabric of the tent in front of me. Very slippery, thin stuff that appeared to take on the colors of its surroundings. I wanted it.

Of course I had to restrain my wants. It may be something useful but only if you were in survival mode. It was the important things that I really should stick to. The coat with the pockets. I wandered back to the clothing display.

This was neat- it had that same shimmery fabric and it seemed to fade into its background. Oh yeah. It felt like a smooth cotton fabric but it was so thin I could fold it in a pinch between my fingers and it seemed to not be there. It had lots of pockets and it was long, even had what appeared to be matching leg coverings. I pulled it from the display and lifted it.

It was featherweight stuff and the interior had a silky feel to it. The sleeves were a bit long and the coat a tad narrow. I tried it on. Instantly the interior felt warm and soft. I could tell that I was going to like this. I ran my hands over the insides. No seams or obvious stitching, but here I found three large pockets above each other on the left. A matching pair on the right and a small holder of some sort for perhaps ammo or glasses; it was almost exactly what I was looking for. Lyt was checking it also.

I examined the somewhat elastic adjustments and was able to get the basic shape a little friendlier to my body, as compared to some sort of upright lizard. The coat was always going to billow a bit at the bottom and had a strange ruff at the back where I would assume a tail would emerge, but overall it was workable. A strange T-shape at the back seemed to take up excess fabric a little as I shifted in it. Clothing makers on Earth could learn a few things from this odd garment.

With a little experimenting, I found that the neck pulled out and could be turned into a hood. The fabric stowed into a place under the collar, completely hidden when it was pulled back down. I pulled it up and closed the front. Lyt looked a little surprised. "Oh."

I pulled the hood back down. "What?"

"It matches the background and seems to vanish. Truly a hunter's coat. I must consider one of these for myself. Very useful." An excellent find. Perhaps I could find one a little closer to my size.

It took some rummaging around and I replaced the display model, just to be neat. I found a box that contained the coat and leggings, but shoes were going to be a real problem. These guys had feet that were a little toenail-heavy. The sole was half as long as mine, the heel was lifted like a dog's leg and ran another foot-length up and back. Well, some standard black or brown boots would have to suffice.

"Okay, I have a coat. You know, this is fun. I could spend a lot of time just window shopping and checking things out."

"It is rather addictive but you must also be wary. What if the store computer insists we pay? How would we react to that?"

"Excellent question. I wanted to ask about that also. Why have we not been challenged? Either the economics here are different from what we expect or there is something that the system is allowing due to unusual circumstances. I expect that some programmer somewhere probably built some sort of emergency contingency program in, like if everybody dies or something, everything is free. Survival mode or something."

"Perhaps. To what end?"

"Maybe if nearly everyone was dead, the system would allow survivors to take what they need so that they can start over with the minimum of trouble. If something killed almost everyone, they wouldn't want the machines denying them access to necessities because they didn't have cash or credit cards. That would make the machines part of wiping out the few survivors that were left. Not an acceptable option."

"I do hope that is correct. If so, we would have free access to most anything, as we seem to, and it would explain it logically." Lyt activated his new computer. "I shall put the question to the system." His fingers rapidly pushed a few keys and the display shifted around.

He spoke carefully. "Store clerk. Where are all the people today?"

The hologram appeared and spoke. My computer said, "No people seen have been or detected. One and sixty passages of year since."

Lyt: "Is there a supervisor or manager who I may speak with?"

The hologram locked, waited. Then it shifted and a different hologram figure appeared in its place. It looked official. "Greeting. Operations perhaps helpful I shall be."

I shifted from foot to foot. The hologram seemed to look each of us over carefully. Lit chose his words carefully. "We are concerned that there are no citizens to be found. We are visitors and wish to be helpful. Will you tell us what happened to the citizens?"

The official looking hologram was somewhat more aware than the store unit. "Apparent disaster biological. No citizens accounted. All systems in emergency supply mode. We will give information and assistance." My translator was getting better. Finally.

"Is there an information repository or library where we can learn and preserve your data? It is most vital now that your data be learned from and saved." Lyt was pushing the humanitarian side of things. "Perhaps some citizens live and we can locate and render assistance."

Official hologram said: "That is desirable. Suggest a course of action and we will follow."

I spoke. "There may be sheltered or safe areas in this world. You must send machines to scout them and locate survivors. Render aid and supply food and tools."

The hologram regarded me. "Logical. We cannot travel far from the power system. We have limits of range."

That was easy. "I commission you to carry portable power units and to construct a power system that allows you to reach all areas of the planet that might contain survivors."

"But there are environmentally sensitive areas that we are not permitted to enter."

I looked at Lyt. He shook his head. I pressed on. "Since lives are potentially at risk, you must do this. Start a new program. You will expand the power grid to reach all areas where survivors might live. You will create a system of vehicles and assistance machines that will carry food, tools, clothing, and medical equipment. They will search for survivors and give aid to them. You must do minimal damage to those sensitive areas in this project. Is that an acceptable program?"

The hologram considered it. "You are not citizens. You are visitors.

However you are the only authority that has appeared in sixty one years. You are sentient beings and not machines. Therefore, the logic of your statements and your position of authority will be evaluated."

He then went on. "As the only living sentients that we are aware of, we must provide you with guardians to assure your safety. Until such time as a citizen is found, you are considered to be the authorities. Stand by please."

Lyt was looking a little worried. "This could be not good."

"Oh, I don't know, we're doing the right thing. If anyone is still alive, they need to be helped." The hologram faced Lyt and then me.

In English it said, "Yes. You are doing the right thing. We will provide you with support and assistance." Whoa.

"Lyt, are we done here?"

"Indeed. We should go to our transfer locations and leave. We have been here for quite some time."

"Okay. I think we should make certain that the system understands that we are going to travel. That we need free passage to do the most good. Officer."

The hologram looked at me. "Yes."

"We are going to be traveling to various places. Sometimes we will leave this world and then return. There should be no interference or restrictions. I would like to receive a report when I ask for it, telling me how the project is going. Okay?"

"Of course. State a name for yourself."

"I'm Mike. This is Lyt. He and I both are concerned about your world and its citizens. Do you have a name?"

"I am Prizka Security."

Two slender robotic looking aliens rolled into the room. They were almost like the mannequins but with treads instead of feet. Each was painted to look like the hologram of the alien security program. "Here are your guards. They will provide for your safety."

"Thank you Prizka. Lyt, let's go."

We left the store with the two robots in tow. "Hey, do we have time for that library stop?"

Lyt shook his head. "We can come back another time within the next couple of days. Perhaps we can find a resonant world for this one that we can step through from. I will do a scan."

He produced the resonator and took some sort of readings. "We have perhaps two that might work. I am not familiar with either of them. Shall we go to the transfer point first? That way we will be most ready to leave in a hurry if we must and not worry about being lost some distance from your home or the workshop."

"Yeah, whatever."

We walked back through the glass roofed plaza to the spectacular fountain area. The bus stop was just steps away. The robots followed. As we sat at the bus stop, we chatted lightly about detectors and the universe in general. After a few minutes the bus floated up and dropped wheels. Doors slid open.

One robot got on the bus first, its treads splitting into two sections. One lifted onto the steps and the robot leaned and rolled forward. It made funny stepping motions of the tread halves and perched near the back of the bus. Lyt and I entered and the other robot followed. The bus took off with the customary projections and chirpy voice announcements. The course carried us through the city and round a loop.

"Well, at least we found what we needed. And, we might have done a good deed for the whole planet. Maybe some of these guys are alive somewhere and we've helped get them on the path to recovery. I would love to meet them." I watched as the bluish buildings swept past and we left an arched entryway to the city. The long and featureless road ahead led back to the bus stop we had first used. Lyt touched the long stripe near the ceiling and it illuminated along its length. Soft chiming sounded.

The bus slowed and dropped wheels again and we prepared to step off. I looked at the closest robot. "We are leaving now but we will be back later. Do you understand?"

"Yes, Mike." Lyt didn't even get off the bus. He gripped my arm and said "brace for a short drop". We stepped into the space just above the grass and he landed gracefully, I a little harder.

"Why did we do that?"

"You must be prepared for most anything. Sometimes we end up a half a meter above the dirt and so you need to be developing a stance for it. The last world is moving out of alignment soon and as it does, we will get sloppier entries."

The sun was much higher now in the yellow grass world. "What's this place called?"

"Melios. Primitive and quiet. No really aggressive predators, the insects appear to have eaten many of them. Stay away from them. They are aggressive but mostly defensive."

"You don't have to tell me twice." I followed him as he walked a few meters this way and that. "What are we looking for?"

"Doors in the air. This is it." He grabbed my wrist again and we were behind my apartment. My ears popped that time. I swallowed a few times and got the pressure back to normal.

"Oh, my keys are inside. Not sure if the door is open or not." He tried it and it opened easily. "Okay."

I pulled out the sandwich and ate the rest of it. We had been gone well over three hours. I spent some time examining the computer and seeing how to set the display a little differently while Lyt did things with his computer. "Mike, I am going to send you a download. This is a schedule of some worlds and how they align. Also you will be needing the frequencies of each. And once you finish your food, we will go back and check those other transfer points."

"Great." I chomped rapidly and gulped down some juice. Lyt did something and my computer chirped plaintively. I saw a block floating in the display volume that said "Accept?" I did. The thing made little squarbly noises and said "done".

A little box that might have been a file holder appeared. I poked it with my fingertip. It expanded and filled the area. The top opened back and a neat little sheaf of folders appeared. At least they looked like folders. I selected one. It slid up and folded open, revealing a list of little pictures and notes. I poked one of the images.

It obediently swelled into a full color picture of some alien place. The image swam forward until I could push my head into it and see it in wrap-around. "Oh, cool!" I kept swinging my head around inside the picture, trying to catch the edges or limits. The three dimensional effect was great. The colors were slightly weird. Even though I could see right through it, the image was very good. In a dark room it would be wonderful.

I pulled back and touched the dark ring at the bottom of the picture which then collapsed and retreated back into its folder. I touched the dark bar at the bottom of the folder and it went back into the box, which then shrank to an icon.

Lyt was watching me play with the computer. "Get your coat, Mike. Develop a routine and put your tools and items where you automatically know how to get to them. Time is critical when danger is present."

True. The strange coat was in a small box that came straight from Boro, the gray tech world. Time to get dressed for travel. Stretching into the coat, I found that curious soft warmth and slick cloth very comforting. The computer went into an inside pocket, another sandwich and drink I placed in the outside pockets.

"Ready as ever." I watched Lyt change some settings on his resonator and then hum with satisfaction.

The grasp, switch, and ear effect did not catch me unaware this time. The second shift left us just meters from the bus stop, where the two robots waited patiently. "Ah, well met" said Lyt.

"Now to see if either of these other resonances can be used." He slid something downward with his thumb, touched a button and grabbed my wrist. It was dark.

It was dead silent. Only the faintest of light could be seen. There appeared to be stars and some scattered ragged clouds. It was warm and damp, overly humid. Lyt stood absolutely still. I held my breath. After a moment his hand loosened its grip and he found a small flashlight. It faded on instead of the rapid snap of brilliance from a normal light.

"Oh." Thin wavering stalks of chalky white were moving like tentacles. There were thousands of them standing erect in the place of grass. Just meters from us they stretched up the side of a small rocky bank. Lyt slowly turned and shown the light, then grabbed my arm and we were back by the bus stop.

I exhaled, unaware that I had been holding my breath the whole time. Lyt turned off his light and put it away. "Well, at least we know it is usable. But desirable is another issue. Perhaps in a pinch."

He showed me his computer. The scene had been recorded in a hologram using his little light. It showed the "grass" was little wormy stalks, each with a tiny eyeball on the end. What I had missed was the dark mass in the center of the stalks. Some sort of animal was wrapped securely in the fibrous tentacles and was struggling slowly against them. Ugh.

In the other direction there were few details to be seen but there was a muddy hole that seemed to be filled with some sort of ooze. He adjusted the light and contrast for the picture and I saw ugly, slithery looking things here and there. Wormy planet.

"Care to try the other one?"

"Let me get over these jitters first. Yuck." I took a deep breath and tried to relax. "Okay, whenever."

He dialed up something else. The traditional arm grasp and I thought I would have a permanent bruise there soon. Red leaves blew past me and green grass with violet edges stood barely above ankle height. The smell of burnt cinnamon was in the air. Something like a bubble floated past followed by a train of milkweed and thready filaments. Lyt spoke first. "Looks normal enough."

I laughed openly. "What the hell are you talking about, man?" The sky had a pinkish tinge to it and the trees had bubbles all over them. Red leaves scurried and ran against the wind this time, and I saw that they were thin, flat insects or something similar. Fine bristles or hairs gave them an appearance something like velvet. A tree released a batch of bubbles and the wind carried more scorched cinnamon smell.

Lyt walked a few steps toward a large stone, stopped and backed. The stone rotated slowly with a huffing noise and showed itself to be a tortoise of some sort. Its vast bulk made dragging noises as it turned. It cast an eye at us, a rather solemn golden iris moving strangely like a fish in water. It brayed.

That made me jump. Turtles don't have voices. But this isn't really a turtle now, is it. The neck stretched out long, longer, and the head rose nearly to eye level. It was chewing on something and a long line of turtle drool slowly stretched to the ground. I stepped a few steps to the right, Lyt was heading slightly left. The turtle thing dipped its head down and rooted something from the soil, started chewing again. A clod of grass turned over and exposed white roots as he rooted and chewed.

I grabbed at a passing bubble and was rewarded with a pop noise. The bubble was a gummy material like sap but very thin. The smell was like cinnamon but earthy. I started to wipe it on the coat and thought again. I lived with it on my fingers.

There was a spot where the turtle had been digging that showed a couple of shiny stones. I took the few steps and picked one up, pocketed it. Lyt was also looking for something. "I got a stone. It might have crystals."

"Very good. Pleasant enough place. Nice really." I watched as the pinkish clouds and light shifted and colored. It looked like an eclipse was coming. Lyt was trotting down to the left, apparently seeing something that caught his interest. I was more wary, went widely around the tortoise and followed Lyt. There were rather large flat flowers here and there in the grass. Their petals were similar to the grass in color but pastels, light green and light purple.

Lyt was recording the scene and doing some general surveying. Some shrubs ahead lined a small thread of water. He stepped carefully around something and stooped toward the stream. He then rose and came back toward me. "Very good. This is a nice place, at least so far." He prepared the resonator and grabbed my wrist. "Shall we go?"

"Yeah. Great screaming turtles, yes." We appeared back at the bus stop but in the middle of the road. Lyt was happy.

"Two new worlds, that is very nice. We can now record how they will be in resonance with Boro and we can add two new detectors to our repertoire, once we start making them. From the survey data, I don't expect that they will be in resonance for long however." He sniffed something he had in his hand. Probably a bit of plant life, possibly something that would make me sick. "Let's go to the workshop and get things taken care of."

I followed him to the bus stop and we waited for a bus. He consulted his old note pad and stylus and then his new computer. Apparently satisfied, he sat quietly at the bus stop. A bus arrived shortly. "Lyt, there always seems to be a bus when we need one. How is that?"

"They are being dispatched from a terminal near here. This time we go to a new route that will take us near the workshop and we step through." I had another drink of juice and we boarded the bus with the robots. The route was the same into the city and once there we skipped three stops and got off near a large transportation hub, like Grand Central Station. Lyt selected a route and we walked to a moving sidewalk. The train station at the end had only two cars but both were ready to go instantly.

"This is it. Not far from here now."

The train was much more plush that the bus. The robots seemed to not mind being tagalongs, and the ride was through a dark, steep tunnel and at very high speed. As the train emerged from the tunnel, the sky was seen clearly at last, and the clouds seemed to be breaking through. For the first time I could see the sun here.

It was very normal, exactly like the sun on Earth. Something in the air seemed to create the blue color, but what? I suspected some particles in the clouds or at high altitude. Lyt got my attention. "See that?"

"Yeah. Wow." In the distance, over the rock lined sea coast I saw a slender, dark form rising from the waves. It looked like a glassy black needle with a broad base. "What is that thing?"

"Hard to say. Not a natural form however, that much is clear. I cannot imagine what it might be for." The shape was like an arrowhead or a long, thin dart. It appeared to have a hole through it near the top. It must have been kilometers tall. I turned to the nearest robot.

"What's that thing?"

The robot turned and looked. "Star cradle."

I waited for more information. Nothing. "Oookay." Another mystery. What would life be without them?

The train slowed and stopped, we disembarked and found a short moving sidewalk. Lyt led us along.

"We shall walk from here." The robots moved along silently. Lyt found a place near an intersection and halted. "We will return in a while." He grabbed my wrist and we were standing in a field of yellow grass, not far from the flat stony area. He walked to the stones and took a pace past them. We stepped into the interior of the building as my ears popped. "And done."

I may never need to buy gas again at this rate. We had used transport systems on other planets to get a few miles from the apartment, and seen sights along the way that would have been difficult to explain. I slumped into a chair and Lyt started putting things out of his pockets on the work bench.

I looked about and saw that he had been very busy. There were three work tables now and lots of drawer cabinets lined one, all filled with parts of all types. The soldering iron was complemented by a power drill and some hand tools. Little parts were everywhere and some sort of thing made of metal tubing with wires draped all over it and pieces of things scattered nearby occupied the center of the table.

"So many things to do, and so many distractions. But all good, I assure you." He started sweeping parts into pile, sorting them rapidly by hand. Some went into drawers, others into more distinguished piles.

"Mike, have you ever done any small assembly work?"

"Not really, I didn't have the patience for it. But I'm willing to learn whatever."

"Here is the short term plan. We must make detectors and fit them into a computer that will go in a pocket. We must also make new small resonators. There is a program that we need to expand; one that tracks the movements so that even without a resonator we can know when worlds should be aligned. You must be trained."

I whistled. He looked at me curiously. "That's a lot of stuff to do. I'm going to need some time off work. What is the long term plan?"

He looked almost sad for a while. "Recover my stones, find my home world, and save a world."

CHAPTER 4

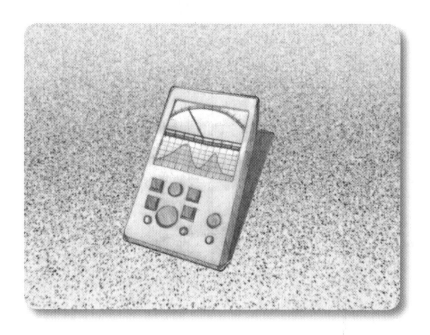

I spent the whole of Monday with Lyt bringing new tools into the shop. He bought a small lathe and a couple of drill presses and some bits and welding equipment. I learned how to change the tools and a bit of resonance theory. He explained how the orbits of planets were not really circles but ellipses.

"You see, if you lay an ellipse over a circle, there are one, two or some other number of places where they will touch or overlap. Picture a world that follows an ellipse around its star, and the farthest point of the ellipse overlaps a larger, more circular orbit. If both planets are in the same overlap area at once, and all other factors are correct, then resonance can occur.

"The issue is that the planet on the elliptical orbit will be as a lower velocity than the planet that is moving in a more circular orbit, so matching the two speeds can be tricky. In that case, there will be very little time when the two speeds and directions match up well. The windows of opportunity will be small and tricky to work with."

"I see." And I did. The two planets had to be of very similar mass and average density, their suns had to be of the same mass within a small window of error, and the planets had to be in the same places in their orbits. But more to the point, the speed that the two worlds moved at had to be close as well.

Lyt sketched a picture in the hologram space from his computer. "Now if the two orbits are nearly circular, there is usually a place where they can match for a month or more. Of the two, if one is slightly elliptical, it is possible for it to match up on both sides of the star for about a month or even longer. Those worlds are very favorable for traveling." He showed me the overlap of the circle and the ellipse. So far it all made sense.

"If a world has a broader ellipse, it can sometimes line up for a few days here and there, like so." He drew a new picture where the ellipse was off-center a bit and crossed the circular orbit four months apart. The rest of the year it showed no intersections and therefore no resonance. He then drew four circles and ellipses and then overlaid them with one another in sequence.

"Now we can see that this set of worlds will overlap like this: world A will align with B for a while and then A will align with C for a while. Then B and C will overlap a little, and D will overlap with A." He made the orbits change colors so I could see how it all came together. Then he made a dot circle all the orbits and I could see when they lined up.

"Here are the chances to travel from one world to another. Now we can model this in the computer and see how and when we can use the resonances." I watched as the planets were made to glow like the gemstones. It came together for me there.

He concluded the lesson and I came away with a better feeling for it. "Speaking of which, should we go to Boro and download those library records? Or we could tell the robots to do it and have them ready for us."

"Very good. Yes. We can tell them what we need in a few minutes. Then when it is out of resonance with us, we will have plenty to read and study." He hummed again, put his computer away and set me up making simple parts on the lathe. "Stay on that for the next half hour. I will return shortly."

He vanished like a fade-out, becoming transparent in a twinkling. I just stared at the empty space he left behind for a few seconds and then went back to learning how to operate a lathe.

I spun little pieces of tubing, cutting them in to a certain depth and radius. I cleaned the ends up and measured them. It was almost hypnotic work once I got the hang of it. A small pile of pieces built up as the time passed. My pocket detector clicked and I knew that he must have returned.

"Most effective. You learn quickly. I shall be using those parts now." He removed the small pile and went to his metal tubing thing. The pieces snapped in without any fuss and Lyt drove fasteners in here and there. The shape grew and it looked sort of like a folding divider screen. There were six panels that hinged together. They could be extended in height and width and folded as well.

Next Lyt started cutting pieces of wire and soldering them into connectors. I finished the last of the lathe work and watched as he put tiny bits of plastic heat shrink tubing over each solder joint. A hot air gun was applied and the tubing shriveled into a tight fit, making the assembly very neat. Lyt tagged each wire and measured them with a meter before bundling them into cable assemblies. He obviously had done this before.

"Mike, let's try an experiment. I don't know how much weight I can move with my resonator, but I want to see. I know I can move a couple of people easily but I expect that there are real limits. What are they and how do we expand them? We must find out."

As I watched, he loaded some sandbags onto a sheet of metal that was near his frame. I grabbed a few and helped him move them. He then placed the frame on the sheet metal and fastened it with clips to the corners. He stood on the pile of sandbags and activated his resonator. The whole assembly vanished. Moments later he reappeared.

"Well. The frame made it, the sandbags mostly made it." He scratched his chin.

"Where is the frame?" He looked distracted.

"Oh. I will need your help." He grappled my wrist and we appeared in the yellow field of grass. The frame was slightly twisted, there was sand in a swath and some of the bags were apparently okay. We moved them off the sheet metal bottom and I noticed a hole in it.

"Looks like it was eaten. Or sand blasted." He examined the damage. "Most curious."

I poked through the remaining sand bags. Some had large holes and the fibers looked frayed somehow. "These look like that bottom. See?" He spent a moment checking the bags and the fibers they were made of. A small magnifier came from somewhere and he was looking them over with great interest.

"I see, I do see. We will need more resonator power."

We got the bags to one side and retrieved the frame back to the shop. Lyt went through with the frame first, leaving me for the first time alone on the wrong side of the universe. It was rather chilling to think about. What if he had a heart attack? Was there food here? Suppose something attacked me. I was halfway through another scenario when he appeared and grabbed my wrist.

"There we are. Home you see. We must make a larger resonator and soon."

I gave the frame a good inspection. It was mostly intact, the twisting was just the joints themselves flexing as they should. It was minor scuffs mostly with one section showing some sort of abrasion. It was that funny sandblasted look.

It wouldn't take very long to make the new parts and adjust the others. A couple of hours at most. "What about the sandbags? Are we going to leave them there?"

"They are safe there. We can use them to do the next test, and that will be very soon. We have one other piece of machinery that we need to do the next stage." Under his hands the frame folded quickly and compactly. He had some sort of trick hinges in certain spots and I realized that there were bungee cords hidden inside the tubing. When folded up, the frame became limp and compliant.

But once it was unfolded and reached a certain point, the bungee took over and things snapped into place and locked. A very clever piece of design, no question about it. Lyt was stretching some of his cables over the frame and measuring them. I took the next drawing he gave me and started measuring pieces of metal rod and cutting them on the bandsaw.

After a few minutes of sawing and sorting the pieces into a little plastic tub, I started thinking about the rock I had snagged on the pink planet with the bubbles. Screaming Turtle world. Lyt could go anywhere the resonator could find a frequency for, but the rocks were just convenient indicators. I had to try something though.

I had three stones from Boro and the rock I had picked up. There may be some reaction with some of the stones. I dug out the three gems and looked in the pocket of the long coat for the rock. Those two worlds were in resonance now, or at least I thought so. I tried the diamond. Nothing.

The ruby also showed nothing. The topaz weakly responded. There was a soft tugging but I couldn't see any light. That was enough for me. Lyt was still deep in his work. I resumed cutting metal.

Over the course of the day the frame was repaired and I had made a number of odd metal pins and pieces. I was getting pretty good at the lathe and there was real satisfaction in making things. Lyt looked ready to try the frame again. I stopped the machine and cleaned up a little.

We made the step into Melios, the yellow grass world. I started dragging sandbags to the frame and loading them onto the sheet metal bottom. Lyt had replaced the eroded sheet with a new one. Once the bags were loaded he told me to stand to one side and he activated his resonator. He and the frame vanished but it appears that the bags were slightly delayed. The lowest bags took the longest to make the switch.

Lyt came back and got me.

"So what did we learn?" He made that funny head movement. I had no idea what it meant.

"The bottom bags are still not doing well. This is about the same as it was. The resonator clearly has a limited capacity and now I have some concept of what it is." He was examining the abraded area with a magnifier again. "Fascinating. I wonder where the metal and sand went. It might be anywhere in the cosmos."

"Lyt, we need to make some sort of probes or something. It seems to me that we are in danger any time we step through and if we have something that could look ahead for us, we could improve our safety." Could a resonator be operated by automatic machinery?

"This has weighed in my mind for some time. Let us confer on the idea and decide what we would need."

"Well, first, how small can a resonator be? And second, can it be operated by a timer or something? We would need to put a camera or a computer in it, so it can take pictures and report back. Maybe something to measure air pressure and temperature. Or better yet, a robot." Lyt straightened slightly.

"Yes indeed. If we could get one of the Boro robots, we could use it as a probe. Perhaps they would loan us one." He gathered a few small objects. "Let's get your coat."

We prepared quickly and stepped through to Melios, then to Boro. The same two robots were present and waiting for us. I took the lead. "We will require one of you to accompany us for an extended period of time. Is this possible? What are your power requirements?"

The closer robot responded. "We are powered by the radiant grid. However, we have internal power supplies that can operate for a few days. We can be operated by nearly any power source with a direct connection."

I felt that this was the right course. "We may be in situations that place us in danger. We will need your protection during this time. Will one of you come with us?"

"Yes."

Lyt carried the robot through without a hitch. He came back for me. This was going to be interesting.

<hr/>

After a few hours of tinkering and working with the robot, we had a recharger worked out. We also had a simple program set up that allowed the robot to check an area, take video and audio, then return to us. It assured us that it was water proof and capable of withstanding pressure and temperature.

Lyt started laying out the design of the resonator. He spoke with the robot at length and showed it how to operate the lathe and the saw. It took over the task of producing parts. After seeing a couple of examples of its work, Lyt seemed quite satisfied with the results.

"Well, Mike, we now have a new recruit. It will make whatever we need within reasonable limits and we can make more resonators. Let's get started." He showed me the odd tuning fork and the set of coils that drove it. There was a simple enough circuit made of a couple of oscillators that would have to be duplicated using Earth-made parts.

I was getting hungry. I talked Lyt into pizza and we ordered delivery.

"So Lyt, why the need for a larger capacity resonator? You said something about saving a world, I suppose you mean to move large objects to do it." He was silent for a bit.

"Yes, it will not be an easy task. Destruction is coming their way and it will take a large effort to convince them and then get them to do something about it. They are not presently reachable but they will be in a few weeks."

I had an idea that might help. "If we could send robots or probes through to do as much mapping as possible and gather stones from everywhere, isn't is likely that we could find a path to this endangered world that might be different from the one you know about?"

"It is possible. We would have to do a great deal of sorting and testing."

I felt confident. "What we need is simple. We collect rocks from everywhere, test them against the stone you have for that world, and then we can see if one of them is in resonance with that stone."

"Yes, yes. It is an excellent plan. The obstacle to that is a simple one however. I am missing some stones, as I mentioned. We must recover them before we can do this."

Damn. "Okay, I see. But wait. We can still start a mapping effort. We need automation. If we can make a fleet of probes and send them to these worlds for us, with some sort of search programs, we can map out all sorts of worlds and get them in the computer. Then we're already prepared when we get your stones back."

There was a moment as he thought about the idea, and then he brightened. "Yes, that is brilliant. I must admit that I have not been very clear on some of this myself. Emotion can cloud your thinking. You have given me a real hope of completing this task. Thank you."

Lyt started sketching and getting a design for a new resonator together. I answered the door and accepted the pizza. In a short while we were eating and relaxing a little and getting ready to build the new resonator.

It was late and the robot had stopped. Lyt showed it how to make metal rods in various sizes and bend them to form. Meanwhile, I was rolling wire onto plastic bobbins and making certain that the coils were neat. Lyt would don a helmet and start welding bits together and then judge how well they were coming along.

Wire winding is one of the most boring things you can do. There must have been miles of the stuff, shiny coppery magnet wire being spun slowly and carefully into coils. Some were long solenoids and others were flat like discs. When I got them done, Lyt had me paint them with some clear plastic stuff that really smelled toxic. They were set to dry next to a fan.

Lyt was happy and humming along. The robot was delivering parts for a new cage that duplicated the last one, which had also been repaired once more. I was thinking about the plan and how to best carry it out. Something struck me.

"Hey Lyt. I just thought about something. Do you have any sort of base of operations?"

"No, Mike. I've been more or less a wanderer for years. I sometimes have settled in one area or another for a while but never anything permanent."

"Ah. You know what you need?" I had a feeling coming on, one that was absolutely right. He looked up from his work. "You need a permanent base somewhere that is safe and neutral. Or more than one. Make certain that whatever worlds are open to you, you can get to at least one base. It's not like there are land owners that are going to evict you or charge rent."

"True enough."

"Look, you have wealth that you haven't even thought about. You can get any building materials, any supplies, machines, tools… you have no idea what your strengths are. Maybe it's been the perspective that you need. I can get something laid out for you in no time. I have friends who know all kinds of stuff about construction and wiring, and we could find all the design information on the Internet."

I was getting fired up. "This is easy. We're puttering around in a shop here with just the two of us when we could have a lot of things done for us, and done better than we know how. Real experts are on hand. We could have buildings, generators, water supplies. Computers, even robots and machine tools. All of this stuff is easy."

Lyt looked thoughtful. "Perhaps some of what you say has merit. I have been reluctant to make too much of travel between the worlds. There are possibilities that are not very nice. In the wrong control it could be a disaster."

"Well, true. So then we need to plan for that. Get there first. Let's set up some buildings here and there so that no matter what happens, we have backup hardware and safe places to be. Wouldn't that make your mission a little easier?"

"I will give this matter some thought. You are correct, it is sensible to have resources within easy reach."

I went back to winding my coils. Lyt did more welding. The robot made more parts on the lathe and then started assembling more tubing.

After about half an hour, Lyt was done. He held up three identical mutant tuning forks that were much larger than the one he showed me before, and two smaller ones that were the same as his. "We can test these easily enough." He took a coil from the drying rack by the fan and fitted it over the stem of a large tuning fork. Then a smaller coil pair was placed over the two upright rods.

Next he carried the assembly to the workbench and applied some screws to hold everything in place. He connected a small circuit board to the coils and hooked a battery to the whole mess. "Let us see if this can determine the resonant frequency of this world." He applied power and turned a control. The detector in my pocket rattled.

"Ho, very good. Simple to make actually, simple." He removed power and disconnected the battery. Now he started searching through boxes and realized that he wasn't even sure where things were. Too much stuff and no organization.

"Hey you, robot. I need to make a name for you. Lyt? Any ideas?"

"At this time, no. Nothing emerges to me."

"Hmm. You're from Boro, maybe I should call you Boron. Yeah, what a Boron." Lyt got a quizzical look. "I'll explain it later. Anyway, robot- you are now known as Boron."

The smooth metal face turned my way. "I understand."

"Great. Now Boron, see those cartons over there? Large cardboard boxes. Yes, those. Open them and assemble the shelf units that are inside them. Line the shelf units up next to that wall with the doors facing out. Thanks."

Boron stopped his machine, stepped back, and rolled smoothly toward the boxes.

"Okay Lyt, that will solve your problem with finding stuff. Wow, it must be 1 AM already. Anyway." I started looking through cartons and sorting them out. "What exactly are you looking for anyway?"

"A small enclosure to put this circuit in. The resonator will need a box just large enough to contain it and the circuitry."

"Ah, those are project enclosures located over here." I hauled up a large but light carton. "Here you go."

"Delightful. Thanks. I have not been well organized lately. Very tired, a little travel-worn. I am not so scattered normally."

I understood. "You have a lot to think about. I know that trusting somebody with your secrets is a big step and it could have been a risky one. I have to thank you for that."

He continued looking through the enclosures. "Well, you strike me as a good person. Everyone needs friends and sometimes somebody to trust. Ah, here we have it."

He extracted a moderate sized metal box and pulled the cover from it. The core of the resonator fit neatly within. He began marking mounting holes and fitting the parts into the proper places.

"Be a dear fellow and drill these please, all with the three millimeter bit."

"Sure. Hey, aren't we near the end of the window to visit Boro? We should get that data and make certain things are in order."

"Yes. We should get three more of these computers as well. They are very simple to program and then we can make identical programs and interfaces for them." I saw a road trip coming. Lyt appeared about ready to do it as soon as I had the screw holes drilled.

I spent a few minutes doing the drilling and cleaning out the holes. A small file and a conic tool got rid of the burrs and smoothed things out nicely. Lyt accepted the box and started putting the assembly together. It took only moments.

"Now for the functional test." Lyt placed the completed box on the first frame and it fit perfectly into a recess with a flat sheet metal back. He fastened four pins and the connection was solid. "Simply done. And very nice results." He consulted his tablet and then installed the battery in the new resonator. A small click from the cover and it was ready to try out.

"Winds and thoughts. I shall be here again." With that, he activated the resonator and the old man and the tubing frame were gone. After a few seconds, he reappeared.

"Very well done. Now we must try something of mass. Do you remember those strain gauges, the devices that measure force? I have installed one in the floor of the frame. It will register how much we have it loaded with. With your help, I would like to try loading it with more sand bags and then seeing how it performs."

I wondered then why we had a robot. But without complaint I started loaded those stupid massive bags and trying to get into the spirit of exploration. It took some work and I was thinking about my back when Lyt was satisfied. "Four hundred kilograms. That should be sufficient." I certainly hoped so.

Lyt stood on top of the sand bag pile and reset something. "And again." The frame vanished once more. After a few seconds, it reappeared. Nothing to report and that was the good thing. Lyt was smiling instantly.

"As you see the load is still the same. Therefore, none was lost in the translation. We have succeeded. This frame can successfully carry itself, myself, and the sandbags. Let us add a few more to be certain of the load capacity."

Oh sure. I added sandbags and when Lyt saw the gauge read six hundred kilograms he stopped me. "Sufficient. Winds and thoughts." The frame was gone. This time it took a little while. I was started to fidget. It reappeared a meter to the left. Lyt was smiling broadly now.

"Okay, what?"

"I added some of the remaining sand bags from Melios and now the gauge reads seven hundred kilos of cargo and still it works. I am reluctant to try more at the moment but at some time we shall. We must find the limit of this frame before we can know what our capability is." Lyt was very happy and clearly had the feeling of triumph.

I was getting worn out. "We should do that data gathering and then get some rest. What do you think?"

It was after 2. I really needed to sleep but I was still pretty excited. We had built an interplanetary travel device from scratch in a few days! Lyt sat for a few moments and just stared at the wall. I pulled a couple of the sand bags off the frame and felt fatigue. He spoke.

"So much we have done and so quickly. Yes, let us get the data. It will take very little time." Lyt removed the battery from the frame resonator and looked at the four new shelf units that Boron was standing next to. "Good job. You should recharge now."

Boron nodded and connected his charger. "We shall return shortly with the data about your planet and its inhabitants. This could be very helpful in finding survivors. And then we have a new job for you. Guard this property and do not let anyone enter until we return, except for us that is."

"Yes."

Lyt set his resonator and grabbed my wrist. I was thinking that this would soon be unnecessary. We emerged with the ear popping pressure change and a world of darkness. Lyt immediately was surrounded by a ring of light blue glow. "Wow, that's a neat trick."

"Oh, hologram flashlight. The light is projected all around you from midair. It is nice, even, and shadowless. I will have to equip you with one. Perhaps your computer can do it. Many are programmed to act as light sources. After all, if they can project a hologram, they can make a light."

True. I hadn't thought of that. Lyt set the second translation. My ears popped again and I swallowed a few times to equalize them. Night here also, no surprise. But wait.

In the distance, toward the sea a thin violet line extended from the water up to the sky, like a laser. Every so often something would twinkle in the light, and a cloud slowly floated in front of it also. The thing, whatever it was, seemed to penetrate the cloud and go beyond. Lyt saw what I was staring at.

"Yes. The star cradle. Whatever it is, it certainly is large. I believe it is a skyhook."

"What's that?" I was mystified.

"A cable that reaches from the ground into space. Or from space to the ground. It depends on your perspective."

Huh. "Why would anyone do that?"

"Oh, it becomes an elevator for cargo and people. You can get into space without a spacecraft." Lyt walked toward the bus stop and there were two robots waiting for us. Obviously Boron had been replaced.

"But Lyt, we travel in space without a spacecraft." I followed him to the robots.

"Indeed and my shoes are the worse for it." He waved at the robots. "Greetings and we are here to retrieve the data. All is well. We will be traveling for a number of months and may not return for that period of time.

"How goes the search program?"

The farther robot turned to face Lyt. "Construction of many explorer vehicles has begun. Radiant power units are now being installed along travel corridors to reach into the wild areas. No survivors are yet located but we have found many remains."

I nodded at the news. "Good work. Continue, you are doing well." Lyt raised his arm and looked at me. "What is it?"

"The resonance is starting to change. We must go quickly."

The nearest robot gave Lyt a small device, like a cell phone. "Ah, yes. My thanks."

He immediately grabbed my wrist and translated.

We were back on Melios and I went through ear popping again. "That was abrupt. I thought we had another day."

"There are some inaccuracies in the model. I haven't a clue why but sometimes it will resonate longer and other times it will fail sooner. It could be most anything such as a shift in the planet's movement or the star itself. But when your detector starts to show changes, you must pay heed. We will likely not see that place again for months."

I sighed. I liked it there. I could imagine exploring it for months. Too bad there weren't any restaurants or other people. Lyt took us home and we returned to little more than a stationary robot and a cluttered shop. I kept seeing that violet line reaching into space.

"So this means that we can't get other robots to act as scouts. Or at least, not soon. And that was sort of important I think. Of course, there could be other things we could do."

Lyt dug at his wrist. "Well. I see options. This is not a loss truly." He produced a small circular thing that looked like a crystal ashtray. There were spirals in the glass bottom and small dark circular things embedded within. "This could be of some help."

"Jeez man, where do you get all this crap? How is it that you don't clang when you walk, carrying a hundred kilos of stuff all the time?" He got a funny look and laughed strangely. "You will learn many things as a traveler."

He placed the glass ashtray thing in midair and it began to emit a soft whine. One tiny blue-green light came from its lower face. The ashtray hung there without falling.

"This is a floater. It cannot carry much, but it could be made as the base of a small scout robot and carry a camera and resonator. We will outfit it with a test model and program it to take a trip for us." The floater hung there and did not avoid his outstretched hand, which turned it off and deposited it on the workbench.

"Oh, yeah. Very cool. I want a big one!"

"Where would you use it? It would draw far too much attention here since this world is not very highly technical."

"Not high tech? What about all the electronics and tools? That's pretty high tech."

He had only a smile. "This is technical but I chose this world because its equipment is low tech enough to be used by hand. You cannot imagine the trouble of things that are too complex to fix. We can make this and that means we can fix this. You can stand a good chance of winding a coil or making a detector here, but if a microprocessor or a frilwen fails on you, there is nothing you can do. All of this hardware can be operated by hand, should need present itself."

Well, he had an excellent point. We're only a few short decades from the vacuum tube. Even transistors are mostly gone now. Chips do everything and when they go bad, you trash whatever it is and get a new one. We couldn't do that in a non-peopled world.

Yes, Lyt's hardware could be made from wire and batteries mostly. He operated everything by hand for a darn good reason. My convincing him to go with the new stuff was a radical change for him. I hope it was a good change, and I knew that he would make everything with a manual mode. I had a lot of learning to do.

"Ah, man. I just thought of something. With Boro closed to us, we have no subway system now. How am I going to get home?"

Lyt seemed to be energized. "Let me show you something that might help a little in your understanding. You have seen how orbits can overlap or cross, but there is a better view that can refine your understanding."

His new computer was set on the table and with swift fingers he activated a program I had not seen before. Instead of overlapping orbits, it showed spheres, each representing a world. The central one was Earth and there was a minor cloud of perhaps two dozen little spheres. They seemed to move at random but some would approach, some would recede and slow, turn around. Overall the mass of spheres would pass each other, sometimes overlapping or intersecting and other times isolated.

"In this program you see the worlds in movement. When two spheres touch, they can be traveled between. Sometimes as you see you can get clusters of worlds that can be reached like stepping stones. Other times a world may be isolated. This shows only a few of the worlds, and even though some spheres may overlap, if they are moving too swiftly with respect to each other, you could not cross.

"As you will see here, there are many times long strings of worlds that allow a traveler to reach three, five, or eight worlds. Others are isolated from the string but can sometimes reach other worlds. Groups and clusters of worlds will be moving through space and only when the speed and energy are right, and they are overlapping as this diagram shows, will you be able to reach them."

I watched, enrapt with the tiny moving spheres. It was amazing to see, and it helped my mind to lock onto a firm picture of what was happening. "Hey Lyt, what would happen if you were on a pair of worlds that overlapped, but were moving too fast- and you were in a fast vehicle going at just the right speed and direction. Could you cross over then?"

He looked at the display and fell silent. He stopped the program, ran another and did some figuring. "It seems possible. Perhaps. If so, you could then increase your range of travel immensely. We would need a powerful and space-worthy vehicle to do it."

"Yes, that's what I thought. But we would need to try it with an unmanned vehicle to find out. We don't want to be sandblasted to bits like the frame bottom."

"There will be some opportunities to try some experiments soon. We need to know just what is possible." Lyt was still ready to work. I was exhausted.

"Man, I need a nap. It's really late. I might just stretch out here instead of worrying about getting home." I found some bubble wrap and foam rubber from some of the boxes and made a small pile that looked rather inviting. In minutes I had found a bit of peace and nodded off. Lyt and Boron continued doing… stuff.

I had strange and twisted dreams. I saw carpets of white tendrils and eyes on them sweeping in little animals in the dark and smothering them. White mice and strange shapes cavorted under an orange sun and strange, pencil thin clouds flew by as a violet line reached into the skies. It was troubling and I didn't really rest very well.

I awoke to raw sunlight coming in an open door. The breeze was nice and helped to clear my head. Boron was putting small parts into a box and fastening cables to it. Lyt was writing a program and playing with what appeared to be columns of numbers, but I'm just guessing. It was all scribbles and punctuation.

"Hey guys."

Lyt turned and said hello. Boron continued working. I had a mild stuffiness but was fine, just achy. Lyt stepped away from the computer and hooked a small wire to his latest resonator, something he must have assembled while I slept. In moments the resonator was lit and doing something. Lit checked his display. Then he disconnected the wire and stood back from the resonator. After a moment he placed it on the floor and watched.

The resonator vanished. After a few seconds, it reappeared. "Yes, yes. Very good." I understood immediately.

"You made it travel somewhere under program control and then return. Cool."

"Yes, we can now install it on the floater and get some scouting information without risk." He placed the resonator, a couple of gadgets, and lots of tape on the table, then started sticking things into a bundle. The floater was taped on the underside and Lyt did something on his computer. The bundle came to life.

"Now a quick trip through three worlds and back." The floater rose slightly and the package faded away. "Would you like some breakfast?"

That got my attention even more effectively. "Sure, what do you have? Alien fruit salad?"

With a gentle laugh he produced a box of doughnuts and some bottles of fruit juice. "It is simple enough to get groceries delivered here, thankfully."

I had to admit, he was making good use of his resources. I grabbed a doughnut and some cranberry juice and started eating. "How long do you expect the probe to be gone?"

"It should return very shortly, a matter of a few tens of seconds. Nothing really straining for this first trip, just some verification." I finished a jelly doughnut and went for a glazed. The probe appeared and was dripping wet. Lyt was happy. "Excellent."

He played with the computer and a display appeared. I laughed at it. "Travelogue for the lazy!"

First there was the workshop, then a picture of a windy arid place. Scrubby little bushes stretched in all directions and distant green and brown mountains could be seen. Next the scene shifted to a plain of grass with large boulders. It looked very overcast and ominous. Far off there were sheets of rain coming down and they were probably headed this way. The scene then shifted again.

This was the edge of a forest. The trees however were like sequoias, immensely tall and sparse with branches. There was a bluish haze to the air and it appeared like the northwest or the west coast. I wanted to step through and go hiking. The scene also showed some birds, dark and long-winged. A flock of them cruised slowly through the scene, passing between some of the giant trees.

Then it hit me- those birds must be absolutely huge! They passed in front of a trunk and each had a wingspan that dwarfed it. Sunlight shone on glossy gray feathers just as the scene shifted back to the plain of boulders. I was startled by the change, wanting to see more of the trees and birds.

The boulders were nondescript but had reddish-orange bracket fungus on their lower edges. Then the scene changed once more to the desert place. Finally I saw my own face in the playback from when the probe returned to the shop.

The floater settled to the bench top and Lyt disconnected something from it. I was amazed.

"Lyt, how many worlds are connected to Earth right now?"

"Oh, three at the moment. But some of them have paths to other worlds. At this moment we could reach a total of six or seven worlds. Realize that if you step to a world that disconnects from us, you could be stuck with its connections for months. Like the spheres you saw, there are ever-changing and shifting connections all the time. It is wise to plot many months ahead and make your map through both space and time so you can decide which chain of connections to follow."

More ideas came. 'What if you traveled to another planet within a solar system? Wouldn't it too have worlds that you could reach that you would not be able to any other way?"

"You are a veritable fountain of ideas. Yes, in theory you would have access to many, many more worlds. The numbers of connections are phenomenal then."

"Well then, what about being in free space? Like off the planet and in orbit around the Sun? Could you step through to other solar systems that way?"

"I think not. You must have a large mass to resonate with. Without that, there is nothing to find a resonance of." I was on a roll.

"Okay, what about this. How large does a world have to be? I'm thinking that a big asteroid might work, and you could find millions of connections all over the universe easily then. Right?"

He seemed unsure. "I have not thought along these pathways before. It is clear that even though I have done this most of my life, I have a large amount of learning to do." His eyes nailed me. "Are you thinking of getting a spacecraft? The mass would be considerable, we would need a very powerful resonator."

"Oh, well, it seems to me that it would solve a lot of problems. Start mapping connections and getting samples. It would be a big job, but look at the payoff. Look, all you would need is a large floater and something airtight. Some engines, a power supply, a decent hull. I'm not saying we have to build a space ship but you must know where to get anything we need."

This made him hold up a hand, warding off any further ideas. "Too much. Too many things to consider. I must follow my task without great distraction. You have presented wonderful thoughts and many of them should be explored, but please. I have become somewhat unfocused of late.

We build resonators and detectors, and we recover my stones. All other considerations must come later."

I was a little put off, but I could see his point. "Okay, what do we need to do next? I want to help you get done."

His hand went down. After a sigh he said "we are doing very well with the resonators and the frames. We need some simple controllers to make everything operate. We also need to start making some detectors to see what works best. You should be hearing from your friend about lapidary equipment, true?"

"Sure, probably today." I picked at my fingernails and thought about cutting crystals and stones.

"We are at an advantageous point. Boron could easily continue working. I need to give you some resonator training in actual practice. We will practice manually setting and reading the resonator. You must be capable of making a transition safely by yourself. You must also be able to locate new resonances so we can start making a larger and well connected map.

"Prepare to travel, Mike. You need the training."

Well, tired as I was, I wasn't going to turn this down. I thought of monstrously large redwoods and dark birds the size of light airplanes. The coat was not far, I was ready in a few moments, and Lyt was putting batteries in a small box with buttons.

"This is your life. You must not lose it. You would be very hard-pressed to survive anywhere else in the universe. Protein incompatibilities, you know."

Not really, but I would take his word for it. He handed me the resonator. It was a little heavier than I expected but that comes from lots of coils and metal. I surveyed it with interest. Lyt began to introduce it. There was a small flip-open metal door and the face had a few knobs and buttons.

"This is the power switch. This is the Q meter. It indicates resonance and how strong it is. This is a frequency meter with the lights over it. I will explain those later. Here is the primary and secondary frequency control. The world you are on will resonate the primary control, the world you are traveling to will resonate the secondary. Here is how to set them."

He activated the power and a small blue light came on. His fingers gently spun the recessed frequency knob. The Q meter began to rise. With a few fine adjustments, he had it pegged at the top.

"Now that you have your home planet frequency, you need to lock it in." He pushed a button below the primary knob. A red light came on and the Q meter dropped to zero. "That's got it. Now you can look for other worlds."

"Lyt, what makes a world's resonant frequency?"

"I wouldn't know. I work from empirical data, my friend." He then indicated the secondary frequency control. "You do this. Adjust the secondary slowly and see what happens to the Q meter."

With somewhat fearful fingers, I slowly adjusted the knob. It too was recessed into the case, probably to prevent bumping or changing it. Then I understood the small metal door that was open on the front of the resonator- closed, it would keep the front undisturbed.

I could feel a faint humming or throbbing from the resonator. It was below any frequency I could hear but it was there. As I turned the knob, it changed to a hand-tingling level and frequency. The Q meter was starting to rise. It slowed, began to drop.

"I found one." I backed the knob up and fine adjusted until the Q meter was at its maximum. "Got it, right here."

Lyt pressed on. "Now lock that frequency in as well using the secondary button." I pressed it and a yellow light came on below it. "That's it. Now, you are at the resonant frequency of the world you are in. But if you were to change that frequency to that of a world that is in resonance with your world right now, you would be shifted there. Do that by pressing the center button."

"Now?"

"Yes."

I pressed it and felt a change to hot, dry air. The sun beat down and a faint breeze brought a dry, woody smell and the tang of alkali. I was standing in a scrubby, barren desert.

My heart thumped hard. I had done it. I was standing alone on an alien planet. Where was Lyt? I looked about and saw short bushes that might have been creosote except for the tiny yellow flowers on the tips of some of the branches. I stepped a few meters this way and that, looking at the mountains, breathing in the air.

Perhaps Lyt was expecting me to figure it out. Sure. If I were to tune the box again, I should find my home planet, right? I started to turn the knobs but then I thought about it. Lyt would be gone and back in an instant sometimes. That meant that there was a simple way to do this without tuning.

The red and yellow lights were out now. What did it mean?

He had told me to "lock in" the frequencies. That meant that the box knew them, right? Perhaps there was a really simple "go home" button. I looked at the small button between the two lock buttons and right above the go button. It said "exchange". Now, what do you think that meant? Swap the two frequencies perhaps?

I pressed it and the red and yellow lights came back on. Ah ha! I pressed the go button and was standing back in the workshop. Lyt smiled. "Very good. You see how simple it is, if you just think about it. I made it as simple as I could."

"So, I understand now. If I tune the primary for the planet I'm on, the secondary for the destination planet, and I lock each in, then it will be ready to transit. Yes, that's a good word. Then, once locked, if I transit the two frequencies are no longer right. They should be the opposite.

"So then I swap them with the "exchange" button and transit takes me back to where I started from. Now, what if I were to tune the secondary around without locking it?"

"Try it." He watched me.

I found the unlock button under the secondary lock. I pushed it and then realized something. I needed to tune my home frequency first, right? I unlocked it also, tuned Earth and locked it. Easy. Then I tuned and found the frequency I had just used, but kept going. A second resonance started to appear on the Q meter. I went past it and found nothing more. Then I backed up to the last resonance. The Q meter peaked and I locked it.

I looked up at him. He nodded slightly. I transited.

My ears popped and I was in a field of yellow grass. Melios! I was delighted. I took a few steps and turned completely around. It was certainly the place I knew. There was a smear of sand on the ground from the experiments with the frame. I hit the exchange button and the transit and was back in the shop again.

Lit was ready for the next phase.

79

"You will often wish to save frequencies and be able to get back to them. You see the second meter? That string of lights over the top will show you what frequencies you have saved. When you set the two frequencies you noticed that the lights above the meter came on, and those are the memory lights. Every time you save a frequency, a light will come on over the point the meter was at. The red one is the frequency you set in the primary. The yellow light is the frequency you set in the secondary."

"Ah, got it."

"Yes, that way you can tell if you are close to what you expect. It helps a great deal when there are many frequencies.

"So, you should be safe enough exploring a little. If you get in trouble, push the green button and it should retrace your path to here. I will be here programming and working out some details."

I grinned and set the frequency for Melios and transited. I was getting used to the pressure difference. It was early morning there and rather nice. This was a good opportunity to try the controls.

First, I hit the exchange button. That put the frequency of Melios in the primary. Good enough. Earth was in the secondary and I could see it on the memory, above the meter. Now to tune the secondary and see what I could find. I unlocked the control and started to watch the Q meter.

The first peak I found was Earth, and that made me feel much better. It matched the light on the frequency meter. Good enough. The second was higher and a bit stronger. I locked it and transited.

Instant downpour. I hid the resonator under my coat and pulled my hood up. The world was slate gray and the water was nearly thunderous. The coat was completely waterproof fortunately. I could see the chill of my breath in front of me.

Bare rocks and large leaves like elephant ears spread before me. The ground was matted with a thick grassy base that had small vines woven through it. I squatted down a little and tried to see anything. It was hopeless; the downpour was too great.

I thought about it. I could keep going, there was little risk of being lost. Lyt seemed to think it was safe and I know he wouldn't send me off somewhere to get hurt. But I did have to use common sense also. I hit the exchange button and looked for new frequencies. Almost immediately I got one. I locked it and transited.

What the heck- this was familiar. I knew this place but I had never been here. It was the boulder world from the floater earlier today. I stood slowly and the water sluiced off the impervious coat, leaving an out-of-place splash of water on the ground.

The grass was gray-green and the sky a pale robin's egg blue. Mournful calls could be heard somewhere to the left. I took a look and spotted some animals that looked a lot like moose but much smaller. They had pale bluish heads, horns, and backs. They were grass colors and tan otherwise with faint bluish stripes almost like leopard markings. The stripes were at their backs and got smaller toward their bellies.

They looked almost like grass and sky. Those were the weirdest looking animals I had seen before. I pulled down my hood and in a flash, they bolted. Oh yeah, they probably couldn't see me before because the coat takes on the appearance of its background. Very effective. I must have appeared out of nowhere to them.

I cleared the primary and secondary frequencies and feeling cocky, decided to set everything from scratch. I locked the primary on the planet, found a secondary that matched the memory and transited.

Desert and scrub. Very cool! I knew where I was, had not only seen it but had been there before. I hit exchange and transited back to the grass and boulders with the weird little moose things. Time to search for another frequency. I found one after a little twiddling. I set it and transited, expecting something amazing. And I found it.

Monstrous trees that would put any redwood to shame surrounded me on all sides. Distance bluing to the air told me that these were so huge, so far away that they possibly could compete with mountains. The air pressure was significantly higher here and I had to swallow a few times to equalize my eardrums.

My feet scuffed lightly through resinous dried needles on the forest floor. The air was cool and dry, almost tangy. The smell was starting to take on a slightly fishy touch. I couldn't quite place it.

Something *slid* over the ground not far behind me. I turned slowly and saw something that looked like a scaly tail disappear behind a tree trunk. I immediately pulled up my coat hood and squatted slightly. That tail was big. I quietly hit the exchange button and made certain that I could be out of there in a flash. Then I slowly walked away from the tree and made a wider circuit of it. My thumb was over the transit button as I moved.

I spotted the tail; a patent leather glossy thing that was covered in scales the size of a nickel. They had an oily iridescence to them with faint little rainbows of color. Taking my time, I moved carefully and quietly to see from a distance just what it might be.

The tail grew higher and thicker as I circled the tree. It was up to my waist and as thick as my leg now. I could only imagine the worst. I stepped on something that snapped.

The tail jerked and moved around the tree, then disappeared. A few steps and a head appeared around the other side of the tree. I froze.

It had a long, powerful beak of dark yellow with a darker brown stripe outlining the mouth. Tiny yellowish eyes sunk in thick wattle like that of a turkey peered in my direction. The wattle was red and fleshy, hanging and warty. The eyes looked this way and that, the head cocked at an angle and the thing tried to figure out what it was looking at. The head rose slowly and turned in various degrees with little jerky movements as a chicken might move.

That was one ugly looking thing. Was it a bird? A lizard? I couldn't tell. I was too busy trying not to pee. A feathery looking arm with long and glossy claws reached around the tree trunk and grabbed bark, steadying the animal. I could smell something really unpleasant, probably its last meal.

It couldn't have been more than fifteen meters from me. I had no idea how fast it might be, but I also knew I didn't want to find out in a footrace. I didn't dare move, but I figured I should wait and see what happened. There was a noise and the thing jerked its head to the right, then started moving slowly and deliberately toward the noise.

I saw it then, like a raptor or some other bird of prey, but covered in scales and pinfeathers. It was thinner and bonier than I thought, and then I realized that it could not weight very much for its size. It looked almost skeletal but the muscles that showed were corded and defined.

I raised the resonator and the swish of fabric made it snap around and start moving toward me. I yelled at it and it stopped with a skid and jerked its neck back. It couldn't see me probably and was surprised by the noise. I didn't wait any longer. I transited.

When I got to the boulders I was covered with sweat. I sat down hard and breathed for about three minutes, just shaking. It took a little while to concentrate on the resonator. I hit the exchange button, tuned the secondary and found the frequency for the desert. That was a short jump and the sand and scrub were a welcome sight. I took enough of a break to drink some water that I had stashed in the pocket and then just to laugh.

I laughed so hard that it was hard to breathe. The danger was minimal because all I had to do was hit a button and I would be, what- fifty billion light years away? Nobody knew, or could know, just how far those worlds were from each other. After I calmed a bit and felt better, I decided it was time to get back to Earth.

I arrived just outside the building and spent a few minutes just enjoying sunlight and fresh air that smelled right. I wondered about the places I had been and that none of them had anything intelligent or like a civilization. Then I remembered that Lyt had said that three worlds connected to Earth right now and that six or seven could be reached at the moment. I had seen... let me see, Melios and the desert world, so there was one more that I had not. If you added up the rainstorm world and the boulders with the mini-moose and the giant tree world (with the raptor thing) that was five.

It was easy enough to tune Earth and then look for Melios and the desert world. I started searching and found a third signal of middle strength. That had to be it.

I locked it and transited, this time with my hood up.

CHAPTER 5

I am not really an adventurous type. I do enjoy travel, and new things excite me. But really I am quite happy to be at home enjoying a video or reading a book. Now yes, travel is fun but I often expect that there will be a good hotel, a nice pool, and a respectable restaurant at the end of the journey.

Lyt had taught me a lot and made me learn things as well. I was really having fun with him. And Boron was just a robot but very neat. Not a friend, but almost a friend. I mean, he wasn't really alive or anything but he was much more than a tool.

And then Morris was cutting another check for a ridiculous amount of money in a few more days, and another a week after that. I was not one to quit a job without some prospects but if Lyt or I could bring in the kind of wealth that seemed to come from traveling between worlds, then there was really very little rational reason to keep a job.

Of course that was the issue. What was I going to do when Lyt was done with his task? He sure wasn't going to settle on Earth, he had worlds to see. It was pretty clear that he had big things to do and he was never going to be satisfied with staying on my home planet.

And then, what about me? Truth was, I could not see myself in a retirement home somewhere. I was going to be a traveler. I would walk the paths between the stars, see strange, new worlds, and gather resources and things. One day perhaps I would find a little world somewhere that had just what I wanted and settle down, but even that was not a certainty.

So I transited from Earth to the third world and stood dumbfounded.

The ground, if that is what it was, looked like matte finish smooth white ceramic. It was one unbroken expanse. The sky was the same, a smooth eggshell thing that had a soft white radiance. What was holding it up?

I saw no pillars or columns. The fact is I couldn't really be sure that the ceiling and floor weren't one and the same. Perhaps they blended there in the distance, but it was a mystery to me.

I transited back to Earth momentarily, then back to the eggshell world. What the hell.

I knelt to the floor and felt it. It was not hard as I expected but almost rubbery. A look at the surface showed that it had tiny pores and really did look like magnified eggshell. It was compliant and seemed to have a harder base but a tough rubbery coating on the surface.

I took a stroll along and saw that the light was unchanging and the floor was as well. No sound came to me except perhaps a soft sigh of air. What a puzzle.

Now think. Lyt was sure that I would be safe, so he probably knew everything I would see. But then, what about the raptor? Did he know that there was something that might eat me in the forest world? If not, then this place could have hazards also.

The mini-moose things were oddly colored and striped for a reason. Predators? Camouflage most definitely. In the grass, looking up at them, an animal might have a hard time seeing them. That meant that it was very likely that something preyed on them and I had the same chance of being eaten that they did.

But I have my camouflage coat. Nothing is likely to see me with the hood up. And, I can be instantly away from danger. Two points for intelligent hominid number one. But this place is inexplicable. Lyt surely knew this was here, right?

So that means that either he knew it was here and was sure it was safe, or that he was mistaken.

A third alternative occurred to me. Perhaps when he was here, it was different. I checked my resonator. I hit exchange and locked the primary frequency for this world in. I transited to Earth. Again, exchange frequencies. Then I carefully tuned above and below. No other resonances, that was it- or maybe not.

I did a slow, slow adjustment and found something interesting. There was a second strong resonance very close to the previous one. I locked it into the secondary. Here goes nothing. I hit the transit button.

This was a surprise, it looked like a park. This was very Earthlike and the area was a small valley, completely enclosed. Low mountainous ranges surrounded it and a clear lake was off a few hundred meters to my right. Idyllic picnic spot, I would say.

Lyt must have found this place and thought it was all there was. Think about it, the new resonator was sure to be better than the old one. He had had plenty of practice making it and refining it. This was possibly a better machine than the one he had.

As such, it could split two very close frequencies and that was what had happened. He probably found the one and didn't look any further. I might have done the same. So what was the eggshell place?

That got me. I went back to the eggshell place. Four worlds intersected Earth right now. Very cool. I had visited seven worlds on my little walking tour now. I sat on the floor and looked. Not much to see but this had to be some technical artifact. A building perhaps.

After a few minutes of simple thought and observation, I decided to explore it a bit. My only concern was that I had no way to make a mark or show my entry point. I looked through my pockets and found that water bottle. I drank about half of it and then placed it on the floor where I estimated I had come in. Then I picked a direction and started to walk.

Every few steps I would look back and verify that my water bottle was still there and that I was going in the same direction. I saw that the ceiling was indeed closing down toward the floor up ahead but that it was so evenly lit that I could not easily see the difference. Finally I stopped.

I could see the bottle behind me. I walked a few more steps and at last spotted the wall. I trotted ahead a little faster, not wanting to lose sight of the bottle but I figured that at this point, there was very little else to see as a landmark and so I continued to the wall. I reached it at last and was not surprised to see how it curved into the floor as one continuous piece. It also seemed to emit a little light of its own.

Before going any further, I set the resonator to take me back to Earth at the touch of the transit button. Ever get the feeling you were being watched? I had it. I lowered my hood and tucked it back into the collar.

"Hello?" My voice fell flat into the soft chamber. I touched the wall and it had a slick, soft feel to it. Almost like it was alive.

Then I noticed something that I had not seen before. The floor close to the wall had a pattern faintly in it, something you couldn't see unless you caught the light just at the right angle. This was hard to do here but I saw a pattern of hexagons that were maybe thirty centimeters across. I touched the spot and could feel an outline of harder material like a lip and a softer zone in the center. I pressed it gently and felt my fingertips just sink into the material a little.

The rim rose slightly and took on a more defined look. The center material became positively soft. I pulled my hand back and some of it seemed to stick like tacky gelatin. It rebounded and the center of the hexagon began to bulge upwards and rise like taffy. I stood back a few steps and watched the material extrude upward and take a rough form. It looked like a body in a rubber bag.

In a few moments it stood like a morphing statue of off-white glistening material. Arms and legs were soon defined and they pulled free of the trunk of the body and lifted a little. Fingers began to form on the ill-defined hands. The head rose and straightened on the now thinning neck. In a little more time it looked like an abstract sculpture of wet marble. I was feeling a little alarm and wondering how quickly I could get back to the entry point. But I didn't need to; I could go at any time. I could walk back on Earth or in the park valley. So I waited, thumb poised over the button.

The form straightened and reached a size and form similar to that of a young woman. It was not yet close enough to be sure; it might have been a boy but it was taking its time becoming something almost human in shape. The face developed some color in the eye sockets and dark orbs began to form. I did step back about three paces then.

A milky white skin split across the eyes and they opened. Red orange irises showed and the pupils took shape as ellipses. The split skin became eyelids which opened and closed rapidly, flick, flick. The skin began to color as well, a translucent honey color that seemed to be filled with tiny flecks of silver and brown. Now I could see that this was definitely looking female. The end came rapidly as the process sped up.

Her right foot lifted from the hexagon with a soft swishing noise and touched the rubbery floor. The left foot lifted free and did likewise. The hexagon seemed to be fading back into the floor. Her head showed a bulge at the back that was stretching into filaments like hair. They were white and golden and each divided and subdivided into finer hair until it looked natural. The shape formed up and solidified. Most definitely female.

She looked at me and her mouth parted and said something like "ahhm." I was about to step away when she looked like she was leaning, going to fall or faint. Instinctively I reached out and supported her. I expected- well, I'm not sure, perhaps a rubbery feel like a squid or a mass of silicone but instead there was firm flesh. "Ahhm heer do welcom youuu."

I was jolted. She strengthened and then said it again, almost perfectly. "I'm here to welcome you." She stood upright and supported her own weight. I felt her grip on my arm, warm and gentle. The face which had been a little too narrow broadened slightly and the nose flowed and conformed more nicely. The skin became less opaque and took on the look of dark glass. The lips, which had been a slit now expanded a little and filled out. A touch of darker honey color came to them.

"I, I mean, thank you. Who are you?" After a moment I blurted "I'm Michael."

"I am Nyos. You travel the worlds. I do as well."

It was hard to describe what I felt then. This was very high tech or something completely outside my imaginings. This made Lyt look like a piker. This put the Boro world to shame. I couldn't think of anything to compare to this. I was simply awestruck.

"Nyos, what is this place?"

"This is a traveler's place. It moves as do the worlds. It can reach out to many worlds and be reached by many. You are welcome here and your needs will be met." She indicated the room around us. I saw nothing other than the eggshell ceiling and floor but it was clear that if a whole person could be made of stuff out of the floor, probably anything you could think of could also be made.

I saw her skin flow with tiny flakes of something, like glitter. Glitter in honey flowing in slow currents seemed to cover her entire perfect body.

"Thank you. I think that I have everything I need for the moment. Information is probably the only thing that really would be helpful to me. I would be happy to share what I have but it really isn't much."

She looked at me gravely and then offered her hand. She had something small in it. "This will help. Come here when you are in need." I opened my hand and she placed something small and crystalline in my palm. It looked strange but familiar all at once. "You will find many things there."

She stepped back carefully and stood over the hexagon area. Her features began to soften. She waved once before starting to be absorbed by the floor area. I waved back. "Thanks again."

I decided to head back to the water bottle. It was the only landmark I knew and at least I would be somewhere near a known return point. The bottle was undisturbed and somehow seemed welcoming. I picked it up, not wanting to leave something in this pristine looking place. I took one long look around at the lack of detail and hit the transit button.

I was about twenty meters from the building, in a pile of weeds and brambles. I didn't feel like climbing through them and figured that a quick transit to the valley park would be easier. I got an idea of the location of the building and transited to the park.

From there I was able to walk forward a few meters and then transit back to Earth. It was just a few steps to the building. The door was still open and nearly noon sun was shining in. Lyt looked up and peered at me over his glasses. "Back you are. It was about time that I look for you. In your absence much has been done, and I hope that you are refreshed and inspired."

"Yeah. Quite. That little valley is something. The giant trees were a bit of a surprise, they have large reptiles or birds or bird-tiles or something. I got a scare from one of them."

"Oh, as soon as they smell you they take off. Anything out of the ordinary scares them. They look far more fierce than they are." He turned back to his work. He had a small circuit module with a wire running to his computer from Boro. The hologram was showing what looked like a circuit diagram made of shields and circles with lots of connections.

"I am programming the new resonator to accept a detector card and automatically search for links. It can be operated manually of course but it will also have a computer that will save travel paths and frequencies. Best features of both modes. And, as a happy result, it will automatically communicate with your other computer."

"Sounds great. I have to spend some time with my computer also. Get familiar, learn some more about it."

"You haven't said much about your travels. Was it what you expected?"

"Much more. I have a lot to think about. The scenery, the wildlife. The rainstorm planet was a real eye opener. I got drenched instantly."

He chuckled at that. I had to ask him something.

"Say, have you run into any races of higher technology? Really advanced?"

"Oh, my. Well, some most certainly. But they tend to be far too... self assured if not downright lazy. Their citizens are often immortal, have no needs or wants unmet. They have mastered their environments, go anywhere and do anything they wish, and in the end tend to retreat into themselves. I don't understand what they intend or what they accomplish. It is a very strange existence."

"Are any of those worlds going to be available to see or visit soon? I'm really curious."

"Ah, all things in time. I am certain that you will come into contact with them at some point." He seemed done with his explanation and went on with the work.

Boron was constructing some sort of machine from a drill and some motors. It looked like the motors would move the drill around and make it dip down to drill holes. A boxy frame lined with sensors and wires held a flat table with clamps, apparently to hold the work piece down. I didn't spend much time looking at it; just enough to see what it was all about.

Instead I went into the office, pulled out my computer and activated it. I also took the small crystal thing out of my shirt pocket that I got from Nyos. Now I knew why it looked familiar. The end of it had a tiny plug that exactly matched the computer. The material itself was translucent honey colored stuff with those little silvery flecks in it. It almost looked like it could have been the same material she was made of or pulled right out of her skin.

I placed the little crystal up against the receptacle on the computer. The display shifted immediately. Was that normal? A new icon started forming and it looked for all the world like a hollow cube thing and water was pouring into it. As the liquid level in the cube icon grew, I understood that this too was a sort of progress bar. When the cube was full, the data transfer would be complete. What was going into my computer?

At last it was done. The icon took its place in the depth of the display, then the little crystal detached itself from the computer. I picked it up and felt that it was slightly warm. As I held it, it squirmed and formed into a small flattened sphere. The connector was now gone as if it had never been.

I murmured "Nyos" and shook my head a little. The spheroid seemed tacky and clung to my fingertips like rosin. Shiny bits seemed to flow inside it like a viscous fluid was moving slowly. I placed it back in my pocket and looked at the computer. The new icon waited there with unknown purpose. I touched it.

The program began to execute. A geodesic shape appeared that was a twelve sided thing of pentagons but sort of softened, black with a foamy texture like a sponge laid open by x-rays. Tiny colored points appeared within the multifaceted form. "Huh." I noticed that one had a blue circle with a crosshair inside it. I touched it and it zoomed and zoomed. The crosshair remained the same size but the foamy stuff resolved into strings and knotted threads. The threads turned into fuzzy motes, which grew into clusters of…

…galaxies. This was a map of the whole damn universe! The blue cross hair continued to sit front and center as the group of galaxies expanded and zoomed into one that showed a football shaped center and a bar with two large arms and two smaller arms. It continued to zoom into a spot halfway to the center and not far from the edge of one arm.

Soon there were patches of fuzz that turned into stars and clouds of dust. One yellow star was at the center and soon it showed a blue dot with a large moon- Earth. Absolute wow.

I pulled the crosshair back and the zoom stopped just shy of showing me the satellite view of the building I was in. Pulling back further showed the galaxy and the local group, then the threads and foam.

I played with the icons and controls and worked it out pretty quickly. I could choose a quick zoom in or out with one touch, and could also see a catalog of places I had visited. The rainy world, the boulders and mini-moose, the eyeball tentacle things. Every world was there, along with its resonance frequency and its images. I could see the solar systems of each world, the planets in the system, and the actual place in the universe.

This was the most addictive program I had ever seen. Lyt would be astounded. There was more.

I found a map of spheres moving in slow motion, showing the worlds that were approaching resonance with Earth. So many! I thought there might be a dozen or so, as Lyt suggested. There were at least a hundred. But some were moving too quickly and others were at odd angles. Many would be difficult or impossible to reach, clearly.

But some could be reached easily if this image was correct. Why did they not show up on the resonator? It was clear soon. They had frequencies that were just outside the range of the resonator. Some were high, others low. But the resonator itself had one limitation and that was its tuning fork thing. Something had to be done to change it a little.

I found that the program had an index. In it was an article on resonators. And there in the open, with plain drawings, was a diagram of a different resonator fork. This one had a sort of bar and coil affair that moved on the main rod, obviously changing the way it rang.

How could I keep this quiet? Should I say something? Lyt should know that he missed one of the worlds; that it had a frequency so close to another world that he could not resolve it or had missed it. I thought furiously for a few minutes. Lyt had a plan, he had a goal. There were steps that had to be taken to reach that goal. He was making great progress and things were coming together, but I could potentially help him get it done sooner.

What do I do? Did Nyos want this information shared or was it an implied secret? She obviously knew so much more than we did. What was her purpose in telling me this and what possible motive could she have? Too many questions and too little thinking. I had to take the rest of this day off and sleep, then get back to Lyt once I had considered the ramifications.

I mean, Lyt had given everything. So much in terms of knowledge and financing, not to mention just plain friendship. I couldn't be deceptive or dishonest. I had a big problem here. I turned the computer off and pocketed it. I had to get home and rest.

"Hey Lyt. I'm going to the house and sleep awhile. Is there anything you need? Left-handed framble spanner?"

It was clear that his translator hadn't made sense of that. He had a curious look and shook his head. "No, nothing. There will be some new machines and tools delivered today or tomorrow. Check with Morris if you can. Boron and I will do some work."

"Cool. I'll see you soon. I can't stay away from here for long you know." I called a cab and burned time looking at Lyt's work and playing with the map of the universe in my computer. When a knock came at the door, I was ready to go.

Lyt waved me off. "Bye Boron. Take care." The robot paused long enough to acknowledge with a nod.

I rode back home deep in thought and wondered about many things. For some reason I kept seeing Nyos and those large red orange eyes. What do I tell Lyt? I could not shake that idea.

Once I arrived I felt at a loss. I had traveled literally from one end of the universe to the other. Here I was in my apartment which seemed deathly silent, listening to an old clock tick on the wall. On my shoulders was an unearthly coat and in its pockets were a computer, a resonator, and my little detector. My shirt pocket held a small honey colored flattened sphere from the eggshell place, which even now seemed warm against my chest.

I drank a long draw of ice water from the refrigerator and started to take off my shoes. Curiosity got the better of me. I set the resonator for the valley park and hit transit. There was a gluey feeling and nothing happened. The resonance was good, it must be that was some sort of object in the way. Lyt had mentioned that.

I set the desert world and transited. Easy. I was near a stand of strange cactus plants that had spines with sticky looking pads on them. A leathery looking bird circled high above. The air was too warm but it smelled good. A thing like a scorpion crawled across a partly shaded area of sand, leaving funny tracks and dragging marks. I went back home.

So the best thing to do was take a nap. I got undressed and then remembered to call Morris. He answered right away.

"Any news on the lapidary equipment? My friend is feeling creative."

"Yes, I'm sending you an email with a local man's address and phone number. He was a hobbyist for years and is now retired. Gem and rock collector, used to cut and polish stones. He made a lot of wall clocks out of geodes and rock slices. He's going to be spending the rest of his life traveling the world and he hasn't touched any of the stuff in at least a couple of years. Just cluttering his garage."

"Well, great. I'll call him right away and see what we can do. Thanks for your help."

Morris sounded a little hurried. "No problem, gotta get back to work. Talk with you later."

Good enough. I wanted to sleep but the email was more important. Not much effort to do it, so I booted up the old laptop and waited. Funny how it is that every year they make faster and more powerful computers but the software then grows even larger and eats all your gains. What was the point then?

It was only a few minutes work to get the email and call the fellow. He was happy to have somebody interested in the equipment. He said he was available right away so I conceded that I could see him in a few minutes. Might as well get this done.

I cleaned myself up a bit by brushing my teeth and rolling on some deodorant. A fresh shirt helped a lot, and within five minutes I was ready to go. The car was getting a real workout these days. At that I paused. Had it really been only a few days since Anlyt Vood showed up and told me his tale? So much had happened.

The street was easy to find. Phineas (what an unlikely name) was sitting in a lawn chair in his driveway and aiming a water hose with a spray nozzle at the base of a tree. He had striped shorts and a white tank top shirt that had to be years old. He waved as I parked out front, rather than dislodge him from his post.

"Phineas, Michael. Call me Mike please."

"So you got the bug, huh? Rocks will be the death of you, I tell you. I spent the better part of thirty six years crawling the hills and dragging my poor wife along. If she didn't enjoy it nearly as much as I did, things would have been much harder.

"Been collecting since I was a college kid, found dentistry and thought it was pretty neat that many similar tools were used for dental work and jewelry, and the rocks just fell into place with it." He turned the sprayer off and stood creakily.

"Yup, I cast my own inlays and did crowns and inlays. I started making jewelry on the side and then had to have better rocks and I enjoyed the collecting and it pretty much took over my life. What got you into it?"

I tried to look noncommittal. "Oh, a friend showed me a really interesting rock. Crystal of some sort that looked like a sapphire. An attraction sort of revealed itself. I'm helping him and he's interesting in cutting and polishing stones. And there are travel opportunities that have already come up as a side benefit."

He had a perfect grin. "Yeah, that happens. Let me show you the setup." He clicked the remote in his pocket and the garage door slowly rose with a minor racket. "Gotta fix that."

We entered the dim and perfectly orderly space inside. Three very neat work tables were in place, two along the wall and one in the center of the room. There was no place for a vehicle. "Damn rocks take over your life, you'll see." He showed me a large circular sawblade thing that had a water nozzle next to the blade and was rough with fine diamond dust. "That's the saw. I have three good blades for it and a couple of savers. I hate to throw them away. Tough steel, good for all kinds of things."

Then he revealed from beneath a small cloth some sort of lighted work station. Next to it were three small barrels or buckets on their sides. "Those are my tumblers. Each has a different grit in it so I don't have to spend a lot of time fussing around with the mix. You know how to tumble a rock?"

"Er, haven't thought about it frankly."

With an easy laugh he went on. "Well, you put your grit in there, rough stuff first. Add a handful of small rocks just about the same size to help carry the grit. You have to make a slurry out of it. You mix some sort of agent in it, I use plain dish soap most of the time. That helps keep the grit floating. You'll get to recognize the sound it makes as it runs. You'll find out that the soap will foam up a bit and that's how the grit floats. Keeps it from sinking and staying in the bottom of the drum.

"Now, be sure to inspect the rocks you tumble every day and vent the drums. When you tumble rocks they build a little gas pressure. Nobody knows exactly why. If you don't vent the drums, they can leak all over, they ooze like sores. Just stop the drum with the switch here and set it upright. Pull the lid off and check the progress."

I was getting a whole lesson in tumbling and polishing. I didn't want to beg off, it seemed like he needed somebody to talk to. Besides, he probably wanted to know that I was going to take care of his equipment once I bought it. I can't blame him.

Eventually we settled on price and I took everything, not sure what Lyt may want or need. I wrote a check and Phineas accepted, then insisted on helping me carry everything out to the car. I also came away with a nice wall clock.

It took altogether too long but I wasn't going to begrudge either Phineas or Lyt the time. Besides, I sometimes don't seem to get out enough. By now I was really beat but felt like I had my second wind.

The Sun was a little too bright and the day was a little too real. I stopped in a small sports club and grill for a decent burger and fries. I hadn't really been eating well except for the pizza the last night. I'd been on seven or eight planets in the space of a few hours, not counting this one. Surely I deserved a good meal.

Nyos. Why did I keep thinking of that woman? She was too far out for my tastes but I really don't spend a lot of time with women. Hell, she wasn't just alien, she was a *liquid!* But I had a small piece in my pocket that had to be part of her. I pulled it out of the pocket as I sat there waiting for my order.

That was when I realized that I was wearing the coat with all the stuff in the pockets. It was a natural outgrowth of not wanting to leave the resonator or the computer lying around. Also the need to vanish in a moment gives one an amazing confidence. I could walk into the restroom and step to another world in a flash. And back again, without a stir or a ruffle.

I ordered a large iced tea and the meal, then waited for it to show up. I decided to do just that- go to the restroom and have a look around. I wondered what might be just over the horizon or on the other side. The little piece of crystal stuff went back in the shirt pocket.

I took the walk down a wood paneled passage past the waiter's station and past pictures of sports figures that had stopped in here or simply sent a signed picture. One plaque proclaimed this the best themed restaurant in the country for the last three years. What an achievement.

Once inside the restroom, I pulled out the resonator and checked the secondaries for hits. I found that there were three strong ones (known) and a second strong peak still present for the eggshell place. Four choices. I tried the valley park. No good. There must be some rock or something in the way.

I tried Melios and stepped out into yellow grass. Simple enough. It took a few seconds to survey it and to get a feel for the land. I barely noticed the pressure difference this time. Not far from me was that white glittering mass of insects. I wasn't going to explore because I didn't want to come back somewhere in the kitchen or the parking lot.

I transited back to the restroom. Lunch was rather quiet after that but I knew that there were worlds literally a step away, just around an invisible corner.

The burger was good, the fries very good. Some places have it. I sat quietly eating and every once in a while would finger the little piece of crystalline stuff in my pocket. Eventually I took it out and looked at it carefully. It was a crystal after all, wasn't it? Perhaps it had the same properties that other crystals from across the universe might have.

I tried the small, glistening thing against the stones in my detector and got nothing. I also tried it against the stones for Boro and likewise nothing happened. I didn't have enough samples to get any ideas of what it might react to. But it wasn't really stone so it was just an idle thought that made me try it at all. What exactly was it, and by extension, what was she?

Materials have properties. Some are solid or liquid, some can change state based on heat. What about something that can be commanded to be solid or liquid? Did such things exist? I was tempted to try the alien computer and see if I could get an internet connection. Well, why not? I could tell people that it was something new from Japan. They'd probably believe it.

So I did. I took out the computer and activated it. There was an "interfaces" icon. I tried it. It showed signal strengths and bands. Some pulsed and chirped, others were fairly steady. I could see a whole picture of the radio spectrum lined up for me. I did remember that most household appliances and phones used 2.4 gigahertz or something like that.

Concentrating on that band I saw that there were many signals clustered there. Some showed regular changes like a sound wave and were possibly mobile phones. I discarded them. Others showed tiny bursts of data on a regular train, then would settle to an occasional pulse. That was probably data.

It didn't take long for the computer to figure out the coding and data rate. But I couldn't really use it because I had no idea how to create a browser and I'm not a programmer. I didn't have the right software to get online.

I decided to put it away and avoid drawing any attention. So far I had no problem and it was best to keep it that way. The computer was turned off and put back in one of those capacious pockets. The nugget of honey-colored stone stayed on the table.

It was then, sitting there at the end of a meal and in the middle of the day that I had my moment of doubt. What exactly did I want? What was it that drove me on? I spent years in school learning a trade, did some engineering design work, ended up entering data in insurance forms, worked in a boring office with some real goofball people and had no idea what came next.

Just what was my goal?

I thought long and hard about that. I held that tiny piece of oblong glassy stuff that I had gotten directly from the hand of somebody miraculous. It felt warm and slightly pliant instead of hard and crystalline.

There was a future for me and I was sure of that. I just wasn't too sure what my plans were. Was anyone?

Phineas, the old rock hound, knew exactly what he expected. He was done with rocks and would travel until he died. He was not resigned to that, but accepting or perhaps embracing it. He knew that the end was coming and it was going to be good for him. Life had promise even for an old fellow like him.

Morris. What did he want? He spent his life in a small box dealing with coins and metals, people who were high rollers, businessmen, or of questionable nature and intent. What did he do for fun? I had no clue.

I knew that I wanted something more. I wanted to see worlds, to travel the stars and have a wonderful time. I wanted to help people and do significant things. I wanted. That was the thing that outlined me. Unfortunate, I thought. But was it?

I had a chance and this was driving me. I *had* done things now, but they were not of my making. Lyt was the factor here, and he had brought mystery and excitement to me that I had never imagined. I was definitely going to help him and to do what I could to find his missing stones and his world. That was a start. But other than that, I was ready to see what came next. And it could be anything.

Did I really want to keep that job? No. If I could afford to travel the stars and at least have a safe haven here, that would be sufficient. That was it. I felt the need to secure a solid income. But income was not the key, it was adventure. The doing is what is important. Income was just a means to an end.

Final approximation is this. I simply needed a place to sleep and eat, some sort of stable base. And, I wanted to travel. I could do that. And when it came time to make the next decision, I would. I just didn't want to end up like-

Lyt. Yes. Old, isolated, no home. As magnificent a figure as he seemed to be, he was alone and homeless. Somehow I now felt almost a pity for him. At least I had a solid life here on Earth and could have continued that way until I died. Lyt was likely to come to a bad end in some strange setting far from friends and anyone who would care. I couldn't let that happen.

My resolve was firm then. I didn't actually know any more than I had, but I did have a sense of direction. It would be a good and entertaining life and one with real meaning. I would help him and others as well, and I would travel and see things that nobody else had.

The tea was getting low and the waiter came by and refilled it. He cleared my plates and brought the check. I kept kneading the little amber bit between my fingers and felt it soften and change a little. A quick look at it showed nothing outward but it was definitely becoming pliable.

Time for me to go, and to get that long needed rest. I pocketed the bit of Nyos and paid my tab.

The afternoon was a little hot but it felt good. Slow traffic made a little comforting noise and the asphalt was too warm and smelled slightly of mothballs and tar.

The drive was quiet and uneventful. All that equipment had been in the car and had given the interior an interesting smell. Not a bad smell, but one of earthy and metallic quality. There was an odor to soil and this was similar. It also carried a hint of the soap Phineas had used to tumble his rocks. Overall the effect was quieting.

At my apartment I stopped as I rounded the building and picked up another pinch of the white builders sand that had been spilled on the ground the week before. I let the pinch flow between my fingers into the palm of my hand. How small could a crystal be and show a reaction?

The sand remained in my palm as I unlocked the door and went inside. I took a napkin and dusted the sand into it, cleaning my hand. I idly pulled the softened honey colored bit from my pocket and held it over the sand like a magnet. There was no reaction, of course. I brought it closer, thinking that it might be weak. The sand did nothing.

Still closer, peering intently at the sand and the gap between it and the stone. My fingers slipped from the grip and the bit fell into the sand and on the napkin. It a flash I had reached to pick it up and missed. The bit lay on the white sand. Well, it wouldn't hurt a thing.

The bit lay there for a few seconds. I moved it with my finger and it felt much warmer. Then I saw that it was slowly flowing over the sand and absorbing it. That was a shock. Pushing it away with the tip of my finger I saw that the sand and part of the napkin had been taken. I looked at the bit of Nyos but saw no sand or paper inside it.

I thought of silly putty and how it was impossible to get hair or stuff out of it once you got it in there. Was I ruining the stone? There was a magnifier in the kitchen drawer. It took a moment for me to rummage through the stuff in there and find it. Behind a rolled up piece of string, under some matchbooks and past a small box of six year old birthday candles I found it.

After wiping it carefully on my shirt I brought it close to the stone. There was nothing inside it other than the tiny silvery bits. The shape of it had changed back to the flattened sphere that it had been. That was a relief. But where had the sand and paper gone?

The paper napkin definitely had a small hole in it. Did stones get hungry? I hoped not. But it meant that new experiments were in order. I tried the end of one of the candles. It swallowed it easily, string and all. No trace could be seen inside the stone although I was certain that it seemed larger.

I was now at a crossroads. Again. Do I feed this thing or do I simply put it away? Do I want it to get larger? What happens if it does? Decisions, decisions. I did the right thing.

I took a nap.

CHAPTER 6

This was going to be a good evening. I slept really hard but felt rested. I woke very late in the evening just as the sunset was spreading in the west. The sense of indecision was gone and my head was clear. The realization came to me that I needed some self defense lessons and survival training.

Could I make a fire without matches? No. I couldn't count on the resonator working forever. Did I happen to carry spare batteries? No! If something had gone wrong I would be stranded and unable to eat the food and with no plan for getting drinking water or anything. What an idiot.

Lyt made a lot of sense. He knew exactly what to do. I realized something else. I had no idea what he was carrying but you can be absolutely sure that he had spare batteries, matches, weapons and probably- logically, a spare resonator. Man, why didn't I think of this before?

It was time to start at the beginning.

If I knew that I was going to be stranded somewhere, what would I need? Suppose it was for a day, then three days, then a week. Since resonators weighed next to nothing, a spare was blatantly obvious. Okay, I got a notepad and my computer and started making notes.

First, spare resonator and batteries. Second, I didn't even have a flashlight. What about matches and water? I did have a water bottle usually but I really needed a purifier and filter. So three and four were water purifier and water filter. Five was matches.

This was turning into a game. Try to pack the absolute most of everything into a small space. What about food? You could go for days without it but if you had dried stuff like jerky and hard candy you could last a long time. So six was some sort of rations kit. Sure, something compact and with a high food value. Next, what about a mirror? Maybe.

Put that at the bottom. Ah! Plastic bags or sheet. Like those silver survival blankets. They weighed nothing and could keep you alive. As a bonus they were also waterproof. Seven was the plastic survival blanket.

What about a good knife? What an idiot to miss that. You had to have a knife. It was a universal tool and come to think of it, many had matches, water purification tablets, and even a compass in the handle. They had small items like needles and thread, all kinds of stuff could be rolled up and put into a hollow knife handle. Definitely number eight.

Finally, number nine should be a small first aid kit. Those could be gotten cheaply most anywhere. Some were not much larger than a wallet or deck of cards. And still, plastic bags were a good idea. Maybe a couple of small hand tools. A little roll-up kit with monofilament line, tape, foil, bits of stuff.

All of that could be fitted into the coat and the knife would strap onto a leg. Sometimes you didn't need much but if you didn't have it at all it could kill you. Even small things like matches can make a huge difference. The computer was not exactly bulky but it wasn't small either. Still, it was a solid need. So the basic travel gear boiled down to a few items, under a dozen. The list was not very long and I decided to formalize it.

1. Resonator and a spare
2. Computer
3. Spare batteries
4. Survival knife (with water tablets, compass, matches, monofilament)
5. Bottled water
6. Dried foods
7. Plastic silver survival blanket
8. First aid kit
9. A multi-tool with pliers, cutter, screwdrivers
10. Miscellaneous small items in a little roll-up pack

Once I saw the list I knew I was on the right track. Lyt was sure to have all of those things and more. He had bags of doodads that I couldn't even name. I knew then why he also wore a blazer- extra pockets. I had to get one right away.

Another thought- these computers could probably be used like cell phones. If we knew the right commands, we could probably talk to each other. Sure. There was another thing to do.

I turned on my desktop computer and then turned on the Boro computer. I started the communication protocol thing that I had tried in the restaurant. I watched as I used the desktop to get on the Internet. The computer tracked what was happening. Soon it produced a box that said "enter keystrokes and transmit."

I typed a request for a web site on the desktop and watched it come up. The Boro computer recorded and analyzed. A window appeared like a flat plate in the hologram space. It showed characters of traffic and I knew it was cracking the communications. It only needed to understand the formatting and it would be ready. It was already monitoring web traffic and was probably capable of sending it.

The message "done" appeared in the window. Problem- there is no keyboard on the Boro computer. What now? I had to create one. Since the hologram was interactive, I would have to show it a keyboard and then use the hologram image of it to type. This was way more involved than I expected.

I set the Boro computer up to see the screen and I began browsing and using the web. This would provide lots of examples of what it should be seeing. I had no hope of using it to get online any time soon but at least it could monitor and was starting to build up an association between the things I typed and what showed up on the screen.

I checked email, looked for information on minerals, and started searching for compact survival gear. This was one of those times when I was completely focused on what I was doing. After over an hour I was ready to see how Lyt was doing. And then it hit me- we always walked or used local transport when we crossed to other worlds. But what about a bicycle?

There were lots of really compact ones and some would fold up. A trail bike that was lightweight and would fit on your back would be a perfect thing to have. And then another thought struck me. Why didn't Lyt make the frames with wheels or something? A large resonator could move a whole vehicle, right? What were we thinking?

I started thinking about the basic assumptions. Most worlds will be wilderness and unoccupied by people. Lyt had found that most were so similar in environment that he had lived through how many decades of traveling without breathing equipment or a space suit. But basic transportation could change a lot of things.

So maybe there was a much better way to do things. Minibike? Moped? Dirt bike? Yes! The computer could be used to match up the landscape of two planets and tell you where you would be emerging, and then you could drive around anywhere and step across to the other world when you needed to. What a concept.

It was not too late yet. I packed everything in and took a ride to a local bike shop.

<hr/>

The salesman showed me a lot of things and I really wanted a lot of them. But I had to be firm about weight limits and ruggedness. I selected a small dirt bike and an oversized fuel tank. I equipped it with a spare gas bottle and a small carrier rack with saddle bags. I also added extra bright halogen lights and a spare battery for it.

This was going to be phenomenal! Everything fit into the trunk and the back seat. There was a feeling of triumph when I drove to the metal building to see Lyt and how he was doing.

The door was closed and I unlocked it and went it. It was dark and I entered the alarm code. Boron was gone as was Lyt. The workspace was neatened up and three large frames were completed with resonators in place and there were even headlights mounted on two of them. Lyt was thinking ahead.

The hole drilling machine was done and had been in use. There were some plates of metal near it that had identical patterns of holes in various sizes. The workbench was also clean and everything in place. Where could they be?

I unloaded the bike and all the accessories. After about a half hour of assembling and testing I was ready to take a trip and do some exploring. It would be dark on the other worlds presumably. No problem.

I got on the bike and did a transit to Melios. It worked perfectly. There was only the sound of breeze rippling the grass. I switched on the headlight and did a slow pan around. Nothing.

I switched the light off and transited back to Earth. Hmm. I tried the valley park.

Soft yellow light from a moon half the size I expected shone down. A smaller dot moved rapidly along towards it. Could there be a small, second moon as well? I stared at the unknown moon and saw that it had its own random splotches and craters, light and dark like our own. Very neat.

The headlight was turned on and another survey of the land was made. I saw what appeared to be glowing marbles of blue-green in the dark and realized it was the eyes of some animal. I transited back to Earth and turned off the lights. Where could he be?

I really didn't want to get lost in the dark on a strange planet. I started the bike and rode, more in thought and frustration than anything else. It needed to be broken in and the battery charged anyway.

After a few miles in the cool night air, I stopped at a place beside the road and transited to the desert world. It was quiet and cool, soft sand under the wheels. The engine ticked as it cooled. I swept the light over the landscape and thought "snakebite kit" and mentally added that to my list. I spoke the request to the Boro computer and made certain I would not forget it.

I set the kickstand and got off the bike. My shirt pocket showed a warmth and on inspection I found that it was glowing softly. What was this about? The crystal bit from Nyos was reacting to something. My fingertips found it and it felt warm and soft. When it was extracted from the natural lint-gathering cavity I could see the flakes inside roiling and moving slowly from its own emitted light.

As an experiment I tried some sand and a bit of rock. The crystal flowed over the rock and seemed to dissolve a piece of it about the size of an acorn. It was satisfied and it retracted from the mineral. I remembered the concept of collecting crystals for detectors and pocketed the rest of the rock.

I had been slacking. Each world had rocks and crystals and I was supposed to be collecting them and making sure I knew where they were from. How do you mark a rock? I had better start carrying a felt tip permanent marker. Add one more item to my list. And what about a rock hammer and one of those little fishing tackle cases for the samples? I was going to be a walking junk collection before the end of the week. If I fell in a puddle, the excess weight would drown me.

The crystal was still glowing softly. What else would it want? A sample of plant life perhaps. I tried it with a leafy looking thing and it took a sample of that as well. It seemed as bent on sample collection as I was. So be it.

After a few more minutes of watching and listening I decided to get back. The bike was a wonderful tool but I would need full daylight to make the most of it. And markers!

I got the idea of planting flags so I could see where my entry point was. That was an excellent idea. If I was going to be traveling a lot, there would have to be some sort of idea of where I should be instead of popping up in a field of briers or rocks. Or a lake.

The computer had some sort of inertial navigation and I decided to explore the desert at night by headlight. I could ride along the approximate path of the road on Earth and do so right here. It was a good way to get familiar with things.

The computer could be used in audio mode but there was a problem. The bike was so noisy that I couldn't hear it. I would ride a little and then consult. Constant stops were the price and the next thing that I would need was a helmet mounted earphone and microphone. Those should be available somewhere.

It took three times as long to get back to the shop but the ride at night was wonderful and I felt joyful and refreshed when I finally killed the engine and transited back to the front of the building.

Entering it, I saw something surprising. Lyt was there with a fourth cage and half a dozen robots identical to Boron. "Ah, times are excellent and well greeted you are."

"Well, I thought that Boro was closed for six months."

He was grinning madly. "There was a factor that I did not take into account. You made me think of it with your talk of changing velocities and matching up to the movement of a world. The moon! It is moving around the planet and it is changing its velocity!"

Oh! I hadn't thought of that. Lyt went on.

"After checking and doing some calculations, I saw that the velocities might match again and so it is. I traveled to Boro and recruited some help. And I also got six more computers and plenty of power cells for them. And at last I understand why the resonance was ending so rapidly and unexpectedly. The moon was the cause."

So something I had said did prove useful after all. Lyt had to be at least a little impressed. "This is all great news. What about the resonance though, when does it end?"

"Oh, in a matter of hours but that was expected. We may see a small but temporary extension but not safe to use I would say. You could be stranded there for months."

Well, that was an undesirable thing to have happen. "Oh, I got the lapidary equipment. But I left it in the car. We have to bring it in. Meanwhile, I had this idea and I tried it out."

I showed him the bike. "I gave this whole thing a lot of thought. I realized that I had been approaching it the wrong way. I was just jumping in with no idea of what it really took."

I explained my thinking about survival gear and what I should be carrying. I could tell that he was more than satisfied with my realization. I went through my list of materials and goods and said that I was open to suggestions.

Lyt looked at the robots and the bike, and rubbed his hands together. "I knew that I had made the right choice. There is something about you that defies explanation but I could feel that you would see the proper course. I am well feeling about your presence. You have brought much to my purpose and are a true asset. And a friend."

Lyt proudly showed the new frame and said it could carry over fifteen hundred kilograms. "I have derived a simple law of resonator power and mass. I can now reliably make a resonator that will carry most any load."

"That's great. Hey, there is something I have been thinking about. Suppose there are more frequencies than your resonator can reach, like higher or lower. There could be other worlds there that are just outside your range, and you would be unable to find them or reach them."

He was interested, clearly. "That may be. I have not put much effort into designing a new oscillating element however. The design would have to be modified a bit."

Somehow the whole thing made more sense to me, I can't explain why. I borrowed a screwdriver from him and opened my resonator. "Okay, here you have the tuning fork thing. See how it is driven by each coil here? Now the problem is that for it to reach lower frequencies, I think it would have to be much bigger, right?" He nodded agreement.

"And to reach higher frequencies, this part would be too long and so it can't uhm… oscillate that fast. I think that's the right term."

"Yes, the mass is too great and is extended too long. It would simply heat up."

"So what if you could change the ah- springiness of the metal? How hard it can resist ringing or whatever." I grabbed a notepad and started sketching. I'm terrible at it. But in a few moments I had the general idea laid out.

"We make a piece of short metal bar that normally does not attach to the rod, but when we activate this coil on it, it couples to the rod with magnetic force. Now this makes the rod seem longer without actually making it longer." I saw the light come on in his face.

"And, if we make the coils on the tuning fork run to oppose each other, the fork seems stiffer and rings at a higher frequency, right?"

"Oh. Oh, this is… brilliant. I can build one right away. I can modify all of them to work this way if it actually works." He was excited at the prospect of a whole new sheaf of worlds to explore. "Boron, please assist me."

One of the half dozen robots came to his side. "We will need to make some coils and rods, and some pieces of mounting hardware. Get two of your associates and we will begin at once."

Soon three robots were making things and Lyt was drawing a new oscillator driver and amplifier circuit. I was feeling a bit out of place and so I got one of the robots to help unload the car. The lapidary equipment was installed and occupying a bench in a matter of minutes.

After that I felt a little naked without my resonator and I reassembled it carefully. But I did take a few minutes to look it over with interest. Yes, somehow I did understand what it was doing or at least how. That was mildly surprising. I'm not much of an engineer; that's why I changed careers. I just use things, not invent them. I couldn't say anything about where I got the design of the new resonator mutant tuning fork, but at least he knew that I was always having ideas. That gave me some basis for credibility and would forestall too many questions for the time being.

The resonator was really a simple thing when you came down to it. It was creating a field, not electromagnetic, but similar. There was a contained magnetic field that made the space around it ring like a bell and made the contents of that space move to the other resonant space of that frequency- but only if the energy levels were just so. I could see something like two sheets of rubber, one above another. Each was at a higher or lower level and that level had a frequency or vibration associated with it.

When you ran the resonator you were stretching your part of the rubber sheet up or down to match the other, and then the contents were simply transferred, like hopping off one stair step and landing on another. You obviously belonged on the rubber sheet that was at the same frequency.

It was hard to explain how I understood that and for so many years I had been completely unable to fathom batteries and electronics. Mechanical stuff made sense of course, but electricity seemed too abstract. For some reason things were starting to make sense to me now.

Lyt was deeply engaged in his project and I was certainly learning what he wanted me to know. I had the thought of doing a quick jaunt to the other worlds I could reach and trying them for resonances. Picking up a few sample rocks would also be good. I could catch up on my samples.

I grabbed a box and a marker and consulted the Boro computer. My map program showed too many worlds but the ones I had traveled to were colored orange. In a moment I found an option and selected a range of worlds that fell within my resonator frequencies. Now the display matched what I knew and the places I had seen. Very good. With one exception, it was perfect. The eggshell place wasn't shown.

That was a little alarming. Was it gone? Could I no longer reach it? I set the resonator and scanned it up and down. No, there were three and only three frequencies now. It was gone. All I had left of Nyos was the tiny bit in my pocket.

It slowed me down but it also made me realize the need to collect samples. I transited to the desert world and confirmed that I had the rock still in my pocket. Plain magic marker wrote on it and I put it in the box. I transited to the grassy mini-moose world. It was noisier than I expected. Things were galumphing about and mooing at each other. I remembered to pull up my hood and then it hit me that the bike was still dead obvious.

I would have to figure something out for that. More fabric from Boro? Perhaps I could get one of those camp tents. That would do it. Should I risk it?

It took a few minutes to get to Melios and then Boro. The resonance was strong but would not last much longer. I appeared not far from the plaza where I had first transited there with Lyt. The store with the hunting goods was some unknown distance from me. But at least I knew that there were stores here.

Soft lighting was indirect in the darkness but there were little floating blobs of blue-green near the ground. They outlined the walkways and the planter boxes. I started to walk the bike but decided against it. I used the headlight to help match up the daylight scene with what I remembered. There it was, the store where I picked up the precious stones.

I entered it and it lit. "I need assistance please."

A strange hologram appeared dutifully. "I will help you."

"How is the search for survivors going?"

The hologram shifted to the officer. "We are making progress in the power grid. The vehicle fleet is growing and some are now scouting new areas. No survivors have yet been found but we have located many decayed remains."

"Thanks, Prizka. I am happy that progress is being made. I have need of a large tent made of the same fabric that my coat is made of. A hunting tent. Is one available here?"

He bowed slightly and vanished, replaced by the store hologram. "Follow me please." The English was getting to be really good. These things learned fast.

It was only a matter of moments before I found what I needed. I grabbed two of the tents and a number of long, thing rods that looked like fiberglass. "This will do very nicely. Thank you."

The hologram vanished and I made my way back to the plaza. Before mounting the bike, I took the crystal bit from my shirt pocket and fed it a little bit of the vines in the planter boxes and pressed it up against the sidewalk or floor. A small nick appeared. It was indeed getting larger. Back in the pocket it went.

I transited back to Melios and then sat there for a few minutes. The tent fabric could be folded over the bike or draped over it. Maybe I could tape it or tie it with something clear. There had to be a simple way to get the tent fabric on it.

Maybe if I simply draped it before I transited, I could scope out a

SIR CHARLES SHULTS III

situation without being seen or heard. Then I could remove it and take off riding. I would think of something. Now for those poles.

I had the bright idea of putting orange flags and also cyalume glow sticks on them. At night you could easily find the flagpole by the glow. In the daytime it would stick out and allow you to locate a marker easily enough. Later I would think about radio beacons or something similar.

What if you had a light airplane or an ultralight? Could you transit using one in flight? You could be almost assured of finding a good landing spot and no danger of falling in the water. If not you just transit back and land normally.

The thoughts were coming fast. More ideas than I could possibly try but some of them might be of use to Lyt. He wanted to get his stones. That was mission number one. I needed to get weapons and I had missed the chance to do so. Would they be available on Boro?

The idea was attractive. But hunting weapons are generally not small. They can be powerful but there are definite limits. More than likely a good pistol would work as well. I had to remember to keep things simple.

So what about the Moon thing? If the movement of the Moon could actually change the speed of the Earth a little, it could make resonance moot. How much was there?

I consulted the computer. If you were under the Moon itself, on the part of the Earth facing it, the difference was small, just about 12 to 13 kilometers per hour. On the far side of the planet, away from the Moon, it could be about 80 or 90 kilometers per hour. I saw the Moon was up before I transited.

No, no. That was wrong. This was Melios, not Earth. How could the Earth's moon make the difference? It couldn't. I was scratching my head. Melios must have a moon also. And yes, a dim orange colored crescent was just making its way up on the horizon. Bingo. It all made sense now.

What exactly had Lyt said? He said "the moon", not "Earth's moon". I had made an assumption. Melios had a moon and it moved the planet a little, just enough to put things out of whack. But that velocity *had* to be small, and I could reach perhaps a hundred twenty on this bike, pushing it. I could actually match the difference and get to a world that was just barely out of reach on foot.

That was a major wow.

It would be risky, you would want to know exactly where you would end up. But if you had a clear field in front of you, you could do it. At least at your destination. I had so much more to think of. I started back to my sample collection.

After feeding the Nyos bit (which was a much better label than "that crystal" and all the other variations I had been thinking of) I left Melios for Earth and transited to the valley park. I found a small patch of soil and plants and touched the Nyos bit to them. I also found a smooth stone that had a light vein of what looked like quartz in it. I wrote "valley park" on the stone and put it in the box. Next, back to Earth and then to the desert.

I had already fed the Nyos bit here. I also had a rock. I pulled it out and labeled it "desert landscape" and put it in the box.

All told I went to each of the worlds, even the downpour world. Fortunately it was only a cold drizzle at night there, and I found some mud and plants without event. The Nyos bit accepted each and was now almost as large as my palm. It was picky and would not eat much each time but it was growing rapidly. It was then that I knew something more was happening.

How did my computer know which worlds I had visited? The software had to be getting the data from somewhere. I had to try an experiment. The scenery was boulders and mini-moose world, just one step from torrential downpour land. It was also one step from giant tree world.

I placed the Nyos bit in the box with my rock samples. There were some misgivings about leaving it there, but I had to see if my suspicions were correct. I set the resonator for the giant tree world and transited. I waited breathlessly in the dark for a full three minutes and then transited back.

When I arrived back in mini-moose and boulder land, I activated the computer and looked for the worlds I had visited. The giant bird world was already in the listing. That wasn't it then. I was stumped. How did the computer know?

Oh. Duh! It had already known when I acquired the Nyos bit. This world was in the directory of places I had visited. Somehow it was already known data. That meant that either a) each world left some sort of trace on you or b) Nyos had some way of seeing what I was doing before we met. Was there another possibility? Who could say, not me.

I made another transit to the giant tree world and smelled the thick, resinous air. The headlight made a bright beam in the moisture laden night and even with its great brilliance it did not reach those distant trees. For a few moments I was thinking of the bird-tile thing and didn't do much moving around.

Satisfied that it was quiet, I found a small rock and a handful of tree needles. Nyos accepted them and the rock was labeled and put in the box. The pleasant night was attractive but really, I had to get back to Lyt and see what I could do to contribute to the effort.

For fun I tested the tree world for other resonances. A faint frequency seemed to be coming in but it was very weak and I got the impression that it was probably a passing world somewhere in the universe. I consulted my atlas of the universe and yes, there was a world just out of range that would have been available if not for some small effect.

I saw the orange worlds marked as visited and the other invisible and unreachable worlds that swam just barely away from the sphere that represented this planet. It would be fun to see just how many the modified resonator could open.

I transited in two steps back to the desert world and searched for resonant lines. Nothing new. I transited to downpour world and looked for lines. Nope. The computer display showed two worlds that might possibly be reached but they were out of range for my resonator.

I finally gave it up and went back to Earth.

Lyt had finally gotten five of the robots doing things. The fifth was making more power adapters for charging the other robots. The sixth was listening to Lyt who was patiently explaining what he needed made and how to do it. The old guy finally was done and started in on the diamond saw wheel for cutting crystals.

"Here, I have some samples to work with." I handed him the box with all the rocks I had collected.

"Splendid! We can make and test some detectors with local worlds now. I had hoped to get this done quickly. Here, take this." He pulled the cover off the saw and started hooking up power and water. I folded the cover and placed it on the shelf just below the workbench. In a few minutes Lyt had a piece of rock from mini-moose land being sliced into a thin section. This was going to be fairly slow.

The rock had some small but serviceable crystals within. These could just about be cracked apart with a hammer to yield small quartz bits. If the rock from the giant tree planet also had some quartz or similar crystals, this could work well. As I thought of the things to do for making tiny bits of crystal, I said "vitamins" and put notes on my pad and in the computer.

"Hey Lyt, can you use these computers as communication devices?"

"I would think it is possible. We can try that when we have time. Very useful."

"What about between worlds? Is there a way to talk from one world to another?"

"No, nothing can move a signal faster than light that I know of and nothing hand held will send a message across the universe. The worlds are isolated."

Thinking about what he said, I fiddled with the rock tumbler in front of me. There was a grain of something there. "What about detectors? They're detecting something instantly from a world that is so far we don't even have words for it."

He stopped what he was doing and looked at me.

I pressed on. "And resonators are reading that world even though it is far away but doing it instantly. So something has to be able to travel faster than light. When we step across to another world, we must be moving faster than light, right?"

"Not at all. You are stepping across a very tiny space. The space of the universe is right next to our planet and the other planet. You are moving at no speed at all. And detectors cannot send a signal, just detect resonance."

"Well then, by your logic if we are not moving at any speed at all when we transit from world to world, then our signals won't need to either. Those two worlds must already be right there. Surely there must be something that can be done to send even a simple dot and dash code."

He clearly had thought about this some time but had come up with nothing. "I cannot see a way to transit a radio signal or a dot code."

"Okay, theoretical case. I see that sometimes when you step across, there is a noticeable fade out period, not an instant flash and you are gone. Where are you during the time that you are fading out- here or there?"

He looked irritated. "In transit. You are in neither place during that time."

"In transit. Yes. I can see you and I'll bet that somebody over there can also see you at the same time. See where this is going?"

I had something here. "When you activate the resonator in transit mode, you have the tuning fork at one frequency for your destination world. But what if you had it at *two* frequencies at once? What would happen? If you kept the two frequencies balanced at the same time?"

"You would... well. In theory you would be anchored to both worlds at once."

"Yes! So what would happen if we had a radio transmitter and receiver and it would receive one frequency and transmit another, and we placed it in between the two worlds. It would be capable of talking across the two worlds at once. Right?"

"My goodness, you have another device you want me to make? You will wear me down to nothing!"

I laughed that time because I had a feeling that this would work. I sketched the idea out as a block diagram. So many ideas and so many things to do. Something would have to give. I made more notes on the computer. There had to be some time to try this before things got too busy.

The lapidary saw was nearly through the first slice. I had to try a piece of the desert rock next to it and see what would happen. And there I saw a faint light from the two pieces. The rocks were compatible and we would be able to make the detectors. Not that I was worried about it working, I just thought that having to poke around for the right kind of rock could be a problem.

Personally I was sure that there had to be a faster way to do this. In a moment of digging around I found a small hammer. I carefully tapped a few times on the desert rock and got some small bits that looked like crystals. They were about the size of sesame seeds and glistening.

With even more care I took one of the tiny fragments and held it next to the rock in the cutter. Yes, I felt the pull and saw a faint light. This would be perfect. The sawed-off face of the mini-moose rock was still there. I tapped a few crumbs of it as well and found one of the right size. It reacted nicely and so I had a pair of stone chips that would indicate resonance between those two worlds.

Yes, something had to travel faster than light because I was nowhere near those planets yet I was getting a signal that showed me they were aligned. I checked my computer and looked at worlds that were moving around slowly like majestic bubbles. There appeared to be a world coming into touch with the valley park world but it was moving too fast.

It would never connect, that was clear. I saw that the speed was a few kilometers per hour too high. But I knew how to match it. I got my resonator and some heavy tape. I had an idea. "Lyt, you want to try an experiment? A world is going to match up with us shortly but it's moving too fast. I'm going to try and catch it."

He had a concerned look. "Isn't this a little foolhardy?"

"We have to know that it will work." I lined up the direction and speed and saw that this would be an easy test. Twenty kilometers per hour should just do it. I set the frequency for the valley park world and got my dirt bike ready. The tape held the resonator nicely on the handlebars. I could reach the button well enough.

"I'm going to try it now, while the timing is good."

Lyt grabbed a few items and stuffed them into his pockets. I transited to the valley and waited. The sun was just starting to color the horizon. That showed me east and I confirmed that it matched what the computer had said. Lyt materialized in a few seconds.

"Michael, I am concerned about this. You have no idea what you are going to face. Take this instead." In his hands was the floater probe. "It is programmed to move up to speed, find the resonance, and transit. Then it will reverse its movement and transit back after about ten seconds."

That was actually much smarter. I liked the thought of the advance scout taking the risk. Lyt released the little floater and it sped off and vanished. It worked! I was trying to find a resonance on my resonator but it wasn't showing up. Yet there was one for the moving floater. Perfect.

Shortly after the floater reappeared and settled in Lyt's hands. He activated the hologram playback. "Wonderful. It does work. You have connected to a fast moving world." He had a beatific smile. "This is very helpful. We can connect to many more worlds with this and reach some places that I could not have gotten to. It greatly simplifies some things for my task."

"Does it look safe?"

"It seems to be." I saw what appeared to be a stretch of grass with tiny flowers in it and a lake not too different from the one we were near.

"Okay, I'm going through." I aimed the bike, revved the engine and got up to speed. It took some juggling to adjust the resonator frequency but it got a good spike and I locked it. Time to slow and turn around.

I rode back to Lyt. "Okay, I have it locked. Now for the real deal." I circled back and lined up on the tire marks and gunned it. In a moment I was at the proper speed and I hit the transit button.

The wheels scuffed hard and I realized I was standing still. The bike lurched and I laid it over. What just happened? This was most definitely not the valley park world. There were pink looking mountains ahead of me. But when I came through, I was stationary relative to the ground, and the wheels were still spinning. That was it, then the engine caught and made the bike try to move at 25 kilometers per hour but we were standing still.

That was why I laid it down and the engine died. I would have to be prepared for reentry. I looked for a rock and as I leaned over the Nyos bit fell from my shirt pocket. Whoops, have to watch out for that. It sank into the grass and to the ground. There was a hiss and it seemed to burrow into the soil. I scooped carefully around it and extracted it from a muddy mass of dirt and roots. Some sort of puffball or mushroom was mushed all into it.

It took a few moments to sort things out and the Nyos bit, which was now larger than an egg, flattened into a thick disk and I placed it inside one of the coat pockets and sealed it. Turning the bike and starting the engine, I hit the exchange button and was ready to transit back. It took very little time to get up to speed and hit the button.

I was ready this time. The bike was stopped immediately and the wheels scuffed but I kicked the clutch and put my feet down right away. Perfect!

"So it works. Lyt, you need to learn to ride a dirt bike." I prepared to transit back to Earth. Wait. I had no sample. I exchanged the frequencies once more and told him my plan.

"I'll just be a few minutes and grab some rocks." Lyt didn't look happy.

"Mike, you are unprepared for this. You should at least have your basic survival materials."

"It's a walk in the park. Ten minutes, roughly. And you can send the floater to see what is going on. Right?"

"Very well. You are an adult. I will wait for you here."

I checked everything, feeling a little chastened but unwilling to back down. The bike reached speed and I transited without incident. A new world!

I planted a flag on the entry point and recorded things on the computer. I took a few minutes to find some stones but they looked too rockish and no crystals that I could see. The territory was pretty enough, like a national forest. Stands of pines with too-dark needles lined the west wide of the area. Pink mountains now behind me were still a mystery.

The lake showed rings and splashing noises were heard. Probably some fish. It was far too normal. I scanned the resonator and found another frequency. What luck. I tried it.

This was a dusty, barren place. I coughed from the smell of sulfur and fumes. Gray dust covered everything and not a bit of green or any sort of life could be seen. I spent a few seconds feeding the Nyos bit some of the ash and what looked like Swiss cheese rock. Large bubbly holes and glassy gray looking stuff, I wasn't sure what it was called.

The smell got worse. I transited back to the fast moving world.

Surely there would be some rocks here, something useful. I found nothing. This was going to require a search and I had no time for that. I might as well scan for other resonances. I found two weak frequencies but didn't feel like trying them. They were probably too risky and might fade at any time. What about dust world, the sulfur smelling place?

That would be easy. I transited to the dust world and scanned. Three lines! Wow, a veritable treasure of worlds.

Now, if I had been smart I would have left it at that. But no, I was feeling in control and knew that I could handle whatever came. I scanned the three lines, knowing that one was the trip back to the fast moving world with the pink mountains. I set the lower frequency and transited.

This place smelled bad right away. Soft muck was squishing under the wheels of the bike and my shoes. It was darker than it should have been. No rocks here and only dark slimy stuff with kelp-looking leaves for plants. There were thick clouds with a touch of reddish-golden light that moved over at high speed.

I then spotted what looked like fish flopping on the ground. They had large heads and were whiskered like catfish. The ground seemed to tremble and there was a low roaring noise in the air. Some deep subsonic rumbling filled the world.

The air had the smell of not just slime and decay but of ocean water. A fine mist of salt spray was in the air and a tang of burning.

I exchanged and transited back to dust world. I waited a few minutes and thought about the place.

Perhaps one more quick look.

I transited to the mucky world and saw a strange sight on the horizon. A golden light was blooming and rising, the roaring noise was growing in intensity. The sun was not rising, something else was happening. It grew until the light was nearly too bright and I could see rocks and debris forming a monstrously large wall of incandescent stuff rolling my way. I transited back to dust world fast.

What was that? Maybe a major meteor impact or something. That place was going to be in a bad way for years. I was far too close for comfort. I set the other frequency and transited.

My ears squeezed in hard with high air pressure and cold. Ice field. This was a seriously cold place. Ice age weather was the rule here. I couldn't see anything but white. The ground rose and fell in sheets of wind sculpted ice. The air was nearly still however and so the cold didn't seem too bad. I wrapped my coat a little tighter and it was a fine shield against the weather. No rocks, no plants, just packed snow and sheets of ice.

Well. I scanned for more lines. Nothing.

I transited back to dust world. The smell was probably going to stick around. This must have been the result of a large volcanic eruption. That made sense. A lot of dust and sulfur smells made it clear that maybe something like Mount Saint Helen's had blown recently. Like hours ago. From there I went to the fast moving world.

Well, at least I could go home. I set the resonator for the basic frequency here and I got up to speed and scanned for valley park world. The line was weak. This was not good. I went faster. The line got a little stronger. I was running out of straight, firm ground.

I wheeled back and sped along to get to my entry point. I made a second run and got a little more firm frequency but it was fading. I transited. Nothing happened.

I made a large circle and scanned. No lines showed that I didn't already know about, like dust world. Time to regroup.

I settled down to a nice spot and consulted the computer. Okay, there were the worlds I had visited from here and their movements around this fast moving world. I could see the fast world and the valley park world overlapped still but the speed was the issue. Why was it changing?

It was clear that the speed was going to prevent me from making the transition. It was changing and speeding up. This was bad. Was there any world that might fall into place for me?

Looking at the screen and running things ahead a bit, I could see that I was actually in worse shape than I thought. The fast moving world was like a stepping stone but it was moving away and would leave the vicinity for some months. The dust world was at least stable and capable of reaching two other worlds. But the fast world I was in was going to be lost in a few days and it had no coming connections that I could reach.

Wait. I could just look for a broader range of movements. Set the program to allow worlds that were up to... fifty kilometers per hour faster. That might help.

It did. Now I had three possibilities but they were still days apart. The first opportunity was a world that would act like a stepping stone from the ice world in two days. That would carry me to a potential rendezvous with the torrential rain world two days later. Could I make a jump on the bike into rain like that, blind? Perhaps.

I had only to get up to thirty to make the jump to the unknown stepping stone world, and then two days there would carry me to torrential rain, but doing about twenty. It was moving back and away from the previous world. It was hard to describe but things could line up for this.

Could I wait here and see what would happen? Maybe. Water was the big issue and shelter was next. Perhaps something would change.

I set the computer to alert me if any favorable change would happen, like the worlds falling into place by a miracle. It was time to explore a bit and find out what I had to deal with here.

CHAPTER 7

A light rain that was more like a mist began to fall. I found a sheltered spot under one of the pine trees. I kicked a couple of branches and found some small wormy things that lived just under them in the loamy forest floor. The lake was still visible from this vantage point and it was very pretty. I pulled one of the camp tents out of the bike rack. At least I had had enough foresight to put those in place.

How many hours had it been since I was on Boro? Not that many. Today was Wednesday morning. Friday would bring a jump from ice world to somewhere new. Then I would ride that world for two days and try to make a jump to rain world. From there I was two steps from Earth.

I could camp out for a couple of days. I had no food and limited water but there was a lake and maybe I could boil some water just to be safe. How did you make a solar still?

Wait, there was ice in the glacier world and that was likely to be cleaner. And at least I had transportation and a spare battery for the bike. I hadn't even unpacked it from the box or filled it. I reached into the sealed pocket with the Nyos bit. It was large and warm, seemed to cling to my fingertips. I pulled it out and examined it.

Yes, it was really large now. It was as large as my fist and filled with slowly turbulent flecks of silver. Had I really given it that much material to eat? It flowed smoothly like a large amoeba and then hardened. It was conformed to the shape of my hand, more or less. I had an idea.

I gave the shape a little kneading motion and it softened. I formed it into a ball and flattened it a little. It smoothed like a squashed sphere and became solid. Perfect.

I took the lens-like shape and held it in the sunlight. On the ground beneath it a small wisp of smoke emerged. Ha! I had a lens that could perhaps start a fire!

I put the lens shaped thing back in my coat pocket and gathered some of the smooth stones and formed a round fire pit. A little scratching with a stick yielded bare dirt beneath and the stones ringed it nicely. Now I gathered some of the drier pine needles and leaves along with some grass and a few sticks. The light rain hadn't gotten under here and so the material was pretty dry.

After a few moments of arranging, I got everything as I needed it. I took out the now lens-shaped Nyos bit and held it over the grass. Smoke began to appear. A tiny flame started after about half a minute. This was going to work.

The flame grew and caught the grass and needles. I gave the lens a little squeeze and put it back in my shirt pocket which was getting uncomfortably tight now that the bit was so much larger.

The flame took a little nursing to get to a stable state but soon it was burning nicely and the heat was very welcome. My coat kept me warm of course but there was some comfort in a fire that went beyond simple warmth. I gathered a few more sticks and kept it burning without much trouble.

The tent was ridiculously easy to pitch. It came together in a few minutes after placing an anchor post in the ground and attaching one corner loop of the frame to it. You just pulled the other end and it blossomed open and snapped into a locked state. The cloth went over the top and it fastened with little fuzzy pads that seemed to have magnets in them. The bottom was already attached to the frame and unfolded with it.

Once in place the appearance of the tent seemed to take on the movement of branches and leaves over its surface. It would be pretty hard to spot if you didn't know where it was.

The computer beckoned. I had to see what the worlds were doing. Was there a chance that I could match speed with the valley park world again? I read the differences and it looked no better. It was time to look at how the worlds would be moving over the next few days and, reluctantly, weeks. It might take that long and I knew it.

I watched the simulation from different angles and for different time frames. The worlds each looked like bubbles and the bubbles would move and stretch out in long chains, then break into singles or doubles. The chains would move and reform, strings and clusters of bubbles that would collapse into a point where a dozen worlds could be traveled easily or none seemed to even touch. For an hour I watched the chains and groups of worlds form and break apart. No mercy there.

Lyt had to know the same things I knew from the standpoint of world movement. He would be doing this too, working out the best chances and most likely cross over points. He would see the ice planet and the fast stepping stone world that I would likely try. Surely he would be ready and when I stepped through he might even be waiting.

Yeah, to kick my ass. And I deserved it. He was the seasoned traveler and he gave me advice that I ignored. I had let him down as well as myself. But there was no time for recrimination. I had to do what was necessary for survival. I also had to keep an eye on the worlds and how they were moving.

The fire was dying down but I could always make another if I needed it. I covered the ashes with damp soil and made sure it was out. I left the fire pit because I had the feeling that I would be back here again.

The rain was ended and a large rainbow was showing up in the west. Sunrise had been quiet and only strange bird calls had marked that transition to daylight. I stood with the little stick in my hand that I had stirred the ashes with. It took only a few minutes to prepare for a trip around the area.

I placed a marker pole not far from the trees and set three smooth stones in a line from it pointing at the camp. Making note of the landmarks near the trees and directly across from the lake, I set off on the bike and cruised over territory to see what I could find.

Within a few minutes I had an idea of the landscape and could see that the pink mountains really were pink, not just a trick of lighting. There were some sort of grazing animals that looked like deer and ran like crazy when I passed. What was odd is that they looked like they were made of leather and had no fur. Also there were little things rather like beavers but they were scaly all over. When I thought I saw a rabbit it turned out to be something like a wallaby but it did have fur. It was the first mammal I had seen.

This was a weird place. Very few mammals, most of the life here was reptile or similar to it. The lake was going to be interesting. I approached it cautiously and watched. Something was moving up out of the water and back again. There was a brown dirty beach-looking area covered with glistening wet logs. I rolled a little closer with the engine off and just pushing along on my feet.

One of the logs moved. It had large fins and lots of toenails on it. A closer looked showed that it was some sort of thing I was completely unfamiliar with. It looked like a lungfish sort of, with large gill slits and dark brown, slimy skin. It breathed in rasping wet heaves and flipped at insects with the flippers. The whole body was covered here and there in little toenails.

Was it a fish or an amphibian? Each of the logs moved in sympathy when the active one heaved itself toward the water. The entire beach was deep in toenail-covered slugs with emphysema.

I backed away quietly, not wanting to disturb the sunbathers. They reminded me a little of hippos, large and slow on the land but quite capable of defending themselves in the water. I wondered at the carnivores that might be around.

One thing I was thankful for was that the flies didn't bother me at all. No mosquitoes, no biting flies. It was easy work backing the bike out of the area and returning to the faint trail I had been following. I knew that wildlife would want access to the water so it was a logical thing to follow. Now I was pretty sure I didn't want to struggle to get fresh water from that lake.

The glacier world was looking more attractive for that. I went back to the camp and on the way gathered some dry sticks for my fire. I had to drink some of my water and knew that it wasn't going to be enough for a whole day.

I wandered slightly from the path in the grass and slowed. My front wheel sank into a hole. Great.

The bike was not very heavy but the hole was deceptively deep. It had a thin cover of leaves and things floating on the watery mud within. It took a few minutes to get a firm foothold to release the wheel. Just off the pathway the ground turned to mush and was covered in juicy ferns. They stank when I crushed a few stepping around the hole. Something nearby smelled strongly of peppermint.

The bike was freed and ready to go. This expedition was not going badly but it also was not what I could call a success. It would be terribly embarrassing to be found in this state. I had to do something to fix it. First, I had shelter and could make a fire. Second, I had transportation both on worlds and between them. Third, I had my computer and could figure out what was coming in terms of resonances.

I had to get water. It was supposedly first on any survival list. I got back to the camp and set my resonator for the dust world and then the ice world. I left the bike next to the fire pit and went on foot, carrying the little tire iron from the bike toolkit.

The step to the dust world was odd. The dust had mostly settled and I found that I was standing on the side of a large hill with thousands of cactus plants on their sides. They were as large as trees and spinier than hell and the dust was covering them pretty deeply. The skies were incredibly bright with sooty clouds and orange light. I held my breath against the dust.

The ice world was unchanged. Nothing lived here. It was even hard to breathe a little, although the air was clean. There was a lot of air pressure though. It took a minute to adjust my eardrums by swallowing a lot. Then the tire iron proved its use as I chipped and pried a large chunk of the ice free. It was fairly low density with lots of white and bubbles inside it. Now all I had to do was figure out how to distill it. Maybe.

I transited back through dust world to the campsite. Nothing unusual there. I decided that since I had no way to boil the water, I might have to risk it. The question was, did I wait until I was really thirsty first, or try it now? If it made me sick, I stood a better chance of recovery if I was not already beaten down. If I waited until later, I might have more time to do something before I got sick. Hmm.

I dug through the bike's saddle pack. There I found the plastic bag from the tools and another from the battery. That could work. I broke the ice into pieces and stored them in the two bags. At least I had water now.

At that I decided to take the trip to Dust again. It gained a name then. I had to start naming these worlds or I would never keep them straight. I checked the computer and found all the worlds I had visited were again outlined in orange. I saw that each had a number of sorts and that my display showed frequencies and some little files that proved to be hologram movies of my visits. Excellent, I could know where and when I had been anywhere.

I transited to Dust and found one of the downed cactus plants. This world seemed not to have trees, just stand-in plants. Or maybe that was a local thing. A planet is a huge thing and you can't really characterize it from one tiny spot. That was a thought that really hit me then. I was only seeing the tiniest of samples of each world. Nobody could even explore the Earth in a lifetime and do it justice, who was I to think that I had knowledge of a world when I just stepped onto it, looked around, and left?

I had given the Nyos bit some volcanic dust but no plant life. I could remedy that now. It sank into the cactus a bit and then extruded back out. It was growing rapidly now and was almost too big to put in my shirt pocket. What was I going to do when it got even larger?

I could picture myself carrying a large blob of glittery stuff from world to world and having to put it in a sidecar. How would I explain it to Lyt? What would I tell him it was and where I got it? This was getting serious.

There were a lot of questions that would arise soon. I felt like I was getting myself into something and not able to back out. I had, come to think of it. I was stranded on a strange world and unable to return home. I wondered where home was even located?

I transited to camp and looked at the sky. It was close to ten in the morning by my watch. The day was going pretty slowly and my stomach was growling. I searched my pockets and found the receipt for the hamburger and fries in the sports bar and grill. Wonder of wonders, there was a peppermint folded in it! Well, you couldn't say that I had no food now. All I needed at this point was a ketchup pack.

That made me start laughing. I sat on the ground and laughed until my sides hurt. Great explorer living on glacier ice, mints and ketchup! The picture was too much for me. My computer beeped.

What was that? I checked the display. No way! I packed my tent quickly and put everything in the saddle packs. The fire pit was cold, no danger there. Tent was packed, stake pulled up and stowed, everything back in its place. I transferred the Nyos bit, which was more like a chunk now, into the coat inner pocket where its warmth was tangible.

The bike started and I rode back to my entry point just a couple of hundred meters away. I consulted the computer and lined myself up for a quick acceleration. After setting the resonator and taping it back to the handlebars, I was accelerating hard.

Yes! The resonator had the frequency! I locked it in and swung back as quickly as I could to start a new pass. In moments the bike was up to speed and I transited.

The look of the valley park was exactly what I had hoped. I had made it back! I hit the exchange button to lock the valley park in primary and scanned for Earth's frequency. I had it. The transit took no time and I was happily back outside the metal building. I could have yelled with joy.

I parked the bike and walked inside. Lyt was already on his way to the door.

"Mike! So wonderful to see you, foolish thing that you are!" He actually embraced me. "Very well met. I greet you."

"Yeah, that was sort of scary. I managed to make camp, start a fire, get water, and see the impact of a giant asteroid. I have to show you my movies. This is great stuff."

The impact world was staggering once I saw the playback. Lyt was just shaking his head. "You must have arrived directly after the first impact shock wave. The plasma wall had not yet reached you." I thought about an alternative.

"Or, I figure that there were two hits, a small one nearby that splattered the ocean all over the land, and the larger one farther out. Two impacts and I was just lucky enough to come right between them."

He was amazed. "You are very lucky to be here at all. I was unable to see any simple path to your world location. There was a time when I thought you may never return. But you are resourceful, admirably so. And I know what happened."

I had thought about it. "The moon thing all over, right? I had to wait until the planet had turned enough so the difference in velocity from its moon was smaller."

"Precisely. You must have arrived right as the world was reaching a resonance but it was not yet stable. You learned a valuable lesson I am certain."

"I did. You are an experienced traveler and have a lot of advice that I should listen to, that's number one. Number two is that I am going to get some real supplies and survival equipment right away!"

"Proper. I have to eat. I suppose you have not, being on that planet all day."

Well, yeah. I was very hungry although it wasn't as bad as all that. But a good hot meal would be great. "Lyt, let's go for lunch. What do you think would be good?"

"Anything that does not include coffee."

———◦———

We ate in an Italian place. Lyt liked garlic bread and spaghetti but said that the parmesan cheese was too "minty" for his tastes. We theorized about worlds in movement and how to better our chances. Lyt was getting ready to try a new resonator design based on the information I gave him.

"I have been working on the so-called mutant tuning fork and with the help of the Boro robots I have a test model ready to try. I would like to have you there for the test."

I sopped up some tomato sauce with a piece of bread. "Sure. Do we have time to get my supplies? I really would hate to go anywhere without them."

"Oh, of a certainty. We shall get your supplies."

"I have a question Lyt, and you are the person to resolve it. I heard that space is supposed to be full of worlds with civilizations, lots of them, and that we should be able to hear their signals. People have been searching for years and it looks like they've found nothing. Why is that?"

He looked at his hands and thought. "There is a likely explanation. There are many. Some worlds do not use radio very much or stop using it soon as their technology develops. But many technical worlds destroy themselves. And so many more worlds have no technology at all.

"I would say however that one cause is a faction known as the Archivists. They have been in the universe for billions of years, very old and very advanced."

"Archivists. Okay. What do they do, kill off civilizations?"

He sighed. "In a way, yes. They have advanced to a point that they have retreated from any world that I know of, and are hard to find. Clearly they do not live on a world that can be reached through resonances with these worlds. But they can get around to most any place."

"What are they like?" He had my attention.

"They are very resourceful and tricky. They can change their appearances to any form. You cannot defeat them or even battle them. They find worlds that are technical and on the cusp of making huge leaps in technology, and they destroy them."

I shook my head. "Why? That makes no sense."

"Perhaps a new technical world might pose a threat of some kind. Some feel that they are there to store the experiences of those worlds, their developments and learning, art and music. Thus the name Archivist. It is rumored that they create archives of the worlds they destroy and preserve that unique experience of each civilization."

Considering that the sky was quiet, and that Lyt had been on many worlds with people and technology, it seemed sort of spooky to think that just making radio waves could alert some enemy in the darkness that would swoop in and wipe out a world.

"So Earth is making a lot of noise right now. Isn't that dangerous?"

"It certainly is. I would not be surprised to find that the Archivists had already found your world and were planning the right time to step in. I am trying to save this from happening to a world; that is one of my goals."

The thought was just horrifying. I had to get equipped and ready to do whatever I had to. We finished at the restaurant and hunted for supplies.

I spent about three hours going to stores, picking and choosing, and finding just the right things. I couldn't buy a pistol without a long waiting period but I went ahead and filled out the paperwork. I also got a high-powered slingshot. Don't laugh; these things are serious weapons. I've seen them drive a steel dart through 8 millimeter plywood.

In the end I emerged with everything and a few more things that would fit in the saddle packs of the bike. Lyt also was looking at some of the devices. "A small pair of these binoculars could serve you well."

I thought about it and got a pair. They didn't take much space. I also got a decent flashlight, a box of small glow sticks and a roll of duct tape. The next stop was a shoe store. I needed a real pair of hiking boots to do this properly.

I found some nice leather boots with high sides. They were comfortable and not too badly priced. I picked a neutral brown that would probably blend in well with most scenery.

"Okay, I think I'm done. I have proper cook pans that nestle inside each other, dried food for a couple of weeks, a knife and water purification stuff. Any suggestions, Lyt?"

"You are far better equipped than I was when I started out. I have no suggestions of merit."

On a whim I also grabbed a few packages of vegetable seeds. That may seem fatalistic but at least if I was stuck somewhere for a long time, like months, I had a chance of making it. These I discreetly wrapped and packed in foil and plastic.

Now that I was properly prepared I felt a lot better about being adrift between worlds. I took Lyt back to the workshop and spent some time with the robots watching their work. I also went back to the small bits of crystal I had been testing before I took off.

The lapidary saw was finished. Four sample rocks were sliced into thin sections and were ready to be cut into tiny pieces. Lyt had prepared a list of which worlds these were capable of resonating with and had even included some of the faster worlds which I had figured out how to reach. Each slice would be turned into a vial of little pieces, perhaps a few hundred of each.

The labeled vials would have catalog numbers to match the worlds they came from and a detector for any pair could be prepared by selecting two tiny pieces and mounting them with a sensor. One robot was installing a small milling machine that had arrived and was preparing it to make a form to build detectors.

Another was wiring the large frames and adding things to them. A third was installing more work benches while the fourth added shelves. The fifth was putting new resonator forks together while the last wound coils. Lyt had a little army making interworld travel equipment.

Somewhere in all the stuff I located some small clear plastic tubing and some epoxy. With a hobby knife I cut a short length of the tubing and place the crystal from the mini-moose world in the end. A drop of hot glue secured it. Then I put a tiny scrap of plastic in the tube and finally the crystal from the desert world. It drew toward the other crystal and both glowed softly. I squirted a little more hot glue in and secured it.

The whole thing was less than five millimeters long. If I had one of those optical sensors it could be a functioning unit right now. "Here you go, Lyt." I gave him the tiny thing. "I can even make it smaller once we have the right things to work with. I need smaller spacers for the crystals and of course neater crystals. Those were hand made.

He watched the tiny thing glow. "This is what we need. We can make these for every combination of world we are likely to find now, and place hundreds of them on a single sensor card. The most important item for us to have is organization."

His computer display changed to a matrix. "This is the row and column of each world and which matching crystals we want to use. Each world has a number and a code and each crystal we have does also.

"Each pair has a specific code that tells us what it is. We need to put the identification code on the sensors so that means we have to label them somehow. I have a system worked out."

A picture of a detector appeared in the display. One end was painted white. Along the length of the tiny thing there were colored dots. "This is a color code that tells us a number. You read it from the white end. That way, you can see the identification easily and even if we happened to spill them and mix them up, with patience we could sort them out and use them anyway."

It looked like a little electronic component. But in a sense it was. Now Lyt showed me a new module in his computer display. "This is a pair of circuit cards. The top one is covered with detectors. The bottom one mates directly to it, face to face, and it is covered with optical sensors. They can read the glow of a pair of crystals."

Finally he showed me the really dense model. "This long, thin rod is twelve crystals in one assembly in a specific order." It was only three centimeters long. It was like a white pencil lead with colored dots on it. "When this is assembled it will fit into the new resonator which has a processor built in."

At last he said "now we can test the new resonator with your modifications."

I was ready for this.

Lyt powered the new device. It was much more refined looking than the one I had, and I remembered how things should be simple. But as long as it could be manually operated, we were fine.

He swept the primary frequency control under computer control. The primary light came on and locked. He scanned the secondary. A new display showed a list of frequencies printed out, with a button by each. Lyt touched the first button and it automatically locked the secondary.

"Wow, nice. Melios?"

"Yes. Now we go to extended frequency range. He pressed one more button and the display showed "scanning". Five frequencies showed up. "Two new worlds in resonance with Earth as we speak. I also added something else. If the frequency is stable, you get an orange light. If it is shifting, you get a green light. If it is too weak or looks unstable, you get a blue light. Now you can tell if something may be unstable before you transit."

The two new worlds were at low frequencies and both were stable. Lyt selected the lowest and smiled. He grabbed my wrist tightly and hit the transit button.

Thick yellow mist and a strong smell of ammonia and sulfur. High pressure ice picks hit my ears. The sky! There was a huge splatter of what looked like lava in the sky, and it was moving slowly in a shifting, tumbling streak. The ground heaved.

Lyt looked about casually and pocketed a rock. I was fighting a strong headache from the smell and pressure. Still, I grabbed a handful of glassy looking rock shards and dropped them in my pocket. He grabbed my wrist and transited us out.

The relief was immediate. My eyes were watering and my lungs burning. Lyt seemed unphased. "Very productive. And we have three more frequencies from that world. We have four worlds on that connection now. Shall we try the other?"

Why not? Whatever does not kill you is supposed to make you stronger. I just don't know where the break point is. Lyt punched up the second new frequency, marginally higher than the last. "Here we go."

My poor wrist! I thought it would have a chance to get some recovery time when I got my own resonator, but I guess not.

We were ankle deep in sloshing seawater. The sun was fairly high and late afternoon was approaching. Little fish were flitting around in the gravel and shells under my feet. I took a deep breathe and exhaled appreciatively. "This is more like it."

I scanned for frequencies and got one. Lyt said "Two frequencies. You have outdone my expectations." He set the one we could both get. We transited.

"Ah. Wow." Another beach. But what a beach! The water was so blue-green that it hurt to look at. We were on a beach of pure white sand but the grains weren't sand at all. It was tiny bits of coral or limestone as small as millet. To our left was a tiny island that you could have walked out to. Three trees with ringed trunks sloped lazily out over the water with palm branches hanging low. To the right was a high cliff of black rock with a thread of water pouring over it, rainbows in the air like haloes. Green stuff of all descriptions hung down the cliff face like vines and creepers, ferns and philodendrons.

I had never seen so many flowers. Lyt sighed. "Truly astounding. This is a wonderful find." I dipped my hand to the beach and grabbed a small handful of the soil. It was crumbly and light, didn't stick to your hands at all.

Lyt looked for rocks but came up with nothing. "It looks like a paradise. Just too green, should be more pink and violet." I had to shake my head. It was perfect as it was.

"Well, scanning. No more frequencies here. We shall go."

We took the two transits back to the shop. He was enthralled. "This is very, very good. We can find whole new categories of worlds now that we can use to get from place to place. We may be able to get to my stones sooner instead of waiting for the resonances."

I thought about my computer and decided to take a bit of time to see what it had to offer. I went into the office.

Now, looking at my atlas of the universe I could see more dots showing where I had been. The computer was getting the data with each transit and somehow matching it to the atlas from Nyos. So whatever happened, I would always know where I was, even if it did me little good. I pulled up the map of moving worlds and selected all frequencies. The three we had just visited were there, along with some video footage of each.

My hands went to the pocket with the Nyos bit and extracted it. It was much larger now, and I fed it samples of the last two stops. Why did I keep doing that? Wasn't this going to be impossible to keep quiet soon?

The map of moving worlds was revealing. I had been on other worlds that could conceivably connect to even more worlds, and the range of travel was now amazing. I realized that I could map the worlds as connections, instead of moving spheres. That would be far more useful.

I selected worlds that would connect to Earth and listed only those first order connections. For the last three months and for the next nine months I showed what looked like a train schedule. I could see each place I could step to from here, with the new resonator.

Next I made the program list the connections to other worlds from those first order or direct connections. Now the number of places tripled. Since the computer could show any connection at all, I played with a list. Suppose I wanted to go from here to the fast world I had camped out in without going through valley park? There was a six step method that took two days but I could get there.

What if I included using the bike so I could match speeds? Yes, a two step process that took one day. How about the giant tree world? Hmm, my three step from Earth was the shortest and fastest route. If I cut out the mini-moose world, then I needed to wait a week but there was a four step route. This was amazing. I could get anywhere I knew about in just a few days, no matter what. I pondered that.

Lyt would be needing a route that could get him to his destination. I was sure he didn't have this program, or for that matter this database. His need of the stones told me that.

We had to get those detectors together. We also had to get those new digital resonators with the extended frequency range. Once we had those, we could set a course and do his task easily. But, I would have to tell him of my information. It was probably worth the risk just to let him know that I had a database I got from somewhere. I would have to tell him the whole thing.

I wanted to see what would happen next before I committed to that course of action. Time for a little privacy.

"Lyt, I'm going to do some field exploring with my new gear. I'll be back in a little bit."

"Surely. Get more familiar, see the sights. I will have much done soon. The detectors are the next big task and the robots are working on them within a few hours."

It was great having free help. I set the bike and my equipment and then transited to the desert world.

Here was an evening scene of peace. Something yipped in the distance like a dog but I saw nothing and decided to plant a flag at my entry point. The bike roared to life and I started on a more or less random cruise.

The sand was not too soft, just right. Every so often I would hit a harder patch of ground that was broken into polygons and sounded like loose tiles as I drove over it. I came to an arroyo and stopped, slid the bike slightly.

It wasn't very deep. It was actually a gully more than anything. I cautiously started to go down into it, then thought about it. Perhaps a little farther down it would be less steep.

I transited back to Earth and found myself on a broad grassy field. I drove forward a few meters and checked the computer. Keep going. I drove a few more and the computer said I should be back over solid ground. Transit.

Yes, I was on the other side of the gully now. Cool, I didn't risk my tires or anything. The drive continued and I came to what appeared to be an oasis. This was as good a spot as any.

It was a few minutes to check the land and see that nothing was coming, and then I parked the bike and found a rock to sit on. It was next to the dark little pool that seemed to have a small spring beneath it. I was amazed at the number of little creatures in the water. I unconsciously removed the Nyos bit from the inner coat pocket and started kneading it between my hands. It was almost doughy now.

I'm not sure of the exact thing that happened next but the stuff just slithered from my fingers, dropped right at the edge of the dark pool and as I watched it seemed to flow into the water and vanish. Oh hell. Now what?

Was I stupid enough to put my hand in there? There could be snakes, roots, anything and you wouldn't know what you were touching or what might bite you. Even the fish, I realized, might be venomous. This was an alien world after all.

I watched carefully and thought I might see the stuff glistening in the water. I even got the flashlight and shone it into the dark to the bottom, which wasn't very deep, but it appeared to be covered with slimy leaves and muck. Oh man.

There was no way I was going to lose the Nyos bit. Something about it attached itself to me. Or vice versa. It was the only remainder I had of that strange meeting and while it was inexplicable it was also somehow comforting to have. It seemed almost like it was alive and this was really a poor way to have it end.

I didn't want to just transit back to Earth, I was a considerable drive from the entry point. And I wasn't going to simply leave it here. There was little choice. I had to get it out of the pond or stay the night here until I had better light and could figure it out. The sun was getting low, whichever sun it was, and this was not a good fix.

Okay, so it wasn't an absolute necessity to get the bit back, and it was now getting so large that it outweighed the resonator. And I could swear that it *slithered* out of my hands and into the water. This was almost like intention.

I pitched the tent and set up a camp. This was a good time to try out my equipment. Sure, I could transit back to Earth and go to McDonalds but what's the fun in that? So I settled in and got comfortable next to that pond in the desert.

Shortly I realized that this was actually a good thing. I knew that this would tell me what I really needed. The first thing I felt the urge for was tunes. I had to get one of those little MP3 players and load it up with music. The light was fading quickly.

The first stars were starting to come out. I looked at the pond again, shining the flashlight deep within and shook my head. I would find a stick or something and try to get it out in the morning.

The tent was very comfortable. Even on the flat grassy area near the pond, the floor seemed thick or quilted. These guys knew how to make camp gear. I threw the other tent over the bike to give it a little camouflage and hauled all the important stuff inside my tent.

I spotted a fine outline in the fabric once I was inside the tent and had my things settled. Wondering what it was, I ran a finger over it. A soft white glow came from the strip. Yeah! Built in lighting. It was dim but just right. I decided that this was as good a time as any to get some sleep. Far too early for my usual bedtime, but it had been a busy day again and I was ready to just sleep.

There was the thought that it might be hard to get comfortable on the ground but as it turned out, I might have been on cinderblocks or pillows. It made no difference to me and soon I was in a dreamless sleep.

What woke me? It's not an easy one to answer. There was no sound that bothered me, and the tent light had gone off. I couldn't say what was right or wrong. But I woke and felt that something was different. There was a sense of a presence, somebody familiar or harmless, just watching me.

Lying in the darkness, I listened to the quiet. There may have been a faint rustle that was little more than a breeze might have made. I knew that I could stick my head out of the tent and see stars, and that drew me. I wanted to know what this sky looked like in this distant part of the universe.

The flap parted and the sky revealed itself. My breath stuck in my throat.

Instead of the usual faint band of the Milky Way, there was an immense braided cloud of stars across the heavens. Nearly glowing clots of dust and gas swirled about a darker broken line of soot. A large lens-shaped bulge just peaked over the band of stars and about two dozen clusters of stars dotted the sky in all directions. Some looked like a pinch of salt on a black tablecloth and others looked like random spatterings of blue-white and yellow points. Halfway to the horizon on the glowing band of dust clouds there was a dark blot as large as my hand and within it like a cocoon there was a glowing blue-white mist with enshrouded stars floating inside.

This was outrageous. A sky like this, and I had missed it before. Why?

The answer was slow in coming but I saw it at last. My eyes were dark adapted now, and before I had been driving with headlights or just transited from the workshop. The night here had rolled on and I had seen nothing for hours, sleeping as I was.

Lyt had to see this! Hell, he probably lived somewhere like this. There was no point in making a big deal of it. I just enjoyed it for a while, watched the skies and reached a state of peace. This was really what getting away was about.

I must have spent about an hour just watching the stars and once in a while, a small meteor would flash by. No matter where in the universe you were likely to go, there would always be something homey to find. I felt my eyes getting heavy once more and returned to the quiet and warmth of the tent.

I took my ever present coat off and stretched out with it rolled slightly like a pillow. The boxes and things in the pockets hardly seemed to matter.

The thin but strange fabric made it all seem softer. I nodded off and then rolled on my side.

An awareness of something warm snuggling up next to me at some point got my attention. In the beginning I was thinking that I was in the bed as a child and the dog had found a spot next to me. The soft warmth was good and so I started to go back to sleep. Something however came to me, traveling strange worlds and I hadn't owned a dog in years. What was this?

Slowly and without moving I parted one eye and tried to glance at the snuggler. A faint light filled the tent. I saw something smooth and glassy with silvery flecks shifting within.

Both eyes snapped open and I started. The mass was shifting and rounded, and very large. This couldn't possibly be the fist-sized chunk of material that slipped out of my grasp hours earlier. But what else could it be? I carefully backed away a little, wondering if it might decide to take a sample of me as it did so many rocks and plants.

It slid back and tried to maintain the body contact. It didn't seem threatening. But how was this ever going to fit in my pocket? It was almost as large as I. The time to decide how to handle this was long past, clearly. As I tried to sit up without disturbing the Nyos mass, it began to move and reshape. It appeared to be forming limbs. If this was leading to what I thought, it might be even harder to explain.

Yes, in seconds it had formed into a head, arms, and torso. The legs were emerging and shaping up. The translucent, glistening mass was morphing into a person. I had some trepidation about this. Who was being made here? The shape of head and face were clear, the slender limbs were filling out. Eyes darkened and congealed.

This person was identical to the one I met in the eggshell place. I watched as she solidified and opened those red-orange eyes. She was lying on her side and gently lifted her head. "Hello, Michael."

The voice was soft and smooth. I was unable to speak.

She reached out and gently stroked the side of my face. "I will assist you in your travels." Well, I could have been knocked over with a feather, except that I was already on my side.

"How did you…" I wasn't even sure what I was trying to say. I started over.

"Are you Nyos?"

The eyes seemed to get larger and brighter. "Yes."

"But I thought that I left you back in… in your world."

"Yes. I am in many places."

I wasn't sure how to handle this. "And you are going to travel with me now."

At this she smiled, the first real emotion I had seen in her. "Yes."

She wasn't one to run on, was she? Simple answers, simple statements.

I laid there not sure if I should get up or lay down. She started to snuggle up again, and that made my mind up. I lay there next to her, unable to think or know what to do next.

I was awake most of the night just feeling her weight against me, totally in awe and wondering what would happen next. There was a barely perceivable scent; mild and intriguing, something that I had maybe smelled in the eggshell place. It appeared to be coming from her.

Eventually I wrapped an arm around the soft form and started to drift off. The decision was making itself.

The morning came far too soon. I woke and she was still there, simply lying quietly. I noticed that she did not seem to breathe. Looking at her skin I could see that about a millimeter below the translucent surface there was a darker zone and within this cloudy interior a light colored mass. No bones, muscles, or tendons were in evidence.

She looked like a living glass sculpture. The tiny flecks seem to have settled and were joined by small translucent light and dark brown flecks that were about half a millimeter across. The fluid skin was about the color of honey and was entrancing. You could stare at it for long stretches and just watch how it moved.

In the morning sunlight the effect was beautiful. The light refracted through her and made strange shadows and caustics. Living glass, that was all I could think about her. She was definitely alive though.

I packed everything carefully and made certain I had not left anything. There was a thought of breakfast but I decided to save my supplies and return to Earth. I had to be certain that she would be safe on the dirt bike with me.

"When we ride, you must hold on to me. I wouldn't want to see you injured. Do you need anything?"

"No. My needs are met."

I wasn't moving very quickly. I had a reluctance to take Nyos to Earth and have to explain things to anyone. But I knew that I was very pleased to have her with me. She was like a happy secret and it was an unwillingness to share that made me feel this way.

Did I think she was going to run off with somebody? I don't know. But I knew that she was with me here, and had said that she would travel with me.

That was good enough for me. I mounted the bike and started the engine. She got on the back and clung to my middle. Time to ride. The path was fairly easy to see even without the computer. I stopped at the gully and saw my tracks from yesterday. Transit to Earth was uneventful and I drove the short distance across the gully and transited back.

The rest of the ride was revealing. I had not seen so much wildlife. There were plenty of birds but they seemed to have burrows. I saw some large masses like mud nests and clouds of little birds emerging from them. A small hill turned out to be burrowing bird nests and the noise was amazing.

There were snakes and the birds, scorpions and pretty mundane looking plants. You might have been anywhere on Earth in a desert. Something was different though in the air of the place. A softness and slowness seemed to dominate here.

At length I reached the original transit spot. I pulled up the flag and stowed it. "We're nearly there. I want to say that I'm glad you're with me. I'll introduce you to Anlyt. He brought travel between the worlds to me and made it possible for me to meet you."

The more I said, the more like an idiot I felt. And I realized something else. She had no clothing. What was I going to do about it? I couldn't offer her the coat. What did I have that she could wear? Would Lyt care? The robots certainly wouldn't.

Hell, once she was in the building it wouldn't matter. I decided to transit because there was little chance she would be seen between the parking lot and the building.

So I did.

The cable company had picked that moment to show up and connect the Internet service. So here I am appearing out of nowhere on a bike that should make a lot of noise, loaded with all sorts of gear and a nude glass statue on the back. That should be easy to explain.

And then another thought hit me. Robots! The cable guy would see all sorts of equipment and robots like nothing ever seen, building things. Anlyt was probably dashing in and out between worlds and all kinds of things were going on that would never be explained.

I had a sinking feeling as I walked to the door with Nyos in tow. The bike rolled in on those knobby tires and making that funny buzzing rubbery noise. Inside, the place was neat and organized, not a robot to be seen, and all four cages missing. Lyt was sitting at the desk chatting lightly with the technician who was splicing a cable together.

I saw Lyt's eye snag on my companion for a moment and then he continued as if nothing had happened. He was keeping the fellow distracted!

I walked Nyos to the restroom and closed the door gently. The bike I simply parked on the kickstand and walked over to Lyt. "Ah, great. We've been needing this. I'm Mike."

The cable guy continued crimping and said "nice to meet you." Lyt looked at me oddly and I knew there would be some talk later. I made my way to the restroom and closed the door.

Once inside, Nyos was waiting quietly. "The people on my world are rather ignorant about life on other worlds, and certainly about travel between worlds. They have a hard time accepting these things. We'll be out of sight for a few moments while the man outside completes his work."

She looked up with those big eyes. I wanted to touch her. She moved close and put her arms around me and I wrapped mine around her. We stood there for a long time doing nothing but hugging. This was strange and I felt very self-conscious. Don't get me wrong, I happen to really like women a lot. It was the unearthly nature of the woman that got to me.

I'll admit, alone with her I was fine. I was happy. Thinking of being seen with her by others I felt odd, like they were going to stare or say something. How do you handle that? I decided that it was none of their business. I was capable of making my own decisions. They would have to find their own unearthly traveling companions.

So I stood and held her and began rubbing her back up and down with my hand. It was a natural thing to do, and she tightened her hug a little. After a few minutes of this I peeped out of the door and saw that the technician was handing Lyt some papers and stapling something together. He must be near the end.

There was still a matter of breakfast. Did Nyos eat? Sure, rocks, cactus, volcanic ash, candles. Pretty much any sort of matter. I needed to get some food and I didn't want to leave her alone, but was concerned about taking her out in public. And to top it off, I realized that I was spending a lot of Lyt's money. Every shopping trip was funded by Lyt when you got down to it.

He didn't mind, but that wasn't the issue. It was the principle of the thing. I had to throttle back on the spending. So I held Nyos longer and deep in thought, put one hand on the back of her head and pulled her even closer. I smelled her hair and stood there thinking... well, none of your business.

I heard the door close and thought that the cable guy must have left. I waited until I heard the van start and then came out. Nyos was pretty much under my arm. Lyt looked at us with a knowing eye.

"She is a pretty one, Mike. Very pretty. I must be polite, I am Anlyt." He extended a hand to her and she took it gracefully.

"I am Nyos."

That was easy enough. "Lyt, she's a traveler between worlds. She has decided to become my partner."

"I see. Well, we have much to do still. Will this interfere with my task?"

"I don't think so. I've promised you to help you."

He seemed to accept that. "Well then, we should retrieve the frames and the robots." He opened the desk drawer and removed the little floater and activated it. It rose and vanished. In seconds, the frames appeared in the room, each carrying robots and equipment. The floater reappeared and settled back into the desk drawer.

Robots spilled out of the frames and rapidly put the equipment back in place and resumed their work. It was like magic.

So things were more than amazing. It was Thursday already, and-

Oh no, work tomorrow.

I had to buy some clothing for Nyos and settle my affairs at the job.

I needed to answer a need. Perhaps an extended leave of absence? It could work.

"How are things proceeding, Lyt? It looks like a lot has been accomplished."

"Oh, indeed. I am nearly ready to take the first part of the task to completion. It will be difficult but I think I can do it. With the new resonators I can reach my target in three days from today. It will remove at least two weeks of waiting."

"That's great. Will the detectors be ready by then?"

"No, but I will have some completed. The whole range of detectors is something that will happen over the next two weeks. I am getting the robots ready to do the actual assembly and cataloging."

"Okay. What part do I take in this?"

"Winds, you have done a great deal so far. The intellectual work alone has been so helpful. Still, I think you need to practice your defense and learn about weapons. If you accompany me on this trip, you will be exposed to dangers and the possibility of injury or worse. Are you willing to do that?"

"For you Lyt, yes."

I turned to Nyos. "I'm going to get some clothing for you. In this culture it is required that people wear clothing." My car was still in the parking lot. How many days had I spent nearly getting lost in space and hauling rock cutting machines and finding Nyos? It was Thursday and getting awfully close to noon. My stomach reminded me again.

I found a shirt in my trunk and some swim shorts. Tacky but enough. A pair of flip flops completed the outfit. I took Nyos into the restroom and showed her what to do with the clothing. The effect was enough to draw a person's attention to the outfit, or so I hoped.

I stepped out while she was putting things right, adjusting and looking in the mirror. Lyt took me aside.

"I must warn you about consorting with aliens. It can be dangerous."

"But Lyt, you're an alien."

His mouth opened and closed a couple of times soundlessly. "I believe you know what I am telling you."

"I really don't think she's going to eat my skin or something. I feel a strong attachment to her that I can't explain. I know I look like a fool but just allow me my little foolishness."

He shrugged helplessly. I fetched Nyos and we went outside and drove to the town with the big ugly surplus store. They had clothing and restaurants.

CHAPTER 8

How do you estimate a size? I have no clue. The numbers for men's sizes are so straightforward. When I buy jeans or slacks, I get the waist size and inseam in centimeters. For shirts I get a large. It can't get simpler.

But women have sizes with numbers on them. The numbers have nothing to do with anything except that larger numbers mean larger clothing. I think.

They start at one and go to twelve, then they go to one again and you start over. I still have nothing except a vague, theoretical sense of what sizes are for women. I might win a Nobel Prize if I could explain some of these things.

Dressed in a tee shirt and swim trunks and looking like glass, I couldn't easily walk her in anywhere. I kind of guessed at things and got a pair of generic jeans that can cover a lot of skin area and a long sleeved cowgirl shirt. Her hair was just hair and it was fine. A floppy hat and sunglasses also covered a lot. For underwear I was at a loss. Something stretchy and that would be forgiving as far as size went.

So with this big bag of clothing I came back out to the car and tried to figure where she was going to change. What a dork. It took me a few moments to realize that privacy was just around the corner. I pulled behind a car wash and got out of the car. I led her out also and we transited to the desert world.

There we had plenty of time to do as we had to. I got the trunks and old shirt off her and gave her the new things. After a few minutes she looked very casual and if you didn't look at her feet (still in flip flops), hands or face, she would pass just fine. I should have gotten some sort of cosmetics or something to cover the exposed skin or glass or whatever.

Once dressed I figured we could be okay for casual exposure around town, as long as we were moving in traffic or just passing through. We transited back and I put the bag and old clothes in the trunk, helped her into the car, and drove back to the main street. I wanted lunch or even a breakfast. I wondered what to do for her.

"Nyos, I know this is all strange. Do you eat? Is there some sort of food or fuel that you need?"

She looked around at the surroundings. "I need no food. You must eat."

"Okay." I sacrificed quality for time and went to a drive up window. A sub sandwich was just fine. After that I found a quiet spot to park and we transited to Melios, to sit in the grass and enjoy the day.

The sun was warm enough to make me sweat a little. A fine slow breeze passed by and riffled the yellow grass. Tiny things like butterflies flitted about. A group of rough boulders and smaller rocks stuck up and provided a nice improvised table and a place to sit.

I removed her hat and sunglasses. "You don't need these things away from other people. I like the way you look without them." She gave a smile which made me feel funny. Concentration was difficult. I started to eat my sandwich, not only from hunger but a little from shyness. I hadn't felt that way in years.

She liked to touch. That did help a lot by putting me more at ease. With little more than a few words of conversation I ate my lunch and spent the time with her enjoying the landscape. After I was done, we walked a little and I automatically took her hand. Somehow the clothing made a change in my perception of her. A lot of the alienness was suppressed and she seemed more like a normal woman.

"So you like to travel between worlds?" She took a moment to answer.

"New experiences and new places are important to me. I like travel."

A flock of birds passed over with thin squeals and squeaks. I looked up for a moment, then back to her. "Lyt has a mission. He recruited me to help him. He wants to find some lost crystals that he had. He's also looking for his home world. And he has a world to save."

She listened with interest. "A great quest, like an adventure," she said.

"Yes, I suppose so. That's exactly how it looks." She moved closer and pressed against me.

"I will travel with you and help you." At this she wrapped her arms around me tightly. Should I? I moved her face gently to mine and looked into her eyes. Her pupils dilated. Sure.

I kissed her lightly, exploring. She pressed her face inexpertly forward and I in turn showed her how to do it. I felt soft lips and skin and kissed her harder, tongues touching a little. It took a few minutes to get it just right but it was all good. Hell, it was excellent.

She leaned her head against my chest and stayed there. We stood for a long time, just being together, my hand stroking her back gently. What an amazing turn of events.

"Nyos, I want you to stay with me always. I. You know." She held me a little tighter.

"You do? That is good."

After feeling my back start to cramp a little, I knew that we had lots of things to do. I shifted around and said "It's time for us to go back. For a while. There are many things to do."

She lifted up and smiled at me. "Then we should." I watched those eyes and the glassy face for a while and after a little time I felt secure that she was earnest, that she was really going to stay with me. There was a lightness to my chest as we stood. Life was good.

We transited back to the car and life resumed. I found a trash can and threw away the drink cup and sandwich trash. I was holding her floppy hat with the sunglasses rolled inside. The sunlight on her was amazing. There was a deep tearing feeling inside me, between wanting the world to see her and knowing that she had to remain inconspicuous. I reluctantly gave her the glasses and the hat.

We drove back to the shop. Nyos watched every tree, every bird and each road sign with interest. It was a strange drive where there were things I wanted to say and hear, but I also didn't want to strain this new and odd relationship. So I remained silent mostly, driving and watching her as we traveled.

We went inside and I saw that a frame was gone as well as Lyt and a couple of the robots. Field test?

The lapidary saw was running and a small stack of slices with labels was on the table next to it. One robot was carefully sorting bits of stone with tweezers and placing them in little bins.

A rack on one table held half a dozen of the new resonators. A stack of plywood and a few sacks of concrete were in one corner and all sorts of building supplies as well. There was a box for a generator and some wrappers from some solar panels. What in the world?

It looked like he was planning to build a house.

Something tickled the back of my brain.

"Nyos, let's try the world next door." We transited to the desert world and there I found Lyt, a frame, two robots, and a building site.

"Ah, Michael, well met you are. You said we should have a permanent base somewhere. This isn't quite it, but it is a good alternate work space in the making."

It was. Forms had been made and concrete was being mixed and poured into them. A pad for a generator was also in place and the generator already on it. It was simple pavers instead of concrete but if they needed power, it was already in place.

One robot was erecting stands for solar panels. The other was mixing concrete. Now the generator made even more sense. It takes power to recharge robots. "Lyt, this is great. We can move a lot of the stuff here and nobody will be able to get to it. No privacy issues."

Nyos wandered around the site and picked through the local sparse vegetation. I watched her for a moment, saw that she was entertaining herself, and shifted my attention back to Lyt. "So when do you expect to make the raid for your stones? A couple more days is all we might have for training and layout."

"True."

"So we should get a layout of the plan and if there are people or places we need to know about, this is the best time to learn anything. When do we start?"

"This evening is a good time. Tomorrow all day we will be planning and preparing. There is a specific place that I must scout carefully first. I will introduce you to the people we will be facing."

At last, a bit of action. I admit I suddenly had butterflies. This could be dangerous and tricky. I wanted to see this done and marked off on that timeline that Lyt had in mind.

I spent a few moments seeing the building and what he planned. The temperature was mild here even though it was a desert. Perhaps water as a rule was scarce on this world or something else made this region a desert. Or maybe it was much hotter during other parts of the year.

I had to resolve that one personal issue that was left. My job.

"I have a question. I expect to be disconnected from my normal life from now on. My issue is being able to live and pay my bills. How do we generate income as travelers?"

"What sort of debts do you have? You will not be in need of most of the things that you presently have. I know that it is desirable to maintain a home and possessions. I would suggest a small cottage in the mountains that does not require electricity or water service."

Actually, that was smart and it was something I had considered. Living off-grid was really a good idea, as long as I could get Internet access from time to time. Groceries and water and power were the only real needs. It was just hard to do in the city where everyone is tied together in so many ways.

"You're right. I should think about that. So what do we do to get money to start that out?"

"Ah, Michael, I thought you would have figured that out by now. There are whole worlds of artifacts and goods that are there for the taking. A traveler can gain much from the dead worlds. We locate a technical world that has collapsed and you find what you need. Simple enough. If it will help, I shall provide six cubes of the iridium for you to start out."

I nearly choked. I would have to resign my job tomorrow. "That's extremely generous of you. My thanks. It will be more than enough."

Nyos was looking at me with a funny expression, one I couldn't quite puzzle out. I soaked in the thought that I was being given enough money to cover a couple of years' salary. It was too perfect. I had to be certain that something couldn't mess things up.

Within a few moments I realized what could. Sudden wealth, quitting your job, selling rare expensive materials… where does it all come from? Business people, tax people, everyone wants to know. I would have to find some sort of front business to make it legitimate.

Lyt lowered his voice, conspiratorial. "Michael, be careful. With her. Please be certain you know what she wants from you."

"Sure. I know she's an unknown. But I like her, can't help but like her.

I feel like I can trust her for some reason." His warning seemed strange and out of place.

I put a few notes in the computer. Find out where iridium comes from, buy some land there, open a small mine. Put a business in locally and sell iridium. Make a few shipments of metal or materials from time to time. That might cover it nicely. Pay your taxes and fill your forms out. Hire a business accountant and manager.

It was probably not that simple but hey, it was worth looking in to. And in the end, it didn't matter just how the business ran as long as the books were right and the metal sold.

So okay, I had an outline of a plan, if not a real plan. And I could easily travel the worlds and make scouting expeditions to locate the resources as Lyt had done. Yes. I walked over to Nyos and couldn't help but smile.

"I think everything is just right. Do you want to see anything or go anywhere?"

"I want to see everything and go everywhere."

"Well then, I'd better put that on the schedule." I set the resonator for the shop. "Let's get some things. I want to look around somewhere. Are you ready to explore a little bit?"

"Yes." She looked excited as a schoolgirl. We transited to the shop and I loaded the dirt bike and checked everything. Plenty of fuel, all the stuff in place. Very good. We mounted the bike and I quickly transited to desert, mini-moose world, and to the giant tree world.

The resinous smell of the trees was strong. I didn't see the bird-tile thing anywhere. She surrendered her hat to me and I packed it in the saddle rack. I took a moment to plant a marker flag and got back on the bike. "Hold on."

The engine started immediately and we rolled slowly at first because needles and leaves can be slippery. Soon we were riding along in the direction of the open space and the mountain. Sunlight spattered over us through leaves and branches. I curved carefully around an embankment of red-orange dirt and slowed for a large field of blue-green melons on long vines, spread out near a mound of brown earth that was low and completely different from the surrounding dirt. The melons appeared mostly to be rooted in the dark dirt and had grown outward and formed the leafy patch.

We circled it slowly, and I wondered at the placement and shape of the mound. What would put it there like that? It didn't look man-made but it somehow was out of place.

We resumed driving and I slowed for a second, similar mound. Odd. I noticed that we were driving over a lot of depressions in the earth below us. Regular depressions. Nyos made an odd sound that was almost a squeal.

I stopped the bike and looked around. There was a mountain of leaves and mud not far from us and it was moving. Landslide? No. Dinosaur!

Well, that solved the mystery of the mounds. It also told me what was in its diet. Clearly it liked melons. I circled back to the first mound and we stopped there. From that point we could get a clear view of the behemoth.

It was very long, very tall, and narrow from side to side. It neck soared when upright but was normally lower to the ground and was at least as long as the body. It tapered but made me think of a suspension bridge in the way it curved.

The head was frilled but with fleshy vanes, almost like an umbrella. The tail was a long fleshy counterbalance and when the head moved suddenly, the tail did as well in almost the same manner. I couldn't tell the natural body color for all the leaves and mud on it. It looked like it had rolled in a swamp and carried most of it back with it.

It probably used the mud for cooling when on the land. Curiosity overcame my caution when I felt we were in no danger. "I want to see those melons." Nyos looked as if she didn't understand. "See? In those droppings over there, those plants grew from seeds it ate. I think that this must be its regular home or maybe a number of these animals pass through here."

I dismounted and walked over to the pile. It was old, barely had a smell at all. The plants were huge, each vine was as thick as a broom handle. It looked like any squash or melon vine except for its size. The melons were oblong, narrower at the vine end and puckered at the flower end. Each was a meter in length and slightly flattened. They had a dark greenish color tinged with a darker blue gray.

Nyos followed me to the melons. The muddy plant eater stayed where he was, munching. I kept one eye on him while we explored the fruit. From this side I could see that a couple of them had huge bites and holes in them, revealing a bright yellow interior. Black seeds the size of my thumbnail ran all through the inside in rows.

Carefully stepping around twigs and crushed branches, we walked up to the nearest open melon. It was just a melon, only larger. I reached inside and pulled chunk of the soft, dripping flesh out. It smelled sort of like a cantaloupe with gym socks mixed in. Pretty nasty. That dashed any hopes I might have had.

But I already knew that anything I found was very unlikely to be edible. The chemistry would probably be wrong. Nyos took the chunk of melon and ran a finger over it, through it, leaving a gap where her touch passed. It looked like her finger was dissolving right through it. She dropped the rest.

It was uncanny, her hands were absolutely clean, not a trace of the sticky stuff. She looked at me and smiled. "Sugars, fibers, some proteins, nucleic acids and water. Many other things. Adenosine triphosphate energy cycle. Mixture of levo and dextro amino acids and proteins, mostly levo sugars."

"Well, what does that mean?"

"Don't eat it."

"Yes ma'am."

I got some disinfectant wet wipes out of the carrier and wiped my hands clean. Instead of littering, I placed the used wipe in a small trash bag and snapped the carrier shut. "I don't want to leave a mess all over when I travel. Now, let's try something."

We got on the bike and moved a little ways off from the dinosaur. I used the resonator and scanned for worlds. Only one, and we had come that way. Now I used the computer and checked for worlds that might be accessible except for their speed. There was one.

I made certain that this one looked stable, that it was not changing speed or doing anything unusual. The signal looked good. We would have to be going west at thirty three kilometers per hour to catch up.

"Okay, here we go. First pass to get the frequency." I got out my tape and stuck the resonator on the handlebars and we took off. The secondary frequency locked and we were ready. With a turn of the handlebars, we circled back and started a second run.

"This is for real." We got up the speed and we transited. I immediately killed the throttle and dropped my feet. Touchdown.

"Ah. Very nice!" I was looking at a runway. Or at least it looked like one. I looked back and saw that we had plenty of space to get up to speed.

Good enough. I scanned for frequencies and found one. "Shall we try this other one first?"

She nodded. We transited.

It was a foggy world, and large glistening mushrooms a meter tall were all around us. They smelled really good. There was a smell of almonds and ginger I think, and something I didn't know that was warm in the throat like brandy. Nyos dismounted and touched the nearest mushroom. A small nick appeared in it. She then touched the ground and sampled it. In a moment she had returned with a mossy rock that had a clear, glassy bit like amethyst showing.

As soon as she was back on the bike, I scanned for more frequencies. Nothing. I was oddly attracted to this place. The mushrooms had stripes all up the stems and the edges looked like they were dripping with moisture but the droplets were golden.

"This is incredible. What is that smell?"

"Ester compounds and polycyclic aromatic hydrocarbons." Wow, that was not helpful. I looked up at a brassy glow in the dense fog. The sun, clearly.

"That one is edible for you."

"Really? I supposed I could try a bit, just for scientific curiosity."

The kickstand was dropped and I stepped carefully on the wet ground cover. It looked like millions of tiny green dots on hairs, and my footsteps left crushed areas that released a spicy smell. The mushroom itself was fleshy and firm, damp and a little crunchy like soft celery when I broke a small piece off.

"Are you sure this is safe?"

She nodded and had that smile again.

I placed the corner in my mouth and let the taste settle on my tongue. It was rather bland. I bit gently into the mushroom. It was developing a flavor. Something odd. I couldn't really describe it except to say that it was not bad, sort of like a washed-out rhubarb. I chewed the whole piece and had to say, it was pretty good.

"Well, we don't find many worlds that are compatible. I've never heard of one. Great."

We transited back to the runway. I fired the bike up and we rode over to it.

On looking at it again, I saw that it was simply a natural rock strip that was surrounded by low vegetation. Perhaps an eruption or something that eroded that way. The stripe was nothing more than a coincidence; the yellow-white color was some sort of other mineral that seemed to be loaded with tiny fossils. Twirling shells and rounded ovoids were all throughout the stripe. Little circles and ovals were interspersed with branching things.

"Funny, it really looked like a runway at first." Nyos sampled the little plants that were something like mimosas with tiny pink flowers. They were flat on the ground and a couple of layers thick. She also touched the runway in two spots, one with the fossils and the darker area without.

We reached speed easily and transited back to the giant tree world and the melon patch. "That runway was uncanny. I know it was natural but sometimes the oddest things can be found."

"Cepra," she said.

"What?"

"That world was Cepra."

"Oh. Okay, I'll make a note of that." We rode back to the entry point and just listened to the sounds of birds and insects. Once there I stopped the engine and got off. I took her hand and led her off the bike also.

"Thank you for being here. For coming to me." She looked up at me with the glistening face.

"You are welcome. Thank you for accepting me."

Well, I had to hug her. She kissed me and I just wanted to hold her. I had only known her for hours, literally, but she was very dear to me, and I hoped that she would not grow bored or unhappy with plain old Michael Winston from Earth. It was time to get back and see what Lyt had planned. Evening would arrive rapidly, and I had to deliver on my promise to him.

"We'll have time to each other tonight, Nyos. I promise that."

We transited to the shop, seeing Lyt's progress in the desert world on the way.

"Now that we are gathered, we shall see the nature of this task. Farlin Dola, a fellow I have had some bad dealings with, has my stones. He lives on the world of Kyochotz, which we will be able to access very soon.'

Lyt started a holographic projection of this fellow, and I must say that he looked pretty strange. I thought of a dragon at once, but was he a reptile or a mammal? He had a dragon face like a lizard but instead of the flat tympanum you expect with reptiles or amphibians, he had mobile ears almost like a cow's.

I think there has to be a new category for this species, like "beaked mammals".

"Farlin is a businessman whom I befriended during a bad time, but what he really wanted was the secret of interworld travel. He understands some of the principles, but he has not the intelligence or access to the method.

"In an effort at extortion, he stole some of my stones, very important stones. I became aware of his plans to create a team of raiders to go to other worlds and gather the resources of other civilizations. He also wanted to set up camps to mine for gems and metals on primitive worlds. This would not be a bad idea except that he planned to use forced labor to do the mining."

I raised a hand. "Lyt, what exactly is his business?"

He scowled at that. "Wagers, gambling. He places wagers on cargoes making it safely to port, and on sporting events. He takes bets on the safety of the cargo and the ship's crew. He provides coverage money for events and extorts high prices from people in return to assure that nothing goes wrong and calls it protection. I do believe your world calls this insurance."

I stopped short and my jaw dropped. Insurance. I was filing forms for this exact business just a few days ago as a regular job. Wagers, yes. The whole insurance industry got started as business people placing bets on whether ships would make port with cargoes and pay off on the trip. Dutch sea captains and trading companies, all rooted in commerce. This early betting industry was now Lloyds of London and the like.

"So he's an insurance agent. Okay, uh, I guess that's… pretty low. What is this about forced labor?"

"He operates what is considered a legitimate business, indentured labor. However, be aware that he has some close associates and henchmen who will stop at nothing. They will do whatever he says. His power is great, he has influence over some civil law and that is how he expands his worker base. People who are arrested and convicted end up working for him quite often."

So Farlin is a bad guy. Okay, he wanted to travel the worlds and make a profit, but using unwilling workers. "Lyt, how technically advanced is this world?"

"They have simple electronics, excellent kinetic weapons, and a large steam and coal driven industrial base. Fuel is plentiful so air quality is poor but there is plenty of work. Labor is always needed and there is quite a market for it. Think of your world in 1920 or so."

Easy enough. Kinetic weapons, like arrows, bullets, projectiles. No lasers or spy devices. But that sort of implies well developed hand to hand skills as well. True fighters.

Lyt showed more images. "He has a building where I believe he has the stones. I can get much better information once we transit to his world. All my items have tracking devices and spying devices inside them. Very sophisticated ones."

That helps us a lot. Information is the most important thing in an operation like this. "So we transit in and break into the fort, retrieve the stones, and make our getaway."

"In essence, yes. Remember, he will do anything to get a resonator or to figure out how it works. My stones are the only way I have to know some of the specific worlds I have traveled, because this was done before I had full computer records of everything. I need the stones to confirm some worlds are where I think they are, and to carry out the other two parts of my task."

Through it all, Nyos was quiet. She sat patiently, seeing the holograms, listening to Lyt's descriptions and plans, and laying out how we were going to get the stones. Lyt explained that we were to get the stones first and foremost. If not, we were to get Farlin himself and find out where the stones were. They had no intrinsic value to anyone but Lyt, so they are useless to Farlin but used simply as bait.

"What do we do for transportation? I'm thinking that he will be nowhere near an entry point that corresponds to our location. He could be anywhere on his planet." I was trying to think of the worst case scenario.

"A very good point. As it happens, since my entry point was walked to, we are going to be quite near. Less than fifty kilometers. The worlds move a little and entry points will as well. But we do need some sort of transport and to that end I will provide it when the time comes."

It seemed that Lyt had other resources. Of course he did. He had learned from dealing with this fellow and perhaps countless others just how many cards to show. It made me feel a little better about not explaining Nyos and telling him about the eggshell place. Or my map of the universe and the new resonator design. I had secrets as well.

We finished our briefing with maps, pictures of buildings and descriptions of what the security might be like. Lyt had selected a world that would be in parallel with Farlin's own where we could step back and forth easily, a place where we could transfer things at need. It was a staging area.

Kyochotz, Farlin's home world, would be in parallel with a rocky and desolate world Lyt called Karoom. Between the two we could contrive to reach any point inside Farlin's compound and get the stones. I hoped it was as simple as Lyt made it sound.

After parking and cleaning the dirt bike, I refueled it and checked the oil. It had to be ready to go at a moment's notice. It was already dark outside, and I didn't see any more travel between worlds today. Nyos was quiet, watching everything with great interest.

Lyt was engaged in telling the robots something in great detail. Four of them entered the large frame which was loaded with building materials and transited. Apparently they were pulling an all-nighter making the new building in the desert world.

I said good night to Lyt and he assured me he had food and other things taken care of. I didn't. Lunch was a distant sandwich and drink and I was pretty famished. Time to take Nyos and get something to eat.

We drove back to the apartment, quietly discussing some of the upcoming raid on Farlin's office. She made notice of how adventurous it sounded and that it was likely to be exciting and dangerous. That seemed odd to me, but I can't judge what alien tastes or preferences are. She clearly had an adventurous streak.

I decided that we could risk a booth at the sports bar. It was dark inside and it was a Thursday night, not likely to be very busy. I went in first and secured a quiet booth in a corner. She entered after and I escorted her back. Nobody seemed to notice anything.

"Would you like anything? Perhaps some water or something?"

"No. My needs are met."

"Let's get you some tea at least, that way it will be less obvious. You will need to have something. People won't pay any attention if you look and act more like them. Besides, you might like tea."

I ordered a Reuben on rye and potato salad. The waitress didn't even look twice. Nyos was under her large hat but without the sunglasses, and I could see her face completely. Under the dim lighting, in a completely normal setting it made her look even more exotic. More beautiful. I realized I was grinning.

"You look very happy, Mike." She was looking intently at me.

"I have never been happier. This is all great. Wonderful. We're on a quest and we're together." Which reminded me.

"Tell me about your world."

She looked a bit strange at that. "There is little to say. It is ideal and nearly perfect. So much to do and to occupy a person. But it sometimes needs novelty. There is little new and exciting. We prize adventure but few are willing to leave our world. It is very secure."

That seemed to resonate with what Lyt had said about advanced cultures. "You must have a very high level of technology there. Control of matter and forces, things I can't imagine. And of course, travel between the worlds."

She nodded. "We control matter on a scale that might be difficult for you to understand. We can alter mass and curve spacetime. We use what you would call nanotechnology but on a very broad scale."

Ah, yes. "Is that what you are? Your body? That's amazing."

She smiled. "Yes, this body is a composite nanotech structure." Somehow the phrase "this body" made a chill run through me.

"So… you're… not really what I see, right?" This was touchy. "You're something completely different, your mind is something completely different from myself or Lyt or anyone else."

Her face became concerned. "Oh. Mike, please don't be unhappy. I want to travel and be with you. To help you and meet your needs. You must live and enjoy yourself, do what you really want to do. So few beings have that chance." She reached across to table and placed her hand on my face. That warm, supple hand that flowed with tiny flecks of silver and brown.

Some subtle fragrance was in the air, something that set my nerve endings on fire.

Her eyes met mine and stayed there. Her lips seemed to pout slightly and her pupils dilated. I felt something, I can't put my finger on it. I was hooked, no doubt.

"I, yeah. Thanks. I suppose you have needs as well, and if making me happy is part of it, then I'd be a fool not to accept." The waitress walked up with the order.

"Okay, Reuben with potato salad, nothing else?" She saw Nyos' hand on my face, glassy and translucent. We both looked up at her instinctively. She froze.

I spoke first. "Oh, thank you. Good timing." I decided to bull through it. "Could I also get a glass of water? With lemon. Uh, anything for you, dear?"

The waitress' eyes flicked to mine, then back to the hand. Then to Nyos.

I spoke rapidly. "Oh, it's a new fashion. From Japan. Like body piercings and tattoos." She seemed to relax a little.

"Oh, it's very… different. Pretty really." Nyos smiled lightly at her and withdrew her hand from my face.

"Thank you," she said. The waitress started to move a little. Her rigor was beginning to relax. She placed my food on the table, all the while watching Nyos carefully.

"My god, that's the damndest thing I've ever seen. I want to call a friend over to have a look."

I spoke rapidly. "Ah, well. This is a sort of a trial. We don't want too much publicity just yet. Market test. We want to be sure that it won't uh… rub off or wear badly." She looked at me. "You know, we have to be sure that we get it right before we can sell it locally."

She looked a little doubtful. I went on. "I'd appreciate it. If you leave me your name and phone number, we'll contact you when we release it." Her look changed.

"Oh. Oh, yes." She wrote on her order pad and tore a sheet from it. "Here you go." She looked more closely at Nyos. "Oh, that's amazing. Wow." When she tore herself away from the table I felt a great relief.

"That was close. I suppose this wasn't such a good idea after all."

Nyos looked up coyly. "You were very excited."

"Yeah, I didn't expect the reaction. I guess I didn't really think about it. I thought that we would be… I'm not sure. Just not noticed."

She sat a little taller. "But you knew what to say. You reacted well."

Yes, I did. There was still an edge of panic to things, like just being missed by a speeding vehicle. But I did react well. "Thanks. I had to think fast."

The waitress came back with a small carrier of condiment bottles. "Is there anything you need?" She kept looking at Nyos and just shaking her head. "That is so cool."

"Oh, no. I'll let you know. Isn't she beautiful?"

She gawked openly. "Yes, she is. She has the face for it, the bone structure."

"Well, imagine how it would look on you. A little pricey right now but we think we can make it realistic for anyone in a few months." I took a bite of the sandwich.

"This is pretty good. Compliments to the chef." She looked at me for a moment.

"If I didn't know better, I'd think she was an alien or something."

Nyos looked her straight in the eye and said "I am." The waitress froze again, then laughed suddenly.

"Oh, you are too much! I'll let you eat your dinner!" She walked away quickly, still laughing. I had that tight-in-the chest feeling and realized that my hands were shaking a little.

I closed my eyes for a moment, just breathed deeply. "It looks like you know just what to say also." My stomach had flipped and was just settling back into its proper place.

Eventually I could eat my sandwich.

We didn't have any more visits from the waitress until I had finished. Nyos did drink a little of her tea, more for appearance than anything else. I could feel that there were eyes upon us, and kept things as normal as possible.

I started to use a card but on second thought, paid in cash. The smaller my footprint the better. We left without incident and waved at the waitress as we exited. Best to be open with her, make the situation seem normal.

When we were safely out and gone, I started to laugh. It really wasn't a healthy laugh but I needed it. My apartment was not far and this, like all my recent days, had been adventurous. I wasn't eating well and wasn't resting properly. Too much excitement and too little normality could make you a wreck.

I parked the car, closed the garage, and open Nyos' door for her. We walked quietly around to my door and I had a hard time getting the key in the lock. I felt excited, really hyper. There was a sense of something about to happen. Something impending and wonderful.

"This is my apartment. I've lived here for about six years. I hope you like it."

She walked slowly around and looked at everything with interest. The walking tour only took a few minutes. After all, the place wasn't that large. She found little things that seemed to hold her attention, like the computer and the cabling, how pictures were on the wall. She seemed fascinated by strange things. Odd details, things that would never have been important to me. But who knows what catches a person's interest?

"I need to shower and get cleaned up. I've been neglecting some of the basics. Um, would you like to shower also?" I know that sounded kind of brazen. She turned from her examination of a glass vase with a plastic Calla lily in it.

"Yes."

Well, that was straightforward. In a few moments I had gathered fresh towels and washcloths and had the shower running. She followed me and checked out the bathroom carefully. It was like she was memorizing every detail. I started the water and disrobed. She also removed her clothing and I remembered that I needed to get her some real shoes and not just flip flops.

The rippled glass door swung open in its aluminum frame and we stepped into the stream of water. I set the temperature to moderately hot and the nozzle to fine soft spray. It was the first good hot shower I had had in a couple of days. Nyos looked upward at the ceiling light and then the spray head and spread her arms out slightly. I stood aside to allow the spray to strike her.

She obviously liked it. An expression of delight spread over her face. "Ah." She turned slowly, a beautiful vitreous form being pelted by fine, hot spray. She almost seemed to disappear where the water struck her just right. It was then in the heat of the shower that I started to feel a little odd.

It wasn't disorientation, but a mild dizziness and heat. It passed quickly.

The soap led my hand to it and I started to lather. The sensation was gone except for a mild background. With a washcloth in hand I started to scrub and lathered some more. She ran a hand over my shoulder and then my chest. With slightly shaking hands I started to lather her and turned her around so I could reach her back.

She was now slippery with soap and felt good under my hands. I was massaging as much as washing, seeing how the droplets of water slid over the skin and lensed the little bits within. It seemed that she was very warm.

Again I had that flash of dizziness but the nervousness passed. I was clasping her and rubbing against her, feeling hot water and warm flesh. She squirmed around and looked at me carefully with that piercing gaze. Memorizing everything like a camera.

The priapic effects were nearly overwhelming. We embraced tightly and stood there sliding against each other as the shower ran. That perfume or fragrance was back, boring into my head. I smelled her hair and her skin, kissed her earlobe and ran my tongue gently over the pinna of her ear. I thought I heard a little gasp. Good.

I pulled back slightly and said "I'd better turn this off. Let's rinse the soap off and get out." It took little time to get dried. I fluffed her with a large towel, buffed her down. She closed her eyes and enjoyed the sensation. So did I.

I led her to the bedroom by the hand, still wrapped in towels. I left the bathroom light on, and delighted in seeing the refractions edge through her. Strangely, her hair was dry and not sopping. What a neat trick.

At the edge of the bed I lifted her lightly and felt a strange energy like the dizziness. I turned and placed her gently on the covers. She laid back and peered at me, red-orange eyes seeming to glow. I lay partly over her and began to kiss her and fondle her. My breath seemed on fire, and there was a taste like brandy in my throat. The mild flavor of the mushroom came back to me.

Ah. That must be it. I was having some sort of reaction, a delayed response to the strange plant I had eaten on that foggy world. I didn't care really. I nuzzled that translucent neck, eliciting another little gasp from her. She smoothly rolled into my arms, rubbing and cuddling me as I touched her.

My mind was almost foggy, heated and taut. I can't explain how I felt or why, but I wanted her more than any woman. I heard her words over in my mind, that she wanted to travel and be with me, to help me and meet my needs. My needs were simple right now. I explored her a little more closely and felt her respond. We rubbed as if oiled and slid and groped for many long minutes, enjoying the simple sensuality of it.

Her little gasps and sighs led me on, brought me to more daring ground. My mind was locked into simple want. To make her gasp more, react more. I carefully and slowly entered her. Her eyes opened widely. Softly and low, she said, "oh." We slid together and rolled in each others arms for hours that night.

The sun was a little too bright. I had a gritty sensation in my eyes. There was a faint throbbing to my head and a funny taste in my mouth, like rhubarb sort of. I will never eat an alien mushroom again.

Pressed closely to me was my new lover. I watch the diffuse sunlight through the cream colored drapes as it illuminated her, like a glow you see in those religious painting. She was absolutely gorgeous. Her smooth translucence held my mind for long minutes, and discouraged any move that might disturb the perfect scene and perfect sensations.

Soft warmth against me, memories of our night, a growing sense that this was it. I wanted her to be with me everywhere, always. How could anyone ever feel otherwise? In that quiet time, I lay at peace with her. She slowly shifted and turned to face me. Those eyes opened slowly and locked onto mine. I spoke softly.

"Good morning, my love." She smiled slowly.

"Mike. It was wonderful. I knew not what to expect."

She said the right things. This was a great day, and a great sense of peace descended on me. I had little to do, no plans…

Oh hell. Work. That jolted me.

"I just realized that I have something I must do. I have to go to my job and give notice. Well, to quit really. Wow, I'd forgotten about that." I sank back a little, wondering what time it was. Nyos rolled over on me, embracing me and looking into my eyes. It became hard to concentrate on the responsibility of the day.

We kissed for a long time, stroked each other. "Mmm, I want to stay here, but I must do this. Certain things have to be taken care of." I rolled her back gently, kissed her neck and her breasts. She smiled with her eyes closed and caressed my sides.

"This won't take me long. I have to get dressed." I reluctantly got out of the bed. We had torn it up pretty well; everything was bunched into a pile at the left side. No matter.

I washed up quickly and shaved. I looked pretty scary with the stubble. No problem. Nyos came into the bathroom and saw the process of running the razor over the flesh, removing the whiskers and washing the razor off. "Here," she said and turned my face to hers.

She ran her fingertip lightly over the skin and I felt a strange coolness. I looked in the mirror and saw a clean strip of skin, free of whisker. She did it again. Wow. Scary and fascinating. How did she do it? "That's incredible."

In moments she had simply rubbed my face and the stray hairs had vanished away. I could feel no stubble or roughness. It was sort of scary, thinking that those fingers could probably penetrate steel or diamond. What could stop her?

Hot water on the cloth and a steamy cleansing, and I was brushing my teeth. Nyos was back in the bedroom looking at things, lifting books and knick knacks, examining the undersides, looking at things from all angles. I heard the closet door open and the rattle of some coat hangers. Let her. She was curious about everything. She wanted to see it all.

Once I was done with cleaning up, I combed my hair and put the towels away. I chose a pretty standard work shirt and slacks, knew that I was late. It took little time to get dressed and then I had an issue.

"What shall we do? I have to go to the office and clean out my things. I need to let them know something. Not sure what. But what will you do while I'm at the office?"

"I wish to be with you. To share your experiences."

Hmm, this was thorny. "Can you change your appearance a little? Like imitate my skin color? Just temporary you know." She looked at me closely for a few seconds. Then she stood very still. In a few seconds she seemed to grow cloudy, then to solidify. She had the same honey coloration but now it was far less obvious. The skin became less shiny, slightly rougher.

When she was done, she looked like a human woman. Why didn't I think of that before?

"Very good. Okay, let's get you dressed and you can come with me. If anyone asks, you're my… fiancé. Do you know what that means?"

She brightened. "You mean to join with me always."

Wow, had I just proposed to her? My heart pounded pretty hard. But she was smiling, not turning away.

"Yes. Yes I do. That's exactly right."

She looked at me gravely and said "I am happy. Yes, I will join with you." She hugged me hard and was smiling. So easy, and it felt right. I really was going to join with her. Marriage. What an unexpected turn of events.

We got dressed and I took her to the office with me. The supervisor was in his office and saw me in right away. "Good morning. And who is this? I'm Jeff Gordon, the supervisor here." He reached out to shake Nyos' hand. She looked at his hand and then took it briefly.

"I am Nyos."

"Nice? Sorry, I didn't catch that."

"I am Mike's fiancé."

"Oh. Well, congratulations to both of you."

He turned to me. "Did everything turn out okay? You look actually pretty good for having a family emergency."

I nodded it off. "Well, a wealthy family member passed away, put me in the will. I've got a lot of things to handle now, and I have to put in my notice. I've had a good job here and I hate to just drop out like this."

"Mm hmm. Well, we're going to miss you. You've been reliable and always gotten along with everyone. You sure you can't give us the two weeks?"

"I'm really sorry, I have to travel right away." I suddenly felt naked. My long coat and resonator were in the apartment, far from reach. I hoped that they would be okay. "I have to handle the family's business and it will require a lot of traveling and negotiating."

He didn't look too happy, but what could he say? He keyed his intercom and asked his assistant for my folder. "What business is the family in, if I might ask?"

"Er, precious metals and gems."

He seemed taken aback. "Well." After a moment he said it again.

"Well. That's wonderful for you. It's a pretty cut throat business, I hope you'll be ready to handle it."

"I think so. It can get exciting." He shook my hand, gave me some papers to sign. Termination of employment and insurance benefits, stuff like that.

"Now, I can't authorize your severance pay, due to leaving without proper notice."

I was reading and signing things. "Okay," I said rather casually.

"Is your mailing address still good? We can send your last check."

"Oh, sure." Finishing the paperwork, I passed the forms back to him.

"Well, it's been good having you work with us. Good luck with your new work and with your new wife." He saw her eyes for the first time then. It seemed that his head went back marginally. Nyos smiled nicely to him.

"Thanks, Mr. Gordon. Have a great day."

He was still staring at her eyes. "Mm. Oh, yes. Thanks."

He shook my hand, then took hers once more. He barely looked away from her face.

I went to the door and opened it. "Let's go, sweetheart." She drew away from Gordon and walked out first. I allowed myself a rather sly smile at Gordon before leaving. I couldn't say what emotion flashed over his face.

I took a few minutes to find a box and empty out my desk. There were really only a couple of items. I gave my plant to Chloe in a nearby cubicle. Funny how little you can accumulate in three years at a job.

The elevator was just arriving as we reached it. Three floors is an awful short distance and I often used the stairs but today I rode down, Nyos on my arm. This was the end of a boring but useful job, and I had no plans of ever coming back. Now it was time to go see Morris for the second check.

CHAPTER 9

The whole day was ahead of me. Ahead of us. We were in the car on the way to Morris' place. It felt like a spring morning with the fresh air and early sun. I had a sense of great liberation, not having to deal with the day to day pressure any more. No more office gossip or politics. Just life as it should be.

When we arrived in the parking lot at the coin exchange, I turned to Nyos and looked at the face that brought excitement to me with every glance. "I have to say this to you. I've only known you for two days really. I can't imagine not having you with me and I don't want to be without you."

I swallowed and worked up the courage to say it. "I love you." There, I'd done it. She leaned over to me and kissed me.

Her face was clear and happy. "It's perfect, Mike. I am with you."

We walked into the coin shop hand in hand, and I met some sales person at the counter. "Is Morris in?"

He shook his head. "Not today. He's on a trip. May I help you?"

"Probably. I'm Mike Winston. There should be a check for me."

"Yes, one moment. Do you have your ID?"

I produced the driver's license. He took it and walked around to a lockbox. Nyos wandered away and was looking at the cases of coins and objects. I watched as she peered into a case, holding her hair back like any other woman.

At that moment, I saw her reach her hand forward and touch the glass, then something very odd happened.

Her hand seemed to slip right through it and she lifted a coin from a velvet display cloth. My mouth dropped open. "Er, dear, we probably shouldn't do that." She looked at me, smiled sweetly and replaced the coin. Her hand slipped back out of the thick glass plate.

The clerk glanced over and then back to his work. Nyos came to me and said "these things are valuable?" I nodded.

"Yes, a great deal of effort goes into finding and making gold and silver objects. The cases are meant to allow people to see them without the risk that they might be stolen." I then pointedly and softly said, "If somebody were able to reach through that protective glass plate, it would cause a lot of trouble." She nodded sagely and continued to survey the contents but this time without touching anything.

The clerk came back with my license and an envelope. "Here you are. Please sign this." He presented a slip with the business header of Morris' shop. I opened the envelope and saw the check inside, then signed the receipt.

"Okay, have a good day. Let's go, dear."

The next stop was the bank. I made the deposit, checked my balance, and decided to talk to a business specialist. But who? I could scan the phone book and look online for recommendations. That was a fine place to start. And Lyt- I had to see what he was up to.

"Does gold help you?"

"Uh, well. Sort of. It has a lot of uses but it also is mainly put into jewelry. Just trinkets. People like it and are willing to pay good money for it. It's rare enough and pretty enough that it is considered hard currency."

She thought about it for long seconds. "But gold is everywhere. Many metals are."

"Well, not much of it and it's too hard to get at. It takes a lot of effort to extract gold and it ruins the landscape with mines and equipment. Concentration is the problem."

"I see. Which metals are most valuable?"

"I don't really know. Gold, silver, platinum, palladium, iridium. Stuff like that. There are others but I don't know them." I drove in thought. "Say, we should buy you some shoes and some more clothing." I turned toward the small shopping mall at the west end of the town. Nyos looked at a large cliff face and said "stop here."

I was slow to respond. "Here?"

"Go back some." I slowed and stopped, then put the vehicle in reverse. After a moment she said "here." She got out and walked across toward the rock face. I had to see what she was up to.

I parked the car and crossed the road to the cliff. She stood there surveying it. Then she rolled the shirt sleeve up and pushed her arm into the rock face. She slowly trawled it around as if it was moving through syrup. She ran her arm up and sideways, all around inside the rock. It seemed undisturbed. After a couple of minutes of this, she drew her arm out slowly and rolled the sleeve back down.

I wasn't sure what to expect next. Her arm extended to me, hand closed. When it opened there were three small beads in her palm, one golden and two silvery. The golden bead was almost five millimeters across, about the size of a pea. The larger silver one was about seven millimeters across, and the smaller one was about three millimeters.

"Whu, what's this?"

"Gold, silver, platinum. It is dissolved in all rock in varying amounts. The concentration of gold in this rock is about 1 part in two million. That is 1.26 grams of gold."

"Yeah. That's just amazing."

She gave me the spheres. "You seem unhappy."

"No, not at all. I just can't see having you swizzle rocks to make a living. It's miraculous, really. But you're worth far more to me than just pulling money out of rocks." I felt winded. "Thank you, thank you so much. You're wonderful."

She smiled at that. I went on. "I want you to be happy, not working like a miner. We have other ways of getting money. Okay?"

It seemed to be the right thing to say. This time her smile was all teeth, and I felt that something in her was changing, becoming more responsive. She was cool to some things at the start, and now she was feeling more. We drove on to the mall and her smile did not lessen as we went. I kept her hand in mine as we drove, feeling like a king.

The shopping seemed to make her feel happier. I helped her select some things and a sales clerk did the rest. Between them we found enough to have about a week's worth of clothing. And shoes, we got her some decent hiking boots and some practical flat shoes, along with one dressy pair. I was planning to take her out again real soon.

It was nearing noon when we finished. I got online and ordered some things Lyt had requested; machinery and tools and parts. Nyos had a new outfit on and was looking amazing. I packed a few important items I had, feeling that the apartment was just about ready to lose its usefulness. I had brought the long coat and my survival gear inside, along with a new blazer with a lot of pockets. That was harder to find than I expected, until I looked into fishing gear.

I had just put my coat on and was getting the last items ready for a drive. Nyos had put most of the clothing back into bags. There was a knock at the door. I rarely had company.

Through the peephole I saw a man with dark glasses wearing a gray coat and red tie. I had no idea who he might be.

Carefully, I pulled the door open and said "yes?"

"Good afternoon sir, are you Michael Winston?"

"Yes. What can I do for you?"

"I'm agent Jim Krueger with the Sheriff's office. I wonder if you would have a minute to talk to me."

"Well, sure. Come on in."

I led him into the living room. "Do you want something to drink? I have cola and water."

"Oh, no thanks. This is just a courtesy call really."

"Oh. What's it about?" I had that sinking feeling in the pit of my stomach.

"Nothing really, most likely. You've recently made a large transaction in a strategic metal known as iridium. This was laboratory grade, single isotope material. How did you come by it?"

"Oh, I have a friend from out of the country who just arrived last week in town. He works in precious metals and was considering moving out here. He doesn't usually carry local cash and he sold some of the metal to help pay for his move." It sounded lame when I said it, but what else could I have said?

"I see. What is his name please?"

Think fast. "Andrew Wood. Older fellow, about sixty. He may be around here later today."

He wrote in a notepad. "Okay, does he have a local place of residence?"

"He has been staying here a little, but he gets around. I don't know if he has rented an apartment though." That was a true statement.

Officer Krueger wrote a little more. "You quit your job today, is that true?"

"Why yes, I have a much better job offer. Better pay, travel. It would have been silly to pass it up."

"Where would that be? Do you have a company name?"

At that moment, when I was about to stumble over something, Nyos walked in wearing nothing except a smile. His eyes darted up and he turned, stunned.

"Oh, dear, we have company. Sorry." She stepped back a little.

"I apologize." With that she turned and walked back into the bedroom, quite slowly. His eyes were riveted. I was thinking furiously, watching her derriere.

Officer Jim turned back to me. "Uh. Oh, yeah. What's the name of the company?" He was having a time focusing.

"DeRay Metals." Derriere. DeRay. Yeah, right. "They're in Sweden. I'll have to move there to do the job."

"Oh, lucky guy. Who is that?" He jerked a head toward the now vacant doorway.

"My fiancé, Nyos."

Time for him to scribble. He glanced back at the doorway, maybe hoping to sneak another peak. "What's her name please?"

"Nyos. Melios. Greek name I think."

"She's a very pretty woman."

"Thanks, I'm a lucky man. The luckiest." I decided to ask. "What really is this about? Is it illegal to sell iridium?"

He leaned back a bit and exhaled. "No, not at all. The transactions were rather large and the metal itself very unusual. It raises a lot of red flags. And you quit your job with an insurance company who has a large client who deals in precious metals and altogether it just looks unusual."

"Oh. Well, life's like that. Sometimes things look strange when there are perfectly reasonable explanations." He looked at me directly, inquiringly.

"After all, everything I've done is completely legal and on the up-and-up."

"Well, you can understand that we have to check these things out. It's our job."

"Sure. Is there anything else you need to know?"

He folded the notepad. There was something on his mind and it didn't make him happy. "Yes. You recently filled out papers to purchase a handgun. What will be the intended use of the gun, if I may ask?"

"Well, I will probably be handling and transporting a lot of precious metals. It's much safer to be able to protect yourself. From robbery, you know."

"I see. Have you planned to take a handgun safety course?"

"Oh, the new job is going to take care of all that stuff. Anything else?"

He seemed a little irritated. "No, I think that's it. Are you planning on leaving town any time soon?"

"Well, I have to move to Sweden of course, but that will be a few days off. I'll be around town here otherwise."

"Do you have an airline flight for that trip? A ticket reservation or flight number?"

"Actually, no. It's a charter flight. Private plane."

"I see. Very well. We'll be in touch if anything comes up. Thank you for your cooperation." He stood and was ready to leave. I did as well.

"Oh, officer, could I have your card please?"

He dug into his inner coat pocket. "That's an unusual coat you have there."

"Thanks. My friend Andrew helped me find it. It's imported."

He felt the fabric and said, "It looks pretty comfortable. Synthetic?"

"I'm not sure what it is, but probably, yes."

"Well, have a good day. We'll be in touch."

He left without incident.

This was bad.

"Nyos, I think…" Something stopped me from speaking. "Well, let's get ready to get something to eat." I had a crawly sort of suspicion. I walked into the bedroom and saw her standing very still, clothed. I leaned to her ear closely and whispered.

"Excellent. Thanks for the distraction. Now, I think that the place is bugged. I mean that there is a listening device somewhere in the place."

I leaned away. She watched me closely. I could almost see the wheels turning.

She walked slowly into the living room and past each piece of furniture. She stopped in front of the couch and pointed, then walked back to me. I led her into the bedroom.

I spoke out loud: "are you ready to go?" Then I leaned to her and whispered "great."

"Yes. I'm dressed." She then whispered to me. "An object is radiating pulsed coded electromagnetic energy behind the couch."

Giving her a smile and a nod, I walked into the living room and peered behind the couch. I didn't see anything. I looked underneath. There was something glistening in the dark on the carpet. A cell phone. Bastard.

We had little choice but to play it out. I walked back into the bedroom and said "I'll be right back" and transited to Melios. Then I carefully paced along until I was sure I was outside the building, somewhere near the garage. I transited back to Earth.

Wow, was I ever off. I walked sheepishly away from the trash bins and to the side of the garage. I transited.

Now, on the Melios side I could simply step into the garage and have access to the vehicle. I walked to where I estimated the car was, hoping the space next to it was empty. Transit. Bingo.

I opened the trunk and made space. I left it open and grabbed a couple of flags. The transit to Melios left me standing where I wanted to appear in the garage. I planted a flag. Then I walked back to the spot where my footprints ended. That should be the bedroom. I transited back. Nyos watched as I gathered her clothing bags and other things I wanted to keep. "Why don't you go to the car? I'll be out there in a moment."

She took a small bag and carried it. I vanished.

It was a short run to the other flag, transit, then stuff everything in the trunk. Transit, run to the other flag, pop into the house and snag anything of value. The computer, yeah. I gathered things I wanted and left everything else. Two transits and stuffings later and I was done. I opened the garage and let her into the car. Now I had to leave the house normally and so I went back once more, but left my flags in place, just in case I needed them again.

This was so stupid. I really didn't want to leave under these circumstances but what else was left? I appeared in the bedroom, looked around once more and decided that if I never came back, it was fine. I could buy more silverware and towels.

That walk to the front door was with a heavy heart. I felt I would never see this place again. The door swung open, I stepped out, closed and locked it. There was a real struggle not to trot to the car. I took my time and checked the mail, sauntered to the garage, and drove off with my dear one in the car.

"Shall we go back to the sports bar?" She was agreeable. We made the drive and chatted lightly, I was somewhat suspicious of another bug. When we stopped in the parking lot, I asked her.

"There are no audio transmitters but there is an electronic device. It is sending a pulse every few seconds. The data appears to correspond to your vehicle's location." That was probably a GPS unit. I thought about how to handle that. I got back in and found a better parking space, one that had shrubs along one side and a large truck on the other.

"Can you show me where it is?"

She knelt down by the rear bumper and pointed. I looked. It was a small black box with a magnet holding it to the frame. I pulled it off gently, put it under the frame of the truck. With a wicked smile, I said "Let's go get dinner."

I took my time, ordered the steak. She had another glass of tea. We got the same waitress and she looked at Nyos and said "oh, you look much prettier like this. But the makeup is very striking. You kept the contacts I see." Nyos smiled at her. She does that a lot.

We ate in peace and attracted no attention. I felt like I had accomplished something significant for once. After the meal, it was still early afternoon and the drive out to the metal building was almost a delight. I knew now that I had been watched, at least some. That there were people very interested in my purchases and movements. Why?

I didn't buy the metals story. It was too weird. And what company did my old job deal with, the precious metals company that the officer had mentioned? I should have known if there was something like that. I filled a lot of forms and I would have expected to come across the name of a firm at some point. My mind was a blank on that account.

We rolled into the parking lot and my first instinct was to grab the things out of the trunk and move them inside. "Hey Lyt, some police officer is asking me a lot of questions. They may show up here and try something."

He waved it off. "Not to worry. They cannot find us and we are doing nothing illegal that I know of. But the laws here could be very different you know." He indicated some new cabinets. "Put anything you wish to save in there for safekeeping."

The robots were all gone except for one. There was something odd I could not quite pin down about the place. The trip to the car had Nyos and I getting everything in two loads. Was there anything else I might want? I couldn't think of a thing.

"Well, we can't go back to the apartment. We're going to have to find a place to stay." Lyt's eyes crinkled with fun.

"Try the desert world."

So Nyos and I transited. Major surprise!

We were inside a large building. There was a metal floor beneath us and plywood walls all around. Machines were everywhere, robots were making things and large open doors allowed a breeze through. Lyt was a wizard! He had everything thought of. Skylights lit the place, work tables were everywhere and odd machines were doing things I couldn't even name.

Outside I found two small buildings. I entered it and found three rooms- a kitchen, a bedroom, and a bathroom. It was sparse but perfectly livable. There was no decorating and no bed, but we could fix that.

We walked to the next building and it was identical. Lyt had thought of everything. "Wow. So cool. This guy is a genius." Nyos wanted to wander and explore it all. I transited back to Earth as she looked it over.

"Lyt, sheer genius man! You've done everything I wanted. Perfect!"

"Mike, is there a legal document for this building we are in?"

"Sure, we signed a lease. If they wanted to search for it, they would find it."

He frowned a little. "We may only have hours left to prepare and get what we need. I ordered some things that will make this easier." He produced a small cash box.

"Oh. Well, I wondered why you had me order stuff when you have the computer here and can do it yourself."

"Deception. If you are being monitored, and you surely are, then those orders would show you working from the apartment and not here. If the materials arrive, fine. If not, at least we can get more."

I opened the box. He had purchased various silver coins, each in a cover. His slightly hoarse voice went on. "We can convert these to cash anywhere easily. Then we can purchase other supplies and materials as needed. Plywood is a wonderful material, and sheet metal as well."

Wow, he really had planned it out. A real survivor he was.

I grabbed the bike and its hardware and transited it to the desert world. Nyos was finishing a circle of the place, was actually happy at the look of things. She looked at me. "We are on a quest. Perfect."

"Yes, we are. It makes things a little tougher having the cops after me. But we'll manage." I gave her a hug and walked the bike to the second cabin. "I think this is ours. We need some furniture."

We transited back to Earth and I called a furniture store. "Can you deliver today? I'll pay extra." You could hear the phone guy talking to somebody in the background.

"You can? Great. I need a king sized bed and frame, nothing real fancy, no headboard. I need two dressers that match, oak is fine. Yeah, blonde finish is fine. A couple of floor lamps. Night table, yeah. Make that two. And uh, make that two king sized beds. Yes. And another dresser. You have all that? Super. I'll be here."

I gave him my card information and the metal building address. Next I called a major store chain and ordered silverware, dishes, towels and whatever else I could think of. Then a grocery delivery place and ordered food, paper goods, and other things.

The appliance store was next. A small refrigerator and a flat surface stove, and washer and dryer. What else would I need? Freezer? Sure, why not. All to be delivered no later than tomorrow.

That ate a few thousand dollars but what the hey- it might not be available after a couple of days. Then I called Morris. I reached him on his cell.

"I need to ask you something. For some reason the police are asking me questions about the metals. It's pretty senseless. I haven't broken any laws. So here is what I need. The last check should be in a cashier's check or… a bond. Bearer bond. That way I can cash it without them tying up my bank account."

Morris sounded unhappy. "That takes time. I can't really do that right away."

"Morris, if you're my friend and want to keep my friendship, and my business, please do this for me. I'll even give you a five percent commission."

I heard him fume and sigh hard. "Make it ten."

"Well, for that, I want to see it tomorrow. After all, I might not see it at all in a week."

He actually cursed. "Mmm, well. Tomorrow, hmm? Okay, at the store tomorrow. 2 PM is the earliest I could do it."

We concluded the talk and I hung up and laughed. Lyt had a surprised look.

"I got the rest of the money coming tomorrow. We can get cash and not have to waste our time." Lyt looked at the ceiling and then back.

"Very good, Mike. You are learning to be a survivor." He turned back to the thing he was doing and then showed me.

"Here we have the first try at the detector card. It will work regardless of what the computer schedule says, and for worlds I have not yet gotten into the computer."

He held up a small thing, a little larger than a credit card. It was covered with tiny long thin rods about half the size of a toothpick. I could see dark and light things inside the rods. Crystals!

Some had a faint glow to them, most were dark. Oh, man. This was great.

"Wow Lyt, you have enough to make a real dent. Oh, I ordered a few things for you also. Stuff for your little house in the desert world. You need to live better."

He looked touched. "Thank you my friend. I appreciate it. Those are some of the things I often overlook."

We had a few hours for the first shipment of furniture and goods. I checked out the frames Lyt had made. This one was large as the others but had treads under it like a tractor. It was actually mobile, he was taking my advice. Excellent. I moved it experimentally to the big warehouse rollup door. Piece of cake.

Nyos was watching the robots and had slowly morphed back into her wondrous glassy self.

Lyt was speaking. "The problem with every technical world is that once the computer arrives, the end is near. Every device is soon outfitted with spy equipment and tracking codes. Every conversation, every transaction, every move is heard and seen and recorded. Somebody watches you all the time, and can monitor everything you say and do."

He went on. "Many devices will simply not work outside of the web. They become contaminated and corrupted from their original purposes. Your world is already there. I am happy to say that the simpler devices, those that require a mind to program and operate and build, are usually clean enough. PIC processors, logic and analog devices, small microchips are still clean. You can make devices that actually do as you plan without reporting your actions."

I didn't see it. "We have computers and cell phones, we have… oh. Wow. I never saw it before. Cell phones send sound and sight, somebody could sure listen in. The cop dropped one under the couch and it was transmitting."

As I thought about it, it dawned on me. "Computers are faster and faster but run slower and slower. They could be doing anything. I knew I was right to disconnect my webcam and microphone."

"Surely." He took the detector module and continued putting little pieces on it. I wandered away wondering just how much of my life had been a play for others to see.

Lyt was moving things into frames. Two robots were helping. The shop was nearly cleared out; only workbenches and small items remained. The desk in the office and the wireless internet were still in place. I spent a few minutes online looking at news and checking catalogs for anything I thought we might need.

Nyos came in and sat behind me, watching intently as I worked. I could feel her presence. "Hello my love."

At that she placed a warm hand on my shoulder. The work noises continued unabated outside. Small high speed drills would whir a bit and stop. There would be tapping and clicking noises. Occasionally a flare from welding would light up. Such a comforting set of sounds, directed and honest production.

At last the noise of tapping came on the large door. I figured it was the delivery but couldn't be sure. I ran out to the door, transited to desert world and ran past. I transited back and yes, I could see the delivery truck. Why didn't I just get security cameras?

A few steps later I was opening the big door. The delivery man had an assistant, a too-small woman who did a lot of the work. Between the two we had everything unloaded in a matter of ten minutes. They followed my lead and loaded everything into the big frame with the treads. I signed the papers and realized that they were seeing two robots making things. Wow, what a blunder. They watched with interest.

"Oh, those are foreign models. They do a lot of small parts work like electronics." The two nodded.

"Oh yeah, I've seen some things like that on the Discovery Channel. Cool."

I rolled the big door down as they left, reminding myself that I had to be more aware of things like that. I set the frame for the desert world and sent it on its way.

There was still a grocery delivery for tonight and that general department store. What else? I couldn't think of a thing. And within minutes the groceries arrived.

That really amounted to eight large bags and a couple of boxes. I transited those to the desert world and then I recruited Nyos to help. "Here's how to operate the frame. Transit here to go to the other world, exchange here to set it to come back, then transit."

She had no problem at all. We soon met on the other side, and I recruited a robot to help move the furniture into the little houses. Nyos watched as the dressers and lamps went in, then started adjusting and moving things a little. I took the frames back and waited for a few minutes to see if the department store would deliver.

So far, no luck. Lyt was calling on the robots to do something with him. I felt useless and wanted to see Nyos so I transited back. She came to me immediately. "I want to change something. With your permission."

"Okay, what is it?"

She led me to the solar panels which were about to be installed. "I can help with these. They are a very bad design. I would like to fix them."

"Sure, if you like. What do you need?"

"Barium and cerium. Just a little. Could we go to Danid 225+2? The lava sky world?"

Wow, she had a name or number for most anything. "Sure, but I'll need a new resonator or one of these frames. It's below the frequency range of my unit."

"Acceptable." We transited to Earth and I was going to ask Lyt for permission to use a frame. He looked up, somewhat surprised.

"Well, surely. Where are you going, to need one of these?"

"Remember the world with the lava all over the sky? Like a splattered moon? Nyos needs some materials from there."

"I see. Well, of course. You know the operation. If your delivery comes, I will have it transferred inside the other building."

"Thanks man. We won't be gone for long."

The smaller frame would be sufficient. Power switch to on, scan for low frequencies, and there it was. I locked it and we transited.

How did I forget the ice picks in the ears? I was in agony and swallowing madly. The stench of sulfur and ammonia wasn't quite as bad but still...

Nyos looked with concern. "No, go get what you need." I waved her off, held onto the frame firmly. She backed somewhat reluctantly and turned. The lava splatter was spread out overhead and moving slowly to the east. Wow, even in my state it was compelling. It seemed to be darker, and globules were wheeling slowly in the mass.

Even in the daylight you could see this thing.

Nyos took her shirt off and started sweeping her arms through the ground. I watched, fascinated, as she stripped all her clothing off, wadded them and tossed them onto the cage floor. She was fully glassy all over and slid like a bather into the ground, seemed to tread water through the mass of rock as easily as I might walk through a pond. Something really weird was happening.

A glow began to spread around her, and the ground was becoming crumbly, like old bread. She stood up and out of the rock and her arms seemed to be lined with filaments and five metallic blocks emerged from her hands to clank onto the floor of the frame. Then she dove once more.

I could see that she was larger, literally growing in size as she swam through the ground, absorbing things I couldn't name. This time she must have been almost twice my bulk, and she stepped into the frame and said "go now."

I hit the exchange and transit buttons. The relief was exquisite.

Nyos extended her hands and produced more blocks in various sizes. Some were coated in a clear gel material. She diminished in size as each block appeared. All told she produced a dozen blocks with a total volume similar to her own. I felt her radiating a baleful heat.

Squinting at her, I could swear I saw heat ripples in the air around her. She looked up at me from her restored height and held a hand up, warding me off. The heat was intense, radiating. It took about a minute for her to cool off. I just watched and gaped.

"These are materials that we can use. Some are harder to find in many places so I took advantage of the trip to gather them. Others are to help you."

"What's the gel stuff?"

"A protective coating. Many materials are very reactive with oxygen and would quickly corrode or ignite. This will prevent that."

Lyt was watching her with trepidation. "Not many races have that sort of capability. You're not organic at all, are you? Nanotech, I believe." He scowled and turned to me.

"Michael, we need to have a talk."

She was cooled and back to normal, at least what I let myself believe was normal. She came to me with a look almost of worry. I let her know I was fine with everything. "Come here, dear."

I grasped her hand and rubbed it gently. "You know I love you. I have a lot to learn about you but I accept you. Okay?" She shook her head up and down. Why did she have that look?

I pulled her to myself and kissed her nose. "Don't worry about anything."

Lyt was waiting to have that talk. We walked into the office together.

"Michael, I am terribly worried about her. She is not a simple traveler. Where is her equipment? Have you asked yourself that? Where did she come from? You didn't just happen to meet her at random. People of her type do not simply wander up to you and say 'I want to share your life and your bed.' You are far, far out of your league."

He paced back and forth. "This could be very bad. You understand that I am going to Kyochotz shortly and I will recover my stones. I need to know that I can depend on you to be there, and I do not trust her."

"Lyt, she's high tech, sure. But she's promised me to stick with me, and to be there for me. To meet my needs and to travel with me. How can that be bad?"

I couldn't formulate what I wanted to say properly. "Look, I love her. I know I only met her a couple of days ago but she's perfect. She tries real hard to make herself perfect."

"Ah, yes. Too perfect. This raises an old dread in me and I'm going to have to consider it carefully. Where did she come from, Michael?"

"It's sort of complicated. That first day I went exploring alone. You said there were three worlds that connected to Earth, and that everything was safe." He watched me carefully. "I found Melios and the desert world, and then I found a place that was some sort of artifact or building. I was inside a white room. There were hexagons on the floor and this white fluid just grew up and out of one. She formed right out of the fluid. Well, not her, but…"

He was contemplating, thinking. "Did you touch the fluid?"

"Well, yes. I thought it was a space in the floor, and it was like gelatin."

"Was it before or after it formed?"

"It? She. Before, I touched the fluid first."

He made a sound almost like a growl. "It read your entire genetic code, your biochemistry, everything about you in an instant. It grew a body that would be attractive to you. Properly formed but exotic."

I was taken aback. "The body is from my genetics?"

"No, no, not directly. Just the general form. It has no genetics. It's trillions upon trillions of tiny machines, smaller than a bacterium." He was pacing back and forth, shaking his head. "This is bad."

"But that wasn't her. She gave me a little piece like a crystal. Then she melted back into the floor. I didn't see her again."

"You fell for this. It's my fault. You had no idea. It used pheromones on you to get you imprinted. It programmed you, and you followed your chemicals and your genitals and fell right into it." He huffed. "Where did this one come from?"

"The piece of crystal. I gave it samples of rocks and plants from each world."

One eyebrow went up and he stopped pacing. "Truly. Why would you do that?"

"Oh, I don't know, it started as an experiment to see if it would react like a crystal and things just… grew. I lost the Nyos bit one night camping in the desert world, and I didn't want to leave it there. I had to get it back."

"Thunder. Damn. How do we undo this? What now?"

I was getting perturbed. "Lyt, this isn't a bad thing. She's very helpful and I want her with me and she wants to be with me. And pheromones or not, I love her. She and I are going to get married."

His head snapped around. "What? She's not even your species. She's *not even a species at all!* You can't marry technology! This, this is ludicrous. Oh, winds and thoughts."

I stood. "She's doing things that help your mission. This is silly, you're benefiting from her being here. If she really wanted to, she probably could stop anything we could ever try. But she isn't. If she really got it into her mind to do something terrible, we'd all be dead and gone without a trace before we knew what was happening. But she won't."

I was pissed. "Lyt, she's going to be my wife. I'm also going to help you get your stones back and find your world, and help you save a planet. But we have to be at peace, and work together.

"You are the most capable person I've ever met, and you could probably do all this without me. But please let me help you. I want to be there for you if and when you need me."

This seemed to touch something in him. He sank into a chair. "Tough it was, and has been. So many adversities. You've been the first good thing to come along for me in many years. I trust you Michael, I do. But remember something. All things have a price. If something is too good to be true… it usually is."

We sat silently for a moment. I said quietly before I stood, "yeah, you're absolutely right about that."

Lyt sighed and stood, then looked at the big bay doors as somebody knocked on them. "I must complete my work. Let's all be careful my friend."

"Yeah, thanks.

Nyos answered the door, back in clothing and looking like a human with skin and everything. I came over to help her. Three large boxes were unloaded and a number of smaller cartons and cases. I signed the tablet and thanked the driver. The diesel stench blew in before we could get the doors closed.

Nyos looked troubled. "Mike?"

"Yes?"

"The trip to Danid 225+2, I saw you in pain or trouble. What was it?"

"Air pressure. It hits you in the eardrums. Like knives."

"Did you know that it would happen?"

"Well. Yeah, I did. I was there before with Lyt. It was even worse then. I got off easy this time." I had to grin at that. She looked me over, her expression was one of caring.

"And you went with me, even though you knew that you would be hurt."

"Of course."

"But why… would you do that? Risk pain and injury?"

I thought about it only briefly.

"I did it because you asked me to."

She looked taken aback. Her mouth dropped open. "Oh, Mike. Oh."

Her face turned down and I lifted it again, gently. "I love you. I'll do anything for you." Her eyes got big.

"Mike. I love you too. Yes. I love you." It seemed to be a revelation to her and it struck me that this was the first time she had actually said it. And that made me believe it.

Nyos and I sat for a moment, just looking at each other. My mouth came to life of its own accord. "I think that we kiss a lot. I'm not complaining because you've made my life so much nicer. Richer. Thank you."

She looked almost scared as she spoke.

"I didn't understand before now. I was just enjoying the adventure and the sensations. You have depth and qualities that I did not know. I thank you for enriching me. For showing me what it is to live. To be alive."

I thought that it had been nothing really. But it made some connection inside her and that changed the way she saw things. Lyt was wrong; she was a real person and not just a trick of technology.

Evening had come and it was cooling off outside. We had most everything now except the appliances and they would be here tomorrow. If the authorities would hold off one more day at least, we would be just fine. We carried the packages to the desert world and put things away.

We equipped Lyt's little house with bed and sheets, dresser and night stand, all the things that made it a bit more livable. Silverware and plates and cups, enough to take the edge off the atmosphere of camping.

I stocked our cabinets with foods but wasn't sure about Lyt's needs.

The night would be upon us soon and there was still major work to do. I felt no need to go to the apartment but wondered if it might forestall any potential problems. If the authorities thought I was on the run, they might turn up at the warehouse in jig time.

I had a quandary.

If I drove to the apartment, I could surely avoid capture by simply transiting. But then I would be stuck in a strange night time desert world kilometers from the only safe place I knew.

If I didn't go, the law might decide to raid us. How to handle it?

Ah! I packed the dirt bike in the trunk and Nyos and I drove to a spot just a hundred meters from the apartment. I unloaded the bike and transited it and Nyos to the desert world. Now, at worst, all I had to do was walk the length of a football field. Simpler than I thought.

I showed her how to use the headlights. The flashlight I kept for myself, knowing I would need it in the dark. I kissed her and transited back to Earth, then drove to the apartment. One thing though- if I was confronted, how did I hit the transit button without reaching into my coat? A police officer would assume that I was going for a weapon and shoot first. Damn.

I set the resonator once I had parked the car. By shifting the things in my pockets, I was able to leave it so I could feel the switch through the fabric. This would work.

The walk to the front door was tense. What would I find? Would they come out of the bushes like some bad movie? The door unlocked and opened, nobody jumped out, and everything was fine. The light switch was just inside the door. I flipped it and the place lit and nothing looked out of place. So far, so good.

The door closed behind me and I walked around and looked for anything. Nope. Just paranoid. For laughs, I looked under the couch for the cell phone. Ah.

It was gone. That told me worlds. They had been in the place and they saw that things were missing. Removing the phone probably meant that there was something else in its place. I surely wasn't a professional and I wouldn't begin to know where to look. There might even be a camera or two. I knew it was possible.

So they know I'm back, and they surely know about the tracking device on the car. That means they know that I know. Oh well, it made no sense to stick around. I was just preparing to leave when there was a knock. More like booming.

"Michael Winston, FBI. Come out with your hands up."

I stood there quietly, wondering what would happen next. My finger was on the transit button. They didn't knock a second time.

The door burst open, there was a brief delay, and then three armed men poured in with guns drawn. Two had seen me and were turning in my direction. I couldn't resist.

"So long guys." I transited.

Okay, so that was stupid. I had accepted that the place was gone. I was going to lose my car also. Oh well. But I stood in the sand and laughed. I laughed until there were tears. And then I turned on my flashlight and started walking. I laughed a lot more and kept going.

I reached Nyos pretty quickly. There were no animals to get in the way although I did hear weird howling and yipping. I shone the flashlight and the headlight came on in response. That was simple.

So on arriving I told her of the situation. "I think that we are liable to have to pack up tonight. Lyt needs to know. And the fastest way without injury would be to use the roads on Earth. Let's seat ourselves and transit."

We were shortly on the main road from town leading toward the warehouse. I stayed within the limit and took a pretty quiet ride. Once we got near the part of town where things thin out, I stepped on it. One cop passed us and I saw his brake lights. I got around the bend, slowed and stopped. I killed the lights and waited. Nothing. Okay, I decided to start the engine and go. Wait, there he came. Transit.

So now we're back to riding in the desert at night. It didn't really take long, but it was a little slower than I would have liked. We reached the new camp and saw that the machines were still working. Nyos and I left the bike parked at our little cabin and transited to the metal building.

"Hey Lyt, trouble. The cops are coming. They broke into the apartment when I was there. It looks like they were waiting for me.

"I have anticipated this. We are loading the last of the equipment now. And I have some defenses in place."

"Oh. Well, okay." It was the work of minutes to find our last few things and carry them to the new shop. Lyt was packing up his little cabinets of crystals. The robots were putting everything in frames. In a wave, all but one vanished. Lyt looked approving.

"There, that's the lot of it. I would like to save these workbenches also if I could."

We helped him carry them into the last frame. They didn't weigh much and when we stood them on end, three would fit in the frame at once. We sent it through and unloaded it, then came back for more. It took only minutes to have the place literally stripped to the walls.

As we got the last load into the frame, I heard the gravel crunching outside. It was a little late for visitors. There was no point in hanging around so we left.

CHAPTER 10

My god, so much happened in one day. It's just not possible to make it clear to anyone who hasn't been through it. I'm lying here in the bed next to my new companion and lover, whom I will marry once we can get the proper setting. Outside the desert animals are yipping in the night. Let's see what we have to face.

Lyt was just about bowled over when he saw what I had purchased and what Nyos and I had installed in his room. He tested the mattress and checked his night stand and light, and I could see his expression soften. His walk around the shop was one thing, knowing the robots' tasks and the expected results. This was unexpected and perhaps the first real kindness done him for some time.

After the raid started, we really had nothing to gain by sticking around. All the equipment was safe and the robots were busy working. As long as we had fuel for the generator for night work, we were just fine.

Lyt showed us more holograms of the business office and home of Farlin Dola. We reviewed roads, buildings, his security system and whatever else Lyt had for us. I didn't like the looks of these guys, but that was just a visceral reaction. I mean, Lyt and Nyos and the Boro people were alien, but these guys were *alien* aliens. Really different.

We studied the territory of Karoom, the world next door to Kyochotz, and the placement of various pieces of equipment. Lyt planned to take a couple of the frames and plant them in specific locations, then use them for a raid. Hit fast and hard, leave them dazed and wondering what had happened. That would minimize casualties and reduce our chances of losses.

We had walked outside in the night and looked at the stars, seeing the band of this galaxy spread out above us. I wondered what was going to happen with the appliances we had ordered. The police might be there and what would the appliance company do? The stuff was already paid for, and the police couldn't just turn it away. We paid extra to have it delivered and that was in the contract. If anybody was there, the delivery had to happen.

I figured that it wouldn't take the cops long to figure out that there was nothing of consequence in the metal building. It was just a shell, nothing inside except for an internet hookup. We left the office desk that came with the place, but that was it.

So maybe I could hang out nearby and see if the delivery was coming. If the cops were there, see what happens next. If the goods were delivered, we could get them out of there at any time. If not, we get a frame outside the store and take possession personally.

I really wanted a refrigerator. Decadent, I guess. But think about it- I hadn't done anything wrong, this was all stupid. I wasn't going to let them get one over on me. My car and apartment and clothing were already lost. And my music discs.

Lyt had a surprise. I knew it. He had a cache of equipment that he had squirreled away over the years, but it was going to be another day before we could get to it. All he would say was that it was very helpful equipment. I could picture armor and strange weapons, things straight from the movies. He just clammed up and said nothing more.

I received a new resonator, one that was smaller and slicker and had more features. This was the extended range model and more worlds were open to us. It also had a direct computer interface so it could be programmed to do complex trips very rapidly.

I started investigating the possibility of a space suit or at least something protective. The worlds we reach are the size and mass of Earth and have orbits that are so close to identical that it doesn't matter; the suns are the same mass although some are in different stages of their lives. Still, that leaves an awful lot of room for things to go wrong. Lyt has been lucky.

Apparently he was without a resonator a few times and stuck on worlds for years. I wondered why he had only been on about a hundred worlds; Farlin Dola was a part of that problem. In these last few days he has been on more worlds than in the last twenty years of his life.

I borrowed the floater from Lyt and programmed it to watch the warehouse and report back every five minutes. It was almost as good as communication between worlds. We could see people coming and going and keep an eye on things. The floater was to appear fifty meters from the building in the tree line, just about roof level. It would record any movement and then in five minutes it would appear here, squirt the video to the computer and vanish again.

So we knew when the crime investigation team arrived and how long they were there. It took a couple of hours for them to go over everything. Later the realtor came out and walked around the place, and we even saw the pizza delivery guy show up and talk to the police.

After that they went away. Things were quiet and I programmed the floater to come back as soon as a vehicle arrived. I figured that would give us instant warning for anything significant.

"Hey Lyt- I need a big frame! Delivery!"

We wheeled the big frame to just inside the bay doors. I appeared inside the building and unlocked for the delivery truck. The place was quiet, the police were long gone. I rolled the bay door open.

The delivery truck had a hydraulic lift gate and that made everything much simpler. We used the dolly and got the appliances on the frame in just minutes. It took longer to talk to the driver and to sign the papers.

The police obviously left some sort of alert on the doors or the property. Maybe it was a motion detector. The truck was pulling away and I was rolling the big doors down and one patrol car stopped the delivery truck while another pulled into the lot. There was only the press of a button to remove the frame and the appliances. I was feeling pretty smug as we retrieved the order.

I sent the floater back just to record the action.

The truck driver was out of the range of the camera so I can only imagine what happened there. The officers from the patrol car split up, one to the front and one to the back. I know that the driver had to tell them an impossible story, of delivering appliances and taking a signature, and the building being absolutely empty. My sympathy was with him, thinking that they probably took him in for questioning.

Once we had the appliances in place, it felt a lot more like a home. Lyt had one test he wanted to do, which really raised my curiosity. He showed me a disconnect for the power to his cabin. There was a quick transit to the mini-moose world, and I could see that there were cleared flat pads in place. What in the world?

We then went back to the desert world and Lyt entered his cabin. It vanished.

No way!

I transited to the mini-moose world and there he was, smiling. "I believe the term is mobile home." Robots were clearing more area and spreading gravel and stone to make a secure foundation. The whole place could be moved!

This made everything so much easier. There was likely to be a place to go, no matter what. If he had been thinking this way, he could have had a home that could be moved at any time, from one place to another. It can be the difference between saving the things you need and losing them.

One thing that puzzled me was the strange way the roof was framed in the smaller buildings. There were large beams from top to bottom through the walls, and the walls seemed to be almost hung from them. A very thick set of beams was in the roof, almost as if he expected to support an immense weight. It might be for snow load, or that was the passing thought that I had. There were all welded anchors holding the beams together.

So today we were to finish preparing for the mission. We ran through some basic scenes, what could go wrong, when to call an end and when to abort. Lyt knew a lot about combat and I had to wonder what army he might have served in. There is an air to that sort of thing.

We were already measuring out locations and preparing for the opening of the next door world, Karoom. The floater was programmed for recon and Lyt had added a small module that seemed to cloak it in a hologram. I don't know if that was a military stealth trick or something he made but it worked well enough. To make something invisible in the sky, you project sky all over it.

Of course, I'm getting ahead of things. The meeting with Morris to get my money was pretty interesting. I had to be prepared for this. The floater was very important for this to work. Lyt wasn't really happy about this at first but I pointed out that it gave us practice doing pinpoint transits and coordinating things between two worlds. He had to recover stones, I had to recover money. It wasn't so different.

First, we matched the map of Earth to the map of this world. I found the coin shop and we used the computer to plot distances and heights. Then we wired a switch in my blazer so that when both arms went up, it would transit automatically. That was a little uncomfortable but necessary.

Finally we drove the dirt bike to the recovery spot. That was a real pain. They're fun for sports and short commutes but let me tell you, they get to be intolerable for long rides. I was pretty worn by the time we arrived. Nyos seemed oblivious to it but she was getting excitement and travel. She was ready to see what we had worked up.

Once in position we put the floater through to fine-tune our distances and placements. The numbers were nailed and I appeared outside the back of the building with my coat closed and the hood pulled up. I blended right in and watched the walking traffic until I felt that things were clear. Then I pulled my coat hood down and walked around the corner to the front door. Morris wasn't at the counter but I asked the clerk to see him.

He dithered a bit, called Morris on a phone and we waited. Too long, I was getting antsy. I watched everything a little nervously. Morris finally showed up.

He didn't look happy and kept glancing at the front. That was interesting, what was he waiting for? I signed the papers allowing him his ten percent commission and accepted the bank note. Perfect. I was about to turn to go when Morris got a look of relief and two dark cars pulled up out front. The adrenaline was flowing. I looked at him and said "thanks a lot, buddy" and dropped to the floor with my arms up.

Well, all I can say is that they can look all they want. I was out of the store and gone before they could even figure out what happened. I never looked back. I took enough time to make certain that the check looked genuine and then we rode back to the camp. Now the nearest bank outside of town was in the city with the big ugly surplus store, and I had in mind to cash that check right there. We rode like mad to the base and took a few minutes for me to catch my breath.

Another look with the floater showed the bank was open. That was surprising in itself, that they were open this late on a Saturday, but I'm not going to argue. Times are strange with the economy the way it is but I could use this to my advantage. Nobody was nearby that might look like an authority. I dropped out at the front door and walked in, demanded cash and got it. That was the end of that.

So we have funds to work with, I got my refrigerator, and things quieted down. All in all, a very busy day.

She snuggled up to me a little more and that was what woke me, well before the sun was up. I was lying there and for the first time in quite a while, I was happy. Just plain happy to be awake, to be lying in a soft bed, no job worries, no traffic, no taxes. I felt a huge burden lift from me then. We had done it. Now the real job was to start. Time to get up and moving.

We spent some time just laying together and talking quietly. Duty called however and I forced myself to find socks and underwear and clean clothes. A quick warm shower got my mind into focus.

Today we would have access to both target worlds, Karoom and Kyochotz. This was when we would get our new surveillance data and firm up the plans. We had some preparing to do, but that was fine. We had robots with shovels and picks ready for work and a portable generator ready for them. Lyt had a stop to make first.

"Mike, this day is auspicious. I had planned some time before to reach Karoom and I had plotted out the path of the two worlds years before. Because of this, I made certain arrangements. I would request your assistance along with four of the robots to make a trip.

"There is a stepping-stone world that has come into position that is accessible with the new resonators. We can begin to transit in one hour and forty minutes. This trip will be four transits to reach our destination. Once there we will make preparations and then practice our assault." He looked rather grave but with an air of excitement.

"Lyt, I'm ready to go." My coat was on, my pockets were loaded, my blazer had more stuff in its pockets, and I had my dirt bike at the ready.

"We have hard travel to do so let us not be too hasty. Our first transit point will only be available for about six days. It is barely tangent to the other worlds it overlaps but this will be sufficient for us. I have not yet seen it but I am sending the floater through shortly."

He played with his computer and hummed. "Well, this looks rather good. Let me take a quick look at your equipment." He waved the computer and a small electronic box over me from head to toe, then back again. "Very good." He then checked the robots in a similar manner. "All good." Weird.

"What are you looking for?"

"Hmm. I'll tell you later. But suffice it to say that everything is secure."

Nyos walked up and looked at me with big eyes. "You are traveling?"

"Shortly. We're preparing to get some of Lyt's arrangements in place. Then we'll do a practice run and then the real thing."

"I am ready to go." She had dressed in loose fitting jeans and trail boots with a plaid shirt. Her skin was its glassy normal self, shifting in the light.

Lyt looked dismayed. "I am sorry, I had not planned on taking a passenger. An onlooker. But I know some of your capabilities so I cannot stop you. Please don't get in the way, Nyos." I think that was the first time he had directly addressed her like that.

Those big eyes looked at me expectantly. "You're welcome to come with me. I know you want to see this. And besides, we're joined, right? Partners." That made her happy. "I know you'll be good, right?" That was for Lyt.

"I will meet your needs. Let's travel."

Lyt scanned her quickly and went "Hmp. Good enough."

"Now, before we go, I suggest that we take restroom breaks, drink some water, and review the plan. This will include a long walk, some scouting, and some hard work. I cannot say what the condition of my preparations might be after these years."

The excitement was growing and so was a lump in my stomach. I'd never done anything even remotely like this before. We walked back to the cabins and I took Lyt's advice about taking advantage of the facilities. I got a glass of orange juice from that refrigerator and congratulated myself on a rather nice appliance retrieval. If only things would go so smoothly on this trip.

After a long and nerve-wracking wait, we were prepared. Nyos had done her customary walk around and looked at everything from every angle. What an interest in each detail and each object. Again, that uncanny sense emerged that she was photographically memorizing it all.

I snuck a peak at her and then checked my gear once more. I had a smile on my face and it stuck there. We set our resonators for the mini-moose world and transited.

Everything arrived and Lyt seemed pleased. All the equipment was in place and the floater sent ahead. It returned in a few moments and we reviewed the video.

This was a gray place, and towers stuck up in all areas of the display, completely surrounding the horizon in all directions. Some were spare and had shallow hemisphere tops and middles, others were like stacked framework crates. I had never imagined a place so... futuristic.

Even Lyt was somewhat subdued. "Another dead technical world. But sometimes there are some survivors, usually not. It all depends on the circumstances."

Nyos looked at the display and seemed fascinated. "Birga. That is the world's name." Lyt raised an eyebrow at that and glanced sidelong at her. He made notes on his computer.

"Very well, Birga it is known as." After looking at the data from the floater he reported "no radiation, no toxins, air pressure very close to this world's, temperature quite reasonable. We shall go."

Resonators locked and we transited, all coordinated by Lyt's computer. This was turning out to be simple so far.

I stood by a large vehicle, and realized that the hologram had not given us much in the way of scale. "Geez, look at this. These must have been some huge suckers." Everything seemed oversized. The vehicles were on the ground, some obviously smashed and others appeared to have come down gracefully. Apparently there was no electrical power.

"Lyt, this place looks really dead. Like a century maybe." Some areas had vines reaching up into dizzy heights and mingled into the structures of buildings, if that's what they were. Lots of things were impossible to puzzle out, like the tall metallic pole that reached up and terminated in a smooth five-pointed curving star at the top, parallel with the ground. Some scraps of fabric fluttered from poles or building fronts, and a mild but fitful breeze passed through.

Some sort of flying things, not quite birds, passed over. They were triangle-shaped and moved very quickly. I thought of animated kites. The silence was leaden. "I wonder how this happened."

Lyt looked around a little, then preferred to look at his equipment. "We may have to move a few things on the way back, but no matter. The area is actually nicely cleared. His footsteps stirred dusty grayish stuff from the dead grass in the median. I think it was a median.

We were standing in a downtown sort of area. The street was intimidating in another way, not just the sheer size. It ran off in both directions like a laser, no deviation or curves and it was really broad. I just stood and looked around for something, I couldn't say what. Lyt kept walking around.

"Very good. We have the second world. I'm programming your resonators."

"Wait, maybe there's a vehicle or something here we can use. It might cut our travel time."

He considered it. "Very well, we shall see. But not for very long, time is precious."

I took the front. The vehicle next to us was certainly large enough for everything, so if it worked, we could be ahead a bit. I could reach a chromed circular pad with a beveled edge around it, just about an arms' length over my head. I touched it and wiggled my fingers on it, pressed it and was about to give up. I found a dimple in it and it seemed to rotate slightly.

The door made a clunk sound and barely moved. But it did pop out marginally. I tried to pry it open, but to no avail. I called one of the robots over and had him make a step for me from his hands. This boosted my height a bit.

Now I could see the circular thing better and the depression. I placed my fingertips in it and turned. It moved freely but the door would not open any further. I peered into the window. There were bones in the seats.

They looked like they had long heads and thick limbs. I was reminded of elephants or maybe those prehistoric ground sloth things. But that's just a guess. I came down once I had given myself a little time to look things over.

"Ah, forget it. These things are really dead. I don't know what to do here." The robot lowered me to the ground. "But except for the spookiness, this would be a really neat place to explore."

Lyt waved us on. "Then we shall take our leave. Prepare to transit."

This was another plains world but with herds of black buffalo. They were moving slowly and our appearance seemed to bother them a bit, but not enough to send them running. They honked like geese but in a lower pitch. On closer inspection, these too looked like reptiles. Why did we find so many reptiles? Mammals seemed to be the exception on lots of these worlds.

"Setting resonators for Karoom."

We transited to a cool, sleety sort of mist. Flat slippery leaves covered the ground, like some sort of wort. Pale stems radiated from a root knot and connected them, and the soil between was covered with fine grass, very similar to Earth. The air smelled of pumpkins or something like squash, and a waxy sort of smell also seemed to be present. After a few moments, a funny taste built in my throat. Lyt planted a marker flag.

"It will take some hours to reach our destination. Let us begin."

This was miserable. Cold, bone-chilling cold. The coat did its work and kept me warm but every so often I would reach in for something and open the flaps and the sleety mush and the humid, nearly freezing air would get in. My exhaled breath made a string of frosty contrails that I might be able to follow back.

I had to pull my hood up and that made me hard to see, but my ears appreciated it. Nyos walked along as if nothing were amiss, seeming to be oblivious to the nasty stuff that this planet called weather. I wanted to hold her and I glanced over a lot. She apparently could see me perfectly, regardless of my stealthed coat.

The territory was flat, boringly so. We did pass a moderate sized outcrop of rocks. Nyos walked to it and felt it, probably sampled it. She stayed with it a while and then came to me with a piece of rock. "Crystals for you, my love." I accepted the rock and stashed it in a pocket.

For fun I consulted the computer and overlaid the map with Earth, just for curiosity. "Lyt, couldn't we just walk in pleasant weather on Earth? Four transits and we could be in some sort of comfort. Or even the last world. It only had buffalo."

"Not so easy as that. You don't want to spend much time in the last world due to predators. Large, fast, very hungry. Earth, well. We risk being spotted by authorities there. And try to explain the robots and equipment to them. And I really don't know the risks of the dead world, Birga." He sighed.

"No, Mike, this is uncomfortable but a known risk. I wouldn't want to walk on your world with the robots and machines, and if we sent them ahead in this world, we might get separated. There is safety in quantities."

"Ah, numbers, yes." I had to correct him. The translator he uses is great but once in a while, something really weird would emerge. And he was right; it might be more pleasant on some other world, but at least here we would be in one group, not spread all over the universe.

So we marched on, only taking a brief break after an hour or so. I did take that time to get a quick squeeze and warm up next to something better than a coat. On the move, Nyos would walk completely around us in a slow circle, getting ahead of the group, then falling back, circling behind, and so on. Guarding us?

The ground began to break up into patches of greener stuff in circles. The plants were thick and soft, and we had to step carefully to keep from sinking down in dips or holes. Some sort of wicked sticker plants started to dig into my pants legs, like living barbed wire. I had to carefully pull it free, and regardless of how I treated it, I got stuck a few times. The skin puffed and turned red around the tiny injuries.

"Be careful, you may develop some sort of allergic shock. The proteins here are not compatible with your own. Any small molecule could be deadly, although that is unlikely." Lyt didn't seem to be having any trouble with the things.

From somewhere inside I felt the urge to whistle. Colonel Bogey's march just forced its way out. It seemed appropriate and Lyt listened carefully. He smiled and began to hum along after a couple of false starts.

"Very good, I like a marching tune. That is quite clever." He seemed to get into the spirit of it. That only fanned the flames. Soon we were whistling it together.

Our footsteps didn't quite fall into the cadence but it made the time pass easily and after another hour, the ground turned to sticks and rocks. Lyt pointed ahead. "That will be rough going. We may want to transit to the last world for a brief walk, predators or no."

He sent the floater ahead and it reported a clear walk. Lyt set the resonators and we transited. The warmth was very welcome.

"This brief walk will save us a lot of rough territory. Perhaps we can stay here until we detect a predator."

Hey, sure. It was nice here, and we stayed in a group, which can discourage predators in some cases. We followed a smoother and warmer path for about two hours. Lyt was surprised. "Under most conditions we would have encountered something… not nice."

The march went on, at which point we reached a place where the ground sloped downward. We could see a cliff ahead that looked like it would be tough to climb. Lyt stopped us and sent the floater through. When it returned, he said "We must transit here and continue walking."

"Couldn't we go into that valley first? We could transit before we reach the cliff."

He shook his head. "No, we would be too far below ground level. No transit to Karoom would work then."

That had puzzled me. Is ground level the same on all these planets? What are the factors?

Lyt explained as best he could. "Most planets that are in resonance have similar densities and sizes. I cannot say exactly what the issue is, but in most cases you will be translated to a point where the gravity potential is the same, but that is only one of the issues. The other is solid objects occupying your destination. It seems to average out but I have found that in many cases you will be raised in height to match the surface of the object and in others you could be deposited in midair."

"Oh, that's bad."

"Terribly in some cases. It can also draw more power from your batteries. It takes energy to move something and in some cases that power comes from your batteries in the resonator."

Well, good enough to know that it works, whatever the reason. We made the transit back to the cold and walked on. The sleet has stopped and there were patches in a few places of fast melting mushy ice. The air was much warmer finally.

We were past the brambles and stickers and had reached an area where the surface became more rocky. Trees started to show up, like water oaks. There was more ground scrub also.

Here there were squirrels as well. Or small mammals anyway with thick coats and lines of spots on their fur. Nyos went to the nearest stand of trees and looked up the trunks at the little things, watched them as they climbed and chattered at us. I saw numerous objects hanging in the trees that slowed my recognition.

Fruits? Nests? They were hanging all over, and the squirrels seemed to cluster near them. They chattered more loudly. Nyos watched while the squirrels became indignant as she walked below. A spray of liquid, perhaps urine, fell on her. One of the objects dropped near her.

I watched as it erupted into a cloud of black dots buzzing around her. The squirrels called loudly. What the hell? The animals jumped and scampered to another branch, one directly over her. More liquid sprayed and another object dropped.

Hornet nests!

The squirrels were marking her as an enemy and dropping hornets on her- she walked carelessly under the tree and then began to step back from it. The hornets flew around her in confusion and a few tried to sting her. She looked with interest at one wasp or hornet on her arm and picked at it carefully, holding it by the wings. She walked to the group with it.

Lyt was already backing and moving everyone aside. He had programmed a transit and was at the ready. Nyos left the trees and the hornets did not seem to follow. The squirrels stayed in the trees.

Soon she had approached with the little insect. It was just like any hornet, not that I would know the difference. It had the stinger and the large eyes and swept back wings. She showed it to me and held it tightly so it would not escape. The stinger seemed to skitter aside when it tried to sting her, like it couldn't penetrate the skin.

Lyt had a look as well. "Fascinating defense they have. But not too unusual. Commensalisms form in all worlds, and some are rather surprising. The little mammals probably are immune to the stings and they release a chemical on their victims to lure the insects into stinging them. Rather clever."

Nyos took the hornet to the general area and released it. We continued to walk but avoided the trees with squirrels and dark, hanging objects.

Finally Lyt was slowing and checking the area out. We had covered about twenty kilometers by then. He pointed to a peak just a few hundred meters ahead. "There." We plotted a good course and walked alongside a thin thread of a stream that emerged not far from us in a thicket of tall grass. The air was still cold but the weather clear.

After about ten minutes we had arrived at the base of the rock spire. Lyt walked around it and poked here and there. I could see something odd that twisted my sight in there. Under the rocks and behind some slabs I saw something so black I couldn't register it. It appeared to be about three meters across.

"Excellent. This is excellent." He showed me a grin and pulled another of his home made devices from a pocket. "Stand over there everyone, please."

We backed away a bit and watched as he activated something. It sounded like a spell, complete with dramatic waving of his arms. A section of weeds and rock tumbled and ripped and something blacker than black emerged from beneath the slope of material. Soil slid out and overturned, the black spherical thing pulled lazily out of the rock while sheets of weeds and overgrowth fell away. The sphere settled on the ground, denting it in significantly.

"Good preparations always are a blessing." He said something else to his gadget and the black dissolved in a pop, like a soap bubble. Inside was a strange looking cage of metal ribs that was approximately a sphere. Within the cage were machines.

"Shall we travel properly now?" With the help of the robots Lyt removed flat discs that were stacked inside the cage. There were other things that looked like boxes and tubes, lots of them had a manufactured look like they might have come from a high-tech world somewhere. Lyt removed a case and split it open. "For you, Mike."

He withdrew a smaller box that was very heavy. I clicked the latch and looked inside. "Whoa." It was full of silvery cubes, each with a triangle stamped into a face and a rounded dent. Iridium! There must have been three kilograms of the stuff. It was incredible wealth in one small case.

"Hey, thank you." I was trying to calculate the value. Oh, who cared. It was a *lot*.

Lyt distributed the disks and opened another cargo case that held poles of some light, silvery material. It didn't feel like metal. The poles snapped into the discs and form guard rails on them. Ah! Big floaters!

Robots and their packages were placed on floater discs and Lyt slaved them to his controls. We loaded our goods and I had a relief as the weight was off my back. Nyos was nearly laughing as she rounded the scene, watching everything with great interest. This changed the picture greatly in our favor.

Within the hour Lyt had repackaged his tools and supplies and the sphere was turned back on. It snapped into a black matte surface that looked too incredible to believe. Force field? I had no idea. He just called it a safe storage box.

We were cruising along at a pretty good clip. "We shall arrive at our destination in half an hour now." This was great, watching the landscape whip by and not having to deal with obstacles or animals. The air was still chilly but livable. My only complaint was the wind.

Lyt raised our altitude until we must have been a hundred meters up and from there Karoom was a very pretty place. We had a slowly meandering valley leading off and away from us, and we were reaching the higher ground with small escarpments and rock outcrops aligned along our path. Layers of sediments and harder rock curved up and down like a squished and twisted jelly roll.

At some point he slowed our movement and we dropped gracefully to a large exposed area similar to a gravel bed. Long grass runners and sheets fell over some errant boulders like shag carpeting. "This is our destination."

The floaters came down in a double row. Sections extended below them and acted as landing feet. Robots stepped off and under Lyt's direction began to assemble their packages. They were frames, complete with resonators.

The little floater was set for stealth operation. Lyt transited it through and looked around at the scenery when it returned. He matched the buildings and layouts with his computer map. "Perfect. Perfect. I could not ask for better."

Lyt rummaged through his items from the storage box and removed a thing like a walking staff. He placed the tip of the staff into the ground and pushed the top of it. There was a click and a chime and Lyt stepped back a little bit. With a small concussion it shot into the ground about half a meter and was stable. About a meter of it stuck up. To this he attached a small box that look like a surveyor's transit. A grid of green laser lines appeared and seemed to overlay the structure of the building on the small hillside.

The robots were directed to dig there. I ate some lunch and had a drink while the machines did the dirty work. Lyt ate something from a duffel bag he had retrieved from his black storage box. "Ahh, real food. So long it has been." Afterward he set his little bottle cap flame thing up and did some sort of devotional thing.

At the end he said something including "thought, time and culture" again. With the sprinkling motion of his fingers, the little flame went out.

"My friend, I am prepared now for this venture. I am gathering a great deal of information and we will shortly have the location of the stones and the rascal himself, Dola. I see some members of his staff that I recognize."

Nyos was observing the setup and took some time to come to me and give me a strong hug and a long kiss. "Adventure," she said happily.

"Absolutely," I replied.

"Hey Lyt, you seem to get an awful lot of data from the floater. How are you doing it?"

"Oh, not at all. I left surveillance equipment before I escaped. It has been gathering information all this time, and now I am reading out the stores of data. The floater is simply reading back everything."

"They didn't find this stuff? How long has it been?"

"About five years now. It is small, hard to detect. The size of sand." I thought of that first evening in the pizza place, when I had met him for the second time. He had spilled a tiny capsule of black prismatic granules that moved and formed like soldiers. Wow. Those things could be spies, hundreds of them. No, thousands! You would never know that you had been tagged with them, and everything you say and do would be watched.

It gives me the jitters just to think of it.

"I am going to make a brief appearance there, Mike. I have good information that the passageways are clear. There is a place I must search that might put this to an end quickly."

"Is that wise? Maybe they have spy gear also."

"I see no evidence of it, and this is worth the risk."

He moved to the place the robots had dug out. After composing himself, he vanished. We waited a while, wondering how things were going. Was he caught or did something happen? After about three minute he reappeared. "Well. Empty. I found nothing of value. He must have the stones on his person."

At this he went to his floater and pulled out another duffel bag. It split open and he handed me a small thing like a gun. It had a strange handle shape but wasn't too hard to hold. "This is a device that will incapacitate a person. It will make them fall asleep or go numb all over for a period of a few minutes. Don't aim it at anyone unless you intend to use it."

He showed me how to operate it. "If you see anyone at all, try to hide. If they approach you or see you, use this." He programmed our resonators and set the two robots as guards for either end of the passageway we would appear in.

Lyt outlined the plan again. Search for anything within a given area with the door guarded. On any alarm we vanish back to Karoom. On an intrusion we stun them. If we find the stones, the mission is over. Barring that, we find and capture Dola and get the stones from him. It sounded easy enough.

The floater made a quick pass through the building. We had the entire layout and we knew where everyone was. It seemed like a game.

Lyt and I went through and each searched a room that led from the passageway. I had a large room that looked sort of like a wine cellar.

The interior was darker than I liked, and the smell of strange spices and the dust of odd fabrics gave it an atmosphere of a medieval palace. There was a set of three dark stained glass windows in the back of the room and colored shafts of light lit the floors. The shelving was mostly stout wooden timbers that had been finished and polished. There was a reddish hue to the wood and a satiny finish.

It looked like a stone floor but it was something like vinyl floor tiles. That odd juxtaposition snapped me into the moment. This was a real distant world with inhabitants that would not be happy if I were found here. It made my pulse race a little.

Heady smells of things kept coming at me. That distracted me more than anything. The search was rather stumbling at first, but I got the hang of the drawers and boxes shortly. Things weren't where I expected, and latches and fasteners had to be figured out.

There were containers of dusty papers, small spongy hemisphere things, bottles of very normal looking liquids with rubber stoppers. I made as little noise as I could. The robot was at the door, listening and presumably able to access Lyt's spy equipment. There were leather goods, and a box of small leather drawstring bags. Aha!

I raced through the bags, checking each. Bits of hardware, some held spices, many were full of puzzling things that made no sense. But in the end I found no stones. I went to the robot.

"Can you scan for mineral objects, about this size and shape?"

"Yes."

"Well then, please do."

The robot left the door and rolled through the room, scanning things as it went. This was much better and faster. In the end it found a small loose stone and pulled it back. Inside was a small paper box with three rocks in it, but definitely not Lyt's stones. Perhaps this was the cache of some child.

"We're done here." The robot and I returned to the passageway.

There was another room to check.

This was a sort of larder. There were food supplies and even prosaic canned goods. I passed shelves of canned foods, bottles of stuff like dark peaches, and large burlap bags that held wax coated dried meats. The smells were indescribable, like slightly rancid vegetables and cheesy things that made me recoil.

I had the robot do the scan again. Nothing.

We reentered the passageway and transited back to Karoom. Lyt was there and seemed pretty unhappy.

"I've been unable to find the stones. We must capture Dola and interrogate him directly."

I shrugged. "We can at least check more rooms. The robots are good at finding things and surely there are other places to look." Lyt concurred. He worked up some locations that seemed safe enough.

We transited through again, and I felt far more comfortable with the task at hand. This was something that looked like a bath house. I had to say, this guy lived very well indeed. White marble columns with thin veins of darker green lined a long central pool. Three sculptures held jugs that continually poured water into the pool. I didn't see much that would provide a hiding space, but there was a low counter at one end that held towels, scented oils, and other things I didn't have a name for.

I went through the small drawers there and found nothing. Lyt wasn't going to be happy. I had the robot do its scan and we found only some small jewelry and decorations. We transited back.

So here we sat on the floaters, waiting for Lyt to appear. No luck so far, and Nyos wanted to step through to Kyochotz and size things up. "My dear, can you locate Lyt's stones?"

Her look showed expectation. "Perhaps. I want to see this place myself. I will be discreet." I wasn't sure.

"I don't want to risk ruining Lyt's mission. Going there might be a bad thing to do."

She almost pouted. "I must see this world."

I thought about it. "Suppose you went somewhere away from the building. Somewhere that people would not see you." I didn't want to cause any trouble with Lyt's task, and at the same time, I wanted Nyos to be happy. This was sort of sticky.

"Couldn't we do this after the mission? Once he has his stones we'll be free to do most anything."

"I want to help." I was trying to figure out how to do that. Lyt was not to be trifled with.

"Very well. Come with me when I transit next." There was surely something she could do.

Lyt appeared and looked winded. "That was terribly non-productive. Bad actually." He settled and caught his breath. "I was spotted but I managed to elude them. However, they will alert Dola and this will become very difficult."

It appeared that being spotted was a moot point now. "I'll continue to search then, this time with Nyos." Lyt looked like I had jabbed him. He wasn't too happy.

"Oh, very well. It can't hurt anything I suppose."

She and I transited there and trotted through rooms, and I saw that the floater had appeared behind us. "Mike, this is a recording. I have set the floater to give you an alert when somebody is coming and project the map for you."

What a guy. We swept through the place, Nyos alertly watching in all directions. She reminded me of my hood which I drew up, providing me with some cover. We spent about five minutes going through everything, and she located a safe in one wall.

"There is a metal box behind this panel."

I looked for the catch but couldn't find it. Damn, I hated to wreck it. I gave the lip a heave and something split. A faint keening alarm sounded. The safe was revealed, Nyos ran her finger through the steel front and the door swung open, a shining gash exposing the wrecked lock mechanism.

I swept everything into the coat, holding it up like a bag. We stepped forward to the door as we heard footsteps outside. We transited.

I appeared not far from Lyt and dumped everything in front of him. "Well, this was in the safe."

He gave the pile a poke with his foot. "Yes, I've been through that already."

"Oh. Well." Wasted effort.

Still, it had the look of value.

"So Lyt, what was so important that you almost got caught?"

He frowned slightly. "Things are worse than I thought. Dola has a whole workshop down there with equipment in it. He's trying to make a resonator. He may be close, too."

"I see. Then we have to put a stop to that. Can we get the equipment out?"

"Better yet to simply destroy it there and not risk getting caught." At this he started going through his bags. "Yes." He held a thing the size and shape of a lipstick. One end had a blue button and a ring around the base. He twisted the ring and it clicked a few times. "I'll return."

He was gone only moments. The floater reappeared along with Lyt. "That will do it."

"What was that?"

"A fission grenade. It will vaporize most everything in that part of the building. Don't worry, the radiation is truly minimal."

I laughed. "I really wasn't worried."

The floater vanished again for another run. It reappeared almost at once.

"The facial recognition software has spotted Dola. He will be heading through this corridor shortly. You, Mike, will get him into this frame."

Whatever. He positioned the frame so it would appear in the hallway. I stood a few meters in front of it, facing it. Dola would come right to me.

"NOW."

I transited. The cage appeared simultaneously with me. Dola was between the two and at a fast trot. He nearly ran into my chest. His eyes locked onto mine and I had a funny thought. I must have looked pretty scary to him.

That was when the alien monster from Earth, Michael Winston, looked at Farlin Dola, leaned forward as said "boo!"

He screeched and fell backwards, literally rolled into the frame. I hit the button.

We appeared between the robots and in the gravel pit excavation. Dola was terrified, making guttural clacking and rasping noises. He sounded sort of like a big parrot. Some of the sounds were almost painful to hear, keen and piercing.

I walked toward him and relied on the translator. "Where are the stones?" He smelled like earwax and unwashed sweat, an oily sort of smell. I pressed the point.

"The stones! Give them to me!"

He subsided a bit, then looked at me a little better. He swung that large, beaky face around and spotted Lyt. The gravelly voice said "you, wizard, you will not torture me. You cannot get the stones from me."

Lyt seemed to snarl. "No, not like you tortured me. I will not do that. But you will not keep the stones. I will have them. And if I must take your whole building and all your wives away, you will have nothing to bargain with. All I want are my stones."

Dola looked outraged. "I am not frightened of you!"

I growled at him. "And what about me?"

"No. You cannot get the stones. I have allies that can defeat you now. The stones are worthless to you."

Nyos then approached from the side, and he clearly had not seen her before. At this he stopped and watched her closely. His head cocked from one side to the other, looking at her with keen interest.

"AAWWGGG" was something the translator did not understand. Dola reached inside his small tunic and pulled a cord.

The concussion blew me completely over twice. I felt nothing except a slam and tasted nasty, bitter slime in my mouth. The world was roaring.

There was a timeless, stunned world. My face and hands stung and I was sure something had to be broken. I could neither hear nor think.

CHAPTER 11

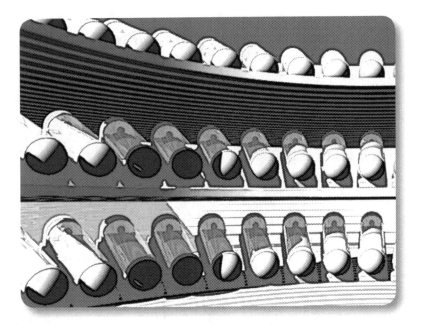

It became obvious that Dola was a poor sport. Lyt was dumbfounded by his response. What could have set him off so badly?

Nyos gathered as much of the debris as she could find and sifted through it. There was a small leather bag with a drawstring that had made it, being shielded by the bulk of his body. I caught the worst of the splatter while Lyt had simply been knocked over. The robots were unhurt but needed a good cleaning.

Nyos was very quiet, not saying anything. She helped me up onto the floater and peeled my hood back. It had been up while I had confronted

Farlin Dola; I hadn't thought to pull it down. He had never even *seen* me, just heard me yell boo at him. All he could tell was that there was something in front of him and he had almost collided with it.

So what alarmed him was not my appearance at all; rather the *lack* of an appearance. It was a good thing the hood was up though.

The taste in my mouth was the slimy mist created in the explosion, and the coat had billowed out around me, sort of spreading out the force of the impact. Kind of like a parachute when you think about it.

I sat up slowly, feeling that I was really going to hurt in the morning. Lyt gathered his senses and came quickly to see how I was. "Can you speak? Do not try to sit up. It's a miracle you live any longer."

Nyos made a broad circle of the blast zone. That frame was pretty wrecked. Bits and pieces were scattered about and I found out that it's not the explosion that usually does the damage. It's the shrapnel and flying debris.

My ears were starting to clear but were still ringing. Nyos pushed Lyt gently aside and said "be very still." He had a look of great concern, but I waved a bit.

"Lyt, really, I've been worse. I'll be fine."

Nyos ran a cool hand over my face and the stench abated considerably. She gently touched my left ear and there was a sensation like water running through and under my skin. Rather unpleasant and it made me want to squirm but she has the grip of a vise. The ringing seemed to decrease a lot. She did the same for the other ear and yes, I could actually hear without the fuzzy effects.

Every so often when I inhaled deeply, I would get a brief stab in my chest. I probably had a cracked rib. After giving me some basic care, she turned to Lyt who had watched this all quietly. She handed him the leather bag.

"Is this your target?" He peered at the bag and his eyes grew.

"Oh my." He accepted the small bag with shaking hands. With great care he spilled the few stones into his palm. "Oh my, yes. You, you found them. Thank you so much, Nyos." I thought he would cry.

I reached to my nose, which felt stuffy. There was a swollen pounding in the top near the bridge. Great, it was probably broken. I sat slowly and with a lot of caution.

My look around was pretty informative. What a mess. But Lyt was now in possession of his stones. First mission accomplished, and I could picture a checkmark being placed on the timeline. "Let's get the hell out of here." Lyt could hardly agree more.

He directed the machines to disassemble the frames and clean things up. The packing started in moments.

After the tasks were started, Lyt selected a stone from the bag and matched it with a stone that he had in his brass disc device. He hmmed and fidgeted and then consulted his computer. "This is very peculiar."

"What is it?"

"This stone should resonate with this in my detector wheel. It does not. The computer says it should be in resonance now. Let me check something."

He adjusted his glasses somewhat and peered at the stone very carefully. "This is indeed the proper stone. I have my scribing within. Why does it not resonate?" He selected another stone from the bag. "This too is the proper stone." He placed it in the brass disc and lined it up. Nothing happened.

"No, he didn't." His expression was turning to one of alarm. There was a mad scramble to find some other piece of equipment, which actually looked like a birch stick with a coil wrapped around it. He waved it near the stone and looked at the stick.

What the heck was he doing?

"He did. Damn, damn, damn. He said the stones were worthless to me. He's heated them and destroyed their signatures! These stones are worthless!"

He made a strangled noise. The mission was a success but the results were a failure. "I cannot find the path without these stones! This destroys decades of my work!"

He pulled his sleeves back and looked at the white scars. "All for nothing. Years lost. Ohh." I have not heard anyone so dejected.

The robots continued to pack and loaded the floaters. This would be an unpleasant trip back. Lyt was devastated.

I looked at Nyos. "My dear, is there anything we can do? Anything?"

She had a troubled look. "I do not know. Perhaps."

Smoothly she strode to Lyt and placed a hand on his shoulder. He looked up but only at the sky. "May I see the stones?" He opened his hand slowly and considered throwing them as far as he could. "Please?"

With a sigh he placed them in her palm and handed the bag to her as well. "It can do no harm."

"I must transit to Kyochotz." I stood up on wobbly legs and set my resonator.

"I'll take you." Lyt was inconsolable. Nyos took the bag gently and came to my side. We transited to a room not far off the central passageway where I had scared Dola. A smell of burning and rancid things touched my nose.

Nyos seemed to sniff the air. She held up a stone and turned it slowly. It looked like she was adjusting something delicate. "Here." Now she passed a finger through the stone slowly. "This may work."

"What are you doing?"

"When you heat a stone, it can capture the local magnetic field as well as other effects. I am aligning it with the field of the planet, and then subtracting it. If the stones were not heated too much, I can perhaps detect a very faint signature from the previous alignment."

"Oh."

With each stone she went through the process, carefully aligning and reforming the little signature of each. Three she could do nothing with. The other six she had some success with. "This is all I can do."

We transited back to Karoom and Lyt. The equipment was loaded, ready to move. Lyt stood half slumped over the hand rail of his floater. He looked up at our approach.

"Nyos, I appreciate your help. I have been rather… unaccepting of you. Not happy with your presence. You have many qualities of an old enemy and it makes me react poorly."

She gave him the bag. "Try them."

With some sense of hope he took out his brass wheel and dropped a stone in. The wheel spun slowly and locked, a faint light coming from the stone. "Oh, this is very encouraging." The computer came out and he entered something. The display showed a set of spheres just overlapping. Lyt stood a little straighter. "This is correct."

He tried another and got similar results. "Oh, very good." He seemed to change from downcast to excited quickly. "Perhaps we have not lost everything."

Nyos turned from the old man and came to our floater, stepped lightly onto the surface. Lyt put the stones away and replaced the wheel in his coat pocket. "Thank you, Nyos." He commanded the equipment into motion and we started on the trip back.

"Hey Lyt, how did you know where to put your safe storage box with the supplies?"

"I didn't. There are six of them at various points around this central point. I put as many out as I could afford to in terms of time and expense."

"Well, shouldn't we gather those other storage containers and bring all that stuff back?"

"In good time, we shall do that. Now we have transportation."

In a few minutes we were back to the safe storage box. Lyt commanded it to become accessible and the spherical cage revealed itself. He moved a floater disc to the top of the cage interior and slaved it to his. Now the spherical cage rose into the air and followed us to the entry point.

It took about an hour for the whole troop to arrive at the transfer point. Lyt had the robots install the large folded frame and resonator inside the safe box and then inspected everything. He was content with the arrangements.

We transited en masse to the world of reptile buffalo things, somewhere over their heads. The shadows spooked a few and started them running and honking in a bass note that carried for kilometers. When the computer stated that we were in the proper place, we transited to Birga, the dead tech world.

I revised my figures. This place must have been dead for much longer than I thought. It was just that their artifacts were durable. We spent little time looking things over but the floaters made it so much easier. I could see down inside the vehicle that I had tried to open before.

"Lyt, it would be a shame to let all this decay away and not know what happened. Like on Boro, we should try to locate an archive or a history or something. At least there we might find survivors but this place looks long gone."

"Well, you will have a few days to recover and do some exploring. The next phase of this task will take some research and time. So you can do as you wish for perhaps as long as a week. And thank you for your help. I truly could not have done this without you and without Nyos."

"Anything for a friend, Lyt." And I meant it.

The return to the little base was quiet but triumphant. We settled slowly to the sand and scrub, making almost no sound. The floaters were quiet with only a small humming when they ran. Looked like magic to me, no moving parts and no flappy things. Lyt now showed his foresight. He had the robots mark the positions of the cabins and carry a floater disc to the mini-moose world next door. Then the robots transited inside the cabins and installed the floater discs in the heavy beam structure in each roof. This neatly got the discs inside the doors that were clearly too small for them.

With six of the discs installed, one in each cabin and four in the large workshop, the buildings themselves could be moved. Lyt did a test and slowly raised the workshop a couple of meters into the air, then moved it right and left slowly. He was a little unhappy with a spot in the floor that seemed to him a bit too droopy.

The robots fabricated new floor trusses. They were triangular sections like an antenna tower. They raised the building up, placed the trusses, and started welding them in place. "Now we can travel as we should. No matter where we go, we will have the proper facilities."

Nyos turned her attention back to the solar panels, something that had been forgotten in all the excitement. She used some of the elements she had extracted from Danid 225+2, the lava sky world, and reformed the cells. It was strange to watch, but then so is everything anymore.

She took each panel and ran her hand over and through it. The dark violet-looking glassy cells changed to a jet black, matte surface with a hint of greenish highlight to it. The surface had before been covered with a fine grid of silvery lines. This changed to a hexagonal array of silvery lines, very close together.

"This will be far more efficient. The panels were about 15% before, and this will yield about 60%. We can now have these installed." It was amazing how much she knew about technical things but how experiences and emotions seemed something foreign and wonderful to learn about.

"So you can take raw material and form it almost any way just by wanting to do it."

"Yes, mostly. There are limits to the complexity, based on speed and energy requirements."

We were sitting on a stack of panels being made into folding boxes. Robots were converting plywood and insulation into accordions that could be unfolded into buildings or boxes. The rooftop units were also pretty slick. Lyt must have been having the time of his life making these things.

The evening was arriving at last. I loved to see the skies here at night, and still had not looked up the location in the universe in relation to Earth. It wasn't important at all, just something that would have been nice to know.

I felt overwhelmed then by it all. Why then? I don't know. It seemed that too much had changed too rapidly, but I admit that I had readily accepted it all. I lost my world and my way of life but at that moment I also gained an incredible new life, so much richer and exciting. It was enough to overwhelm anyone.

"Let's go exploring tomorrow, just you and I. Okay?" Nyos looked happy.

"Yes. Please." It was one of those times when we just sat and leaned on each other, arms around each others' back. My nose still throbbed and my ribs hurt but I was fine, just expecting to be sore tomorrow. I wanted to outfit a little expedition to Birga and do some serious exploring. If I could get a few trophies, fine. If I could learn about the people and what happened, also fine. And Lyt had mentioned that dead tech worlds had things that were worth acquiring. I wondered where he had gotten the floaters and all his odd devices. The answer seemed clear.

I had one other thing I wanted to get for us, if we could afford the power to move it and run it. I was going shopping tomorrow.

⸺◆⸺

I really hurt the next morning. That's true for a lot of Mondays, but not like this. Still, I was driven to get some things done, and Lyt had himself immersed in his safe storage box. There were wonders and treasures in it. He had no problem with us using a pair of large floaters and a resonator frame. I also borrowed one of the robots.

Nyos and I packed the robot and frame on the second floater and then I mapped out Earth. There was a city not much farther up the road named

Adell that had some pretty fair industry. That meant that they would also have lumber and supplies, food, anything we could need. We rode to the coordinates and while still in flight we sent the little floater in stealth mode so we could get the lay of the land visually.

It returned with holographic maps of the area and we selected an area behind an old theater, a secluded yard with high fences. It looked abandoned and was perfect.

Once we had appeared in the yard, I checked everything out again on foot. No traffic, plenty of weeds, and this was the spot. Nyos was properly dressed and looking human. We cut the chain from the fenced yard and walked out like we owned the place.

Around the corner we found a gas station and I got change by buying a drink and some beef jerky. From there I used an anachronism, a pay phone. There was a truck rental place and they also had drivers. Perfect. We arranged for him to show up at the gas station and I gave the driver five hundred up front. For that he was willing to do most anything.

We stopped at the old theater yard and I transited a floater in and loaded it in the truck bed. It had a frame already in place and ready for anything. The driver remained in the cab.

Now we stopped at an irrigation supply and purchased two large plastic cistern tanks for water storage. I also bought plastic pipe and a pump and filter. These were loaded in the back of the truck and we moved on. A solar energy store had water heating panels and I bought two of those plus the pumps and hardware for them. Cash talks.

We made a trip to the theater yard and I transited a robot in to load the floater and frame. Everything was carried to the world next door and unloaded. The floater frame was transited back and off we went again. This was fun.

I stopped at a fast food place and bought some lunch for the driver and for me. Nyos was actually enjoying this. It was like sneaking around and sort of an adventure in its own right. The next stop was a construction materials yard.

After a couple of hours of shopping and buying anything I could think of, we made our final trip to the theater yard. It took moments to transit everything and unload the vehicle. I paid the driver for the day's service and got his number in case I needed any more work from him.

We went home with two fully loaded floaters. It was now afternoon and time to get some things put away,

After loading my freezer with about eighty kilos of steaks and meats, I had the building supplies put in the workshop. We still had a small building that housed the generator and I wanted to change a few things around. I told Lyt some of what I had in mind and he agreed and seemed happy I was taking an interest in the structures and facilities.

After some instruction to the robots, a new building was made that had the generator in a soundproofed room but most of the space open. One of the large floaters was installed. One cistern I had installed in the new room, the other I left on a floater. Now we would have a really useful water supply.

I further installed water heating panels on the roof of the new building and had everything plumbed and hooked up. Hot water was coming up!

As that work was under way, I took the two floaters and Nyos and I transited to the mini-moose world. There was a great lake there and we filled the cistern from it and carried the water back to our new building.

The water was pumped and filtered into the permanent cistern and the water heating panels started. Lyt was going to be surprised.

I filled the floater cistern again and dropped a shock treatment pack in there to kill any potential germs. A small shock pack was also dropped in the cistern in the new building.

It was only a couple of hours to sunset so I would be unable to show my handiwork off just yet. But tomorrow was another matter. My stomach was rumbling by now and there was only one thing to do. I broke out my new grill.

We lay in the dark, a soft bed below us and the quiet of the desert outside. I had the windows opened enough to allow a breeze in. Nyos was quiet and almost seemed to glow. It seemed a shame to speak but I felt like talking a little.

"It was a very productive day. I feel good about what we got done." Nyos shifted a little. "Tomorrow will be even more interesting. We're going to Birga to do some real exploration. What do you think? Explore a world with history and culture that ended suddenly, and we don't know why."

At that she spoke.

"Yes, that is interesting. I must ask something."

"Okay, sure."

"You told Lyt you would do anything for a friend. Is that true?"

"Only for special friends. We all have friends and acquaintances in our lives but very few of them are close enough that we feel that way. Lyt is a really special guy."

"Do you love Lyt?"

"Well, not the way I love you. It's different. Lyt has qualities that make him worth knowing and helping. Nobility and gentleness. He helps others even when he is at risk. He helped me when I was just somebody that seemed like a potential friend. He's a really good guy."

She thought about it quietly. "So the reasons you help me and love me are different from the reasons you help Lyt. And the way you feel about him is different. It can be confusing but love appears to have levels or distinctions."

"Exactly. Each person has a different meaning and you are willing to go to different extremes for them." I thought a little more in depth about it. "I would do anything that you needed done and a lot of things that might seem trivial but you want done."

She rolled to face me. "How do you judge those who are worth loving and helping, and those who are not?"

That was a tricky one. "It can be very hard to do. Sometimes you see something in a person's mannerisms or their actions, or how they look. And other times it's something about them that you want to be like. Some quality that you wish you had in yourself.

"People are like mirrors and we see in them the things we would like to see in ourselves. We can also see things that we don't like and a lot of times, it's something in us that we don't like."

Her look became more intense.

"What do you see in me that attracts you?"

This could be a dreaded question but I knew that I could answer honestly and she would be okay with it.

I turned to her. "When I first saw you in the... eggshell place, the white room I mean, it was sort of scary. Alarming. But as your appearance changed, I realized that how I felt changed. You were powerful but you were about to fall over. It made you much more human, capable of need. It reached something inside me.

"Then when you welcomed me and offered your help, I felt that you were more like me, not so alien. I identified in a way with you. And you were very pretty too. That always helps."

She was pondering what I said. After a while she spoke. "So pretty people are not dangerous or evil?"

I laughed a little. "No, no, they can be the worst. But something inside each of us wants to believe that beauty and goodness are connected. What attracts me to you, to answer your question, is that you show beauty and power and knowledge, and innocence at the same time. All those things are a wonderful combination. Those are qualities I would want in myself, and I guess that through association, I get them from you."

I could see an understanding grow in her expression.

"And so, dear Nyos, I am in love with you partly because of selfishness but also because I want to do what I can to see that you, your beauty and power and knowledge and innocence, all continue. I want to see a universe with strong, perfect, and good people in it. Then we have a chance to face any problem and possibly defeat it. You see?"

Her expression seemed to melt. She pulled herself closer and I felt that warmth and softness. She did indeed have a faint glow to her tonight, a pale foxfire radiance.

"Mike, you make me feel so good. I did not expect this and I cannot explain it. You make me want to be better somehow. I will tell you something."

I rubbed her soft back slowly. "Okay."

"The whole universe is going to end, but not for a very long time. My race, as you might call them, has a way to extend that time by a factor of a million. We are working to explore all the worlds and meet all the people, and to try to find a way to prevent the end of the universe."

"Wow, that's a huge job. Admirable too."

She went on. "It may take all the mass in the universe arranged in the proper manner, to create an opening to another, young universe. One that we can then organize properly so it will last billions of times longer, and then be easy to leave for the next universe."

"Well, can't you make a universe last forever?"

She looked uncertain. "Perhaps. There are some signs that an infiniverse could be made but it would be difficult to balance and maintain."

I hadn't ever thought of such a thing. Moving to new universes? Making permanent universes? I didn't even know that there was more than one.

"Well, how long do we have before this universe ends?"

"The end begins in about one hundred trillion years."

Well, that counts me out. "So you're saying that in a hundred million, millions of years, the universe will start to end. I'm not even half a hundred yet. So this is really a long time off. And you say that your people can extend that by a million times, and that's a number I don't even know if there's a word for."

The immensity of it was something I couldn't even imagine. I must have shuddered a little because she moved against me more closely and I fell into a long and warm embrace.

"Well, I'm glad that somebody is doing something about the end of the universe. I wouldn't know where to start. And a million to one extension is pretty significant, so it looks like your people are making progress."

She kissed me slowly and then laid her head against my shoulder. "We want to save everything. Not lose it."

"Wonderful woman, marry me and we can spend our lives together seeing the universe. Would you like that?"

"The experiences we will have. I can think of nothing more precious."

I spent an hour with Lyt in the morning figuring out what was happening next.

He showed me his progress in detectors first. "Nyos rescued this mission. For that I owe her a debt that I cannot even place a value on. With the effort that you and I have invested, we now have this."

He gave me a small module that was supposed to fit inside the resonator.

"There are three hundred twenty resonating pairs of crystals here, and each is tied into a processor that can tell you which worlds are in alignment at any time. Now I have nearly completed a database of all the frequencies of those worlds, but with the new frequencies we are surely going to miss some important ones. No matter, now that the method is worked out, we can produce smaller systems in times to come."

I accepted the module and admired the workmanship. Lyt was making strides in his hardware. "Man, you've done incredible things. All of this was just a dream less than two weeks ago."

"We have another big job now, to find my home world. That is going to be difficult and will be research intensive. We are going to be moving the whole base to other locations soon. And we may be away from Earth for some weeks. I hope you don't mind."

I couldn't seem to get worried about it. "Lyt, I filled a freezer with food from the supermarket yesterday. I can stay away from my home planet for at least a couple of months I think. I have dried beans, pasta, juices, you name it. Canned stuff, whatever."

There was little I would miss. I only needed those things that kept me alive. But again, it would be nice to have an occasional perk.

Lyt gave a sigh. "Yes, I had my first real food from home when we retrieved the safe storage box day before yesterday. Those little things you miss the most. You are very fortunate to be able to get your needs met. In all ways."

He placed a hand on top of mine and gave it a pat. "Enjoy your explorations today. There are exciting things to see in the universe."

"Thanks. I'll install this card in my resonator right away."

I was feeling energized and ready to explore. This was one more tool that would help, at least in maintaining connections with some of the worlds.

Bees! Damn, I knew there was something I had forgotten. Even though I thought about having to be stranded somewhere off planet for months even, I had felt smart in gathering and packing seeds. But without bees to pollinate the things, there was no chance that anything would fruit. I would have to think of something else.

I got Nyos and we spent a few minutes selecting things that would make the trip easy. If we had had another generator, I might have taken the whole cabin. However, it was more adventurous to just pop in and do what we had to do. I set my resonator for the two-step trip to Birga and we vanished.

On the floater, we appeared in the dead central roundabout. I dropped a flag even though we couldn't get lost, with the landmarks and the computers. The air was still and quiet, although I could hear a constant chirping and squabbling in some distant place.

I took the floater up to about five meters and slowly cruised along the broad street. It was morning, the air was somewhat moist and cool and the sunlight was rather hot. Nyos swiveled her head in all directions, soaking in every sight. I listened and waited, not sure of where to begin.

I decided to rise to the level of one of the flattened umbrella-like parts of a skyscraper. I vaguely pictured the Eiffel Tower with a mushroom cap halfway up. Strange. The curved surface was covered in thin golden lines, tens of thousands of them in parallel. They looked something like a circuit board, with sharp angular turns at the end of each.

"I wonder what this is for."

Nyos looked for a few seconds and then turned back to her survey. "It appears to be to de-ice the surface. Current in the line would generate some heat."

"I hadn't thought of that. So in the winter they would get snow or ice on the surface and this would convert it to water. And prevent it from cracking from the load."

After a few more seconds I shook my head in puzzlement. "Well then, should we assume that the climate has changed here?"

It was her turn to look puzzled. "Why?"

It seemed obvious to me. "If the system was needed when these people were alive, wouldn't it still be needed now? And if it is needed now, where does the power come from to operate it?"

"I see." She looked at the surface a little more closely. "This is partly solar battery but it also appears to store some power in its shell. Like a capacitor. But I see that it would take more power than that to keep it operating during winter nights. Therefore there is another power source or storage unit."

Reasonable. Something is still operating after all this time. Where are libraries located in futuristic alien cities? I had a feeling that it could be a problem.

"On Earth we are slowly moving to the Internet and many libraries are just vanishing. If these people had everything in a network, there may be very few libraries or only small ones that depend on the net. Everything is distributed. We might not be able to get any real information."

I descended to a lower level and floated through the streets. We looked for signs of things, like fountains, planters, parking meters, whatever I might recognize. It seemed sort of barren until I realized that without power, the displays might be invisible. Like holograms.

"Let's get a hands-on look at the street level." Nyos agreed.

The floater came down to within a few centimeters of the ground. Our steps to the pavement raised no dust, made little sound. There was little debris except for the occasional wrecked vehicle.

"Is anything radioactive or toxic?"

"I detect no nuclear radiation and no obvious toxins."

There was a long glass front to something that I couldn't identify. It was like a wall but every tower had them along the walkways. Very bland, nothing identified anything. No doors were in evidence. Through the glass was a blank white wall that was in segments, and each was unremarkable.

The upper portion of each wall was off-white. The lower portion, about two meters of it, was perforated metal. Round holes, hexagonal grid, it might be stainless steel and could have come from any metal shop in the world on Earth. This was the borderline between mysterious and boring. We walked in silence.

Nyos crossed in front of me and stopped at the wall. The ceilings inside were about four meters tall. "Could you get in there, you know, without breaking it?"

She gave me that smile. "Yes, my dear, I can." She shucked off her clothing and proceeded to walk through the wall, with about the same resistance that a strong wind might have. I gathered her fallen things; shoes, blouse, jeans and underwear.

Inside the glassed hallway, there was little as well. I saw her walk faster to the end of the hall where it squared off and make the right turn. When she went around that corner, I felt really alone. What was I doing here, so far from home? Looking up, I spotted more of those triangular bird things zipping along at ridiculous speeds. I'm way out of my depth; at least that was my thought.

She returned as she had come, and then she stopped and shoved her head into the inner wall to take a look around. She didn't spend much time at it but then walked back out the way she had come in.

On the street she was more quiet than before.

"Any ideas what caused this?"

She said very little for a while and walked around observing. Finally she spoke.

"This appears to be the result of a biological agent. I find no trace of one however."

I remembered what Lyt has said; that viruses would not be a threat to us because the genetic codes would be wrong. "Could this agent have been destroyed by time? Things in the environment like weather and age?"

"That is plausible."

"Let's explore a little more. We've only seen what's on this one street."

We got back on the floater and made a long circuit of the area. Very little debris was present other that the occasional downed vehicle. I didn't think it was likely that somebody had cleaned the city up in the middle of the disaster.

After making the long loop, I thought that it might make sense to see things from altitude. We rose to about a hundred meters and hung there for long minutes. "Wow. Look at this." The area we were in was typical for the surrounding few kilometers. An amazing number of identical towers arranged in a regular grid dominated the scene. Very few breaks in the order could be seen.

"What in the world... could this be? It's not like a city. There are no stores or shops, very few vehicles, nothing that seems to be productive. I don't get it."

I chose to move away from the area into something that looked a little more varied. We spotted a loop of road that was lined by what appeared to be buses. They were impressive in their size and I concluded that these people must have been about three meters tall. There were very few remains to be found, and the scene was almost like an abandoned city and not one where there had been some biological disaster.

Another thing that struck me was the lack of any plant life in the area. It seemed prudent to find something that might be alive. That thought was in my mind as we approached the bus area, which was surrounded by areas that might have been lawns at one point.

Nyos peered down over the rail fearlessly. I wasn't so bold and stayed a little further from the edge of the floater. Ground rose to meet us and shortly we were ready to step from the platform and walk across the strangely textured expanse.

"Oh, look at this. Weird." I looked at the lawn and saw strange bulblike objects. The ground was covered in a ruffled mass of bulbs and tubes, all the same uniform gray color. "They feel like sponge. Full of holes too."

Nyos trod lightly over the things. "Machines. Gas exchange devices."

What? "You mean these are all artificial? Like Astroturf?"

Why would somebody cover a city in fake plants? And ugly ones at that. "What sort of gas exchange?"

"They absorb sunlight and carbon dioxide, along with other materials. They exchange it with oxygen and make new gas exchange devices."

Self-propagating fake plants. Now I thought I'd heard of everything.

I tried to think of why they would need them. "Well, maybe something killed the plants and they made a replacement for them. That might support the biological disaster scenario."

The more I thought about it, the more it made sense. "Then they'd have a real problem with food I'd think. We should find artificial food factories here somewhere."

She looked at me. "That is a reasonable conclusion."

"You know, what really amazes me is how we see these technical worlds and how they end up. They have the means of meeting their needs; they have advanced devices and apparently energy and resources. Why do they die out?"

Nyos came back to the platform. I was at a loss. "Something happens to societies with technology. They go away or die. It happens at just about the same time for each of them, when they get electronics and finance and start to make an easy life for everyone. The two big questions are why it happens and what happens."

I looked at her. "Nyos, your people didn't die out. What did you do differently?"

"Mike. You know I was created only days ago, when you met my template. I have not spent any time with my people."

Fair enough. "Okay. But you know an awful lot about things. I just thought you might have some sort of an answer, or at least a clue."

We left the bus area and aimed the platform for some of the other lower buildings in the vicinity. I wondered why there was something that didn't seem right, but it was just a vague sense of something. Ah!

"Most cities are on a river or a lake. Or at least near one. I didn't see anything from the air, so where does the water come from?"

"Perhaps from the air. That is a simple technology."

"Hmm. Yeah, that can be done. Maybe the fake plants capture it. And those big flat domes too, they would catch snow and ice, probably shed rain. I also don't see any power lines. They could be underground I guess."

Nyos was looking intently at the smaller buildings we were approaching. "Most civilizations use broadcast power. Very few use power lines."

"Wow, that would be handy to have on Earth. It could save a lot of copper wire. We wouldn't need those towers and transformers."

"Your world already knows the technology. It is not used."

I was taken aback. "What? When did this happen? When was it discovered?"

"Nearly a century ago."

"No way! We'd be using it everywhere. They've been working on wireless power for years. Once we get that figured out, along with the cheap fusion thing, we'll have more than enough power and no monster wiring system."

"Fusion was solved on your world over sixty years ago."

That had to be wrong. "But. No. That's not right. They've spent billions trying to make it work. Some of the best minds have been working on it for decades. If we had fusion power, we wouldn't be struggling with the coal plants and... no."

She took my face in her hand and turned it to her. "These are facts. I can show you the information. Every technical society discovers the basic principles very early in their development. It is dictated that they will by the laws of physics. Those societies often choose not to use those discoveries. Economics and control are the issues, not difficulty."

I was heartsick. This was impossible. We had fusion power? And broadcast power? Where were they? Why wasn't it being used? This was... incredible. What else was known but not used?

"Nyos, I had no idea. How can it be?"

She shook her head slowly.

"Mike, there are so many things you do not know about your own people and your own world. You want to explore and learn. You feel the need to find out what happened to these and other people *after the fact* of their ends. But what about your own world?"

Her words cut into me. "But I didn't know any of this. What was I supposed to do? What is anyone supposed to do?"

Her arm went around me. "You cannot see it when you are on the inside. I did not mean to make you feel bad." The floater moved on in silence. "Perhaps your experiences on these other worlds will help to give you perspective."

I nodded slowly, but my heart was leaden. We were just like these other races, on a greased track to doom.

"So Lyt is aware of all this and he's trying to stop it from happening somewhere?"

She nodded. "He knows a great deal for an organic life form. He has had many experiences and he may have a chance of preventing the end of a world."

Good for him. At least he was doing something. "And he brought me into this. Maybe he just needed help, but maybe he's looking for a recruit to carry on the fight. To stop worlds from collapsing."

I had a great deal to think about. Nyos was comforting but she also said things that were truly disturbing. This was a mystery that I had to learn everything about.

The rest of the exploration was subdued and by lunchtime I was ready to leave the dead world of Birga.

CHAPTER 12

The return to the base was quiet, and I had so much to think about that it distracted me from things that I would have paid attention to otherwise. Nyos was also quiet; I felt that there was something on her mind that was going unsaid. I didn't feel the need to press her however, so I left things as they were.

The base itself was quiet as well and I felt no need to change that. I was in a more or less neutral frame of mind, digesting the things I had been told. There was an implied assumption that people were actually working very hard to make the world better and to make life easier. I thought that things were as good as they could be, and they would become even better as time went on, and that there were really tough problems to solve before we could have these wonder technologies in our grasp.

But no. I was now being told that all of that was false. That the problems had already been solved many years- no, *decades* before and that for some unknown reason, those solutions were not being applied. But for what purpose?

"Nyos, please. Help me here. I need to see this information. It's just too incredible to believe. I mean, I trust you and I know that you are right. But I have to see this."

"We will go to Earth then. I will show you what you want to know."

"Are we going to some secret government facility?"

"No. We need the Internet."

No way in hell. This is on the net? There were reasons that the Internet is known as the web of lies. It's too hard to tell the crackpots from the real thing. But if Nyos says this is true...

No doubt about it. I knew that she would know. She *had* to be right. We would find out very quickly.

"My dear, how hard would it be to actually build some of these things? I mean to make these machines. Do we have the resources here?"

"It is simple. Yes, we have the resources."

Wow. "Then I want to see this. What is simpler to make?"

"The broadcast power can be demonstrated simply."

She led me to Lyt's workshop. "Locate a spool of copper magnet wire and some flexible plastic tubing." I looked through the cabinets, then resorted to the computer. Surely there would be an inventory. And there was.

Within minutes she had cut two pieces of the tubing and had placed one in a lathe. Then she placed the spool of copper wire next to it and fastened it to the plastic tube. She spun the lathe up carefully and wound a loose coil on the tube. The lathe was brought to a halt and she fastened the wire securely to the tubing.

She repeated the process and soon had two identical coils. Then she heated the plastic tubing slightly and began to curve both coils into curves like the letter C. Once done she looked for capacitors and found a pair of high voltage units. In minutes she had wired them to the coils. Then she attached a set of legs made from T fittings and the coils would stand on their own.

"This is the device. Now I will apply power to this coil and you will see a response in the other coil." She instructed me to set the coil upright on the workbench a few meters away. She pinched one wire with her finger and pointed her other finger at the other wire. Her finger seemed to become shiny and metallic. A fine spark shot from the fingertip and struck the opposite wire of the coil.

I heard a small crackling behind me. The coil on the workbench was arcing! A thread of violet arc spattered between the two electrodes. She stopped sparking the first coil and the second one stopped arcing.

"Oh my god. That's so simple!"

"A man named Nikola Tesla invented it decades ago. It is a known device. It has been in the public knowledge ever since." Nyos placed the two coils in my hands. "Now you have a basic broadcast power unit."

I looked at the two coils in my hands. This could have been built... in the 1700s! How could anything so simple have been...

I just couldn't think. "And fusion power, simple as well?"

"Indeed." She then walked very close to me and looked up at my face with an expression of innocence. "Would you like me to make a fusion reactor?"

"Maybe later. I'm just in shock right now." I gave her a brief hug and hefted the little coils. "Uh, out of curiosity, who invented the fusion reactor?"

"Philo Farnsworth."

"Never heard of him. Did he invent anything I might know of?"

"Television."

That word struck me like a hammer. So many millions of hours of commercials and garbage. And instead of putting the more useful device into practice, the television was made instead.

"I suppose that there are lots of inventions like this."

She looked aside and then said, "Everything is driven by profit. If a product can make a great deal of money without any real progress being made, then it is decided that it will be produced instead of a beneficial product. That is one constant in almost every technical society. There may be a clue to their downfalls there."

My day was really in a shambles now. So much of what I had believed was junk. I had to decide on the trip to Earth. Could I risk some time in a library or a web cafe? Sure, it would tell me a great deal. I had no illusions about saving the world but maybe something I could learn might be helpful. And maybe this mission with Lyt would help me to understand what had to be done to save a world. He felt that he could do it, and surely I could learn something from his efforts.

My laptop had been neglected lately. It was in a cardboard box I saved from the delivery of silverware and household goods. The case was clean, the battery a little low but otherwise fine. I had a wireless card built in so it wouldn't take anything really to get the information.

Nyos dressed and became more presentable for human company. She and I looked up a web cafe and took a floater to the transit point. I must have been pretty depressed during the flight, and said very little. We arrived and landed the floater, then walked to the door of a small coffee shop.

Once inside, I bought a hot tea and set my computer on a table. She joined me and dictated the links and information to search for. And there it was. She was right. But I couldn't have doubted her.

I learned more about what the world could have been and what it was not in that hour than I ever would have thought possible.

I folded up my laptop and crumpled the empty cup. A look at her showed me little. "Let's go home" was my only statement.

We were walking to the transit point and only then did it hit me. "Home" was not on this planet. Was I separating myself from humanity? But this had been all that I knew for all my life. It was only the last couple of weeks that I had been exposed to alien worlds, technology and ideas. How was it that I no longer felt any real attraction to this world?

We transited and stepped on the floater. "Oh. Is there anything we need? Anything you need?"

Nyos looked down at her hands, clasped lightly together in front of her. "Yes."

"Name it."

"I need you to be happy. I see that what you have learned has made you unhappy."

How could I resist her?

"Thank you, my dear. I promise to cheer up."

The cruise over the desert was actually helpful. I wondered what it was that made civilizations any different from other organisms. Animals lived their lives and didn't create an end to their worlds. Give an animal some brains and somehow it would invent fire, wheels, levers, pyramids, and they were doomed from there.

That was a fatalistic way of viewing it though. Some races made it through the gauntlet, and Nyos was proof of that. I had to find out what it was that made things different for her. And Lyt seemed to have found a few races with incredible technical skills, things I hadn't imagined. So some of them survived. Or at least for a time. Boro was amazing but its people were gone, and now to be told that Earth itself was on the road to the end…

There was a solution. There had to be. I would travel and learn until I had the answer. Maybe on the way I would figure out how to make the ignored technologies of Earth openly available. Could I set up a business doing that? If I did, it would have to be somewhere that I could not be arrested for stupid things like suspicion because I sold some pure metals.

I already had the germ of an idea for a business. A metals trade or something. But what if I set up a general technology business and made all sorts of things that could make life easier. Sell licenses or something, make sure that I could have the income needed to get these things out.

Focus!

I had to figure out what was more important. How to do it. I couldn't do it though; I would need to delegate this to somebody who could do it for me. Do I travel the worlds or do I save the world I was born on? Too big a job either way and I was thinking of taking on both.

There was absolutely incredible wealth out there in the dead worlds, and no regulations or anything about who could get it our how much. If I had unlimited wealth, what would I do and how?

That started me on the road to my own quest.

Nyos helped me with the research and then I outfitted myself for a real expedition. The afternoon had worn on but there was still time for this.

We returned to the planet Birga with four floaters and four robots. I carried metal cutting tools and had specific instructions for the robots. We appeared in the big loop and started a search for entrances. We used floaters to reach the higher levels, on an inspiration. And then, just below the big flattened hemisphere umbrella things, we found a vehicle landing pad and a broad archway of glass. "Ah ha!"

The floater touched the surface softly. A door sputtered and slid open halfway under the arch. "And it looks like show time." The robots disembarked and I took one extra precaution. "We absolutely must not transit. If we do, we're likely to fall to the ground on the other side. I don't want to do that, and you don't either."

The robots remained mute. I turned the power switches off on the resonators.

The entrance proved to be cooler inside, so there was either really good building design or even now, something had power. I thought the latter, since the door had tried to open. We moved in silently, listening for anything.

The archway and the adjoining hallway were dimly lit by light fibers. We had no idea where the power was from, or if the light might be natural sunlight conducted inside. The floor was a soft mesh-like material that had little resilience but under heavier feet might have been ideal.

We found some doors that would not open and had no latches. I opted to cut the way in. The robots did so and we removed the first door entirely. It was on sliding tracks into the wall and did not want to budge, so we had no real choice. Nyos seemed lost in thought and followed us almost absently.

I got the same effect then that I felt a few days earlier when I suddenly felt an understanding of the resonators. Things started to click into place, and I felt somehow smarter or more competent. I can't explain any better than that. I saw things a bit differently then and I stepped back from the scene and wondered what I might do if I were three meters tall and weighed around two or three hundred kilos.

I also wondered what this place might be that I would only want somebody with a vehicle entering. No street traffic allowed, clearly. It had to be important enough to make lots of these things, it had to be sealed except to those who had access to vehicles, and it had to be essentially self-contained. I had an inkling of an idea.

"We proceed carefully here. Look for inner doors and always move toward the center. Be ready for anything." The robots rolled on softly buzzing treads and removed two more doors. The inner door was rather stylized and had a cartoon outline of something like a giant ground sloth, but on its side.

We forced the door carefully and expectantly. A smell of decay and sweet rot bloomed from the door. A faint light came on, like a solid state lamp. It was bluish-white and there were hundreds of them, each aimed at a sort of large sconce that held a plastic clear tube that reclined. The room was completely encircled with them.

"Oh gawd, this is awful."

Nyos stopped and if she had been an organism, she would have held her breath.

Hundreds of corpses in tubes, each wearing some sort of headset, and each slumped in relaxed repose.

"Here's your Internet. It's an artificial world and all of them died in it. Like a giant video game or a fantasy land. They died here in their virtual worlds."

I tried my computer on the language. The robots traced a power feed and figured out a working voltage and frequency. Then they located a working terminal once they disconnected the old line and applied their own with the proper power settings.

I set my Boro computer on the top and tried a few of the touch panels. In a short time the Boro computer was doing likewise somehow and analyzing the bus traffic and processor states.

A soft voice came from the Boro machine. "Welcome to Oneiros, the theater of dreams." I got gooseflesh. This was so wrong.

"Computer, locate a map of this city. Download a map of the planet if one is available. Any and all cultural information, any technical information, whatever you can locate."

"Data is limited to local station only."

Yeah, the net was down. Well. "What data can you retrieve from the local station?"

"Local maps, communication access codes similar in nature to telephone listings, some local literature and technical matter."

"Download what you can."

"Working."

It was creepy looking at the sloth corpses. The name of the place-obviously made into something I would understand but there was a sinister, dreadful sound to it all. Oneiros. It was probably Greek or something. The theater of dreams and then you never waken. The world ends while you play and you go down without a struggle.

"Download complete."

I disconnected the computer. "Are there any local art galleries or museums?"

"There are two."

We got the hell out of there and went to the nearest museum.

Nyos had not spoken since arriving in the theater of dreams. She now continued to remain in silence and seemed much less energetic that usual. I felt *sharper* still and could not explain it but was grateful for the clarity it seemed to bring me. The museum was ahead.

I was less subtle this time. Damn them if they would simply lie down and die. This was outrageous and beyond. This door was a simple automatic swing-open-on-a-hinge thing and I kicked the door open viciously. I was madder than I had been for a long time, even more so than after the police incident. This was insanity.

The robots, still without a task to perform, rolled behind me. I entered the gallery and for a moment, just a moment, I was slowed by the scale of it. High windows about three stories up had slanted beams of sunlight and below were large leaf-like tent structures that sheltered various works. The first real color I had seen on the planet was the dark green of the tent fabric.

The floor- well, it was magnificent polished wood of some type that held deep red highlights and twisted, burled grain. Each piece was some sort of interlocking tile and the pattern shifted slowly from one type of pattern to another. It was a real-live M. C. Escher artwork in and of itself.

Now I saw something of the thinking of an artist who had never seen our skies or understood our languages or listened to our music. He had no idea that our world existed, and he had never seen a Van Gogh or a Mondrian. This artist thought in a manner that paralleled Escher, and he produced on a grand scale the floor before me.

I walked faster once more and instructed the robots to make holograms of everything. Only by seeing something of their art or their culture might I dilute the raw anger and horror of the dream theater.

Paintings, amazing paintings, and there I got my first real view of them as they saw themselves. Not the rotting dreamers or the dried bones in the vehicles, these were colorful and vibrant images. I saw fields and pastures, skies and flowers, and people who were very different from humanity. The faces were long and narrow with short tusklike protuberances and the noses were not elephantine but more like a tapir.

The ears were small, flattened near the head and the eyes small and sunken into shallow sockets lined with wrinkles. They looked wise, caring. I stopped and heaved a deep sigh. What had gone wrong?

This was enough for now. Nyos had walked slowly at the rear and was now leaned back looking at something near the ceiling in this new gallery. I tracked her line of vision and saw it.

There, among the high beams which had been sculpted into the forms of lofty branches of trees, there was Icarus himself with long, smooth skinned limbs of a Birgan, and he had the feathers of some great bird fused into his limbs and around them. The form of a Birgan was large and stumpy, thick-limbed and immense and made me think of massive elephants and slow moving sloths.

But this was grace and power, made of some lustrous material like pale marble, and it was done so wondrously as to tax the skills of Leonardo or Michelangelo. I gasped in awe. Nyos stood transfixed, her mouth hanging open.

I stepped quietly to her side as she looked and said to her, my arm outstretched to the Icarus, "There. There is aspiration. THERE is power and love and the will to become." The last of my voice echoed softly. "There."

Something inside me reached a resolution. I knew that at least some of these people did not go down without a fight. The masses will exist always; it is in the nature of all things. But within any group there will be those who make the paths and light the beacons, and this building was the antithesis of the dream theater. Somewhere inside, after the horror, I had a measure of peace.

I placed my hands on her shoulders and squeezed lightly. "Let's go." Her eyes tore reluctantly from the numinous thing above her and I saw something like hurt in that gaze. "Come."

We left, I in a much more subdued state and Nyos moving almost through inertia. The city was still there and I had a plan to save my world. I recalled the robots and they followed just a few paces behind.

Daylight was like a shock. I consulted my computer. "I need to know if there is a precious metals repository in this area."

"Yes."

I turned the resonators back on. "Set the floaters to the coordinates of the repository." We boarded and I activated the floaters. In moments we were homing in on a low building that was completely innocuous. "There will be defenses and systems we cannot imagine here. This is likely to be dangerous. We are entering an area like a vault. Be aware of potential traps and prepare to move quickly to avoid harm."

We landed near false hedges. There were more gray gas exchange machines in the shape of nicely trimmed boxwoods or ligustrums, more fake plants making air for a planet of dead people. Maybe there were some animals somewhere that benefited.

The doors were sealed but that was not a problem. The robots had something like plasma cutters that made very short work of the bolts. They slid the action back and swung the doors open. Now we were inside but really no closer to the goal.

A scan showed no power operating. Good. The rest was sheer mechanical work. We removed something like a ton and a half of metals but I left all the artwork and artifacts. I didn't want to destroy anything important but I would need an incredible fortune to carry out the plan I had in mind. Saving a world can be costly.

At every opportunity I downloaded computer files and data. Perhaps we could reconstruct something of the culture and the people here. And perhaps their death would actually provide the means of saving another planet from their fate.

I was feeling somewhat positive about the Birga trip when we returned. I felt a bit of guilt at the thought of taking something as crass as wealth away from it but I had to be a realist. What I had in mind would be expensive and there was no doubt about it.

I gave Lyt a brief explanation and he looked a little surprised but admitted that it might work. "I have a plan that is a little different, but we may learn enough from my attempt, even if it fails, to help temper your plan. At least you are doing something and that is all I can hope for."

Lunch was next. I was worn out, even though the actual work had not been that great. Mental fatigue was enough and the stress that brought it on.

I checked on my other project in the new building and was very happy to see it working out exactly as I had hoped. I went back to the cabin and made myself a large and rather complex sandwich, gathered a towel and some swimming shorts, and went to the new building. Nyos was nowhere to be seen.

So that is where Lyt found me an hour later. I was getting rather pruney but I was relaxed and had a full stomach. "What, Michael, is this?"

"Ah, Lyt. My friend. Get a towel and join me. This is an Earth diversion known as a hot tub. These are water jets and they provide a great deal of relaxation, and that is ice cold bottled water in that cooler."

He walked slowly around the tub, brows knit in mental engagement. "I see. Well, it is rather sybaritic but I believe that you have talked me into it." He left the room and was only gone a few minutes. The door opened and he stepped in with some sort of loose fitting cloth thing and a large, woolly towel.

Wow, he is definitely not human. His feet had a large cleft from front to back and there were two toes on the left of it and two toes on the right of it. The heel had a toenail also. Hey, whatever.

He slid into the water carefully, then got a big grin and just about submerged himself. "Oh, delightful. This is just delightful."

"Knob up there sets the jets to your liking. No voice control on this baby, all manual." I was pretty settled, taking advantage of my solar water heater panels and the solar electric panels that Nyos had improved.

"So how's the plan to find your world working out? Any progress to report?"

Through the splushing and gurgling it was a little hard to make his voice out but he sounded positive. "I'm constructing the signals from the past. I have some stones but not all the information about the worlds I crossed from my home to a known destination. I am recreating the past positions of the worlds in an effort to find the exact world of origin. It's tricky."

"I see." I took a long drink of cold water.

"So far I believe I have about two thirds of the path worked out. I have some stones that came from other worlds along the way and I am comparing resonance with the known worlds, and that helps me verify which world in the database the stones came from.

"Then I recalculate what worlds would have been in resonance at past times, and see if any of them match my stones. Slow and painful work to be sure. But at last I have resolved some of the way, and it helps me because it often triggers memories that can eliminate false trails."

Running the scenario through my head, I could see that Lyt needed more definite information about the movement of worlds in the past. I must have the complete map while he has fragments. I wondered about sharing that data with him, and I decided it was the right thing to do.

"Suppose you had a larger database. Something more complete with more worlds and maybe even their frequencies. Could something like that help you do this?"

He looked ceilingward. "Oh, most surely. I have a very good map but it does not extend much earlier than when I started traveling, and it is mostly things I have learned and some from two previous travelers."

He turned his jets down a notch. "Traveling is a very rare art. Only a few cultures know of it, even though it is quite simple. And travelers tend to keep it that way. Most learn from another traveler and new inductees are a thin breed. Maps are hard to get and jealously guarded."

"I see." I wanted to give him the map but wasn't sure how Nyos would react. She seemed willing to help but she often said little. And where was she anyway?

"So Lyt, if I could get some data for these worlds, you think you could get the path worked out? I may have something that could help."

His look was inquiring. "Well now, I cannot imagine finding a map of the worlds, unless you found a world that had the data because they use it. And worlds with resonator technology are hard to destroy. At least their people are. They move all over the universe and end up spread quite thin but they don't die out easily."

"I guess you don't have a stone from your world then?"

With a sigh he said, "no, I do not. And that would make this process unnecessary. Remove all of the effort, because it is possible to test a stone for resonance to worlds that I do know, and so we could match it and pinpoint it."

"I'm going to keep my eyes open and see if there is anything I can find. Whatever I find is yours, okay?"

The little snort and laugh was almost completely human. "Very generous of you Michael, generous to a fault. But I thank you. You have surprised me greatly in the short time that I have known you. You may just find a database of resonating worlds."

"Show me what you've been able to work out, if you are inclined, and I'll see if it matches some things that I have found."

"Surely."

So we stayed in the hot tub for a while, and I finally had had enough. I left Lyt enjoying himself there and went back to the cabin.

Late afternoon, and we only had four more days to retrieve Lyt's stash of goods on Karoom, so that was the big task for tomorrow. Then we had three days left for me to explore Birga in detail and gather as much of its wealth as I could for my project. I had no idea what we could accomplish but it had to be limited to an area as large as we could reasonably reach with floaters and the efforts of the robots.

I was now beginning to put all the pieces together and see what I could accomplish. With Lyt's other safe storage boxes as well equipped as the one we did get, I could do a great deal in a little time. What a shame I didn't have access to more robots.

I stepped into the little cabin and there I saw Nyos who had been very quiet, very retiring since our experience in the dream theater and the museum. She was sitting quietly and looking at nothing. She might have been a statue. "Dear?"

She didn't move at first. Her form was as rigid as stone. After a few seconds, she slowly turned her head to me.

"Do you fear death?"

"No, not as much as I fear being useless. Accomplishing nothing. I know that death is coming, and there's nothing I can do about it. I live with that fact." I gathered my thoughts and continued.

"Each of us has something to contribute to the world- no, the worlds around us. Many people are not able to figure out what they're good for and their lives might go unfulfilled. I feel like I have something I can do and so that's what I do. When I die, I'll go knowing that I was doing something worthwhile."

She seemed to think about my words for a long time while I dried off and changed clothes. I was keen on getting Lyt's other boxes back. There was so much to do and only four more days to get it done. I almost could kick myself for spending a day on frivolous things like going to Earth to use the Internet. Each hour was precious.

Nyos sat before me and turned those red-orange, luminous eyes to me. "I have lived only days, but I expect to continue to the end of the universe. I may live many trillions of years. And of all I know and feel, I have learned the most about the value of love and life from you. It seems so paradoxical that you are so ephemeral and you give me the most powerful lessons. It seems sometimes that you are a superior being and I am a child. How is it?"

"For a living thing, every moment can be worth a lifetime. And some things are worth so much that you will risk everything for them, for even a chance of them. My perspective is from the viewpoint that the end is near, and so I want to make each moment count. And that means that sometimes I must enjoy myself and take care of myself as well."

She accepted that and stood slowly. "Come with me. I want to show you something."

"Sure."

Instead of moving she embraced me tightly and I felt a shift of air pressure and saw a change of the light. We were on a beach that stretched for kilometers in both directions, almost a straight line. The crashing of low waves was at my back. Oh, man, what just happened?

Lyt asked me where her resonator was, if she was a traveler. Clearly she had one. But wait.

The sun that was seen was too red and too large, low on the horizon. The position was wrong, it didn't match the position it should be in. And the sky! There was a huge moon directly overhead; that *had* to screw up the resonances and speeds. This was utterly impossible.

"Where are we? This can't be a resonant world!"

"It isn't, not the way you know. It does not correspond to any world in your atlas, and it does not resonate with any world you will ever reach as a traveler. Look over there, in the sky."

And there, a tiny reddish dot was hung. It was a second little sun, something I never would have expected to see. This system was completely hosed up. The gravity potentials would never, ever match an Earthlike system.

"Should I call you goddess?"

"No, never. Mike, I have been engaged in a great internal struggle. The things we have seen and the places we have been have taught me a lot. Some of it goes against what I thought I knew. And we are an old and powerful race. But I am new and very young. I am trying to learn everything I can."

She looked sideways at me. "You have shown me that regardless of the facts that I know, they are only a small portion of what life is about."

We looked at the surf and the sky for a while and she released the tight hold she had on me, a little. "Mike, please. Never leave me."

"Oh, Nyos. I couldn't even think of it."

"I will help you in any way I can, and I am very capable. I want to be as good as you are, as feeling as you are." She rubbed her hands lightly over my shoulders.

"I don't know what to say. Let's make our commitment solid and legal. We need to find a place to get married. I hear you can get anything in California, so let's get a marriage license and find a preacher who will do it, but knowing who you are, not hiding behind a false face. Let's make it real."

She hugged me again and we were once more inside the cabin. I got dressed immediately and put a wad of cash in my pocket. My wallet- I had it here somewhere. The coat was next and I was ready to travel. "For our arrival I think you need to look human, and once I make arrangements, we will do this naturally." She got dressed rapidly and shifted to a human skin tone.

"Okay, we need to get to California. I assume you know where that is. Try- no, wait. Las Vegas. That's the place. It may sound funny but you can get married there any time and easily. Las Vegas, Nevada. Can you take us there?"

"Yes" she said tentatively and then grasped me again. We were standing on a sidewalk near a gaudy painted plywood wall that surrounded a row of apartments that used to be a motel. The bright fluorescent red of the wall just made the fluorescent yellow of the apartments look worse.

Evening was setting in and lights were starting to come on. I walked into a convenience store there and asked the clerk where a phone book was. He pointed at a low table just beside the lottery tickets.

It took a moment to thumb up a marriage license and a preacher. We spent more time walking to places but within the hour we had the license and I had a preacher on the phone. "This is unusual, and I need somebody who is willing to do unusual. And we want the ceremony on video."

She sounded a little high. "No problem, as long as it's not animals or love dolls."

"Fine. I'll explain it when we get there."

We had a short walk, fortunately, although I am certain that Nyos could have whisked us there in a fraction of a second. The place was actually in good repair, and the outside's only concession to tackiness was a large metal heart archway. The woman who met us had jet black hair, clearly dyed. There was a string of Hindu prayer flags fluttering at the entrance and a small brass statue of Gonesh with an incense bowl.

"Welcome to Happy Hearts. I'm preacher Kitty. If you have the marriage license filled out, I can take that here."

I began to explain. "This is a little unusual. My fiancé is a bit different, and we don't know exactly what sort of documentation you might require. She has no birth certificate and no identification because she is from a place where they don't have such things."

She stopped. "Well, we need certain papers for the courthouse." She opened a leopard print glasses case and perched the reading spectacles on her nose. "You don't have a date of birth on here either."

"Uhm, Tuesday of last week. What was the date?"

"Year?"

"This one. This year." That got me a stare.

"Well, she's an alien. I need you to do this, just fill in the truest, most factual information and we will make the commitments. But there has to be a record, no matter what anyone might believe."

"Hey, I've heard stuff like this before. Her green card is needed. But I have to have the proper information on the license or it's invalid."

"Green card? Oh, not that kind of alien. We can prove it. And we're going to have to trust you. Nyos, show her your natural appearance."

She began to remove her clothing. The preacher woman said, "Hey, nude weddings cost more." But as the last piece hit the floor, Nyos lost the skin tone and showed her glassy self. The glasses case hit the floor next. Preacher Kitty looked like she might follow.

"Wait. Hold on there, don't faint. Sit down, breathe, and I'll explain."

I helped her into the chair and she started to hyperventilate. "Oh wow."

"Now, Kitty, we have very limited time. The government is probably after me, so we have to do this and get moving. But as you can see, this is legitimate. We filled in all the required information but there is no way to substantiate some of it. But you must also be a notary, correct? And we have produced evidence that is known to you to be true and accurate, right?"

Something clicked into professional mode in her brain. "Oh. Oh, yes. That's true."

"Now, we want to get married, we are two consenting adults of the opposite gender, and I'm not even sure that's a requirement any more. But marry us!"

"Well, you don't have to be residents to get married, and you do have a driver's license. And she sure appears to be an adult, and... dear, you want to marry this man?"

"Yes."

"Okay. They may not like it but you're right. It's a matter of heart and commitment. So okay."

She set up the camera and started doing what she knew best. "No birth certificate."

"Well, here she is. Do you need proof that a person was born if they are standing in front of you."

"No, no, that's not what it's about. You have to show- or do you. Hmm. I can tell that she's not human, I think. Dear, do you do something that isn't human? Something convincing, I mean you are very pretty and different and all, but what can you show me that isn't human?"

I was feeling a little impatient. "Teleport or transit or something."

Nyos vanished. After a moment she reappeared.

Preacher Kitty was open mouthed. "Will that do?" I was shaking her shoulder.

"Yeah. That's pretty good."

She continued with her preparations. I was feeling pressure to get this done. "Remember, law enforcement is looking for me, so we can't take a lot of time."

"Right." She dropped a video disc into her computer and adjusted the camera. "Ready."

The ceremony was just a few lines, very brief, but it made it official. I added one brief statement as a personal vow.

"I commit myself to you, to love you and to do my best to keep you as long as we both shall live."

And she said, "I will love you and care for you and meet your needs as long as we both shall live."

I think I got the better deal really.

Preacher Kitty was more or less shell shocked but she had done this so many times that she was able to carry it out properly. She gave us the marriage certificate and a DVD with the ceremony on it and I left her a substantial tip.

I then hugged my bride and we said our thanks to her and I whispered to Nyos, "It's time to go home, dear."

And we vanished.

CHAPTER 13

W e didn't think about her clothing. It was still on the floor of the little Happy Hearts chapel. Today we had three days left to access Birga and to get Lyt's safe storage boxes from Karoom. That had priority.

Lyt was enthused about this trip. We had floaters so it wouldn't take very long. We transited all at once with only two floaters and three robots. Lyt, Nyos, and I were on the lead floater. We started out on the reptile buffalo world because it was still pretty cold on Karoom. In about an hour Lyt reported that we were near the first box.

We were in another area of shifted rocks and cliffs, and Lyt had similarly hidden this box at the base of a spire and the retrieval, like the previous one, was simple. Once the box was opened, Lyt pulled out a floater plate and hooked the box to it. This then proceeded to follow us to the next place.

We spent about seven hours locating and loading boxes on floaters but at the last we were nearing our transfer point and had five of the metal cage things following us. Lyt commanded the transit and we brought all the safe boxes down to a perfect landing.

By mid-afternoon we had recovered the equipment and had it loaded into the big workshop while some of the boxes were reloaded and placed outside. Lyt activated those and we had five black spheres in a line like odd storage tanks.

"You see Mike; the trick is to use your resources to multiply your efforts. I could not possibly have gathered the boxes and equipment without paying others to do it. Your efforts must similarly be directed. Use your resources to get others to do it for you. And sometimes, to get good accomplished, you must appeal to the greed of others."

He didn't have to tell me that twice.

This was a happy day for me. Nyos and I had spent our night enjoying each other's company and the day had started with me tired but energetic. Now we had some time left to do things on Birga and a set of targets that would help us recover more data. Our crucial need was exactly that- data.

We were both mentally prepared to do our job and face this world. There were some maps of the planet and it surprised me how little ocean there was, roughly 12% of the surface. It was later in the afternoon that I really wanted to start but this wasn't going to be much of a detriment.

I took Lyt's words to heart. I needed a work force. Surely this planet had robots and some sort of technology that I could put to use. Perhaps the equivalent of construction or police forces or even automated street cleaning existed.

I had the Boro robots look for communications centers and computers and for portable power generators and storage systems. We had some pretty good success and retrieved a lot of things back to the base.

Evening was arriving at an unwelcome speed but we now had assembled power generators and a set of large light bars from what appeared to be a stadium. They would provide plenty of light for our work.

We also had enough data and computers to assemble a pretty complete picture of the cities and facilities of the planet, along with a massive dataset of what appeared to be music and entertainment. I felt that we had accomplished a lot.

After that, I had four floaters equipped with generators and split them into two teams. Two robots formed each team and they were given map coordinates and told to locate and retrieve precious metals and bring them back to the base. I left them to do this all night and spent my time reading through the data of the Birgan world.

One excellent find was an entertainment system that did full holographic projection. I used this to search the data and it provided an excellent travelogue of the planet. You know what struck me as odd? The name of the planet that Nyos had given us was not arbitrary. It was the name that the people themselves used. For some reason I found that significant but why, at the time, I could not have said.

This day was gone but again, we were making progress. Lyt was happy as well.

"Mike, I have found a very close match to the path that I must have taken. I am narrowing the possibilities down now. I may have found a set of worlds that contains my home world."

"Hey, that's great news! How did you do it?"

"As I traveled, I kept a set of stones that showed connecting worlds. Since the worlds move all the time, the configuration changes constantly. I reasoned, and correctly so, that if I had a string of worlds that I had traveled then that configuration would likely be unique. I know the time frame and so I used the times and locations to create a set of connections in the map.

"Now, as I set the time on the map to this specific range of times and I matched the worlds to the stones, I found a small number of candidate paths that lead to only a small number of worlds. One of them is likely to be my home world."

"That's a lot of work, Lyt. When can we start accessing some of them and exploring?"

"One of the lesser candidates can be reached in two weeks. Others take longer unfortunately, but at least there are things we can check very soon."

"Well, when you're ready for a break, I have some pretty neat things to show you. I have it set up in the big shop."

He did a quick set of calisthenics. "I am in need of some diversion. Very good then, I will see what you have. It surely will be interesting."

Outside of his cabin the early night air was dry as usual but slightly cooler. We walked in silence to the workshop, now with its associated set of odd things like black spheres, strange hardware, alien power generators and new stacks of shining metal bricks. At that Lyt pointed and said, "You seem to be accumulating a great deal of that. I hope you know what you're doing. It's strange how dangerous a pile of money can be."

"You're telling me. I'm glad that there is some separation from us and Earth. We'd have every treasure hunter and speculator there is struggling to get to it."

He gave the stack an eye. "There must be about six tons of the stuff. Roughly."

Somehow I felt disconnected from it. "Yeah, probably. I'm about ready to set some things in motion." The workshop was warmer inside, retaining some of the heat of the day. Lyt found a chair and rolled it up to the hardware Nyos and I had installed.

I gave my computer a command and the hologram faded in. We were in what appeared to be an orchestral hall, and before us was a group of about three dozen Birgans. They began to play.

It was a symphony; there is no other word for it. There was an Asian flavor to the music but it would have been at home in any music hall on Earth. There were strings and percussion, winds and brass. There was also some electronic accompaniment but it was subdued.

I had no idea what the subject of the symphony was, but it had one of those tunes that stuck in your head. It started with broad, sweeping deep brass, swelling strings, and rolling drums. Then was a transition to a pastoral theme, quiet and with small bits of trilling flute, and then a dramatic conclusion. That ended the first movement.

We sat through three movements and what seemed like an epilogue in tune. By the end we were just awed. Lyt seemed to be drying an eye. "This alone was probably worth the effort you have put into your project. I have rarely heard such a moving piece of music."

"I guess I'm making an archive of the planet's works. I don't have much time left, just a couple of days. But at least I feel that I'm doing something that will help to preserve some of what they were all about. I'm not just taking and plundering."

Night had fallen and it was quiet and cooling quickly.

There was a minor rumbling noise outside that drew our attention.

"Thunder? Lyt, does this planet have thunderstorms?"

"I suppose it must, but we should see what that is."

I shut down the hologram system. Lyt was out first and I could see that something had his eye. He was stopped in the doorway. I gently pushed past him to see what was so engaging.

Nyos was walking slowly this way, radiating heat waves. She looked tired, and I had never seen her even slightly out of sorts. Behind her was a literal mountain of boxes and cases. I had the picture of a warehouse of goods being spilled haphazardly on the ground, but not damaged.

"I have brought you a gift." She was just about glowing along her back and arms. Slowly she returned to a more normal temperature. In her fist she held a crumpled bit of paper. "Call this number once you are on Earth."

There was a name and a phone number. I took it.

She stood before me and said in a more normal tone, "Good evening my love."

"Hello, wife." Lyt's brow rose fractionally. "It's wonderful to see you. And thank you for... this."

I hit a light switch and a bank of floods came on, illuminating the parched ground.

We approached the pile of cases. I selected one that was easy to reach. It had a pair of latches that required a pull outward and then to twist a pair of fins that popped out. Unusual.

The interior was a thick, soft foam and contained within were blocks of metal with some sort of stampings on them. "This one is platinum." I closed the case and picked another. It was different from the first in all respects. Inside this case I found tough plastic bags that weighed very little. I opened one on a sealed edge and it was full of tiny plastic capsules of some sort.

"Those are nanobots. They are programmable industrial machines. The interface is in that small box." And indeed there was a slot in the foam with an interface box packed inside.

"All this stuff... where is it from?"

"Dead technical worlds. I have brought technology, metals, tools, and information. This should be enough to do what you want."

Lyt walked around the mountain and gaped. "So many things. These are from all over. Mike, you are a very fortunate man. If only she could bring me a crystal from my home world as easily."

Nyos strode over to Lyt. "But you have one."

"Certainly not! I have been searching for my world for ages. I have no crystal from my home." He looked at her strangely.

"But you do. It is in the implant in your left leg."

—————◆—————

Lyt was speechless. We went inside and sat and he explained what had happened and about his life.

"When I was very young, I knew that my family and the town in general had put a great deal of effort into my training and education. Everything seemed normal to me, but we don't know as a child what to compare 'normal' to. The whole of my life was training in such things as listening and watching, remembering details and learning languages.

"I had the best computers, the best training. I was sent into a special military school when I was nine to learn about stealth and survival. I thought it was normal to have such a life. I did not know that this was my preparation for something much larger."

He seemed to think back, his eyes gazing outward. He grasped the fabric of his worn coat and rubbed it between his fingers absently.

"What I was unaware of was the danger that was closing in. My parents seemed to know that some disaster was coming for our world and that somebody had to be trained to circumvent it. There were no outward signs, but it happens that they had befriended a traveler.

"Myan Zeeda was his name and he was quite unlike us. I felt that he was like an uncle, the strange uncle that looked different from anyone else. Very few people saw Myan, but he was known in our community.

"We had a farming village and our world was technical but we had very little in terms of computers and technology. Myan supplied what we needed."

I had a question. "So there wasn't an effort to build lots of resonators and save people?"

"Oh, well. Myan was not a technical man. A traveler to be sure, but even though he had encountered some dead technical worlds, he did not understand enough of what he found to really put it to use. Some hand computers, some small gadgets, but he knew nothing about electronics and nothing about making things from scratch.

"He did what he could. He supplied a small number of resonators and even carried people from my world to other places where they could settle and grow food, create small splinter colonies. I had some contact with them in times past, fortunately.

"In any event, we thought that the danger was years away. Remember that our culture was not a highly technical one. So it was that I was shown the basics of resonator operation and travel. I found two worlds that we could reach, and for many months that was all that we could reach. The planets were not well overlapped for much travel. So I learned to seek crystals and how to use them.

"There came a day when everyone was in a panic. Something in the air, one might say. I had only moments to say anything to my parents, but they were sure that this was nothing more than a minor scare. They didn't want to take any chances however, and they sent me off, more or less as a training exercise. I had to know what to do when the time came. I was given a package of food, water, some books and other small things.

"And so I left. I waited for the prescribed time, followed my course of training. I was to gather water, make a camp, and start a fire. There is a rigor, a set of steps that you follow, so that come what may, you will be ready to take care of yourself and anything else you can manage. And those steps I did follow.

At this he seemed to sink a little. "When the prescribed time came to transit back, I checked the frequencies. Yes, I could see the line for my world. But it was odd, it kept changing around and pulsing. I had never seen or heard of such a thing. I was singularly unprepared for this.

"The frequency of my world then vanished, as if it were no longer in resonance. I knew then that I was unable to return. My training took over and I tried to find those things needed to survive. The frequency for my world did not return, and I took this as a sign that I was not going back. The time for its resonance passed and I was certain. I struck out to explore and see what I could, and I collected and worked my crystals so that I would have the path home ready for me."

That struck me. Questions came to mind. "But Lyt, didn't you have a crystal for each of those worlds? Something that you would always have just in case?"

"Indeed I did. You see, I was not going to make the same mistake that Myan Zeeda did. I learned electronics and I studied physics. I learned how to make a resonator from scratch and how to repair and make most anything. But I was attacked and robbed early on when I arrived on a somewhat civilized world known as Fennio, and I lost everything. Absolutely everything. I was fortunate to escape with my life.

"I must say it was my own pride that did me in. I was the wizard, the mysterious traveler from other worlds! I made the terrible mistake of believing my own stories and thinking that it would shield me from the locals. It did not. They beat me and robbed me, and I was left alone and without my tools.

"Think about what it would be like to have been left stranded on a world where you were a freak, and your only means of escape stolen."

Another point came to me. "But if they had your resonator, they would have been able to travel also. Did they?"

"Ah. I had done the one smart thing that morning. I removed the battery from the device, and I hid it. They could not make the resonator work, and they destroyed it. That perhaps saved me from releasing a thug into the various worlds. But I had no tools and only my skills to draw on."

He sighed. It was clear that some of these memories were painful.

"I was fortunate that I could eat some of the foods, not many, and water is present everywhere. I lost a great deal of weight but I was able to gather just enough material to make a crude resonator and escape that world. I was able to go back one world and get a stone as a marker. I then recovered what resources I could and built my strength. There was another world coming into alignment, a technical one, and they had all sorts of advanced devices.

"With the help of a family that I befriended, they showed me how to synthesize the proper nutrition and gave me a new computer. I built a much better resonator and put a considerable tool kit together as I worked. In exchange, I provided them with brief travel to a resonant world that had mineral wealth at hand, and they made a handsome profit.

"So I left them and made a new map of worlds, and I returned to Fennio to see if I could find anything of my original belongings. It was not good. But I was successful in recovering a data cartridge from my computer and making an interface for it. I was able to save some of my map data at least, or all would have been lost."

It put so much into perspective. "And now you probably leave backups of everything wherever you go, right?"

"Without exception. I have resources all along my trail that allow me to recover what I need. Like the safe storage boxes on Karoom. And all along, I have been creating a trail that I hoped to recover, or to at least point the way to my world. Laboring under the impression that I was permanently lost. But Nyos here says that my parents did leave me a crystal. What's more, it is in a location that I would be very unlikely to have to worry about.

"So how do we go about getting it?"

I looked at her and she looked at Lyt. "I can remove it for you."

"Well. I believe that I knew this was coming. At least peripherally."

She stared at his leg, seeing things I could only imagine. "With your permission."

Lyt raised the coat and his pants cuff, revealing a pale hairless shin and knee. Nyos placed her left hand behind his leg to stabilize it and slowly plunged her right hand into the leg itself. "There may be some discomfort."

Lyt's expression went through a couple of phases. "My, how unusual. Disturbing actually." Her fingers seemed to trawl slowly and make small movements of coaxing. The flesh parted slightly and a dim violet bead emerged from between muscle and skin. Nyos slowly withdrew her fingertips and the bead fell neatly into her palm as the opening irised shut.

The flesh was unbroken and the bead was clean. She handed it to Lyt with great care. "You may find your home world now."

Standing slowly, she turned to the door. I wasn't as surprised by it all as I might have thought, but Lyt seemed unphased. "Nanotechnology can be used to do some amazing things. What surprised me most is her ability to move through objects. That is something else again. I have no explanation for that at all."

I wouldn't know. "She said her people were old and powerful. She took me to a non-resonant world. One with two suns."

Lyt looked at me as if I were crazy. "You are sure?"

"Yes, absolutely. She can go anywhere. Anywhere at all."

He had an expression I couldn't puzzle out. After a few breaths he said, "This is bad. Very bad. And you, you called her your wife. Is this true? Have you committed yourself to her?"

"Gladly. And yes, it's true. We got married on Earth yesterday."

"I see the attractions that she has. I cannot find fault in your choice. But be aware, very aware, that she is unknowable and very powerful."

"She's helped you, Lyt. What motivation would she have to do that if you were her enemy?"

"Very advanced races have inscrutable aims. We cannot know, nor are we smart enough to figure out, just what she might want."

"That's easy. She wants to spend our lives together, to travel and see things."

He nodded. "Yes, but she can travel anywhere with a thought. What does she need from you? It's your viewpoint, your perception. You will see things differently from her, and she needs that from you."

"Lyt, that's true in any marriage. We share and support, we help each other to become more than we are individually. Right?"

He closed his eyes and exhaled softly. "Perhaps you are right; I truly hope that is it. Please my friend, do be careful. You have crossed a threshold with your commitment to her."

We parted in the workshop, he with his new link to his home world and I with a head full of things to consider. I needed to go to Earth and make a phone call.

I took the floater and loaded my dirt bike on it along with the bag of metals that Lyt had given me. There was a set of halogen lights that fit nicely on the railing and a small battery pack for operating them. It took a few minutes to hook them up.

A quick look at the computer showed me something I had known but had not kept up with. The connection to Melios with Earth was going to end soon. The connection with the world of giant trees was also going to end within a couple of days.

The map always changes.

I kissed Nyos and told her I was getting the floater packed. "Do you want to come with me? No more disguises. You can be yourself."

"I will join you shortly. I have some things I need to do."

That was strange but she is capable of taking care of herself. "Of course."

Minutes later I was flying over small arroyos and gullies, watching a spreading field of fine grassy stuff that mingled into the edge of the desert soil. Hardpan and crunchy mud polygons spread below, dotted with scrubby little bushes. There was a resinous smell to the air tonight and it was warmer than usual.

I settled the floater where I could be near a gas station. I should think about getting a cell phone for this sort of thing. The dirt bike came off the floater and I checked everything. Gas, oil, battery. Everything was good.

I transited the dirt bike to the side of the gas station and started it. There was very little traffic since it was just after midnight. A short ride took me to a pay phone and from there I called the number on the paper that Nyos had given me.

"This is Morgan." He seemed to have a slight accent I could not place.

"Hello, Morgan. My name is Michael Winston. I was given your number."

"Yes, Mr. Winston. I am presently searching for a piece of property that meets your needs. Do you have an email address where I might send a report and some potential candidates?"

"Uh, yeah." I gave him my email. Searching for property?

"There is an island off the coast of Africa that can be purchased and is amenable to your terms. We will only need a good faith deposit from you. Your partner indicated that you will be transferring hard currency. I will send a connection for a courier and we will make all arrangements. Can you meet with our agent in Aruba in three days?"

"Sure. Put all the information in the email."

"Very good. Now, your deposit is completely bonded and insured, and will be fully refunded if you are not satisfied with our service. We expect a five percent commission on the actual transaction if it is concluded as agreed."

"That's not a problem." I was slightly winded from the words that were coming from the earpiece. "No problem at all."

"I- just out of curiosity, Mr. Winston. Our firm would be interested to know if you are the same Michael Winston that is presently... uhm, wanted for questioning. It won't be a factor in our transaction, but we have a legal requirement to have certain information for our protection."

Questioning. That's a diplomatic way of putting it.

"I probably am."

"Very well, sir. I will personally get that information to you right away."

"Thank you. Have a nice day."

"And you as well, sir."

Click.

What did she do? Some firm is looking for property for me? My mind was in a loop, trying to fit it in. An island off the coast of Africa. But why not? Once purchased, it would be a logical place to do things from and not be bothered by authorities.

What would it entail? You purchase an island and declare yourself a government. You need infrastructure, like buildings and power, food supplies and communications, living space. People.

This was going to be complicated. But if any small country can do it, I have at least as much wealth as some of them and I could easily get population. So that was the answer to those issues, at least to the first approximation.

So, first things first. I buy an island and I'm going to need to name it something. Then I start building. Well, no. I establish a bank account with something big like a Swiss banking firm, and I deposit a lot of money in it. Come to think of it, they accept precious metals, and really that tended to be their basis for ages. It's probably good enough today. So how do you transfer your money to a Swiss bank, if it happens to be a few tons of gold or platinum?

And that was the need for a bonded courier. I knew that from some of the work I had done. You have an appraiser come in and test the materials, certify it, and then an insurance policy is issued to cover it. Then your courier comes in and transports it with a company of their choosing. You are credited with your balance and the balance is backed by the metals. It remains safely in a vault somewhere and you really don't care where.

I certainly didn't. I expected to spend it. It wasn't like I was going to run out.

So I stopped at the internet cafe and retrieved my email and found the information from the firm that was searching for an island. I could do this. Nyos had provided everything to make this plan, this *dream* become a reality. Nyos, the maker of dreams.

The deposit was considerable. But I didn't have any problem with it; my first retrieval from Birga would cover the whole transaction. I looked over the list of candidates. Some were quite interesting, just a few square kilometers of unused or abandoned island that was owned by some nation or another. They were willing to sell it off with a clean title to help stock their national coffers.

It would be great to be able to figure out where these places would be on the map, and also on the desert world. If it was feasible, we could get there easily and then transit over. Or Nyos would take me.

The day was being laid out for me, but that was okay. I decided it was safe to get coffee and a doughnut. I stuffed the laptop in the saddle rack of the bike.

Not two blocks away was an all night doughnut shop. I rode into the lot and felt jarred by the total normality of it. You cannot tell, I realized, if the person in the next booth in a restaurant or in the next line at the store has just stepped here from a place halfway around the universe. The breath they exhale might have come from some distant world, created by plants under a strange sun.

I got a chocolate frosted glazed and a blueberry cake doughnut and a cup of hot coffee with one sugar and a cream. A television up in the corner was covering the news. The news anchor droned on about financial difficulties and riots and floods.

I ate my chocolate doughnut in about four bites and drowned each one with a gulp of the hot liquid. It was blissful and simple.

The young guy, about seventeen, who was behind the counter said, "Hey, you look kinda like that guy." He was pointing at the television.

I had to look. "Yeah, you're right. The resemblance is scary." I watched the reporter, now a woman; she was saying that the story got stranger with every new piece of information. Then a clip of our wedding was shown. There was a short piece of footage with Preacher Kitty saying that we hurried in, got married, and vanished again.

The announcer went on. "The original search for Winston was over a matter of a highly refined laboratory grade of the precious metal iridium which is similar to platinum but much more rare. Authorities are trying to verify the origin of the metal and suspect that it is part of a stolen shipment that vanished in 1993, which had a similar composition. The metals stolen in that shipment were valued at over 2.2 million dollars."

I saw a short clip of a vault showing bars of gold, which had nothing to do with the story. Then the two news announcers chatted back and forth. The male announcer said, "Well, I don't know if the wedding video is a hoax or not but it sure looks real. Not like a computer graphic. And the preacher who married Winston and his girlfriend swears it's all legitimate. How it ties in with the theft is anyone's guess."

The woman announcer said, "Maybe even aliens have good taste in jewelry." They both laughed and went on to the price of biofuels made from corn.

The doughnut shop counter clerk said, "Wow. That's just weird. What do you think of that?"

"Aw, you know how it is. They make things sound better to sell more airtime and newspapers. Blown out of proportion you know." I bit the blueberry doughnut and heard the door open. The clerk did a full double take.

I nonchalantly sipped and said, "Oh, here comes my wife now." Nyos was dressed but not hiding herself. I invited her over and we both sat. The counter guy was almost dancing back and forth, not sure what to do.

"You're the guy! You're the guy!"

"Hey, please. We're trying to hear the news and have some coffee." He stopped dancing around but was obviously in distress.

He quieted a bit and I finished my doughnut. "Could I get a lid for this coffee? And a refill?" The counter guy looked around anxiously and found the proper lid. I brought my cup to him and he refilled it but was staring the whole time at Nyos. It was getting pretty close to the brim.

"Whoa, pardner." He pulled the coffee urn back with a start. He had the look of panic.

"Is she really an alien?"

Nyos approached him quietly. "Yes."

His face paled slightly. To his credit he did recover his composure well.

"What's the story, really? Did you steal that metal?"

I fielded that one. "No. That's a cover to give them an excuse to arrest me. You're being lied to. That metal has nothing to do with anything. I had some metal, I sold it, they got nosy about it."

"And she's an alien. Wow." He kept staring at her.

"Look kid, don't believe what you see on TV. There's an old saying. Believe half of what you read and none of what you hear. And nothing you see on television."

He stopped his little movements. "Oh. But. I mean, an alien. Wow."

"There are millions, billions of planets out there. More. And a lot of them have life and aliens. I've been to a few of those planets myself." I had an inspiration.

"Kid, you have a phone number? Give it to me. I'm going to be hiring some people pretty soon." He scrambled for a piece of paper and then wrote his name and number on the back of a sales ticket.

"What's your name?"

"Kyle."

"Okay, Kyle. I might be calling you, or she might. Just keep quiet and let things be. But just relax, we're not stealing anything or hurting anyone. We're trying to help."

He went back to dancing a little.

I left him a hundred and we walked out to the dirt bike. "Dear, could you hold my coffee?"

Nyos perched on the back of the seat, took my coffee, and off we went. The transit point was just around the corner. She asked me a question.

"You said that your people don't want to believe in aliens, and I see conflicting evidence in my research. Why do you openly show me to people now when you would not before?"

"For one thing, I love you and I want everyone to know it. I'm proud to be married to you. For another, if a few people at a time see the facts, acceptance grows a little at a time. In ones or twos we can show people and they can't deny the evidence of their senses. Before, I had to keep as quiet as I could so we would not be arrested before Lyt could finish his work."

"I see."

"Dear, as much as I wanted to be seen with you, I had to accept that I couldn't have what I wanted then. I had to be patient. Now I can do as I please. As long as I'm cautious."

We transited to the floater and I clicked on the lights. We lifted smoothly to a few meters above the ground and I took the lid off the coffee and sipped. Drat. No sugar or cream. But it was still pretty good.

"So I spoke to Morgan. He sent me some information. You are brilliant. Perfect. Thank you so much!" She smiled then and became softer and more affectionate. "You seem to know just how to get things done."

"I am helping you on your quest. It is sure to be an adventure."

"Oh, yes. I have no doubts about that."

We rode back in the darkness, feeling the rush of wind and seeing the splash of halogen light on the ground from the lamps on the guard rail. In moments we were making out like high school kids.

The computer alerted us to the upcoming destination and reluctantly I broke a long kiss and sighed contentedly. Adventure and an exciting life. How could all of this ever happen to anyone? I felt like I had some sort of guardian angel. And really I did.

The camp scene was surprising once more. Lyt was directing machines and the floodlight banks were back from Birga. So were the floaters.

"Mike, have you thought for a moment about the responsibility of recovering tons and tons of materials? How, if there were an emergency, would you move or store this?"

Well, he had me there.

"I'm going to be disposing of a lot of it in three days. And I'll build a... oh, I guess some sort of mobile vault."

Lyt shook his head. "Well, I cannot take you to task for this too harshly. You may hear one day of what I did on Thanosa in my early time as a traveler. What an embarrassment that was." He laughed ruefully. "Ah, that crater will still be bubbling for eons." This laugh was more hearty. "Eons!"

"Crater?"

Nyos actually smiled at that. "They use radioisotopes as currency there. Mostly thorium-233."

As if that explained it all.

Oh, wait.

So here I had to confront the issues of activity gone overboard. There was the mountain of goods that Nyos had given me, with stuff I could not even guess at within. Then there was the first day's haul from Birga, which I had committed to a transaction in a short time. It would be gone. But this!

The robots had been called off, the floaters were back and the light bars set up to show my folly.

There were eight huge stacks of bars, nearly blocks, all gleaming and I really didn't know what they all were. Gold was obvious. Silver was present as well, but it took a lot of space. Platinum, hmm, it *did* have a different sheen from the silver. Silver has an almost yellowish look to it. But what to do with it all?

I looked for a robot to ask. "How much of this stuff is there?"

"Approximately four hundred eighty tons."

The ground was compressed and sagging beneath the immense weight of it all. A quick check with the computer showed the numbers to be unbelievable. I actually was short of breath. "I have a problem here."

I walked slowly around the stacks and hyperventilated a bit.

"Okay, I overdid it. What do I do now?"

I was going to have to get another courier.

But other problems were here now. I had instructed Boron to locate and recruit any robots, and so he did. There was a small army of robots now, all sorts of robots. Things that looked prosaic like boxes with arms and treads, and other things that looked just plain alarming.

Of course he had help; there was no way they could have loaded and carried this all themselves. Somehow they had conscripted a load of robots, then activated some local transportation, and hauled all of it to four transit points. Once there, they loaded half of the robots and ground transport vehicles and transited them. Now they had a huge workforce and had retrieved power generators, vehicles, robots, and computers.

In a day I had inadvertently created a small industrial movement. But that also gave me another idea.

"Okay, we need mobile storage and power. Where do we get the materials to make floaters? How do they work? We need to find out how to create a larger resonator that can move a hundred tons at a whack. And I only have two more days with Birga."

Lyt begged off. "I am very tired. You must handle your own interplanetary crisis." He went to his cabin and emerged a few minutes later with towel and swim trunks. The scamp! He was going for a soak in the hot tub.

Well, I set the robots to park all the vehicles a little ways off from the workshop on the far site from Lyt's cabin. Then I had all the computers and other sensitive items brought indoors. Was there the equivalent of a building supply on Birga? I needed materials. Time for another massive effort.

This time I programmed Boron to gather sheets of building materials, structural metal, and whatever else I could think of. Then we created a new building site a hundred meters away and in the mini-moose world so we could work without bothering him.

All through the night the machines worked to some impromptu plans I made in the computer. They imported more generators and welding equipment. A large foundation was prepared and the equivalent of concrete poured. It was some sort of industrial polymer that required two parts plus electric current to set.

Then the building was made but just set on top of the slab, not actually fastened to it. I started with a box beam structure and kept everything round. As I worked the design seemed to grow itself, and the pieces fell into place under their own volition.

Robots began appearing with I-beams and plates, plasma cutters and rivets. The frame was growing as I watched; a large disk nearly seventy meters across and supported by some lightweight metal beams that seemed to be aluminum but worked as easily as steel.

Nearby was a large rectangular frame with moving arms that was creating custom made box trusses from a sizable stock of metallic tubing. It was some sort of automated beam creating machine, weaving heavier tubing into an outline and welding smaller tubing sections into an extended web of triangles. The robots would accept the extruding beams and carry them to their intended locations in the growing structure.

Now a very solid double-thickness wall, all supported internally by some of those triangular box beams doubled side by side, and filled with an expanding foam insulating material. It was welded onto the disc shaped base. It was after three in the morning and I was still jazzed, watching an amazing thing taking shape.

In the meantime, we located information on the vehicles in Birga, and found that they seemed to be very similar to the floater plates Lyt had stashed in the storage boxes. We could get hundreds of floater plates from the vehicles and the factories. We did.

These were fastened uniformly throughout the ceiling and floor of the building and power lines for everything run to a central generator. Five in the morning, and still materials came in and the work continued.

Wall panels were either sandwiched metal sheets with honeycomb interiors or some sort of pressed plastic sheet not too different from plywood. A strange robot with roll welders for hands was moving through the interior of the building putting things together. It looked like an automobile factory run amuck.

Splatters of welding arc and sparks, sounds of metal plates landing and being fastened, and three big plasma cutters slicing curves and plates to match the needs. It was all very entertaining to watch. Sheet metal was being formed, curved, cut. Plates were fastened over the entire outer surface, being applied to some sort of gel-like insulation that seemed to draw up to it greedily. The seams appeared to melt away, leaving a smooth, burnished outer appearance.

By seven AM the sun was coming up and the robots were putting the last of the roof in place. Some had started moving the bullion from the stacks near the camp and placing them in storage rooms equally spaced around the perimeter of the building. The ceiling was high enough inside; I had them make it nine meters and foam everything for insulation. I also foresaw the need for air conditioning and heating and so there were slots located all around the top in eight locations that would support the vents for it.

I was wearing down at last, feeling a little punchy. The robots were building bays for each machine with charger plugs and computer interface plugs. There were four large doors located around the building and the doors were equipped with ramps. Floaters moved in carrying loads of supplies and tools. I had the mountain of boxes and containers that Nyos had given me moved inside, and there were ample storage rooms for everything.

In the middle of the whole thing I had the holographic entertainment system installed in its own room. The room was surrounded by places to put computers. There was a growing network that would allow the machines to communicate with each other and while it was nowhere near ready to use, it was something that could be worked on over time.

Through it all, I saw little of Nyos but she was watching everything with great interest. Lyt would have nothing to complain about because everything would be out of the way. I started to load his safe storage boxes but stopped- they were his and he would want to decide how to handle them.

Now about that resonator. I thought of a solution. If I were to make resonators the same way the floater plates were, I could match them all together and fire them simultaneously, creating a single larger resonator field. The problem was, I know nothing about electronics at all. I turned to Nyos and the robots.

She agreed that it was the way to do it, and she also said it would require a large network of signals to be sent to all of them from one central amplifier. So I could make a couple of hundred mutant tuning forks and drive all of them from one amplifier, greatly simplifying the system.

Boron had built a number of the things already and knew exactly how to mass produce them. Lyt's shop was pressed into service.

He was rather surprised to see all the machines and metals gone. He was more surprised to see me in the workshop puzzling out resonators and their mechanisms. The army of robots and vehicles was gone although the desert floor was the worse for the traffic. "Oh, good morning Lyt. Want some coffee?" I was grinning.

"Winds and thoughts, no! I thought I recognized that hideous stench from my cabin. And what have you been up to all night?"

I had a wicked grin. "I should show you." I detached myself from the circuit diagram and the computer that was patiently explaining things to me and set my resonator.

"We should transit next door to the mini-moose world."

I vanished and a moment later he appeared next to me. The workshop was almost done, only the internal work was being finished. I pulled out my car remote and clicked it.

A klaxon sounded and the ramps retracted. Doors rolled down and shut. The building came to life and lifted a few meters from the ground. I turned to him, grinning.

"Big floater, Lyt."

He nearly fell over.

"You know, that underside is sort of ugly. I might want to cover it over with some sort of sheet metal or something."

He staggered and took a few steps toward it. "You! You did this?"

I was showing more teeth than ever. "Oh, yeah. I need it anyway. On second thought, the underside is fine. Nobody I know will be seeing it. Spray paint, yeah."

"This is- I have no words! Are you insane?"

"Well, probably. I've been hanging out with unusual people a lot in the last couple of weeks."

"I could have used your audacity forty years ago! What are you going to do about a resonator? It must weigh hundreds of tons!"

"Oh, I figured that out, and closer to fifteen thousand tons when I'm done. I had some help of course. The machines are making it now. Oh, and I'll replace the parts from the shop." Going shopping today. You need anything from the surplus store?"

"Oh, you. So you have a world to save and you are not wasting any time doing it."

"Time is precious. I stayed up all night to personally see that this got done. I conscripted more machines, gathered more materials, and made it happen. Is there anything that you might need when you go to your home world? For that matter, when you go to save that other world?"

He began walking toward the floating building. "I am sure to give it my thoughts."

I clicked my key remote once more. The building settled slowly and once down, the doors opened again. Ramps extended and robots seemed to be impatiently waiting in line to exit the building.

Lyt walked up the nearest ramp and looked at the smooth welding and plating. "Marvelous." He walked past the storage rooms and peered into a few. "Organized, yes." Light panels and strips were being finished off and the mass of wires and cables was starting to vanish inside wall spaces.

"See? These will be living quarters, here we have workshops and these are slots for each of the robots. Each one has its proper power system and charger, and they all will be networked to the main computers in here." I showed him where all sorts of alien machines could be plugged in.

"No matter what world we go to, if we can get some computers from it, we can hook them into this network. It's going to take a lot of work, but we'll use one as the control and it will handle the communications with the others. That way it's simpler."

I showed him the holographic system in the center. "This is like our library. We can get to all the data here and see it as it was recorded." Fresh carpeting was in place, but there were no seats yet. I had to give it time.

He couldn't believe it.

"Oh, one last thing. See where the big empty slot is by that door? Our cabin parks there. There's another slot on the other side, just for you. And the hot tub cabin goes there. Only your workshop doesn't fit inside. But I only had one night you know."

When the tour was done, we walked back down the ramp. "Well, time for me to check on the resonator progress. I need one large power amplifier to run things. There's a place I might be able to get one already made, and the robots are looking for it now."

After a moment, I said, "Oh, and Lyt- feel free to use the factory stuff to make whatever. We have a whole industrial zone here now."

I transited back to the workshop in the desert world, leaving Lyt to marvel a bit.

CHAPTER 14

Time was running out rapidly on our access to Birga. I had everything I needed and much more, so I didn't take that as hard as I might.

We saved all the data we could and recovered crystals that were labeled and cataloged, then matched them against the data in my computer map.

I was worn out. The night, while productive, had taken its toll. Two days left but I could spare some sleep time. I had exceeded my needs and that was a great help.

There was more to do such as installing worktables and plumbing, and I had barely looked at the things Nyos had delivered. I wanted to just immerse myself in it all. But after trying to keep moving, I found that I was getting goofy and it was time to relax.

Lyt was excited. He had identified three worlds that might be his, and the configurations of nearby worlds were all encouraging. This narrowed his search greatly. He was terribly excited.

The workshop ran out of parts, and although I did make a surplus store run, we had bought most of the stock of useful parts. I did find an audio amplifier that would world perfectly with the resonators, and it was stereo which was exactly what we needed.

Resonator parts were being installed as rapidly as they were made. The machines scrounged up spools of copper wire and one expedition returned some spools of black, glassy looking stuff that couldn't possibly be wire but it was. It was some sort of superconductor or something. I shelved it against future need.

After it was all done, noon had passed and I knew that a crash and burn was eminent. I was just plain loopy by then. Everything was funny, I laughed too much and too loud, and the sun was too bright and things just way out of proportion.

The cabin looked inviting. I closed all the shades and pulled off my clothing. I needed a shower but that wasn't important yet. The bed was.

Dragging myself there was the last great effort. Pulling back the covers was almost too much. I slid between the sheets and just allowed my head to flop on the pillows. I heard nothing as Nyos entered. She sat quietly on the bed and began to stroke my head. It sounded like she was humming to me. I faded out gracefully.

I had a strange jumbled dream. Lyt was plugging me in to the computer network in the hub of my new circular workshop. "It's all binary. You said yes so that bit is true. She got you and now we have to download everything."

I couldn't struggle and then a smooth, glassy hand stroked my face. "I love adventures. I want to save all the excitement. I live for it, don't you?"

I woke up enough to change the track of the dream, then realized that it was just that. I slept again and it was much more peaceful. I awoke as evening was arriving.

The camp was quiet. Low orange sun was striking long shadows.

Lyt's workshop was quiet as well. The black spheres were gone and all the machines had disappeared.

It took a few minutes to shower and get changed into something clean. Stars were starting to appear and a quiet, warm wind blew from west to east. Tiny fluffy things like dandelion seeds blew by, and that resinous scent was in the air once more. Perfect.

I transited to the new workshop. There was some action going on there. I had to see what was happening.

I took the short walk across the grassy field of boulders where so many feet and treads had trampled it down. The moose-things were making some sort of noise like "ork ork" and then they would hoot a long note. The sunlight shone off the curving metal of the work shop and left slight dazzle spots in my eyes.

The ramp was down and the door open. I walked up the metal deck plate with a soft clump, clump from my thick rubber boot soles. What a difference!

Most of the niches had a robot in them. They were all charging, small indicator lights on some. The floor had been carpeted in some areas and wall partitions were in place to divide the work rooms from the general floor space.

I walked through the larger central room and found a well equipped kitchen. Somebody had done some shopping without me and had acquired sinks, stove tops, pots and pans. The plumbing worked; water bubbled from the faucet as it should. There was a pair of top end microwave ovens. A great deal of work had gone into making things complete.

I wandered through the spaces and saw that all the light strips were done. Doors were hung and everything had that air of newness to it. I heard some voices in the central room. On the way to the entrance it was clear that the computer slots were wired and ready for any sort of machine we might find.

"Ah, there he is. You have good timing." Lyt had some hand tools and was tinkering with some sort of control box he had made.

"You were right to pick up that amplifier. It is ideal for driving resonators. I have installed it and we are ready to take some readings."

Nyos was working with him. This was something that made me feel better; even through his misgivings, Lyt was practical. Nyos was smiling shyly and gave me a hug.

"Thank you dear for helping me relax. I went to sleep immediately when you started humming. It was very sweet."

Even Lyt seemed touched by the words.

"You wife has been very busy. She went shopping on Earth today and picked up all the things to finish off the work here."

Oh?

"You went to Earth and went shopping. Wow. Tell me about it."

She had a playful look. "I thought about what you said last night. I also considered the reaction of the sales person in the doughnut shop. He wasn't really scared of me, just not sure of how to react. He was more scared of what you might do. He had been told you were a criminal."

"Well, probably. I didn't sort things out that way. But do go on."

"I went to a large building supply and appliance store. I took money with me. I approached the sales clerk and she was nervous but when I told her what I was looking for, she became more reasonable and less panicky. She worked from what she knew."

I shook my head up and down. Of course.

"So I listed my needs and she showed me merchandise. There were many people who stared and gathered but nobody was angry or violent. The clerk had the items placed on flat carts and I paid for them. Then I transited the items here."

"So, nobody questioned you or tried to stop you?"

She looked askance. "The clerk asked me if I was an alien and I said yes. She then asked me why I needed appliances and I said they were for my husband."

It was so logical that I just accepted it. I thought back to an old television show where they would hide a camera and then do outrageous things. People would mostly just act like they didn't notice or didn't care. It was true that for the most part, nobody would confront others. Whatever it says about human psychology, it works.

Lyt was powering circuits and testing things. "Good, very good. You know, this is going to work. All the drive signals are moving at nearly the speed of light in the wires, and the signals are all down around the audible range. There will be no problem in creating a single, unified resonator field. Amazing."

Nyos gave me a sunny smile. "Adventure."

"Well, yes, I think we need to abandon ship for the test run. Right, Lyt?"

"Oh, absolutely. While I trust that it will work as you say, I don't want to be in the damn thing when you first do it."

He echoed my thoughts perfectly.

"Okay, let's program the resonator for a quick trip to the world next door, and then back to here. I think one of us should be waiting at the destination, and the other two here to start the sequence and then de-fuse this thing once it returns." I started for the door.

Nyos followed right behind me.

"My wife. I'm proud of you. In so many ways. You did great today."

"I hoped you would think so."

I walked down the ramp with her head on my shoulder and Lyt not far behind us.

The night had fallen. I slept the day away but to good effect. We stood a few meters from the floating building, waiting for Lyt to be ready. I clicked my keychain.

The klaxon sounded, the ramps retracted, and the doors closed. Nyos and I transited to the desert world and waited.

With a thump and a soft rush of air, the workshop appeared. "Oh man, it works!"

It hung quietly for about five seconds, then it vanished with a faint thump.

"Let's go see Lyt."

We transited and watched as he clenched his fists and laughed. "Michael, I should have found you years ago. Now I seem to remember you telling that you have an idea of how to communicate across the worlds. Do you remember what you said?"

"Sure. We'll have to do that next."

"What do you have planned next?"

"I'm taking a cruise to the southeast. Way southeast. We should be in Aruba in a couple of days, and then we'll probably go to an island. Hey, want to come along? It's going to be fun."

Lyt looked at his computer and nodded. "Of course. I wouldn't miss this."

"Hey, I just had a thought."

"Oh, not another one!" He threw his hands up in mock distress.

"Well, we can cruise all over the place but we can also go to other worlds while we do it. So let's see some outrageous scenery on the way. Get some videos and check some things out."

He smiled broadly. "Truly. Well traveled and well equipped we shall be."

We transited to Lyt's workshop and moved it to the new floating building. Our cabins were packed up and transited to the building as well. We parked everything in the bays and tested the water and power connections. The robots were secure, the machines packed, and the generators running. Once the loading was done, we tied Lyt's workshop to the floating building with a thick nylon rope and programmed its resonator to match our own.

We transited to the desert world and checked the site. Nothing had been left.

Lyt had routed the system through the holographic room. There were cameras mounted on the floating shop, which we decided to name the Roundhouse. I was almost trotting to the central room where a large soft couch had been installed. It gave a great view of the wrap around display. It also was very comfortable.

From within the hologram we could set and navigate everything. "Okay, let's take it up to one hundred meters. We're heading southeast and will be moving at one hundred kilometers per hour. Now you know why I made this thing round."

We started out slowly but soon the ground was moving along beneath us at a respectable rate. The view was perfect, and the desert below was coloring red as the sun dipped below the horizon. Soon it was black outside and we could only see because the cameras were capable of sensing infrared. But not long after sunset the infrared sky glow was gone and we were cruising through the inky night with the ground just barely visible below us.

After a couple of hours of this, I gave Lyt the controls. "I need some food. Time to fix something worthwhile and check out the new kitchen."

I had to go to my cabin to search through my freezer. Once there I took out some frozen burritos and carried them to the new kitchen. The shelves were stocked with dishes and glasses and I thought of a potential problem. I hadn't really designed this to be used during rough weather. I would have to add some sort of tiedowns or something to keep dishes and glasses from falling out and breaking.

But the problem wasn't as bad as I thought. The dishes were melamine, so they would survive a fall easily. Only the glasses would suffer. I wondered if we had a vacuum cleaner.

So my first meal in the Roundhouse was a couple of frozen burritos and some cola. It could have been better but then, it could also have been worse. "How's it going, Lyt?"

"Quite nicely I must say. The computer has been matching our progress up with the map of Earth and we are advancing quite well. But we should install some sort of ranging system."

"Good point. Let's slow it down, find a good landing site, and install some of these lights on the bottom."

He dropped our speed greatly and we began to make out the features below more clearly. We were still over desert and scrub so there was no problem with a good landing site. We came down almost to touching the ground.

I gathered a couple of robots and three of the stadium light bars. That would make a nice start. We raised the Roundhouse a couple of meters and the robots began installing the lights up in the recess under the frame. Wiring was another issue. They just drilled a hole for each where they would come up into the hollow wall interior.

While on the ground I took a look at Lyt's workshop, which had been dutifully following us like a cow on a rope. That was my real concern. I had to keep the speed down so it wouldn't end up getting ripped to shreds.

Within a half hour, the light bars were in place and everything reloaded. It took a little while to hook up power to them but once done, we were back in flight.

Now we could see the ground well enough for the holographic cameras to show the scene. After another hundred kilometers of this, we decided to transit to the mini-moose world and see what we might see. We slowed to be certain that the transit would work.

There was a completely different setting here. A chain of lakes was below us, surrounded by marshy territory that seemed to stretch forever. "Lyt, let's raise it to a kilometer, slowly. Better chance we won't run into anything. Wonder what Nyos is doing."

Lyt seemed content to fly the Roundhouse. I brought him some bottled water and asked him if he would like some pizza rolls. He accepted and I heated a few for him. "Well, the pizza itself is much better but these are not bad."

He munched quietly as he piloted the building.

I was impressed by the constant wind and a faint whistling sound. There must have been some leaks that the air was getting through, but it wasn't critical. There was plenty of foam inside the walls and the wind wasn't that great. A good storm would put more wind load on a house on the ground.

The real wind noise came from the large doors rattling and I thought about the need for an outer door of some type that would shield them from the direct wind force. A few sketches on the computer and I had something that looked pretty good.

Lyt was finally getting tired of the piloting. I took his place and we cruised for a while longer. It was going to be another long night for me.

The look at the ground was not really that difficult. The display was being turned into a high contrast outline of the horizon from the low light level, and to help things out we had a fat crescent of a moon rising and giving off a little bit of light.

As the ground flowed below us I played with some designs in the computer. I could get the robots working on the parts and when we took a break at landing, the hardware could be made and installed. At least that was the theory. Where was Nyos?

She kept coming to mind, and I missed her. I didn't want to leave the Roundhouse unpiloted but there wasn't a whole lot going on. My watch said 2 AM. This was getting to be a habit.

I checked the display and saw that everything was flat for a long way in all directions. The house wouldn't care and things looked safe. I locked out the controls and kept my computer in my hand so I could see everything as we flew. Standing and twisting my back slowly until it made a mild crunch noise, I felt like doing a little walking around and seeing if I could find Nyos. The carpet muffled a lot of the sound and the wind made a soft rumble every so often as the turbulence would change.

The hallways were about half-lit. Everything was quiet except for the occasional rattle as the wind might shake the place a bit. I walked past the row of robots in niches and made the big circle of the place. The first stop was the slot with our cabin parked near the big door.

Nobody was inside. It was time for a quick check of the computer display and it showed that the path was still clear and flat. Great, I had plenty of leeway. There were some regular shoes in the closet instead of the boots I was wearing and I changed into them to feel at least a little more comfortable.

We needed some windows. It was a shame we couldn't just look out. Another glance at the computer and it was time to raid the refrigerator for something cold to drink.

Swigging on a bottle of soda, I made the walk around to the next bay and found the generator and hot tub shack. That was a mess. The water had sloshed out of the hot tub and it was all over the floor and soaked into the carpeting. Oh, there was still a good half meter of water in the thing but the lesson wasn't lost on me. Prepare before flight. You couldn't drive a car with a hot tub full of water in it, so why should I assume that you can fly a building with one?

I called on a couple of robots to help clean up the mess. The computer still showed no obstacles. I was getting a little too relaxed with walking around and doing things. It was time to get back to the control room.

By now it was getting close to three. The chain of lakes below had long vanished and now we were flying over a meandering river and some low cliffs. An occasional hill or small rocky protrusion below gave the ground some interesting character. I was playing with the display settings when Nyos entered the room.

"Ah, there you are. I was looking all over for you. Well, half of all over."

She took a seat next to me on the soft couch. I was just finishing my soda and looking for a place to put the bottle.

"I was negotiating."

This was enough to create visions of finances and property sales and who knows what else in my mind. "You seem to be very good at that. Do you call people on the phone or email them or what?"

"I often go to their place of business."

That was startling. "Oh. You just sort of walk in and say 'Hi, I need an island. Here's a billion dollars' or what?"

"Oh, no. I say I am from another world and I need to purchase an island. And I usually give them some gold as a token of good faith."

Sensible. "Well, money talks." I turned to her. "And you never have any trouble?"

She shook her head. "No. People want money and they are much more reasonable about business than you might think. Money overcomes most any fear."

I would have to learn that and keep that lesson close to my heart. The almighty dollar has been known to corrupt and redirect like no other power. "You've probably hit on the single most powerful concept of dealing with people. Pay them. Even the devil does that."

"Oh. Yes."

I consulted my map display. "Looks like we've covered about six hundred kilometers. Very nice."

How could she find us in motion between different worlds? I hadn't even considered that one. Well, it was a question I would ask another time. It was better to just know that she could and to snuggle against her a little.

"I'm going to transit to the desert world and see what the landscape looks like there." I set the resonators and slowed the roundhouse and Lyt's workshop in tow behind us. It was very quiet in the sky, and bright stars sprinkled the blackness around us.

"Transiting."

No perceptible change but the star patterns shifted around. The ground was gone however and replaced by ocean. I raised the Roundhouse another half kilometer or so and felt safer for unmonitored travel. "Okay, let's take it to a steady one hundred again and let things go."

We were in motion once more and below I could see the moonlight reflected and stretching off on the water's surface. It showed nothing but clear water ahead as we flew toward it. There was a better sense of security knowing that any interruption in the light would mean that something other than water was up ahead.

After a few minutes I took the speed up a notch and continued to do so until I was doing about a hundred twenty. Any more might have dire consequences for Lyt's little building behind us. It was being hit with hurricane force winds. Lyt, however, had done some real engineering on the frame, knowing that it was to be hanging from the floater disc.

This really wasn't a desert world at all. We had simply transited into that type of landscape. But really, that was logical. Any world will have all sorts of territory and all sorts of climate. It seemed odd to me that I always ended up on dry land when water was so much a part of a world's surface. That was one more thing to think about, like I didn't have enough already.

The excitement was starting to wear thin. I called on Boron who was in a charger niche and set him in front of the couch. "Okay, here is what we need."

I showed him the controls.

"We are at an altitude of about 1.5 kilometers and we are traveling at about 120 kilometers per hour. We want to maintain that speed and altitude and our same direction. Keep going southeast."

Boron accepted the controls and checked the holographic display.

"Now, if a mountain, volcano, or other obstacle shows up in our path, just gently curve around it and resume our original direction. Like this."

Taking the controls from him, I made a slight turn and stayed at the angle for a bit, then aimed back along the path we had been following. "You see? Simple enough. You have passengers who depend on your skills to keep them safe. If something is too big to go around, slow down and then stop. Call me. Then I will take over and figure out what to do. Understood?"

"Yes." The controls were handed back. Boron began monitoring the flight. Time was long past for a decent break. I'd been up all night again. This was a terrible way to spend a honeymoon.

"Now, we're ready for a nice cruise. We're over the ocean, no worries, and somebody else is driving. What a deal, right?"

We walked out of the central room which was now consigned to be the control room. Our hands found each other and we walked past the empty workshops and to the kitchen. "How did you know what I wanted in these areas?"

"You left notes in the computer. Your design had labels on much of the space and others I simply made into unfinished rooms with power outlets."

"I didn't realize I had written so much down. I was really tired at the end there. But how did you get the kitchen details right? I know I didn't put all that down."

"I saw showrooms and material online. There are only four things needed in a kitchen. Storage, cooking, washing, preparing. A triangle is the basis of a good design."

"So I guess you went browsing through the kitchen section of the building store. You must have had fun."

She shrugged. "After all, the authorities are after you, not me. I have no difficulty in public. I am what I am and people accept that."

"Hmm. I think that if they believe that you are an alien, things will change radically. Right now they probably think it's a hoax. But that's fine. One long standing principle is 'confusion to your enemies!'"

I rummaged through the shelves a bit and found all sorts of canned and dried foods. There was a freezer full of stuff, I had no idea just what or how much. It was overwhelming.

"What made you do all this, dear? I mean, you don't eat or anything."

She was silent but a moment. "I wanted you to be happy."

"I am. Unbelievably so." I think I hug her a lot. But neither of us has a complaint so I plan to continue doing it.

My feet led me to the storage holds where the mountain of goods and boxes were stored. "I've felt sort of guilty that I haven't taken the time to look at all you've given me. Lyt sort of had me on the spot, with all the scrounging and hauling I was doing."

Her mood became very easy and human. I noticed that she sometimes went to extremes of being quite remote and logical and then becoming almost like a little girl. This was somewhere in the middle but toward the girly end, affectionate and happy.

"I brought things that I thought you would like. And things you might need."

Her grip on my hand tightened slightly. "I want to be sure that you're safe and properly equipped. I can't always be right there with you. You mean so much to me."

What can you say?

"Thank you so much, my dear." The storage room light had a standard light switch on the wall. Simple is good. I flipped the switch and surveyed shelving filling the room from floor to ceiling. Every space was crammed with something exotic and unknown. I selected a container at random.

"Okay, heavy latched box, off-green to gray, single button latch. Let's see what's in the box."

The interior had a foam material with a cavity inside it. Packed in the cavity were glassy black cubes, each about 15 millimeters on an edge. There was a sheet of flimsy rubbery stuff separating them. I counted twenty cubes the long way and four the short way, and they were stacked three deep.

"What are they?"

She moved the foam in the lid down and it separated into a compartment that held a manual of sorts. I pulled it out and held it. It looked like a credit card but smaller and thicker.

Her vitreous finger indicated a small dimple on the card. I smiled at her and pushed it.

This was like a hologram but I can't describe it. A lizard-headed form appeared which was only a few centimeters tall. It walked over the contents of the box, pointing to them and explaining things. I didn't get a word of it. I pushed the dimple again and it froze. My computer was the thing I really needed now.

"Okay, let's try this again. Computer on, translate mode on, let's hear the sales pitch."

A click of the dimple and the figure started over. I let it run through its spiel and then started it from the beginning. My computer got a few words right away.

"See now Optimizer unit best. Designs refinement of engineering tool. Best. No rgsbr rbsbfs needed." Some of the words were spits and hisses but most were translated fairly well. I got the gist of it.

"So these cubes are 'design optimizers' whatever that means. Hmm."

The little hologuy continued. "Designing in space of computer cannot to real world. Best better work working prototype. Real space not in computer space. Quantum mechanical model used makes best short path to product."

He sounded pretty excited so I felt like I should be too. Well, this was definitely worth a second look later on.

I clicked the button a couple of times and the display faded away.

"That was pretty cool. Design optimizer for space real world. Got it." It clicked for me then.

"Ohhhh! Got it! It optimizes real objects, not computer models! How the hell would that work?"

It's just like some aliens to come up with something like that. It also irks me that this computer of mine can translate crap like 'quantum mechanical' but it can't verb a parse phrase decently.

"Wow. If those things work, I can think of a million things I could do with them."

"But you only have two hundred forty of them." She looked up at me with puppy eyes.

"Oh, well, then I had better be really selective." I laughed at that and she got a tentative smile. "No, really, I'm awed. This is beyond anything I could have thought of."

That made her much happier.

I set the optimizer box next to the door. That was a keeper.

I chose another container at random. This was a small one. I opened it and saw six pairs of eyeglasses. The frames were a little large and the lenses odd looking. "Huh."

The first pair lifted easily from something like sand, but whatever it was wouldn't spill out of the container. I ran a finger through it and it felt like silky, slippery sand. Crazy stuff, you really couldn't spill it out. That held my attention for about a minute until a funny picture appeared in my mind. Think of a monkey with a binoculars case, being fascinated by the bubble wrap and ignoring the binoculars.

I must have reddened slightly. Nyos looked concerned. "Oh, it's just me. Never mind. It's all good."

The glasses had a little heft to them. The frames felt like a gel or thick liquid. I squeezed them and they started to change size and shape. Ah, the adjustment was automatic.

"Well, when I'm old and my eyes are bad like Lyt's, then I'll wear glasses."

A soft, hoarse voice said from the door, "My eyes are perfect. I don't need glasses either."

"But you're always wearing..."

He pulled them off and handed the spectacles to me. I looked through them and the image was unchanged. But wait, something odd was happening.

They scrolled through infrared, telescopic, ultraviolet, microscopic and thermal.

Lyt laughed easily. "You see?"

I looked at the fronts and they were unchanged, like simple lenses.

He retrieved his glasses from me and replaced them on his nose. "The smart traveler has backups. And tools, lots of tools. If people see you wearing glasses, they assume you need glasses. They have no idea just what they are for now."

"I figured you had some tricks up your sleeve. I got the idea you had armor and weapons somewhere also. Do you?"

In a flash something gray appeared in his left palm. A brilliant needle thin line of light swept over the bare metal floor and left a line inscribed in it. The gray thing disappeared in a smooth motion.

"Hey! I'm gonna make you- hey, fix that! That's my new floor!" I hadn't expected anything so direct. "Don't go lasering peoples' stuff!" I was partly indignant.

Only partly.

My attention returned to the glasses with new respect. I placed the pair where they belonged and squeezed the frame again. There was a crawly feeling as the glasses snugged, moved, and formed to fit my face and ears. It took a few seconds but they made their adjustments and stopped.

Removing them carefully, I saw that somehow the lenses had even changed to match the frames. "Nanostuff probably." I had missed a little silver spot on each earpiece and the bridge of the nose. They looked like electrical contacts.

"Okay, here goes."

Replacing them, I saw a little bar on the left of the lenses that was like a menu. I looked at the first icon and the scene shifted until the colors were just plain weird. "Well, I've got something here. Not sure of what it is, but I guess it will take practice."

Another glance brought the view to normal. Good enough.

I closed the case and replaced it on the shelf. I used my computer and got a picture of the case and stored the note identifying it. Time to see another case.

Lyt was curious. "Are you finding anything interesting?"

"Absolutely everything. I've only opened two packages and I'm already blown away. It's like magic."

Nyos was beaming. "I hoped you would like this."

I kissed her briefly and turned to another package. This one was little glass ampoules of an amber liquid. I hadn't a clue what it was but it might be a computer, an automobile, or a three course meal.

The Roundhouse veered slightly. "Oh, I'd better see what Boron has found."

I jogged to the control room and saw a large island in front of us. "Oh, wait."

The sun was just peering over the eastern edge of the water and the glare was starting to grow to the left of our path. "Hey Boron, slow down to twenty kilometers per hour and make a circle around that volcano thing."

A perfect cinder cone rose dramatically above the water. We made an orbit of the peak and below I saw an amazing beach and palm trees. Well, okay. They just looked like palm trees but nature seems to work that way. I took the controls and the Roundhouse and Lyt's shack, slaved to the same controls, slowly dropped in altitude and approached the beach area.

This was what I wanted to see. A black porous rocky layer stretched toward the water and pure white sand covered its top and created a beach along it. The waves at the far tip splashed over and around it, and a thin line of trees ran along the ridge back all the way to the bitter end. In the distance was a diagonal black ragged rock sticking out of the water and surrounded by its own perfect beach and line of pseudo-palms. I had never seen anything quite so perfect before.

I could see the sun rising rapidly as I made the approach, and picked a spot that was somewhat higher than the apparent high tide line. The flood light bars were still running so I flipped the switch off for them and brought the Roundhouse down for a perfect hover just half a meter above the ground.

Dawn was breaking and the monstrous cinder cone was at my left while the perfect beach was at my right. "Hey, let's see the beach."

Lyt and Nyos had come into the control room when I took over. "Boron, you did an excellent job. Thanks."

"Yes" was all he said.

I opened the bay door that faced over the ocean, away from the sunrise. The long shadow of the roundhouse was ahead of us, and the roar of surf entered the doorway.

"Lyt, let's make sure your workshop is okay. It's been through a real test."

He retrieved another floater from one of the storage rooms and we piled onto it. The emergence into the daylight was nearly tangible. Soft ocean breeze with a tang of salt blew through my hair as we sedately glided just a meter above the blue-green water. Lyt slowed the floater as we came to a small bay. I looked over and thought I could see dark, amorphous shapes and light branching things. It was a forest of coral.

"Wow, look at this." I was like a kid, looking at crimson darting fish and yellow branches of spongy stuff. The color was starting to grow as the light did. This sun was already a little more orange than I was used to and the colors seemed to pop as it brightened.

Nyos was delighted with the fast-moving things below us. We came to a halt and watched the wind blow through the trees. It was idyllic and attractive. I had an idea.

"Lyt, let's go back to the Roundhouse. There's something I want to try. And we need to know how your workshop fared. It would be a shame to have any damage."

He needed to check his boxes and equipment. "I do have to keep on top of the hard-won resources I have. I don't trawl the worlds for tons of material like some mammals I know." At that I had to ask.

"Are you a mammal, Lyt?"

"No, my people are actually descended from something related to flightless birds long ago. We do have hair, but that is simply a modified feather when you think about it. Modified scales in your case and that of all mammals."

"Nyos, what are your people descended from?"

She turned her head at an angle. "That would be difficult to explain. We are composite beings, created billions of years ago. Some of the makers were of reptile descent and others from bird descent. A number of races cooperated to make us what we are.

"I am not of any descent as a result. We are more... patterns of thought.

My makeup is of patterns in nanomaterials and manipulated spacetime geometry."

"So how did you come to be so human?"

"I was organized from the general template of your genetic code. I have a pattern of mental and sensory wiring that is like your own. My senses and my feelings are human, but with billions of years of information in place."

She looked at the sky and the volcano peak and spoke as if to them. "I was formed to be your complement."

"Oh. So you were made from a, I guess a general template with all this information in it. But you have the sensory system and thought patterns of a human being. So in theory you could have taken any form, depending on who had arrived in the... I keep thinking of it as the eggshell place. Whoever had touched that white gel stuff."

It seemed to trouble her.

With reluctance she said "yes."

"But I was fortunate enough to be the one to find you. And I'm glad I did."

The look she gave me was heart-warming.

Something tickled my brain. "Resonant travel has always been around, right? Isn't it possible that some travelers were on Earth long ago?"

Lyt spoke up. "Of a certainty. They could have been there millions of years ago."

"Nyos, has anyone from your race appeared in times past on Earth, to humans?"

She looked down and then said "yes."

"What would they have looked like? Do you know how they appeared?"

She stood straighter and then began to rise lightly from the floater. She stepped clear of the rail moving backwards and hung over the water, began to expand and took on an iridescent sheen. Her form grew, expanded to three times its original size. A deeper, more powerful voice emerged from her as she began to glow with a corona of faint lightning.

"We were the beings of fire and wind, known as the djinn. We learned of the Earth and saw its people and offered some the chance to live forever with us."

She seemed to droop slightly. "Some worshiped us and others declared us evil. The conflict was inevitable and we left. Only some stories now remain but none of us has been on Earth for over two thousand years."

The glow faded and her size decreased slowly. "They were not ready yet. We were divided over the decision."

I was backed away at the rear rail. I'm sure my knuckles were about to pop out of my hands, as tightly as I had clamped onto the rail. Nyos gently touched down on the floater platform and was her familiar size and appearance. I wasn't sure what would happen; Lyt was open-mouthed at her display.

I wasn't breathing. Nyos watched me with concern. "Mike, I hope you're not unhappy with me. I really didn't know this until you asked. I have a huge amount of information in my mind but I don't know what I know until I think about it. I'm only a few days old and learning how to be an organism from you."

It was terrifying, but how could I turn away from her? My wife, the great love of my life; I couldn't simply run from this. She was like a foundation stone for me, new and unsure of some things, and incredibly capable in others. One thing stayed in my mind, that I needed her and she needed me. We were committed to each other.

I relaxed as much as I could; took her in my arms. "Don't worry, it's scary for you too. We're fine. As long as we love each other, we're fine." I hugged her to me, feeling her hot flesh; far too hot for any person.

Lyt stared at me like I was insane.

I just held her and stroked her, and she seemed to sob a little. "I didn't mean to- to alarm you. It was just- like a reflex or something. Like being there, a playback of some other time."

"Shh, don't worry." And somehow, I felt the threat dissolve away. I rocked her back and forth a little, still holding her. I freed my left hand and indicated to Lyt that we should go back to the Roundhouse. He stared at me with an almost wild expression, but moved the floater.

"Nyos, you and I are going to do something together. I've been up all night again, and when I turn in, unless you have something that you must do, let's just spend the time with each other, undisturbed. I know that tomorrow we have to be in Aruba for the meeting, and I think we will be pretty busy then. We need time alone, and we haven't had a proper honeymoon at all."

With a sigh, she looked up and nodded at me. "You're not upset with me?"

"Well, I was pretty... surprised, that's for sure. But no, I'm not upset with you."

Lyt was still pressed back against the rail and was flying very carefully. The Roundhouse was getting much nearer rapidly. What can you do in this sort of situation? Just keep your trust that things will work out.

We landed just inside the big door, touching lightly to the deck. Lyt shooed me off the floater, and by default, Nyos as well. Wasting no time, he directed his floater out to inspect his workshop and to see if the high speed winds had done it any damage.

I walked Nyos to the storage room and got the optimizer package which I had left by the door. This was as good a time as any to test this out. My computer was able to connect to the direction booklet, creating a hologram of the instructions.

Nyos was helpful suggesting what to do. I had a pretty fair idea, and we put our thoughts together. After reading the instructions, she helped to create a program for one of the cubes. We defined volumes and areas, things that were to be optimized and things that were to be left unchanged. It would need some time to do the job.

I removed the keyfob from my keychain and dropped it in the control room before we left the building. We moved the cabins out of their bays and placed them along the beach where we could have a wonderful view if we wished, and the two of us went out on a floater to the top of the Roundhouse.

Lyt was in his workshop, which seemed to have lost a strip of roofing material. Its solar panels were in place however, and everything seemed structurally unharmed. He stayed off at a distance from Nyos and took his floater up slightly to see what we were doing.

"Okay, this is the big test. Let's see if it can optimize something this big."

I placed the cube at the top and in the center of the Roundhouse. The computer sent the activation sequence to the cube. The effect was very odd.

The cube seemed to melt and flow in black lines. Fuzz appeared to sprout outward like the tiny spines in dandelion fluff. The shape of the cube sank almost as if draining away into the lines of fuzz. They seemed to unfold into new, finer lines which then split and unfolded again. In moments the whole of the Roundhouse was covered in black shrink-wrapped fuzz.

Now this is where it got weird. Weirder I guess. The fuzz flowed and moved over the surface of the building. The upper edges started to soften and move. The underside started to do likewise. It was almost like watching a balloon deflate.

It looked like the whole building was being eaten from within. The doors seemed to melt and reform slowly, like foam being created with an air hose and soapy water. Something dripped or drooled to the ground beneath the Roundhouse and stanchions grew from the sand and connected to the building. It settled ponderously onto the stands and its floater panels were turned off.

For a long time after that, nothing seemed to be happening. "Come on, we can see the results later. Lyt will tell us if something happens."

She directed the floater to our cabin, sitting on the beach invitingly. Once the floater parked the two of us walked to the cabin. I was enjoying the smell of the air and the early morning sun, although it was again far too bright since I had been up to all hours.

We sat quietly on the porch a few minutes, glancing occasionally at the work of the optimizer. Nothing seemed to be happening, but one thing I have learned is that those are usually the busiest of times. A fine keening noise and a foamy white noise were growing from the fuzzy, frothy black mass.

Lyt had taken his floater over to the building and was watching raptly as it was being rebuilt. I had seen enough and was getting tired. Nyos escorted me inside.

The windows were cracked open enough to allow a fine breeze in. She raised the cabin slightly off the ground and left it there about tree height. Good move. The rest of the morning was ours and ours alone.

So I didn't get any sleep at all. It was a very private time and one that we both enjoyed immensely. We allayed each others' fears and reaffirmed our commitments.

Some time around noon we started to move around a bit and felt that it was time to get moving. I was tired, yes. The day was before us though, and we had a lot of travel to do yet.

Nyos was up first, looking out the window at the Roundhouse. She said "you might want to see this."

I sat up immediately and grabbed a shirt and some pants. She held the curtain aside and past it I could make out something gleaming in the sunlight. It had eight smooth airscoops at the top, where the air conditioning systems and ventilators were to be installed.

I should have showered, but this was important. I could do it in a while.

We brought the cabin over to the Roundhouse and slowly panned along it, seeing a smooth, unbroken skin instead of the rather crude original work. The ground below it was very strange. It looked eaten or corroded, as if it had been dissolved with a powerful acid.

Three landing legs now stood beneath the building. The bay doors were now smoothly worked into the body, not simply recessed and flat. Everything looked as if it had come from a factory, not a handful of machines and scrounged materials slapped together in a night. I looked at Nyos and said "what do you make of that?"

She seemed impressed and I hadn't seen anything before that would impress her.

"It's really beautiful. It looks like it belongs in flight. Let's go inside."

"Yeah. Definitely."

I maneuvered the cabin to its bay. When it dropped into place, I heard a click and a whirring. Nyos said "the water and power just hooked up."

We stepped out into something wonderful.

The floors and ceilings seemed to flow into the wall partitions. "Oh, Lyt has got to see this." The floors had an odd effect; the metal deckplate and the carpeting had fused together. There was a transition of about a centimeter for the metal to become carpeting but it was all one continuous thing.

I peered at the overhead and saw that the lighting strips were similarly fused into the ceiling metal. There was a bizarre and organic feel to everything. Walking around the perimeter I saw that as we had instructed, the robots themselves were untouched. The charging niches however were almost conformal, fitting each machine like a glove.

From somewhere there was a movement of cool air. I felt the walls but there was nothing humming or vibrating. I looked to Nyos and shrugged. "What do you think?"

"I must say that everything looks far better than I expected." I went to the kitchen, to storage rooms, to the control room. There in the middle of the floor was my keyfob. I put it back on my keychain, seeing no apparent change in it.

"I'm going to get Lyt. This is just too incredible."

But wait- where were the controls? I made a quick survey of the area but nothing was to be seen. I sat on the couch, thinking of where I had last left them.

A display appeared, swelled and filled the room. It was a clear view of the exterior of the Roundhouse. Where were the cameras? I could see Lyt's cabin and his workshop, so he was still there. No, he had been on a floater. It must be inside his workshop.

When I stood the display remained lit, but when I exited the room it faded out. Nyos was almost running from room to room, looking at things and checking their functions. I got the floater ready to go to Lyt's cabin, and to tell him of what had happened.

Eerie. That was the feeling I had. Something was not quite right. I checked his cabin first and he didn't answer. I went to the workshop, thinking he must be working on something. I opened the big door.

Empty.

All the black storage spheres were gone and the tools and electronics were missing. The benches had been cleaned out, cabinets emptied, and the whole place seemed dead. I walked through everything, checked it all, and only the largest items had been left. One was the lapidary saw.

The motor was still warm.

There was a brownish-gray slurry of rock dust and water in the pan, like he had cut something right before he left. In the slurry I found a lump.

Scraping the thick muddy sludge with my fingertips, the lump resolved itself into a small hemisphere. It was half of an amethyst colored bead.

Lyt had gone.

CHAPTER 15

I retrieved the generator cabin and docked it in its bay. I thought about Lyt and what he might need. Should I leave his cabin and workshop here? The weather would surely destroy anything left unguarded for long. He took everything he felt he needed. But why?

This was terrible. He had a couple of weeks before he could search for his home world. Where would he go and what would he do?

I gritted my teeth. What the hell had rubbed him so wrongly that he had to leave? At least he was a survivor.

I knew him; he had to have all sorts of resources stashed away. Those safe storage boxes alone held treasures in floaters, tools, explosives, who knew what else. For instance, he had "real" food in the box that he opened during our trip to Karoom. If he didn't know where his home world was, and clearly it was an issue for him to find it- then where did he get food from?

Perhaps there was a colony somewhere that he could get to, populated with settlers from his home world. He did say something along those lines.

Some things were not adding up. Too many insane things. Some small, some moderate, but this was the last in a chain. I came back to the first really insane thing I had seen.

When Farlin Dola had blown himself to bits, he seemed not to worry about being dead. He was sure that Lyt couldn't use the stones, and that was enough for him. Why was that so important? Just as Nyos came to the scene, Dola was at least talking. What had he said?

He said he had allies that could defeat Lyt now. And the look he gave Nyos was... uncanny. Had he met some of her people maybe?

Lyt had at least agreed that she had been helpful, despite his misgivings.

But he was really spooked after the display today. Like he was seeing something terrifying.

Was he so terrified of Nyos that he ran? I had the strongest feeling that he had left for good. But he left me one thing, and it looked like half the stone that had been implanted in his leg. That stone would lead to his home world.

I knew he wouldn't give up his quest. He had to find his world. But he also had a world to save, and I had absolutely no idea where it might be.

Okay, so he left the cabin and the workshop for good. It made no sense to leave them to the elements. But he knew that there was a place that his workshop might be found, if no other place was agreed upon.

I unloaded Boron and gave him instructions.

"I want you to fly this workshop back to these coordinates. There is a solar generator and backup power, so you won't be running out. Load all of Lyt's furniture and belongings from his cabin into here, so if he comes back he'll have water, power, and a place to sleep.

"I'm charging you with the job of waiting and watching for him. If he comes, you do as he says and help him out."

"Yes."

"Thanks. You've been very helpful. I may come to check on you and to see if he shows up. And don't let anyone except Lyt, me, or Nyos enter the building or take anything from it."

"Understood."

"You're a good guy, Boron."

I left after he had unloaded Lyt's things and I put some items in the freezer for him just in case he did show up. I knew he liked some foods and I made certain that he would have them.

Boron directed the workshop and piloted it away from the island. I watched as it disappeared into the distance, too small and far a dot to be seen. I took Lyt's now empty cabin and parked it in its berth in the Roundhouse. I felt like hell.

"Where's Lyt?"

I just stared at the floor.

Nyos craned her neck and looked inside his cabin. Didn't she have x-ray vision or something? "He left."

She stood back slightly. "Left."

"Yes. While we were in our cabin and the optimizer was working, he packed up his stuff and took off. He left his workshop and cabin. I had Boron take his cabin back to the old base just in case he shows up and needs anything. That's the one place we all know."

There was really nothing I could do. I wanted to be there when he found his planet, to help him do it even. And I promised to help him save a world. But now I was adrift and had no idea where any of this was to happen.

As much as I wanted to get Nyos to help, I knew that Lyt wanted nothing to do with her. I wondered if it had to do with any of the things he had told me. Advanced civilizations becoming lazy or focused on ideas that we couldn't figure out. Having goals that didn't square with our thinking, or being so powerful and unstoppable.

Nyos was something I had never thought possible or even imagined. She was some *one* who was too incredible to believe. Her people surely would have been thought djinn and worshiped. That was completely understandable.

I had to get my mind back on track. This was unproductive.

"Okay, he made up his mind and he's going out on his own. He's a grown man and can do whatever he wants. I want to help him but he has other ideas. Let's get moving so we have a place to stay once we get to Aruba."

I was really wearing thin by now but had to do something. I pulled another Boro robot from a niche and instructed him on how to fly the Roundhouse. I clicked my keyfob and the ramp retracted. The bay door slid sideways and fit snugly into the hull. Yes, it was definitely a hull now.

As the robot watched, I took the Roundhouse up to four kilometers and noticed that the air pressure inside did not seem to leak out or even change a bit. Excellent.

Now to see what it would do. The control was almost intuitive. A volume of space showed all around the display, revealing ocean and the island far below us. I could see the direction we had come in and set our direction to southeast, then grabbed the imaginary control bar that was no more than a hologram and pushed it forward. The Roundhouse began to accelerate.

In a few seconds it was clear that the wind was just barely whistling.

The display showed 50, 60, 70 klicks. I eased it up faster. 90, 100. Still no noise. Faster.

I was up to two hundred very quickly. I didn't want to push it.

Checking the computer was telling. I wasn't going to be able to make it in time at this rate. Experimentally I pushed the control even further. The Roundhouse began to hum slightly but all the indicators looked good. Okay, why not? Something like this was sure to have some sort of safeties.

So soon it was doing over four hundred klicks and there was very little vibration or buffeting. Great. We would make it.

The Boro robot took the controls and watched the path. I made certain that he understood some points, what to look for, and where we were ultimately going. On an afterthought, I named it also.

"From now on, you will respond to the name 'Borneo'. Do you understand?"

"Yes".

Well, that was done. And I still had had no sleep.

My diet had been terrible and my sleeping habits were utterly destroyed. At least we were on the way to the meeting spot. Another thing had to be considered. The worlds were constantly moving and the map changing. It was not possible to keep those connections exact and they had drifted a few meters here and there but now would be really off.

The computer kept track of it so at least I knew where things were. Now we would get there with time to spare and I needed a shower, a meal, and a nap.

My slow walk gave me time to go over things mentally. What would I do with Lyt gone? I knew the answer to that, pursue my course. Something must have happened, or something about Nyos spooked him. He really did have reservations about her. And this threat to the Earth from the Archivists- at least she was going to help me fight that.

She was powerful and probably could find other people to help if necessary. Was Lyt's world attacked by the Archivists? I had to let the pieces sort themselves out.

My first move was to make a sandwich. It wasn't a great meal but it would hold me over. There was plenty in the refrigerator so that wasn't an issue. Nyos watched as I laid out bread, lettuce, sliced tomatoes, and lunch meat. There was cheese and a slice of it was dropped on the growing stack. A bit of mustard topped it off.

It took a minute of searching to find a cloth to wipe down the countertop. Everything was smoothed and altered in the kitchen but not terribly. The most notable factor was that all corners and edges had been rounded, but most small objects were completely untouched.

I needed a place to sit while I ate. The kitchen had an area with a table and some chairs, but I didn't see any of that. There was a smooth, empty space in its place. There were also outlines on the floor. It looked like red tape outlines molded into the white floor space, nothing more. I walked around it slowly, then stopped.

The central area began to extrude upward until a table surface was formed. That was a neat trick. Beside me, a chair began to do likewise. Wow, fold up furniture. It wouldn't take up any room in flight and chairs and furniture wouldn't be falling all over the place if you hit turbulence.

The chair didn't look very comfortable but when I sat on it, it reshaped itself to fit nicely, rather like my funny eyeglasses. I had to think back- where had I left those? Oh, on the night table in the cabin. I had to learn to use them.

Nyos joined me in another of the extruded chairs.

Through bites of the sandwich I chattered. "I don't get it. He must have had something come up or maybe he was really upset. Did you two have words or anything?"

"No. I spent my time with you while the Roundhouse was being remade."

Chewing and shaking my head, I looked at the sandwich and then her. "I think your display, out over the water, really upset him. That's the only thing I can think of."

She sank a little in her chair.

"I mean, he seemed to be really scared. Well, I was too, but it was nothing that big. We're over it. But Lyt seemed to really get upset."

I sat in silence, just holding the sandwich and staring at the tabletop. "I hope he's okay."

"Perhaps he just needs some time to think about things."

"Maybe."

I began eating again, finished the sandwich and carried the plate to the sink. I found something interesting there.

In the splash guard behind the sink was a flat, synthetic stone panel that matched the countertops. It was nearly white with little flecks of gray and black in it, like fake granite. It had horizontal slots in it and each had a little icon molded into the splash guard. They were blue-green profiles of plates and other objects.

Experimentally, I inserted the plate into the proper slot. Something inside grabbed it and smoothly swallowed it. A whirring noise came from inside the slot and I could smell hot soapy water. A one-off dishwasher!

In seconds there was a small clatter in the cabinet. I pulled the door open and saw my plate, on the top of the stack. I touched it with a couple of fingertips. It was still warm. Wow.

It was time for a shower.

Halfway there, I consulted my computer again and figured we were somewhere well over the Gulf of Mexico if we were to transit to Earth now. My curiosity got the better of me and I had to look in at the control room.

Borneo was piloting in silence, and the display showed a range of sandbar islands and atolls below us. They had the same ethereal perfection of the island we had stopped at some time before. This place would be a boater's paradise. Below I could see two blue holes rimmed with broken rings of island, thin lines of palms, and glaring white stripes of beach. They passed below in silence.

It was hypnotic to see such beautiful scenery passing beneath, never before seen by human eyes. A large number of smoothly swimming shapes caught my eye below. They must have been immense.

Gray shiny bodies swam in tandem, sometimes breaking through the waves and sluicing through the surface. Line of white foam trailed and dissipated as they swam, all set on some common destination. I heard a soft voice beside me.

A breathy "oh!" sound was all she made, and her hand settled on my shoulder. "They're beautiful."

"Looks like some sort of whales. But the heads are too long and narrow. And the tails are wrong. And you're right, they're beautiful."

Yellowish sand bars under the blue green water spread below the waves like a rumpled cloth. In some areas there were packs of swimming things, and large masses of silvery fish. I was caught by the beauty of the scene and had to tear myself away from it.

Nyos' hand tugged my shoulder gently. "Let's get you cleaned up and ready to sleep."

"Yeah. You're right."

I had a thought. "You don't sleep, do you."

"Sort of. I am fully aware always, but my mind does go into a state like sleep when I lie down with you and rest. It's like two minds, one a shadow above the other. The aware one is full of information and facts and the human-like part acts and feels as you do."

"So you don't need to sleep?"

"I suppose not. But I like to be next to you. It's somehow very comforting."

We went to the cabin and in there I stripped and took a really well deserved and long-needed hot shower. I lathered extensively and just stood in the hard, fine spray and felt the tensions relax.

It was early afternoon and the trip was exciting. I couldn't make myself actually get into the bed for the sense that I would be missing something. But logically I knew that I had to sleep. It was silly to stay up all the time and then be too worn out to respond if something dangerous happened.

So I made myself towel off and prepare the bed. Nyos had the covers turned back and ready for me, and I could scarcely imagine a more welcoming sight. The curtains were drawn and the lights low. There was a scent of candles and berries in the room.

The smell of fresh cotton sheets and the feel of the mattress were enough for me.

"Sleep well, my love." She kissed my forehead. "Have sweet dreams."

"Oh, Nyos. Maker of sweet dreams. I love you."

Again I felt the soft caresses and heard the quiet humming and without any reservations I drifted to sleep in a very short period of time.

Oh, Nyos.

I slept very hard. When I woke at last, I was alone and it was very quiet. Turning easily and placing my feet against the floor, I found that there was a soft rug at the edge of the bed. The whole interior of the cabin was more or less transformed.

Fine silky curtains hung over the windows, very sheer and airy. The theme was all in melon color, orange and brown. Carpeting, wall covering, everything was amazing. I stepped carefully and gently, unwilling to disturb anything.

There were finely made brass hanging lamps in the four corners. A look at them showed amazing geometric patterns of lines and octagons, an interlocking knot pattern that wrapped their entire bowl-shaped surfaces. Each was lit and burning a small oil flame that was redolent with an incense I could not place.

Even the wooden surfaces seemed to be smoothed, polished and oiled. I felt like I was in a small palace. It had an eastern flavor to it. Moroccan patterns were woven into the new carpeting that covered the floor area. That caught my attention next, the incredible workmanship and detail of everything in the once-crude little cabin.

Somehow she had done all this while I slept. It was dreamlike, bizarre.

My clothing was laid out, a business suit that I had never seen before. There was a faint smell of something in the cloth, something that made me think of really expensive things; those things that I had never experienced in my life.

She knew that I had to be properly dressed for this meeting. This was a big transaction and she was going to be certain that I did it right. So I got dressed and marveled even at the socks, which were so thin and fine that I couldn't imagine them stopping a breeze.

When I was fully and formally dressed, I could feel a difference. Some indefinable air of power seemed to be present. It was in the suit, the shoes, and even the cufflinks which were probably diamond and appeared to be a couple of carats each. This was insane.

Once dressed, I consulted the mirror, another addition. It had a dark wooden frame that looked hand carved. I had seen things like this in the high-end shops but had never considered owning one. It wouldn't have matched the indoor-outdoor carpeting.

The doorknob was new; a glazed ceramic thing with more of those perfect geometric patterns, Chinese red lines on white. I stepped from the cabin into the main area of the Roundhouse.

It was early morning, the doors were all open and a wonderful smell of greenery filled the broad hallways of the place. The silence was astounding. We must have arrived and parked somewhere near a good transit point. On an impulse, I turned back to the cabin and found my new glasses. I put them on and checked the effect in the mirror. It was actually rather nice.

Now, I was uncomfortable not having a resonator and computer on me. I hadn't worn the long coat since some time yesterday when I realized that it was be dangerous to transit while we were in flight. So now I was unequipped and it felt funny.

The walk to the control room was quiet, and I missed Lyt's presence. Nyos must have been out doing what she does, whether it was negotiating with somebody or gathering things from around the universe. She certainly had been busy during my nap.

Borneo was sitting in place, unmoving. The hologram showed an amazing jungle scene below us, a riot of greenery and flowers. The greenery was a little too dark and the flowers a little too brilliant but it was very attractive. This was definitely not Earth.

"Good job, Borneo. Thanks for piloting."

"Understood."

From there I took a walk around the perimeter of the Roundhouse. That was when I saw that two of the Boro robots were missing. Boron was flying Lyt's workshop back to the old base. Borneo was in the control room. So there should have been four left. But two more slots were empty.

Good for him. He needed some help and he has it. It made me feel better knowing that at the least he had some robots to gather materials and do things. He was better equipped now than when he first came to me.

I checked my watch. I hadn't adjusted for local time, which was probably three times zones off from where I had been. Maybe two. But it appeared to be about eight or so, which was fine. My laptop computer had the email with the specifics for the meeting. These things need to be plugged in and operated every so often anyway.

So the meeting was set for 9, there was a local bank that had vaults and meeting rooms, and we would be making our deposit there. I was ready other than the need for a breakfast. The kitchen was just around the corner.

I arrived to a setting on the table. Apparently if you left something on the extruded table it would not retract into the floor.

A wooden tray, again with all the detailed knots and geometries, held a plate of cut fruit and cheese. There was a chilled drink carafe full of cranberry juice. Wow, she had thought of everything. I sat and began to eat, taking my time and enjoying everything.

When I was done, after reaching the point where I was just eating so it wouldn't be wasted, I realized that I should just cover it and place it in the refrigerator. There was about twenty minutes by my estimation, and I was counting on Nyos being here soon.

I was nervous. I hadn't considered how I was going to move the deposit money. I hadn't thought of anything really, but I needed to put a little time into how it would be handled.

I didn't doubt that she had things worked out though. My greatest worry was that I would be facing strange people in a foreign country and hauling a lot of money around. That was alarming. And another thing. Would our government have people around watching the transaction? Would the authorities here cooperate with them?

I didn't know.

Well, it didn't take long for me to put things away. Nyos did appear as I was wondering where the exotic wooden tray should go.

"Good morning my dear. Are you ready for your meeting?"

My eyes locked onto her. She was wearing something I had no words for.

What a sight! It looked almost like a business outfit but with lots of sheer silk stuff that made every curve just pop. Her hair was almost jet black and tied back with a gold circlet loaded with gems and the same geometric detailing. She had a scarf over her face with only her eyes showing, and they looked somehow… different. More gold and less red, more mysterious.

She turned slowly for me, showing off the look. "You like it, my love?" Her form seemed more compact and voluptuous, her honey color richer and more radiant.

"I'm breathless. Wow. What made you change?"

"I took a form that more closely appealed to those we are dealing with. Something that would let them know that you are a man of power and that even your wife is powerful. There is a psychology to things that I have been learning. Trust me, this will be perfect."

We boarded a floater accompanied by one of the Boro robots. He had a metal box in his grasp which presumably held our deposit. Nyos directed us out the door into the brightness of the morning where we were just a few meters above the trees. I saw the bottom of the roundhouse now and it was completely different from my original, ham-fisted design.

The I-beams beneath were gone, replaced by flowing ribs that radiated from the center hub. The ribs were smoothed into the bottom and the three light bars had become slick lines that seemed melted into the structure. It looked like a flying saucer from here.

We approached a clearing and without a warning, we transited.

We were on a small concrete dock, floater and all. Real palm trees surrounded us, some looking sickly yellowish. There was a mild smell of sewage and diesel fumes. Nyos held out her arm and I looped mine through hers, but she insisted on being on my left side. The Boro robot was directly behind us and rolled along on those treads. The floater rose into the air and found a niche up in the trees, not directly in sight.

We didn't have far to walk; we were just across the street from the bank.

The building looked crude in a way; thick white stucco and tiny windows, all the wood trim was painted red. The trim was very thin, almost like an outline of the doors and windows.

The entry was well-kept and had a small patch of grass and a little white stucco fountain lined with tiny blue tiles. Some greener tiles were fashioned into a mosaic of a fish in the bottom of the fountain. Warm ocean air moved along with a hint of the chill that morning sometimes has.

We entered the bank and I was struck by the contrast. It was far more professional looking inside, but it was echoey and dark. Immediately somebody who had to be a bank official came forward with extended hand. His slim, slight form was hung over with a nearly white suit that was a little too large.

"Mr. Winston I presume." He was energetic and amiable with a moderately dark tan and short brown, combed-back hair.

"Indeed." I shook his hand firmly and stopped. The robot also stopped behind us. This fellow was trying very hard not to stare at the robot.

"I am Mr. Ghali, bank manager."

"It's a pleasure to meet you."

"Ah, and your wife I have met."

He turned to her and bowed lightly, hands pressed together.

"A privilege to see you again, Mrs. Winston."

She nodded at him and flashed those eyes.

"We have a meeting room reserved down this hall. It is secure and will be guarded during your transaction."

He indicated the robot. "I do hope that he is not armed."

I really wasn't sure. "He is simply my courier. He will handle the deposit."

That seemed to satisfy Mr. Ghali.

We waited in the bank lobby for no more than a minute, small talk with Mr. Ghali being the course. I wondered how the potted plants could survive in this gloom. They must have a service that swaps them out regularly.

A pair of men, also rather thin and a bit darker, entered and walked in our direction. One carried a small briefcase.

"Mr. Winston, I am Morgan Salihd. We spoke briefly a few days ago."

"Yes, thank you for making the arrangements."

He pressed his palms together and bowed to Nyos. "An honor to see you again."

His face became thoughtful and he said something in Arabic I think.

Nyos looked at him a moment and said "not Shaitan. They and the Ghul are not in alliance with us. I am acting independently under the direction of my husband."

His eyes sparkled as he looked at me.

"You sir are a very lucky man. Very, very lucky."

"Yes, I am. Shall we continue?"

"Yes, of course. This is Aziz, he will accompany us." He indicated his companion.

We followed Mr. Ghali to the meeting room and I had the Boro robot deposit the metal box he was carrying on the table. At a word from Nyos he opened the container and revealed many gold bars. Morgan seemed to inhale and hold it.

Aziz removed a small kit from his pocket and touched something to the topmost bar. In a few seconds he nodded at Morgan.

Morgan spoke. "Beta backscatter machine. He checks my deposits for me and handles the technical end."

"So we have located three good candidates and two backup candidates for you. I hope that something meets your requirements."

He spread some pictures on the table, glossy computer prints of different islands.

Nyos tugged slightly and whispered to me "number 3 is the best choice."

I nodded. "I have decided on this one." I fingered the center picture.

"Very good. Here is the total cost, as communicated to you. We may be able to work that down somewhat. The government agrees to allow this land to secede and will provide, in return for this payment, three years of support by patrolling the coast as well."

I nodded as if I knew what it all meant.

"And when do you want payment?"

"That will be made directly to that government, and it will be due when you sign the documents. We can arrange that in two more days."

"Where should we do it?"

"In the capitol at the main branch of their national bank. The treasury is located there as well."

"Sounds good to me."

I spent some time signing papers, agreements, and documents. A young woman entered to witness and notarize the papers. She stopped short when she saw Nyos and placed her hand over her mouth with a sharp indrawn breath. Her notary stamp clattered to the floor.

I looked at Nyos who was sitting quietly. I turned to the notary and said, "don't worry, she won't bite you. Much."

Morgan laughed almost nervously. "She is a good djinn, just be polite and respectful." I became aware of the tension in the room that I had somehow missed utterly before. Morgan was actually quite terrified, I realized. Only the gold held him at bay.

Aziz too was tense. Suddenly, without awareness of how, my nervousness faded. Things were going as they should. Morgan was in fear because he had come face to face with something of legend. It was all he could do to function, most likely. And I had had no idea that he was from the Middle East.

Of course. Nyos would have selected reputable people, but she also would stack the deck in our favor. He was a true believer.

The notary watched as I signed the agreements. I presented my driver's license and realized that I didn't even have my passport. It was probably left in the apartment when the police came in.

The notary said "I will need to see your passport, please." She kept looking aside from Nyos, but I could see her stealing a glance at her hand every so often. She was watching the flowing glassy skin and its fine metal flake appearance.

Nyos produced my passport and handed it to her.

She took it gingerly and began to copy information to the papers, then stamped and signed them.

The notary slid the passport back to Nyos and repeated the process with Morgan. Soon she was satisfied and took the papers in hand and made a quick exit.

In a few minutes she had returned with copies and each of us had signed and copied versions. She looked directly at Nyos once and then down at the floor and backed out.

"Morgan, would there be any objection to our visiting the island? I will want to see it personally and spend some time there before we sign."

"Please do. As the new owner, you will want to survey and decide what you want to do there." He gave me a package of data showing maps and geological information.

"Well." That was Morgan. "It seems that we are done here. We will handle the deposit from here and I hope to see you at the conclusion of the deal. I will email you with the details, as before."

"Thank you." I shook his hand. Aziz stayed back and remained quiet.

We stood and exited the room, the robot not far behind us all. Aziz remained in the room with the deposit. As we reached the lobby, the bank manager extended his services and his card. I shook his hand, Nyos nodded to him. Morgan then shook my hand once more and we promised to meet at the closing.

He turned to Nyos and she extended her hand to him. He took it and lightly kissed the back of her hand, respectfully. She clasped his hand between hers momentarily and looked at him directly.

"I wish you happiness and success."

He looked ecstatic.

"My humblest thanks."

He retreated quietly and with a radiant smile, bowing deeply. Of course, he had been blessed.

The walk from the bank was quiet and purposeful. "Excellent" was all I could say.

Once again in the sunlight, the sense of a great weight lifting came to me. She had done it! We were going to have an island.

Somehow the excitement was blunted though. I could step around a corner and take a whole planet, if I really wanted to. But the island represented something, more than simply running away somewhere and being king of my domain.

The island was a tool to save the planet.

So the effort was worthwhile, not simply wasted. We walked to the pier and the waiting floater. "I think I should find out what the news is saying about us, because the more we know, the better we will be able to handle it."

"Of course. Is there anything else you want?"

I turned to her and smiled. "A kiss. Would that be appropriate?"

"You set the rules. You are in control. This is your dream, your project."

"We're not going to offend anyone's sensibilities here?"

"Do you care?"

She lifted the veil and I kissed her one block from the bank, just a few feet from the pier. It might not have been my imagination that some fire was involved.

So she retrieved the floater and it landed smoothly on the pier. We boarded and the robot was just behind. Loaded, ready, and I felt that a trip to the island itself would be in order. At the moment she was ready to transit, somebody ran forward from the bushes and grabbed the handrail of the floater, just as it lifted slightly from the pier.

We transited.

"Damn, we have a hitchhiker!" There was a thump from beneath as his arm or leg struck the underside of the floater.

The floater had lifted until the man was dangling by one hand a few meters above the ground. He might not even be aware that we had gone anywhere but if he had dropped off, he would have been stranded on another world forever.

"Robot, help him up but restrain him once he is safe."

He grabbed the arm and lifted carefully, his cargo suspended well over a tree. The man was determined, jaw clenched and gaze flicking to the ground only momentarily. He was dressed in a loose fitting jungle green outfit with a green scarf over his face. It looked military.

The fellow hooked a leg over the edge of the floater and pulled himself onto it. He was gently placed on the surface and then I found out why the robots had treads instead of legs. With a little judicious manipulating, the robot had both of the man's ankles in front of the treads and shackled emerged just above the tread base. With a click they snapped shut on the ankles. His arms were pinned behind him and a second set of shackles emerged from the robot's chest. They clicked shut on the wrists.

Well, it was a police robot. It made perfect sense.

In a few seconds he had stopped struggling.

"So, what's this all about? What's your name?"

"Are you Michael Winslow?"

"Yes, and who are you?"

"I am under direction to take you into custody."

Ah. "Is this about that stupid stolen metals thing?"

"That is one of the charges."

I actually felt like laughing. "Well then, you know that this has nothing to do with stolen metals."

"We know nothing at this point."

I did laugh then. "I couldn't have put it better myself."

Nyos placed herself in front of the man and looked into his eyes.

He seemed to stiffen, then stared right back at her, defiantly.

I thought she actually growled at him. "What do you want with my husband, human?" She pulled the scarf off his face and tossed it backwards over her shoulder. It flamed and vanished like a magician's trick.

He seemed to realize that something was wrong. Perhaps he concluded that those were real eyes and skin, not some elaborate prank. Perhaps he had just felt that maybe he had bitten off a little too much.

"Hey, soldier guy. Look around you. You're not in the U.S. You're not even in Aruba."

He looked around for the first time. His head panned back and forth, saw nothing but jungle and only a distant edge of ocean. Some local bird things were flying over, like little pterosaurs with feathers. Their crackly calls cascaded over each other. The silvery bulk of the Roundhouse floated nearby, silent and unmoving.

I could see the change in his eyes mostly. "Nyos, is he armed?"

"He has a pistol in his back pocket, one strapped to his left calf, and two knives."

"Thanks." I was irritated at having been taken in. I didn't check for anything and I knew that we were wanted. I let my guard down.

"Gee, should we peel the skin off him and stake him out for the dinosaurs?"

She laughed a low chuckle. "There aren't any big ones around right now."

He was looking panicky now. "Well, let's save him for later. I want to get out of this suit and into something more comfortable."

We were slowly approaching the entranceway. Now his head was turning back and forth, taking it all in. "This is kidnapping!"

"No, you're a stowaway. Different laws. I think we're allowed to do things to stowaways."

Nyos landed the floater and the robot rolled off. She led the robot to one of the storage rooms. I followed, more from curiosity than anything else. I didn't want to have to deal with this guy. Still, he was my responsibility now.

I summoned the other Boro robot. "I have a prisoner who will try to injure us. He needs to be restrained and guarded. You can use a cargo hold as a cell for now. Follow me."

"Understood."

Wow, these robots had wonderful command of the language.

Nyos was at the doorway of a storage room and the robot was inside. The prisoner was still clamped in place. "Man, this could waste my day."

The second robot was right behind me. I let it enter and the two frisked the prisoner and removed his weapons. "Take those to my cabin please."

While the second robot was gone, I asked the first if the prisoner had any electronic devices or transmitters.

"Yes, two transmitters."

I followed his direction and found a small transmitter and recorder taped to the small of his back and removed it carefully.

"Where is the second?"

"Implanted in his right hip bone."

He looked surprised.

I shook my head. "Figures. Property of the government. Probably didn't even know he had been tagged. Well, we won't mess with that one." I turned my back to him and grinned.

"Probably has an explosive charge on it, you know. It would blow him to pieces if we took it out."

I was trying really hard not to laugh as I said it. After a moment of gritting my teeth I had control and turned back to the robot.

"Any other electronics?"

"Numerous radio frequency devices in his digestive system."

Huh?

"Er, can you describe the devices?"

"Approximately. I detect over one hundred radio frequency tags measuring approximately one quarter of a millimeter square and of smaller dimension in thickness. All respond to a pulse with identical digital signatures."

"He's got radio tags inside him. Wow. How do you get something like that?"

Nyos smiled at me. "They place them in the food and they are eaten. It can take days for them to work through the system."

This was an education for me. "I guess that's the new dog tag."

Then to the prisoner: "So what's your name?"

"Davis."

"Okay Davis. Here's the deal. You are a stowaway on my... ship. You are now a prisoner. Where we are, there are no laws about anything. None. If I let you go out there, you will be giving some big reptile indigestion in a few minutes. I really don't want to do that, I like reptiles."

He watched me carefully.

"Now, I have to go somewhere but I don't want to take you with me.

It would make your ride home a lot tougher in the end. But I'm on a schedule."

Nyos was standing silently, taking it all in.

"Davis, if you're good, I'll put you right back where we picked you up. I really don't want to deal with you. Does that sound like a good idea?"

He recovered his composure. "I was directed to arrest you. I'm doing my job."

"Yes, I know. But then you should know that your superiors are in the wrong. They know that I didn't steal any metals. And that they have no authority over non-humans."

His look was firm. "I won't negotiate with you."

"I'm not negotiating. You agree to let us drop you off or… oh, I don't know. See, I'm not giving you a choice, so it isn't negotiating. So I am going to release your restraints and my wife is going to take you back.

"Just be a gentleman. You don't want to have her mad at you."

To Nyos I said, "Take him back please."

She made a slight bow. "As you wish."

Nyos pulled the veil off and looked at Davis intently. "Come with me."

"Oh, before you go." He looked at me.

"If you try to get anyone else close like you did, I will incinerate one square kilometer of land. Location of my choice. Do it twice, ten square kilometers. You get the picture."

I stepped back slightly as she moved forward. She clamped his wrist tightly and said "release him." The manacles clicked open and Davis was placed gently on the floor.

Nyos looked him over and said "I suggest you close your eyes."

Davis looked back and forth quickly, eyes darting, then scrunched them shut. They vanished.

She returned after a few seconds. The robots were dismissed and the room aired out. It smelled like sweat.

"Okay, we go to the island next. Set a course due east and full speed. Close the doors first, I don't want anyone getting blown out."

I looked her over and smiled. "Thanks."

She literally grabbed me and kissed me, aggressively. She said in a somewhat muffled voice, "this is fun."

After a few minutes we separated breathlessly. "Yes, it is. Let's go get the Roundhouse in motion."

In moments we had the doors closed and all items secured. I set the course and brought the Roundhouse, the ship up to speed. We would be there with plenty of time to spare.

I assigned one of the Birgan robots to be the monitor. Any hardware was to be stowed and any loose items secured before we took off. That was plain good sense. I wondered at not having thought of that before.

But it was simple. I didn't think of this as a ship before, but a round workshop that could be moved. And in the race to build something large enough to accommodate everything, I had way overdesigned in terms of size. There were rooms I hadn't even seen. There were also unused charging bays and computer bays

I picked seventy meters arbitrarily and figured that there would end up being a couple of hundred rooms altogether. Then I had no idea how much hardware it would take to do what I had to, and how many computers and tools and machines I might pick up from various technical worlds.

A lot of stuff was simply wasted right now, so I thought about what I would really need to make this workable. There were workshops but they were literally empty rooms. There were places for tools and storage, and a lot of those storage rooms were full of things Nyos had given me. It would take a lifetime to sort through all of it, just to figure out what everything was.

So I had to be practical. Given that I had a lot of space to work with, what would I want if I could have anything? Wow, we could use all kinds of stuff. What do ships need?

Power, water, food, all sorts of stuff. Engines, weapons, hospital. I couldn't wrap it all into one idea easily. It was complicated. So like my travel supplies, I decided to make a list.

First, however, I made the walk to the cabin so I could get into some jeans and a decent shirt. And sneakers or some other comfortable shoes. It was slow in coming but then I saw it. Why live in a wooden box, even though it was decorated like a palace? Hmm. While I lived in a box, so did my wife. That wouldn't do.

Well, there was plenty of space for it, so I conscripted a chunk of large, barnlike workshop space and decided to make a home there. That was on my mind as I undressed, making a decent home for Nyos. She had been with me all her existence and that started out in the lint of my pocket. It was shameful.

Getting dressed, I visualized something more fitting. The computer was going to get a workout.

Taking the time to check on Borneo, I saw that we were deep into a spreading jungle and that it wasn't flat as I had envisioned. Real jungles are hilly, and have large peaks and valleys completely interlocked with trees, vines, bushes, and everything in between. I had no idea.

We passed a couple of really beautiful waterfalls and a number of deep pools and lakes. Before us was a spreading area where the jungle thinned and converted to grasslands. Gray-green grass stretched out ahead for some unknown distance, swept into curving waves by the wind. Herds of some sort of two-legged things were running along in long, bounding strides. I thought of ostriches when I saw them.

A marshy land was to the north of us, and the edge of it was covered with birds. I had never seen so any birds before, bright yellow-green things that stood on tall legs. They were wading in mud apparently, and had white undersides when they took off. Reeds and rushes parted and small groups would explode into flight.

We came to an area that had large leaves on the ground, apparently some sort of huge viny type of plant that spread out over the surface for kilometers. This was very different from the previous area and got stranger as we went.

Nyos joined me in the control room. "What do you see?"

"Just amazing stuff. Lots of wildlife, strange plants, beautiful landscapes."

Ahead the ground appeared to get marshy like a tide pool. There were more of the large leaves and some smaller lily pad looking things, but they were just in clumps. Now the trees appeared and I was scratching my head at them.

"Slow down and drop down to a hundred meters. Speed to 60 klicks."

Borneo complied. The ship drifted smoothly to the lower altitude, affording us a much better view of the trees.

They looked like stacks of squishy dark discs, or maybe melted old tires. They were sort of haphazardly made, teetering back and forth like something out of Dr. Seuss. The tops had a shape of branches that spread out like an upside-down chandelier, and large round poms hung one from each tip.

"That's just plain weird. And look at those!"

Scattered here and there with increasing regularity were thick, sausage-like things that had to be trees. They stood upright with thicker bases and tapered to a sausage-shaped top. There was a little spray of branches from the top, dense with little pink flowers.

I looked more closely at the bases of the sausage things and saw wide fins like a rocket. The trunk actually grew fins of wood that spread out and anchored the trees to the ground.

"Now that's an alien tree. Not like all this other stuff you might find in a garden center."

She was watching it all with fascination. "Oh. Look."

A long alligator was slowly slithering through the shallow mud. It was huge, I had nothing to compare it to but it had to be huge as distant as we were. It had a ridge of spiny plates running down its back. They were alternately nearly black and dirty yellow.

"Yeah, let's stay up here. Borneo, let's go back up to four kilometers altitude and four hundred clicks speed."

So I spent some time sightseeing and chatting with Nyos and didn't get a lot of designing done. The day was just right though, and we had plenty of time together and I enjoyed it all.

CHAPTER 16

My schedule was more or less back to normal. It took that long sleep the night before and everything seemed to fall into place afterwards. I spent part of the day designing the new living quarters and just being in Nyos' company. It is hard to imagine a nicer and more exciting time.

The scenery below was phenomenal. We crossed a small ocean and many jungles, even a desert of large dunes. As the territory became somewhat rocky we neared our target and selected a potential landing site. From here we could directly transit to the island and for our meeting very soon, we could get to the capital in less than an hour.

I had mapped out a good spot for a transit to the island and then realized that we might have to move quickly. Better to know what we might step into, even on foot.

I checked the resonances and decided to transit first to Earth and then quickly to the valley park world, just to know what my options were. We made two quick steps and were over a field of boulders and glass. That was unexpected.

"Look, those look like windows. But they can't be. Irregular shaped, between boulders… what in the world. We have to come back and explore this at some point.

"Borneo, make a note. We need to explore the valley park world, field of boulder and windows."

I reprogrammed the resonator to take us to Melios. Two quick steps and we were above a shallow sea, something loaded with yellow and violet seaweed. Black seal-like things with crab legs folded alongside were wallowing on the seaweed like some huge field of sargassum. The seals had segments all over. Crustaceans and insects must rule this world.

"So okay, we don't have any viable jumps here. We have to go to the so-called desert world where at least there is a field that you can walk on."

After making a few arrangements, I put my long coat on and prepared a floater with Nyos. "Let's take just the floater and keep the UFO sightings to a minimum."

We opened a bay door and exited the Roundhouse, leaving it suspended over the rocky field. The transit had us appear directly over an elongated island with a few small shacks on it. It was fairly rocky, having few trees and not much in the way of beach. A lone set of poorly repaired steps led down one side to the ocean and a tiny strip of sand.

"Well, looks like it might be the one. Hard for people to come up here unless we want them to." Nyos agreed. She was holding my left arm tightly.

"We will need to prepare a landing site. Not hard if I put the robots into service."

She leaned on my arm and said "perhaps there is something in the store rooms that will help." Ah, the treasures of the universe, all in handy boxes.

"Right. We'll check it."

The floater dipped down low enough to see some trash on the ground. There were some rusted steel steps, treaders collapsed. A couple of block shacks with flaking stucco were also there; one leaned considerably. "It's kind of a hole, isn't it?"

She shrugged lightly. "Holes can be filled."

"Yeah. Let's go to the meeting and then we'll find a hole plug."

I admit it. I expected to find some sniper or seal or something just waiting for me. But considering what I told Davis before we released him, they might be a lot more circumspect. I didn't even know if I could do it, but it just felt right. Force was something they implicitly understood.

The floater rose and we transited to the Roundhouse.

Moments later we were inside and parked. I closed the doors and yelled down the hallway.

"Hey, Borneo, mark this spot on the map as 'island' and then take us to the capitol." The ship accelerated smoothly and was on its way.

"There has to be an intercom system installed. Something this big is just too impractical otherwise." Nyos agreed.

We took a walk to the storage room we had been checking out a couple of nights back. I had labeled the optimizer and the glasses case. Surely there was some gadget or system that would help out here. I picked a case at random.

"Okay, let's see what we have. Pencils. Great." I applied my computer to translate. It looked pretty hopeless. It said something about anti-protons in stasis. I labeled it and set it aside. Next case.

It was full of red metallic discs like coins. "Fuel charges for fusion reactors. Helium-3 and beryllium-6 mixture. Okay, to the generator room with this one, I guess."

I was starting to move along. A duffel bag came out with a cylinder inside. It split on its axis and hinged open. There was a little wiffle gun thing inside like a child's toy. Three plastic bottles held rows of little brown fuzzy spheres about three centimeters across. The spheres were cut into octants by silver lines. There was an equator and two circles from pole to pole, all at right angles on the surface of each fuzzy ball.

"Wonder what this does?"

I pulled the cap off one of the tubes of spheres. The first one tipped into my palm and it was squishy and rather gelatinous. It positively reeked. "Gah! This could make you sick!"

I was gagging slightly on the smell. "Okay, back in the tube with you." I stuffed the cap on quickly and hoped that we had good ventilation. There was a folded flyer that showed putting a sphere on the wiffle gun, setting some knob, aiming at probably something you want to make smell real bad, and then pulling a trigger. Yield, 4.2 kilotons.

"Yeah, 4.2 kilotons of stink. Great." I sniffed my hand and then wiped it on my pants. Everything in the case had a smell to it, and apparently the more dangerous it was, the worse it smelled. Lawyers ought to be rubbed in it. "Yeah, this is some sort of weapon. Looks crazy enough to be really dangerous."

I put that one on the "has possibilities" shelf.

"Ah, this looks cool." I found a blue metallic case with a shining white button on the top. There were no latches that I could see. It seemed to be a single molded or stamped piece of metal. I didn't want to push the button and didn't want to waste much time. I set it aside.

The black shiny box was next. It had red diagonal stripes on it. This was one of the larger boxes and it took some hefting to get it to the floor. Opening it wasn't a mystery.

The top split in half and opened out like a fishing tackle box. This looked like a weapon.

I oohed at the two rows of cartridges, each about two and a half centimeters across and about seven centimeters long. They had the appearance of big bullets. Complicated ones, too. There were brassy circles around them and black spots here and there. I saw where they dropped in, one at a time. You probably didn't want to fire more than one of these at something. Probably didn't need to, it likely wasn't there any more after the first shot. I looked at Nyos with a big grin.

"This is too much fun! How could anyone not love this?" My laugh must have been infectious. We both laughed for quite a while, and then with my breath coming back, I saw her eyes and was caught. She leaned forward.

"You are very happy. That is wonderful." Those large now-golden eyes were entrancing. She didn't have to lean much more. I was staring at her eyes, her curves, her hair. How had I found her? I nibbled lightly on her lip and put an arm around her.

"Wonderful woman. We will be together always."

"Is that your dream?"

"Oh, yes. And my wish. I hear you fulfill wishes."

"That's nothing but gossip. And thousands of years out of date too." She nuzzled against my face and my ear. "But for you, my husband, I will."

I lay the gun thing gently in its case and returned the nuzzle. The Roundhouse began to slow.

"Drat. Must be here already." Our fingers entwined. "I would marry you again and again. Perhaps we should get married in every country we visit. Bigger event each time."

Her eyes seemed to reshape, to become more acute somehow. She was morphing a little, changing in small ways but the effect was stunning. "I must prepare for our next meeting, my love. There is a suit in the cabin for you."

"You think of everything to make this perfect." We stood together and I repacked the gun. Her skin tone was lightening slightly, more of a radiance to it. The eyes were now more almond shaped, and eyebrows almost golden. Her hair was lightening as she was standing and walking through the door. And her height- she was elongating a little, making herself taller.

She probably had a psychological profile of each important person to deal with, something to use as a lever with them. Time to pack these things and get dressed.

At the end I was nearly trotting down the hallway, hoping there was time for everything. I dressed in a hurry, put on the shoes and my glasses, which I still had not learned to use.

There was some racket as robots were loading a floater with precious metals. The other floater was ready for us, but there was an ornate round carpet on it. Again Nyos appeared dressed amazingly. This was almost erotic, lots of skin exposed and lots of silks. "I play on their cultural understanding of the myths. And I can tell you like it too."

We brought the two floaters to the same bay door.

"For this you will only need the floaters. But we will use them openly. Prepare people a little at a time for what is to come."

She picked the transit point carefully. We appeared two blocks from the bank and moved along a side street, then the main road at only about six meters altitude. We rounded the bank and there was an entrance to a back compound with a high wall.

"Armored vehicles and members of state usually enter here. This is the guard location."

She guided the floaters to the guard station where a tiny red and white diagonal cross arm was dropped down. Large steel posts stuck up from the roadway, denying access to any wheeled vehicle. Two guards, very dark and well muscled, stood at the entrance in pale blue shirts and dark blue pants, both wearing red berets and armed with Kalishnikovs. Both stared at the floaters.

Nyos spoke to the first guard in French, then in English. "We have an appointment today." She handed a paper over to the nearest guard. The other was on a telephone talking rapidly.

"Yes, Mister and Mistress Winston. To the white poles in the back." The roadblocks dropped and the cross arm rose. The floaters moved past the shack and both were looking at the pile of bars on the second floater.

We approached a white roll up door and a set of white barrier poles. The door opened immediately and the poles dropped. A group of six armed guards, these in military green but still wearing the red berets, appeared inside and lined the way like a gauntlet.

Three men in business suits appeared. One was Morgan, the smallest of the bunch. The other two were African and well-fed. They introduced themselves.

"Frederick Ndonga, president of the national bank. I am pleased to meet you sir." I shook his hand and nodded.

"Michael Winston. The pleasure is mine."

I indicated Nyos. "And my wife and partner, Nyos."

He actually caught his breath on seeing her. She nodded to him, flashed golden eyes and offered her hand.

He almost knelt, touched his forehead to her hand.

The second man was the treasurer. "Jean Mkolo, Department of the Treasury. So happy to meet you, sir." Another handshake.

"Thank you, likewise. And my wife."

She also faced him once her hand was recovered. He took it gently, then shook it once. His expression was unreadable.

We stepped from the floater and Morgan met us. "A blessing to see you both again. I see you have your flying carpet today."

"But of course. Wait until you see the living room it goes in."

He smile and bowed, palms flat, to her. She said something in liquid syllables and he beamed. "You look amazing. Thank you so much."

Ndonga, the bank president, spoke first. "I see you have brought part of the payment. We would gladly have sent a courier."

"We have much more coming. A great deal of it is in platinum. I hope that isn't a problem."

"No, not at all. We can start the assay and the inventory right away. We have the documents here for you, ready for both sets of signatures."

I followed them to a table that they had set up right next to a scale and a computer. A platter with bottled water, coffee, and tea had been placed there with china cups. I seated Nyos first, then myself.

"Will you be needing my passport or other papers?"

Ndonga laughed. "We know who you are. There is no question of your identity. I would think that everyone knows who you are. Your wife is also very, very well known. We met of course a few days ago, when she made arrangements for this transfer."

"Certainly. Well, let's get started. I'm sure we have important things to do later today and I wouldn't want to hold you up."

Mkolo laughed. "We do not sell many islands."

The mood was much lighter than the earlier meeting with Morgan. Each bar was carried by a white-gloved guard to the scale. Each was weighed, dunked in a water tank and measured, and then checked with a meter. The bars then passed through a small conveyor belt into a box with a red danger light over the top.

Mkolo himself sat at the computer and tallied numbers. Within a few minutes the first load was counted. Nyos stood.

"I will retrieve the rest. I shall return shortly." She strode to the carpeted floater and in full sight of everyone, transited both away. The gasps were audible. Guards froze, not certain of what had happened.

I watched the jaws drop. "Oh, don't worry, she will return very shortly."

Morgan looked at me. "Can you tell me sir, does she have a sister?"

"I will ask her mother next time I see her."

"You know the mother of a djinn?"

"When we first met, she offered me the hospitality of her home and told me to come back any time I needed anything." Well, that was true enough. The mother bit might be a stretch though.

"Oh, I wouldn't be standing there." I pointed to one guard who had walked down to the floor area and was looking the empty space over. "Could be a problem."

Ndonga called to the man and he literally skipped back out of the way.

Mkolo looked at me, deciding. He spoke finally.

"Tell me, Mr. Winston, what you do for a living if you don't mind."

"I travel between worlds. I used to be in engineering underwriting, sort of insurance business but this travel opportunity came up and I took it. So far I've been on a couple of dozen planets I think."

That caught their attention. "Planets?"

"Yes. All over the universe really. Different worlds under different suns. Animals, plants, people you would never believe. I love it."

Ndonga stared. "And why would you want a little piss hole island here on Earth? You could live anywhere better."

I turned to face him directly. "Because Earth is in terrible danger. I'm going to try to prevent it from being destroyed. You see my wife? Her people are older than the Earth. And there is a race that actually destroys worlds, saves all the people and music and art like files on a computer. Breaks them down to data. They're called the Archivists.

"What we are trying to do is prevent them from destroying everything around you."

Morgan sat back in his chair, pale.

"He knows that what I'm saying is real." I hiked a thumb at Morgan.

I turned back to Mkolo. "I need a place to operate on Earth with no government interference. This island will work. Let me tell you what I have seen."

And I told them of Boro and Birga. Two dead worlds that had technologies far advanced over what Earth knew, both destroyed with no apparent fight from the inhabitants. I told of the theater of dreams and the dead Birgans in their tubes.

As I spoke, it became very quiet and soon everyone was listening.

"You see, there are old, powerful races in the universe and they are pretty much unstoppable. I have to find out why they do this, what attracts them. I have to find some way to prevent Earth from being archived like an old backup disc. And I have to help a friend save a world also. He's been traveling all his life between the worlds, looking for a way to stop the Archivists.

"So that is why I need this island. There may already be Archivists here somewhere, I just don't know."

It was silent for a few moments. Ndonga broke the spell.

"That is an amazing story. Assuming it is true, how do you propose to stop this from happening?"

"I'm still finding that out. There's so much to learn, and these guys are really powerful."

The floaters reappeared. Nyos was on the lead which was loaded with bars, and the rear one was almost sagging. The guards immediately began passing them along, bucket-brigade style.

My wife returned to the table and I stood and seated her. Nobody was speaking.

"Well, we have our work cut out for us. I may need to call on you gentlemen to help me recruit people who will listen."

I thought a moment. "Mr. Ndonga, can your bank accept a deposit in precious metals and issue letters of credit against them?"

"Most surely, sir."

"How much can you handle? I mean tonnage."

He looked uncertain. "Tonnage?"

"Yes, like four or five hundred tons of metals. Could your bank handle that sort of volume for me?"

He looked like he was choking. Mkolo looked at him, concerned, and spoke.

"We would need to increase our storage and our security but yes, if you give us a few months, we could meet your needs. The treasury itself can hold overflow from the bank and so we could make arrangements."

"Great. I need a place to put some precious metals."

"You could buy a whole country, not a little island," said Ndonga.

"I could have whole worlds, but this is what I need. Let's start with an account. I need to open an account and I would like to deposit some three hundred tons of metals in, oh, five days. That should give you time to make arrangements."

"Very good, sir. I will personally fill your paperwork and issue your card and access codes." Ndonga became businesslike. "We will be prepared for everything. Is there anything that you will be needing?"

"Yes, on the day of the transfer, leave this bay clear."

I poured a glass of water for Nyos and one for myself. She looked serious but I saw a tiny gleam in her eyes. "Gentlemen, we will need to work together. Think about what I said."

The first floater was nearly unloaded. "Nyos, my dear, I think we should send a robot down to help them unload the other floater."

"As you wish."

With that, she vanished from her seat, leaving them to jump at the sight of it. Morgan simply said quietly, "wow." The floater, now unloaded, vanished as well.

I had been playing with the controls on the glasses, flipping this and that. I had an epiphany and they made perfect sense. I set them to x-ray and could see that Ndonga was armed. I then used the zoom and could actually read the serial number on his weapon.

"Mr. Ndonga, do you have paper and pencil that I could use?"

He fished around and handed a small pad to me and a black ballpoint. I copied the serial number down and slipped it to him. "I know that guns are illegal in this country but you have a permit, because of your position and need. I want you to know how good my information sources are. That is the serial number of your weapon."

I flipped the glasses back to normal mode.

"I'm not sure I understand."

"Check your pistol. That is the serial number."

He stared a moment, then slowly removed the gun. He laid it on the table and compared the two numbers. The pistol was replaced. He handed the paper back to me. His expression was grim.

Mkolo was looking at him pointedly. Ndonga glanced his way and scowled.

"I'm not trying to embarrass you or cause trouble, what is going on is much bigger. Again, we need to work together. I'll start sending my deposit down in five days."

The floater came back with Nyos and a large robot. They began to unload the metal onto a blue pallet that was stationed near the guards and the scales.

In a couple of minutes the task was done and the robot moved onto the rear floater. I stood.

"Well, I sent more than enough. Deposit the overage into that new account. I will return in five days, about nine in the morning. Good enough?"

Ndonga nodded, now subdued. "That will be very good."

The papers were signed, a thick sheaf that filled three envelopes. Government agreements, sea rights, land usage, airspace, all the things that were negotiated had to be formalized.

I shook hands all around and Nyos nodded to each. We boarded the floater and stood on the circle of carpet. The floaters lifted up a bit and we transited.

"Wow, I'm glad I can relax a little. All that work is a lot of uh, work."

Nyos was almost fiery. "You did wonderfully. I knew you would. This is a good adventure."

Somehow I felt I had overdone it. These weren't the right people to tell this to. I needed to get to the right people and do it again, better. Okay, so it was clumsy and overplayed. But think of it as practice. Next time would be better, I was sure.

"So, we have an island now. Let's go to it."

⸻ ◆ ⸻

We arrived at the proper place in a short ride, made much shorter by my changing back into normal clothing and starting to sort through the things in the storage. I went back to the big gun thing first, not wanting to leave it as an unknown.

"Ah, it's not a weapon, it's a military construction tool. For making base camps. It makes foundations. This is interesting. Okay, it goes over there. We will be using that, I think."

"Next case, and it is full of glass eyeballs. Cameras, different ranges and types. Good, we need cameras for our outside view. It's kind of low resolution right now."

Nyos was doing something like meditating. I rummaged and found an old, plain wooden box. I opened it and it showed a little water damage but the interior looked fine. There was a plain paper flyer inside explaining the contents. I looked at the things in the box, which were slightly dusty. They looked like ceramic coasters you might put a drink on.

Extracting one, the dust flew a little but the coaster looked clean and new. It had a pebbled glassy surface and was white ceramic beneath with an interlocking pattern of loops that ran over its surface. The bottom was matte finished and featureless.

The edge of the thing was coated in rubber, I guessed so you wouldn't scratch your table top. There was a bump and a dent there. I wondered if it was simply dented from being in that case for so long. The dent pressed in when ran my finger over it.

"Floaters! Little ones!" I thought back to the last container full of glass eyeballs. Yes, this could be a winner. "We can make floater spy cameras to check things out before we get there. Great!"

I ran through packages and things, figuring out what we had and putting a simple plan together.

We updated our position data and made certain that we were over the proper spot and I decided to transit the whole ship to Earth and just park it over the island. The sun was starting to dip and it was just about six PM

323

local time. Amazing how much time had passed when I was engaged in sorting and exploring things.

I selected a couple of cases and we walked to the rear ramp which I had opened to show the island below us. I had the robots place a safety rail in place so we could go to the edge without danger.

"Okay, I have this figured out. First, let's be ready to transit on my mark." I could see the island laid out light a map.

I pulled out the smelly wiffle gun and put one of the fuzzy ball things on the tip. "Be ready." I aimed it at the island, junk buildings and everything. A grid appeared over the little plastic toy gun and I selected a target. Island, dead center. Holding my breath, I pulled the little plastic trigger.

It made a soft "thop!" noise and the little rubber fuzzy stinky ball went off on an unnaturally straight course. "Back us off quickly."

The roundhouse backpedaled away from the island as the little invisible dot fell.

The sun came out. "Oh hell! Transit!"

We just caught an edge of the blast and started to buck. The skies of the "desert" world were quiet in contrast, and it was my thinking that it would be good to wait for a few minutes before transiting back.

"After all, we have to wait for the cake to cool."

I got a drink, munched on some of the fruit that was in the refrigerator, and just killed a little time. "Okay, transit to Earth." That was ten minutes, it should be done with by now.

We entered turbulence and a smoky shroud. The island was licked clean and not a stick remained standing. A constant wind was blowing up and away like a chimney, the ground was scorched and glassy. "Phase two, frosting the cake." I slipped one of the big, fancy bullet things out of the gun case. The lines, dots, and patterns were diameter settings and slab thickness settings. I turn the shell end to something like 140 meters diameter and a quarter meter thickness. The shell slipped smoothly into the breech.

This one had a hologram grid also. I locked onto the center of the detonation zone and pulled the trigger. The shell exploded from the gun with a sharp crack. It curved upward, made a complete loop, and was facing directly down over the target area.

A little thing like a Chinese fan unfolded from the nose of the shell and turned into a flat circle. It landed in the center of the zone and the shell spun like a break dancer in the middle of the little origami circle. A fine reddish mist sprayed out from it in strings and streamers.

Immediately the glassy area began to foam and sink as if acid were eating a hole in the Earth. I could see something like snakes or worms forming and collapsing in the boiling zone of sand. There was a perfect circle of activity now.

In moments it had started rising like a load of bread. The foundation was thickening and deepening. "Wow, pretty cool. Borneo, take us directly over the center of activity please."

The Roundhouse moved slightly, slowed, adjusted a bit. Now below I could see the frothing and squirming mass of glassified sand and foundation rock of the island. The perimeter had a thick border that had formed like the edge of a bowl that kept the activity trapped within. Within minutes the activity was slowing. The material had stirred itself to a uniform state and was now leveling. It looked like oatmeal with lots of steam and bubbles for a while.

The light had been dropping and the air was clearing. The mushroom cloud from the explosion was now just a large spreading dust cloud and it caught edges of sunset orange. It made a spectacular display on its own.

Using the odd glasses I had, I clicked to infrared and could see the heat of the slab making operation was dissipating. This was probably the end of the process and it would be ready to use in a very short time. Looking at the horizon around us I then spotted a number of infrared objects both on the water and in the air. Boats and helicopters.

"It looks like the neighbors are interested in the noise."

Nyos scanned the skies lightly, almost with disdain. "They are sure to know about the purchase. The amount of money and the type of buy are things that make news. They have had time to travel here and see what you may do"

She was right.

"Now, we need to attract some businesses here. We want to make this a better world, not just save it from the Archivists. Let's figure out how to become a government and how to attract business."

She went into a machine-like mode. "You will need transportation, power, communications, and basic facilities for living."

"Yes. So an airport and marina, some business space like buildings, water, food, power. I'll bet everything we need to know is in the computers." I took another look at the ground. "That slab looks ready to use. Turn on the landing lights and take it down, Borneo. Land on that pad."

The Roundhouse lowered, centered, then extended its legs.

"Okay, we have four days to figure out our tools and goods. In the meantime we will scout the land here, figure out the best design for our new country, and also do some exploring of dead worlds. We need to find out what happens when Archivists arrive, how people respond, and what draws them in the first place.

"Day five we make a large deposit in the local bank. We need to figure out the best and most effective way to get it there without taxing our resources. I went about it all wrong the first time. I should have brought some carts or something to load and unload easily. Well, I know better now."

I'd given a lot of thought to things and there were just too many to take care of easily. It was time to recruit some help.

"First, we still need to make floaters that can look ahead for us. We have enough hardware to do that. I'm going to have to draw a basic design and have the robots put them together. We need a workshop that makes stuff. I guess that has to happen before the floaters."

I felt a little exasperated. There were so many things to do, but a lot of them had to happen before other things. My lack of familiarity with the jobs made it worse.

"I also need to make some resonators. Lyt had it worked out, I mean to a science. So workshops first. Okay, today we set up workshops."

I grabbed Nyos by the hand. "Let's survey this place before it's entirely dark, just get a layout in mind. And I want to just hold you for a while. It helps my confidence level a lot."

In a few minutes we were rounding the island, checking out the land in detail in the setting sun. It actually was quite pretty with the junk removed, and the sound of low waves rushing against the tiny strip of beach was soothing. I would glance out every so often and see the stationary ships and helicopters keeping their distance but surely watching everything.

"It's kind of scary. The Archivists are coming and might already be here. We just don't know. I hope there's something we can do to stop them."

She had her arm around my waist and pulled it a little tighter.

"I am certain that you will do something marvelous."

We floated serenely back to the Roundhouse and delayed only a little so we could watch the sun setting over the water.

I began by gathering robots. "I need you to start construction of proper work space first. Here are the layouts I have in mind. Let me know what you need. You three." I selected out the most nimble and dexterous looking robots. "Come with me."

The first I explained electronic assembly to the best I could. I gave it resonator designs and asked it what it would need. It was going to produce a parts list.

The second I instructed on machine operation. It was to learn how to operate welding, cutting, and milling hardware. I wanted it to analyze the available tools and create a list of needs.

The third was the smaller and had the most able hands. "You are going to learn to cook and clean. I'm tired of munching on things when I haven't had a real meal in days. You are going to learn all about food preparing and then I'll give you a schedule."

I looked at Nyos with a smile. "I don't expect you to be a housewife by any means. Cooking and cleaning are things that take a lot of time and our time is better spent elsewhere."

Soon we had lists of materials, tools, goods, and another list of the information needed. That actually took longer to figure out.

We found a building and construction supply not too many kilometers from us. Using two robots and two floaters, we purchased wallboard, electrical supplies, tools, whatever we could get. The prices locally were terrible but it wasn't hurting us to pay the premium.

Next we set up some basic communications and contacted a satellite company for Internet service. We purchased a large dish and had it installed in its own little building on the slab.

It was evident that we needed a place for boats to dock when carrying supplies in. I found an excavator tool in the storage room and we used it to slice and nick away until I had a nice deep canal about one third of the way into the island. One box yielded a set of plastic crystal-looking things that would eat into rock and foam it into a block that was anchored firmly into the bedrock. We made a jetty to stop erosion and we lined the new canal with sidewalks and pads to tie boats.

Within the first three days a transformation had occurred. The island was now neater and shielded from the waves, and a set of uniform slabs and pads for buildings was in place. I ordered a boat load of trees and greenery. Then another.

Robots were constantly moving about on the island. I bought a load of earth movers and construction machines and had them brought in. I had no problem with using standard machinery and thought it best to conserve my strange tools for real needs.

Now we were at a point where it was going to take time for many things to arrive. I didn't feel like traveling all over to drag things in on my own. There were other things to take care of.

The construction of a home within the Roundhouse was moving along nicely, but slowly. Most of the robot's time had been spent on the island. They were building a water treatment plant for bringing in seawater and making drinking water by the fourth day. With a sense of getting big things done, on the fourth day I decided to scan the worlds and see how the map was changing.

Melios was no longer in resonance. It had shifted along with the mini-moose world and they were now in touch, but losing contact altogether with us. The valley park world was still in touch and I wanted to explore those windows in the boulder field. I also wanted to see if we could find new tech worlds.

The workshops were now in shape and our first new resonator was tested. One of the boxes in the storage room contained little plastic tubes full of computers about the size of my fingernail. We installed more cameras all over the Roundhouse and also installed radar and thermal sensors.

I felt it was time to travel a bit. I left a set of three robots and a generator to accept shipments and we lifted the Roundhouse. The transit to the valley park world was almost like a relief.

"Okay, time to find out what this is about. Let's scan everything first."

The field of boulders was not odd in any way that I could tell. They were rather normal looking smooth brownish boulders. In some places where the boulders were close together, there was a window that bridged the gap and made a little greenhouse looking thing.

In other areas there was just grass and boulders. It looked very mysterious.

I got a closer look at a window. Inside was very hot, leaving the grass to turn brown and crumbly. In the center of the glass was a red cactus thing.

Now this wasn't a spiny cactus but more like a thick succulent plant. It had dark gray-green coloration in some places but it was outlined in bright red and it split into slices like a loaf of bread. Each slice was outlined as well and so some areas were quite red indeed.

"Well, I guess I can understand the cactus needing a greenhouse, but what makes them?"

The windows themselves were odd. They had the look of sheets of material glued together. There was a strange mineral look to them. I was examining one up close, leaned over it. My shadow fell on the cactus and at first nothing happened. Then a thick fluid squirted from the cactus to the window from the inside.

The liquid was some sort of sap. It was white with a faint bluish look to it. As soon as the fluid spurted something like a little beetle scurried up on the window. Soon other small insects of the same type were behind him. They spread flat comb-like limbs and began to smooth the fluid out. They were apparently eating some of it but the bulk was spread over the surface and as it dried, it became transparent.

After a few minutes the beetles ran back down the window, then disappeared inside holes in the bottom of the cactus. They lived in it and it provided food. They maintained its little greenhouse and it keep them safe from predators. It seemed like an ideal system.

I walked slowly around the boulders and discovered something else. All the chinks and cracks were filled with mud. How did it get air? More to the point, how did the window get started in the first place? It was just plain amazing.

I took the step onto the floater platform. "Wow, beetles and cactus. What will we see next?"

I scanned for resonances. Faint lines, no more. I checked the computer next but nothing really stood out. There was a fast-moving world not far off. I would have to move at a fair pace to catch it thought. "Nyos, are you willing to check out this other world?"

"Of course."

I raised the floater and moved us up to speed. The lines locked in easily. Transit.

Nothing outstanding. Scrubby spiny things and packs of little animals flowing around them in a herd. The vegetation was red and orange like an autumn world. Rodent things were moving in one direction mostly, like lemmings rushing to the sea. I scanned for more lines.

Two more appeared. I transited to the first.

Mud flats. A geyser was spraying in the distance. Bitter alkali was in the wind. Everything was too bright and the ground was slick with pale gray mud and crusted with brown salts. I moved the floater to the drier ground a few meters ahead and saw the mud the color of old creamed coffee, drying into a sheet and fracturing. The salts grew in sparkling crystals on the edges of the fractures.

No more apparent lines to transit to, so I made the trip back to the autumn-colored world. The lemming things were gone now, leaving only a quiet landscape similar to scrub vegetation on coastlines or in swamps. "Makes me think of the Everglades."

I tried the other line.

This was a broad cultivated field. Rows of crops stretched for kilometers. I made the floater rise substantially. I didn't want to cause alarm with the locals.

Plants here looked pretty normal. Some of the rows were particularly dark purple but that was even true on Earth sometimes. Large leafy things like kale or spinach grew in most of the rows. We cruised past a few different fields. Some had large pale squash things under large leaves. The fruits had a pinkish-tan color and a sort of gourd shape. It smelled like Earth and even looked a lot like it.

I saw a person below. The form was thin, attenuated. I called down. "Hello!" I was waving.

The person jumped slightly, then turned in the general direction. "Up here." It looked at us and dropped a hoe. I brought the floater a little lower, just barely over the ruffled greens. "Greetings."

The person below was like a long, thin lizard. Its head was at least thirty centimeters long and had large dark eyes. The neck was also slender and moved gracefully. The legs reminded me of horse legs but slimmer. A glistening whip tail stuck out behind, almost rigid.

It was dressed in a frilly fabric thing like a farmer's wife might wear, a white cloth with flower prints on it. It stared but did not move. I looked at Nyos and then brought the floater down to a place where I could step to the ground. Its eyes were riveted the whole time.

With hands outstretched, I stepped carefully from the floater, avoiding the crops. That brought a small reaction as the head flicked back and forth a little to see what I was doing. "I would like to speak to you."

I placed my fingertips together and bowed slightly, then stopped a few meters from the being.

Slowly, slowly, it seemed to relax a little. It took a slow, tentative step in my direction, watching the floater and me, flick, flick. The dark, liquid eyes never stopped moving. I looked at the crops, bent and took interest in one of the plants. It had a moist, green smell to it, like celery with a hint of a spice. I slowly withdrew from the plant and looked back at the lizard thing. It had advanced maybe two steps.

It looked at Nyos. She waved at it. Then a curious thing happened.

The thing made a high pitched whine and a warding motion, crossing its arms and dipping its head low. It knelt and would not raise its head again.

"Should I approach it? It might bite or something."

Nyos shook her head. "I don't think it will want to put you in its mouth. It appears almost frightened. I don't know why."

"Well, yeah, aliens from who knows where drop out of the sky. I hadn't thought about it, but it appears that I'm an alien on this world." I stepped back and mounted the floater. I called out once more.

"Bye, have a nice day." We lifted off and I went up to some altitude. It looked like a world of mostly farming, but I was only seeing a small portion of it. I checked for resonances and found none.

We transited back to Earth and looked down on the island. A ship was docked in the marina and robots were unloading bulldozers and building supplies. Good enough. We went back to the Roundhouse and docked.

"People are scared of you. I don't get it. Maybe your people have been on other worlds, like the djinn legends on Earth. That might explain it."

She looked at me with concern. "As much as I know, there are some things that I cannot access. Data or memories, call it what you will. It is frustrating and I feel that it would answer many questions."

"Yeah. Hmmm. Well, let's at least see how things are progressing."

I could smell a roast cooking. "That's encouraging." We walked to the kitchen and saw lots of industry going on. "Yeah, that's the thing. Good meals and hot showers. You can live anywhere if you have those two things." I turned to her and took her shoulders in my hands. "I have to show you what I have been doing here. You probably figured it out anyway because it's no secret."

We took a little dogleg around one hall and there was a wooden door. "You see, I never really thanked you properly for the work you did on the cabin. You made it into a little palace while I slept. Now I'm making a proper place for you, with all the things you have never had in it.

"This might help you to have a more human experience of how good life can be. It will also help me feel more at home and I'll have less to focus on just staying alive."

"Oh, Mike." She looked as if something had really touched her. "You are so kind. But I have all I need." Her cool hands were on each side of my face, her eyes bigger and happier.

"Nyos, you deserve the best. I don't have anywhere near your knowledge or power, but I do know that I want you to always be happy. I can at least try to do that."

The door was unlocked; I let her in before me. "Ladies first."

The tour was definitely a good thing for her. She had been doing so much for me and now I just wanted to let her take some time to herself and enjoy things as they came.

"Now, let's concentrate on saving the Earth and then I want to see if we can find Lyt. He has to be somewhere that we can reach him. Or at least you can."

I took a trip to the kitchen again where that roast was about ready to eat. Nyos stayed in the new home and busied herself with things there. She seemed very happy and that made me feel light and happy myself.

I spent some time concentrating on moving a few hundred tons of metals. Tomorrow was bearing down on me but at least I had the proper tools now.

CHAPTER 17

This has been a day of disasters.

First, the main holographic system went down. No explanation, everything simply stopped working in the control room. I checked what little I know, but nothing made any sense. I powered it all down, then rebooted it. Nothing.

I made do with the backup display systems that some of the alien computers had. They carried us well enough but I didn't have my controls. I configured my pocket computer to act as a surrogate.

Next we had problems with a generator. The power output started to drop and there was no explanation for it. I brought the ship down over the boulders and glass world, found a spot that did minimal damage and landed.

The robots filed out and started going over the hull. There was a small metallic object stuck right through it, like a dart. One of the Birgan robots gently pried it out and got it in one try. The hole was a problem but I had a tool for that.

As the robot was carrying the odd metal dart around so I could look it over, it exploded. Scratch one robot. Somebody had obviously planted something nasty in it and didn't want it to be examined.

I checked the hole over after having another robot check for explosives. Only traces could be found. I gave it the personal look and found that something had burned into the interior. The hull was a metal skin over a foamy metal interior and then a foamy plastic interior. That was apparently how the optimizer had rebuilt the hull for strength and insulating properties. But buried inside the plastic were what looked like spent shell casings. A hole from each led off into the plastic foam.

I had one of the Boro robots look into it and I turned my x-ray glasses on the site.

The three shells had held little robots about a centimeter across and they had burned their ways into the foam and gotten inside things. In the middle of the search our lights went out and the computers went offline. Nyos appeared quickly, wondering what had happened.

"Somebody shot a little missile with what looks like little robots or something in it, and it buried itself in the hull. When one of the robots dug it out, it exploded and destroyed the robot. Now we're searching for the little robots from the missile. And the power is down, and the computers are down, and the Roundhouse is stuck in boulder land."

Nyos looked very unhappy. "I will see to this." She vanished in a thunderclap. That startled me greatly.

I found that the power generator was burned through and through. Something had happened to it, I had no idea what. The secondary was not burned out but it wasn't making any power either. "Check it and see what it needs."

One Birgan construction robot started a checkout. "Fuel" was its only word.

I scanned through the room and found something interesting. There was a thumb sized hole in the wall and a scorch mark all around it. Small bits of metal were on the floor. Copper and shiny black stuff was crunching under my shoes. A Boro robot said "this generator has been EMPed."

That was it. "Thirty robots scan the entire hull millimeter by millimeter. Find anything out of place or unusual, any damage. Find it and report to me immediately."

I turned to the Birgan robot. "What type of fuel does it need? Let me know and we will find something."

The computers were next. We took each one off the circuit one after the other. Eventually the network came back up. Every machine was repairing some sort of virus. We checked the last three computers we disconnected and found that one had some sort of virus that was creating new virus codes. It was a sophisticated analysis program that would find out the language of a computer by testing instructions and then it would write a virus specifically to lock it up. It was turning my machines into bricks.

"Fix it!" I yelled. The machines started working on repairing the computers. They assured me that there was a backup memory store in any civilized machine and that they would be working again within the hour. I went into my storage room of miracles.

I was positively growling. I heard a dull thud noise and smelled burning plastic. Damn! Now what?

I followed the smell of destruction and found that my new house was in flames. "Gah! Put this fire out!" Two robots came with bottles and nozzles and started spraying everything. That was probably the second little enemy robot. I stepped back and thought.

These were petty things. Sometimes this sort of stuff is meant to keep you busy while other, more important stuff happens.

"Drop what you are doing and check for explosives. Check for acids, toxins, anything dangerous. NOW!"

I put my long coat on, adjusted everything and grabbed a floater. The big door rolled open and I took the floater just past the lip of the Roundhouse. Something made me stop. I left it suspended there and walked back up the ramp, made half a turn-

Thunder and fire erupted behind me. I was blown clear around the corner and tumbled on the carpeted part of the floor. Something was burning as bright as magnesium where the ramp used to be.

The floater had been rigged with something. Nyos appeared suddenly, mouth hanging open.

"Are you hurt?"

"No, not really. I wiped something wet by my eye. It was blood. "The floater had an explosive apparently. Wonder who put that there."

Davis. Maybe.

I saw a look of fury on her face. She vanished again, this time with the smell of ozone and fire. One thing this ship didn't have was a hospital. I made a note of that.

It was a slow walk to the door. I peered over the edge. The magnesium look was gone and white powdery stuff was blowing all over. The plastic foam wouldn't burn. The door was out of the way and was probably all right but that ramp was a total loss. There was a hole burned and melted into the deck and I could see scorched ground beneath it.

The floater was nothing but twisted metal and stacks of dark metal discs with pale green curvy stuff like wire scattered through them. That was irreplaceable.

"All computers are back online." That was a welcome message.

"Backup generator is now fueled and operating." More good news.

I told the computer repair robots to set up a complete backup network so that if one went down, the other would take over. I had no idea how to do it, but they *are* computers, right? So they should be able to figure it out, I guess.

Then the power generator thing- I told the Birgan robot to find another generator and wire the system so that if any generator is still running, it will still have power, and to add warning indicators so we can tell if they are low on fuel. Off it went to do the job.

Water was sluicing over the floor. Now what?

I followed the path of the water to the main cistern. There was a fist sized hole in the bottom of the tank that looked melted. Near it was another thumb sized hole. That was the third little enemy robot. Oh, wonderful.

"We need the cistern repaired and water brought in!" I was through yelling by then.

Now, how to fix the hull damage? I made that trip to the storage rooms.

I found a lot of things, and then located a couple of neat devices. One was a coating that made the surface puncture and impact resistant. It was a rubbery liquid that contained nanoparticles that would stick together and make an impermeable shell when struck by impact. That sounded handy.

The other was a tool that softened metals. You aimed it at a piece of metal and it got doughy and malleable. Soon after the effect would wear off and it would harden up again. Excellent, I might be able to do something about some of the damage.

I dragged about half a dozen things like that out of the storage and took them with me. I must have looked like the junk man with all that crap dangling from arms and shoulders.

More instruction time for the robots ensued. They understood and started the repairs. "Now remember, don't aim that thing at yourselves or you'll turn into oatmeal!"

I spent a few quiet minutes in the bathroom in our cabin washing the blood from my scalp and face, and then just breathing deeply. This was not a good day.

At last I was ready to face this head on and continue to fix things. We were late for the bank deposit. I'd have to make that up to somebody.

There was a growing noise ahead that sounding like yelling and thumping. It was around the corner in the largest open area, an unfinished workshop. Who could be yelling? I was the only human on board. The noise grew louder. Okay, I had to see this,

The corner brought a sight. Two large robots with guns were standing outside the workshop door. It sounded like a bunch of angry men inside, but the noise would swell and ebb every so often. The robots parted as I reached the door and looked inside.

The room was full of old guys with uniforms and suits. Well, that was my first impression. After a moment of looking them over I saw that there were some young people as well and a handful of women. But they were from all over, many different nationalities and many different uniforms. There must have been about a hundred of them.

This had to be Nyos' work. She must have picked up anyone and everyone connected to this and dumped them in my lap.

I x-rayed them and found that all were disarmed. Nobody had any weapons and for that matter, they had not so much as a pen or a coin on them. Good enough.

It started to quiet. They saw me at the door and the yelling slowed and stopped.

"Hi."

It was very quiet. "You're probably wondering... a lot of things, really. Well, so am I."

Nyos appeared in the open space with a passenger, some unwilling fellow in a navy uniform. He was struggling and shouting. She stood as if made of stone, let the noise go on a bit, then *roared* at him with lots of shiny, ebon-black teeth showing. Too many, in fact. He blanched and drew back and she released his arm, letting him windmill his arms and fall backwards. She walked quietly to me, her back contemptuously to the group.

When had she grown a tail? It had a pointed end and was swishing back and forth like that of an unhappy carnivore. She looked like a demon, long black nails and all. The demon came to my side and bared her teeth at everyone.

"First, I will tolerate no noise whatsoever. If you have something to say, it would be far better for you to bite your own tongue off and spit it out. You will say absolutely nothing. You will make no noise, you will listen. If you have a problem with that, you will be made an example of."

I started to walk slowly across the front of the room, then turned and walked back.

"You have heard many things over the last couple of weeks. You are in fact responsible for much of what has been said in the news. But apparently not one of you knows anything about me or the facts. Now you will find out exactly what this is all about."

I stopped at Nyos and looked at her; smiled a little. She looked up at me with an almost helpless look. Endearing, always.

"A couple of weeks ago, I met a man who told me a number of things, and he gave me some metals to sell. He was a traveler between worlds. He needed to raise a little money so he could continue on his way with a little better equipment and we came to be friends.

"So I sold the metals and helped him. He offered me a chance to travel and learn and to have some adventure in my life. I accepted. Somebody somewhere in law enforcement decided that I needed to be… looked in to. Somebody else made up a story about these metals being stolen. Actually, they were never from Earth to start with. It was all a lie.

"We were forced to leave the Earth so he could continue his work, preparing for a difficult task. Well, the long and short of it is this. He was trying to save a world from being destroyed. But he also told me that Earth is going to be destroyed as well. This was a chance to do something about it. Well, maybe."

Some eyes were wandering, people who either knew something factual or didn't care. Others were following every word quietly.

"So I decided to find out about this enemy, the Archivists. They come to worlds with technology and they destroy them. When they are done, those worlds are dead. They leave nothing. I've been to some of those worlds. All the people are gone. Bones and corpses remain.

"At first, I wondered if this might be the result of warfare or some disease or some terrible mistake. But no. Almost every technological world is dead. Ever wonder why the sky is quiet? We don't hear aliens out there, but they should be everywhere. Well, I know why now.

"They're dead. The Archivists have been there, converted them to data. They convert a world, all its people, its cities and machines, its animals, everything about it into data. They leave a dead husk behind."

I had to stop and take a breath. I was looking at the floor too long.

"So, I have been equipping myself to try and make the situation here better. To learn about the Archivists and see what brings them, what makes them come. To see if we can do anything about it. To find a way to fight them, maybe. And if nothing else, to see if we could somehow move enough people to other worlds so that we can go on and not be destroyed by this ancient and powerful force.

"Archivists have been around for billions of years, since the beginning of the universe almost. They are old, powerful and inscrutable. No way to know what it is they want or why they do this. And so I bought this island to try to set up a place where I could work in peace, and be at hand to do whatever I might be able to do.

"I don't want to take over, or steal your gold, or blow things up. I want to make a difference, to stop the Archivists. At the very least, I want life to be better for the time we have before they do come and destroy us. And what I get is being spied upon and shot at, being vilified and nearly killed.

"What you are doing is stupid. You are directly contributing to the end of the Earth and all its people. You personally are killing the human race. I would have been happy to come to the government, or the U.N., or whatever agency is responsible for taking care of things like this, but I can't. Not one of you can be trusted. You would have me in a cell and my wife on a dissection table in minutes because she's not human.

"Just let me do what I have to do. Don't bother me. You're out of your league. I would like to think that somebody on this planet really wants to make things better but it just keeps getting worse. So here is what I am going to do.

"I issued a statement to a fellow who stowed away once, a man by the name of Davis. I told him and surely he told his superiors that if anyone tried something like that again, I would incinerate one square kilometer of the Earth, and that if they tried again, I would incinerate ten square kilometers and so on. Apparently you didn't get the message. Today you have rung up quite a tally.

"In response, I will demonstrate what I can do, and remember that the Archivists won't stop at that. They will destroy it all in one swipe. They can move worlds. I want you to prove to me that I *should* save the planet. Prove to me that you are worth saving. Meanwhile, I will do my thing and fix up my little island. If any action is taken against me, I'll interpret that as a sign that you are all insane and it doesn't matter what happens here.

"Maybe I'll just go away and let you sort it out for yourselves. But remember that the dead worlds I saw were far more advanced than this place and they didn't have a chance."

I looked at Nyos. "I have a task for you, my wife. I'll tell you later." She nodded and bowed partly.

"Okay, the way I see it, as long as you are missing, I am sending a message. I will not return you yet. You are going to have to fend for yourselves, for a little while. I don't want to have to feed and take care of you, but it's the only humane thing to do. You've caused me and everyone an awful lot of trouble.

"Some of you have tracking devices buried inside your bodies. I can't put you back on Earth because you'll be found pretty quickly. It defeats the purpose. Therefore, I'm going to put you on another world. When I have decided how this will resolve, I'll return you to your homes. If the Archivists come while you are on this other world, then you get to be the last of humanity.

"So while I have important matters to attend to, you will get down to the basics. Nothing you see around you will be edible, because the proteins are different. You can drink rainwater or whatever I supply."

There was a faint voice in the back

I glanced at her. "Bring him to me."

She walked into the crowd and pulled one struggling fellow by the leg. He lurched around and grabbed her ankle and then her arm. His leg swung hard and connected with a crack. Oh, no.

She grabbed his leg and twisted it until I heard the joint pop. Her skin began to color and glow. I could smell burning cloth and then maybe flesh. He started to scream.

Nyos stood slowly, without effort, still holding him tightly. Light flames danced over her skin. She raised him like a toy and threw him hard on the metal floor. He was groaning in agony. She dragged him again, this time by the other ankle and dropped him at my feet. I looked down, shook my head.

I whispered to her. "Take him to another room. Keep him quiet. Let them wonder." She bowed, palms together. The unfortunate was grabbed and they vanished.

I looked at the group, all of whom had backed away and were rather crowded into the rear of the room. "You have probably figured out by now that my wife is a djinn. Some of you call them genies or whatever. They are not. They are a race that is not from Earth and billions of years old. Powerful, but we don't know if even they can stop the Archivists.

"And, you've probably also figured out that I can get anyone, anywhere, any time. There is no place on Earth or off that I cannot reach you. There is no place you can put something out of my reach. There is nothing I cannot get and probably that I cannot do."

She returned, bowed and resumed her stance at my left.

"So, let's get started." I turned and left them behind, strode out between the two guard robots, and down the hall. Nyos was right behind me. The voices began to grow behind us.

"Oh, god, I hate confrontations." I was starting to sweat.

"You made the right choices. I don't see how they can say or do anything."

It was frustrating but at last I had reached people who might possibly be able to tip things properly. I had to do something else though, to get the word out. Perhaps I could.

I stopped and turned to face her. She was waiting, expectantly. I grabbed her tail as it swished once, surprising her.

"And what's this? Demon, huh?" I pulled the tail gently forward and rubbed it between thumb and forefinger. I let it slip until I had the barbed tip in my hand. She smiled and looked down at the floor.

"Most of the people I was retrieving respond well to the Christian images of demons and pitchforks. It strikes deeply into their psyches."

I pulled the tip forward and kissed it. "Yeah, just don't get too happy with it."

She dimpled and began slowly changing back. "That tickled." The tail shrank and vanished, the claws did as well. "You said you had a task for me. What is it?"

"I think we have to let the people know what's coming. Some sort of big flashy thing, letting them know that the Archivists will be here very soon. I don't want to start a panic but I just don't know what else to do."

"You start with something that most everyone can get to."

Yes. That might work.

"Meanwhile, we have to see if this ship is usable. Let me get status reports first. And let's take water to our guests."

The hull was clear of holes, one other explosive had been found and disposed of, and the damage to the cistern had been repaired. I reloaded all the robots and tools. "Let's drop off this gold. We'll take the whole damn ship. I don't care who sees it."

We transited to Earth and started moving along at a couple of hundred klicks. "Borneo, if anything fast and small starts coming toward us, transit back to the desert world please and let me know."

"Understood."

I checked on the rear ramp that had been blown apart. There was a plate of metal in place of the ramp, the hole had been patched and the door brought down and sealed. It looked airworthy at least. We increased speed to just under four hundred. The capitol was minutes ahead.

"Oh, dear. What did you do when you vanished the first time?"

"I incinerated one square kilometer of a military base in a desert."

The bank was below. I was better prepared this time. The metals were loaded on flat dollies and rolled to the remaining floater. "Um, just for fun, roll all those dollies by the door where the prisoners are. Let them get an eyeful. It's not just fluff and words. Like you said, people respond to money."

Nyos altered her look to that of the previous meeting, coloring her eyes golden and growing slightly taller and more bronze. It was eerie watching the transformation. You couldn't see it all happening but you were aware that something was changing.

We started to deliver the gold by floating it directly from the bay door to the rear of the bank, where we had entered the previous time. We met with Mr. Ndonga and Mr. Mkolo, and I apologized about the delay. Oh, geez, she was nude. I hadn't thought about the demon appearance before. Whatever.

"We had a small military matter to handle. It took a few hours to settle things."

Mr. Ndonga looked worried. "There has been some news coverage. It appears that the conflict is at a standstill right now." That was startling. I didn't know there was any conflict that people might see.

He was eyeing Nyos and made no mention of her appearance. She stood motionless and seemed to flex and ripple slightly.

"Well, here is the deposit. This is the first load. If things get busy we may have to come back and make the rest at some other time."

"I understand. Er, is that your craft outside the building?"

"Yes. I hope it doesn't cause any distress."

His troubled look intensified. "It brings unwanted attention, unfortunately. However, we will handle it."

It took an hour to unload three hundred tons of metals. The bank staff was backed up and unable to accept any more. The treasury was unwilling to hold and guard it also.

"This will be sufficient for now, and when you are ready we will bring some more." He provided a sheet for me to sign and presented the bank account package.

"We have credited your account with twenty three billion U. S. dollars based on the rough estimate of the value we see. It may vary considerably by the time we have tallied everything but you will have no trouble purchasing anything from this account."

"Thank you. And now we have some business to attend to." The floater was being used to retrieve some of the empty dollies. We had to wait about a minute for it to return.

"Let's go. Lots to do."

I found a nice looking spot that would provide a safe enough place for the prisoners to stay. I left them with shovels so they could dig latrines and enough bottled water for the next three days. If they kept the bottles they could collect more. I also provided a large cook pot, a bag of rice, rope, and enough canvas to make some covered space. It would be tough but they should be able to make it if they cooperated.

We brought the Roundhouse down low and dropped the survival

supplies first. Then I marched them six at a time to a ramp where they would board the floater. The floater went down under remote and they were to step off it. Then the next load would be escorted to the ramp. The one fellow with the burned leg and arm was a problem.

I'm not a mean person, understand. But sometimes you have to go a little beyond. This might be fun. One of the computers had a really nice holographic projector. I had it loaded with a program that came to mind.

I ordered him restrained to a bed. There were some chairs left from our destroyed home. They smelled of smoke and water. I thought it was appropriate to use one.

The chair was delivered to the room and he actually flinched when he smelled it. I entered and sat by his bed.

"You kicked my wife." His shirt sleeve had a handprint scorched into it and so did his pants leg. I could see a large, wet blister on his leg.

His face was covered in sweat. He looked at the ceiling and then at the door but refused to look at me. "I know that she did not make you deaf. I might have to call her and let her deal with you as she sees fit. I would let her do that."

He shuddered. "Then look at me and talk with me. I've seen her walk through stone and throw lightning. You can't imagine what she can do." He remained silent and shaking a little.

I pulled my chair closer and leaned over a little to whisper with confidentiality.

"Remember the stories of the djinn in the Arabian Nights? All the things they could do to people, like stretching them over beds of red hot knives and hanging them upside down over molten lava? Or peeling their skin off and... you get the picture."

He was clenching his teeth hard and his breath was short and fast.

"Well, those evil djinn might well have been her ancestors. Or her parents. I mean, I have no idea how long they live but it can be..."

There was a rush of wind and she appeared, looking even more demonic, if possible.

"Why, hello my dear. Have you disposed of the others completely?"

"Surely, my master. Their suffering will be great and long. They will never be found."

"Thank you." I activated my computer and set a sequence in motion. The room became slightly warmer. The holograms faded up slowly.

"I was having a little chat here with this fellow."

"He kicked me!"

The fellow gasped hard and strained against the restraints.

"And so he did, which makes me extremely unhappy."

He had to be feeling the heat. The chair was starting to stink and the more I moved, the more the smell filled the room. It was awful. I moved a lot.

"Well, he seems to be unwilling to say anything. Shame really, I thought we could settle things with, you know, civility."

I got up as the holograms were starting to get obvious, showing flames and lava. The room was really heating up. The chair was really stinking. Nyos was moving closer to him. "Well, dear, I'll let you talk with him for a bit. I'm sure he appreciates having a visitor."

She actually hissed. I walked to the door.

I put the last straw in place. "I feel like a snack. Barbecue sounds about right."

He screamed. Really, bloody scared-the-hell-out-of-him screamed like a little girl. His eyes were scrunched down tight and his teeth gritted so hard I thought he'd break a couple. His throat was even clenched. He started to whine with each breath like he was being eaten alive.

I walked back to the chair. "If there's something you want to say, now's the time."

That broke him. He started to talk and the words tumbled out so fast I had to slow him down a few times. I keyed my computer and the holograms stopped and the heat went off. The chair was without help; I had it removed from the room.

First he told me that he was an executive clerk, not a soldier. He worked logistics. His job was to determine supply movement and how to integrate it with the battle plan. The upshot of it was that they had determined that I was dealing with an alien and that there was a threat to everyone as a result.

They had planned to plant a small nuclear device on the island and detonate it, then claim that we had been planning to attack and the weapon had apparently misfired.

It sounded like a load to me. Nobody could think that a plan that stupid would be believed. But he seemed earnest, so I took the information at face value. There was probably a nuke somewhere on my island. I didn't particular care about the rest.

Now I had to do something to treat his burns and possibly a dislocated leg. "I'll get you some medical treatment for your injuries. I'm going to send you someplace for a little while so you can't get in the way. And maybe you would be better off bagging groceries for a living."

I instructed a robot to give him water and feed him after letting him out of the restraints. He was not to leave the room. I would figure the rest out soon.

How can things be so stupid? I sold some metal, now I had to find a nuclear weapon. The frustration level was immense.

Wait a minute. Again, a sense of clarity seemed to descend. This didn't make sense for a reason. This guy was too scared, and then too talkative. If there was really a nuclear explosive on the island, why would the ships and helicopters be hanging around? Didn't somebody know?

And everyone had been told time and again that Nyos was an alien, and it really didn't seem to bother most people. I had the feeling that our talkative captive was not being quite square. And, every moment I spent with him was time I wasn't doing something else.

It was time to step back a few paces and find out what was happening.

First, I scanned the prisoner for tracking devices. He was clean. Then I went to see Mr. Ndonga. "I need a favor. I have a fellow who has been injured. He needs medical attention and he also needs to be isolated for three days. No communication in or out, no chance he can get away. I will pay for the service. Can you arrange something?"

He actually looked conspiratorial. "Ah, prisoner of the conflict. I can see that this will be an outcome of the sort of dealings you must do. I have had to make arrangements for some of my larger depositors and good customers. You may be surprised to know how often this is done."

He steepled his fingers. "Yes, I can do it."

We worked it out, I was given a number to call, and things were made to happen. One issue was out of the way. Next problem.

It was ridiculously difficult to set up on the island. Ships and things all over, hanging around. Waiting for what? I would have to set up elsewhere but the island could still be useful. I needed better information and to fix the damage inside the Roundhouse. We really needed a day of downtime and some supplies.

The obvious solution was a short trip to a large city to buy supplies, which we did. Having one floater was not crippling but made things difficult. In Africa, supplies can be had but the prices are usually outrageous. We paid what we had to and got sheet metal, plywood, carpeting, and electrical wire.

After loading up, we flew back to a couple of kilometers from the prisoners. I scanned for frequencies and checked the computer. We were not due for another resonance for a few days. That was a letdown but that's in the nature of the thing.

We found a decent place to land and cleaned out the fire damage. Time was spent on general repairs and we made small resonators and put some floater probes together. I also experimented with making the resonator key two frequencies at once, in theory keeping the probe halfway between two worlds. It seemed to work, leaving the floater translucent and hazy.

Now we could send data in realtime between two worlds. Success!

Next was the armoring for the Roundhouse. The repairs for the bay door and ramp were not great but the robots made a fix that didn't look patched over. I had the robots apply the liquid armor stuff from the storage room mystery box and it stuck to the surface nicely. I didn't want to test it but it was nice to know we had at least something.

I wanted to find new resonances. Another tech world would be great to find, if possible. But the storage room treasures had only been scratched upon. It would have been more productive to simply spend a day looking at the things there and finding what Nyos had felt would be useful.

My main concern about tech worlds was finding out what happened when the Archivists arrived. What was their arrival like and what did they do? Fire and thunder? Silent and subtle? Perhaps something in the middle.

The process seemed to leave most things untouched, or a lot of things. But Boro, for instance, might have been the victim of a biological accident and that would leave the Archivist's off the hook for that dead world.

What still bothered me was what the trigger might be. Nyos didn't seem to know much about the subject. That too was troubling. She had a monumental amount of knowledge but as she had said, there were some things that she could not remember or get access to.

Well, we had made progress and I had few worries about prisoners. I decided to check on them and see what was going on.

There wasn't a lot of greenery to deal with because this was a pretty rocky area, although there were a few trees. Somebody had organized a little and had gotten some of the rocks and boulders moved around. The meager scraps of wood were lashed together to help make some poles and there was a fire. The canvas had been stretched over the rocks and poles to make a large shaded area.

I could smell rice cooking so at least they weren't going hungry.

At this point I had to tally my pluses and minuses. I had a lot of capital to work with, that was a plus. I couldn't go anywhere on Earth without being recognized and perhaps hunted, that was a minus.

I had gotten an island which now had a marina and some decent landscaping, that was a plus. I had a lot of important prisoners to deal with, that was a minus.

After a few such points, I was kind of depressed. I really didn't want to deal with any of it. It was time to send a small floater through and see what was going on with my island.

We set up a realtime link and started operating a mini-floater and its simple instruments to look for anything unusual. The robots were still present on the property and had unloaded earthmovers and a paving machine. It looked normal enough.

I sent the mini-floater up next to one of the robots and sent instructions. They were to scan everything for explosives and unknown hardware. That ought to be sufficient for now to find anything obvious. Meanwhile they were to proceed with construction and at least it would appear that things were normal.

Next, I outfitted one mini-floater with that metal softening thing and sent it on a cruise to the location where the ships were. Half a dozen various watercraft of a military nature were anchored or at least holding station in the distance. I had the mini-floater drop out a meter from the hull of the first and fly slowly around its hull while firing that metal softener at it. Then I transited it back and went for the second ship.

Within a few minutes it was clear that something was wrong out there. My mini-floater returned and we disarmed it. Now what could I do about helicopters? I started to laugh. For some reason, the whole ridiculous nature of it became clear. They couldn't see us coming and they couldn't hide anything from us. They didn't even know what was happening.

I didn't want to hurt anyone, but things were going to get really rough soon. Things always escalate. So how do you show somebody that you have the upper hand? You have fun with it.

I had the mini-floaters sent out to find things. Junk things. We had some steel cable in our stores and we had anchors and turnbuckles and fasteners. We had spray paint and spray foam. It took a couple of hours to get all the items together but it was worth it.

The mini-floaters became vandals of a sort. The first helicopter had its windows spray foamed and an old, broken cattle cart hung from its landing gear. They never knew what happened or how. They turned away and went back to base.

That was easy. Then we hung boat anchors, old car seats, a bathtub, and some strings of cans. This wasn't a war or even a surveillance action, it was a joke. I kept getting dumber ideas of things to do, and laughing so hard I could barely operate the computer and send commands. This day started out really, really bad but I was laughing so hard by the end of it that I hurt.

I sent two big robots to the workshop to make little silver flying saucers out of sheet metal. They were just as simple as possible, but each had a mini-floater inside. I sent four or five of these things out to the helicopters and had them appear and then start flying around them, circling and moving in all directions just out of reach of the prop wash.

They couldn't keep an aircraft or a boat in the area without something happening to it. But as silly as it all sounds, I had sent one very powerful message to them. That bathtub hanging on the landing gear could just as easily have been over the rotor.

The aircraft carrier arrived just out of sight. I moved the operation closer to the carrier and did something different. I transited the Roundhouse directly over the carrier, turned on the light bars, and hung there for about thirty seconds. A dozen mini-floaters dropped down and starting buzzing the thing. One had the metal softener and was randomly firing it at things all over the place. Any tall metal pole slumped or fell. Radar dishes just collapsed. Railings and stairs sagged like rubber. Spray paint was flying too.

The mini-floaters all vanished and I turned off the light bars and transited the Roundhouse safely out of reach.

That carrier looked like a disaster. It looked like something you would find in an alley.

Finally, I had had enough silliness. This was pointless but at least I felt a lot better. There was something constructive that I could pull out of this.

It was time to send a video.

I made a short recording stating that as long as there were aircraft and ships watching my island, I would render them useless. And for every day that they kept spying on my island, I would render a military base useless.

That went for any government and included satellites.

Time to check on the prisoners again and see if they had any problems. Then I was going to do absolutely nothing except what I wanted to do.

I bought thirty roasted chickens and thirty bottles of orange juice, a case of potato chips and a crate each of lettuce and tomatoes.

"Nyos, I have a request." Somehow I knew that she would appear.

"Have you been having fun?"

"Yeah, stupid fun. Too much fun. This day has taken a turn for the better."

She smiled broadly. "A wonderful adventure. What do you need me to do?"

I took a moment to formulate it properly. "The prisoners have only seen you as the demon, right?"

"Yes. Tail and claws, fire and brimstone."

I chuckled a little because I hurt too much to laugh more.

"Okay, let's do something different. The djinn bit, silks and everything. Let them wonder, they will probably think you are somebody else. Confusion is good. If they think there are three or four of you, it just makes it even better. So I don't really want them to go hungry or live on water and rice. I got dinner for them and I want you to deliver it in grand style."

She looked interested. "The genie delivers a meal? I can do that."

"Great. Do the golden almond eyes and the whole deal. Look magical I guess. Have fun with it."

I let her do as she wished. There wasn't a doubt in my mind that she would make it memorable for the prisoners and have fun while doing it.

What I really wanted at this point was to find Lyt and see what was happening. I also needed to find more information about Archivists. Nothing was happening on that front and it disturbed me to realize how easily I had sidetracked myself.

There were too many things to handle at once.

It was the work of a moment to go to the cabin and find the half bead of amethyst that Lyt had left behind. I had few enough crystals any more, having gotten far too lax in collecting samples from the places I had been to. However...

I retrieved the resonator also and started checking some things. There was a batch of little crystals in it, and if I were to wave Lyt's half bead over them and read the results, I could tell which, if any, of the crystals in the detectors were triggered.

So after connecting the resonator to the computer network, then asking the computers to read whether a change had occurred or not, I could get the resonator to respond to the crystal. I would save all the changes and put those into my computer and ask it one question- which world matched the pattern of worlds in resonance for that crystal?

I could have kicked myself. I should have been doing this all along. Then I would have more data and be able to narrow down the connections. But as it happened, there were six hits and they all converged on three worlds. Then as I waved the crystal over the detector some more, over different areas, some worlds were excluded. Two worlds remained.

I felt certain that one of those worlds had to be Lyt's home world.

I ran plots all night, trying to find a pathway to those worlds. I looked in every conceivable path, every conjunction, trying to find a way to get there. It would take a week at best to be able to do it, and only by making three high-speed connections in the process.

But I was missing something. What did I mean by "high speed"?
Damn.

I was using the numbers from the dirt bike. I had something faster, much faster now. I entered the new numbers and used the new top speed of four hundred klicks as a parameter. Wow, suddenly I had three pathways and they could be done within a day! Either one of those worlds could be reached right away, but the other would be trickier once I made a choice. I could get to both but it would take time. The pathway would be disintegrating behind me and I had to choose one now.

This meant I had to send my prisoners home now. I couldn't risk leaving them to starve if I got stuck somewhere or worse, dead. I had to decide what to do.

Once I thought about what was important and what the priorities were, it was a simple choice.

CHAPTER 18

It was nearly morning when I got my plans together. The prisoners enjoyed their meal and were actually rather jovial when the sun set. Nyos had spent a good deal of time with them, and they seemed to be speaking to each other about the situation. They spoke to her with reservations but it seemed that so much misinformation had been flying around that nobody really knew anything. Now, after a little isolation and some talking, they were much more cooperative.

Maybe they would talk to the right people and get the proper words in the proper places to bring this foolishness to an end.

We took them all to Aruba and dumped them there that morning. They probably thought we were taking them on a long flight between the stars. We were simply floating along in the desert world going from one point to another. Aruba was just as close as I felt obligated to go.

I picked up some of the robots on the island and things got real quiet there for a while. The larger robots remained and did construction and landscaping. If anyone was still spying they would die of boredom soon.

I loaded every conceivable tool, machine, food, and supply that I could think of. My bank account did work; Mr. Ndonga had done well.

Now, at last I had all the legwork done and was going to find out what happened to Lyt and if he did in fact find his home world. I set the robots at work finishing off the home that I sorely needed by now. We were going to be traveling a bit, and I wanted to at least be comfortable. It was early afternoon and I also wanted to see new places.

We transited to the valley park world and spent a few hours there waiting for a high-speed resonant world to catch up to it. The Roundhouse was moving at a pretty fair clip, about 280 klicks. We transited.

More jungle stuff, a bluer sun.

The plants were not impressive or amazing, the planet itself was nothing spectacular. We would be waiting for about three hours for the next connection.

I read four resonant lines and we traveled to each and collected samples and rocks. There was one workshop set up for lapidary work and we made good use of it. Rocks were cut and polished and labeled, machines were busy cataloging things.

When the right time came, we moved up to speed again and transited to another world. This was an ochre place with a dimmer, redder sun. It was bloated and about three times the size of the sun I knew. The ground was darker and cooler and frost seemed to coat most everything. Ropy dark green things lay on the ground amidst orange and brown leaves the size of beach umbrellas. A corroded-looking moon hung over it all with a yellow-gray sheen. I checked for more lines and found two worlds we might explore.

One had a frosted, slushy world with an even dimmer sun, one framed by brilliant orange flares and prominences. The ground seemed burned and crusted. I spotted something and we came closer to it. It was a melted and charred stump of a skyscraper.

We got samples and I made a note that it would be worth exploring at some point. The air itself seemed rancid and scorched. The smell of hot metal and burned plastic was in every vagrant breeze. Nyos pronounced it Murdossa.

There were no easily explored lines here and we went back to see the other world we could reach. There would be a little time to kill.

The transit was odd. There was a strange feeling when we went through that I cannot explain. It felt like a little twist sort of.

"We are near a black hole of great mass. The spacetime itself is curved in odd ways. We are in just the right place in this... manifold... to transit now. We need to go back quickly."

I scanned the area. It was a normal looking world and we were near a sea. But the sky seemed darker than you might expect, and the air pressure was low. I could feel it starting to trouble my ears. We transited back.

"How could we even be in resonance then?"

"The star and planet had the proper masses and proper velocities for it to work but it would not have lasted for long and the Roundhouse would have been stuck there."

That was alarming.

So we waited now for another connection.

It was quiet enough in this dim world. The sun was huge and soft, and the lighting made it look very spooky. I saw what looked like phosphorescent things moving on the ground. Here were mammals that seemed to have glowing spots on their fur.

I turned on the light bars and this might have been the first time in ages that bright white light had shone on this place. The plants seemed to cringe, leaves sluggishly folding into themselves. The air smelled funny, with hints of waxiness and dried leaves. I thought of wet newspaper and candles when I smelled it, like a trash pile but not offensive.

It was time to take a break and look around at things the robots had been doing.

I walked through our house and the smell of the fire was gone now. New furniture was in place and I thought it might be nice to sleep in this room, draped with fabric hangings and a large round bed lined with pillows. The decor looked oriental. There were finely carved dividers of rich, dark polished wood and low ceramic pots with candles in them.

The back wall was a paper screen with low level lights behind it. Large brass urns with circular interlocking patterns held hibiscus flowers and something I didn't recognize. Come to think of it, it could be an unearthly species. The flowers were overlarge and had dark purple edges with veins fading into white in the centers. The smell was very soft with sweet overtones.

Yes, this was a beautiful room. I pulled my shoes off just to walk on the cream carpeting that outlined the polished wood floor that the bed was set upon. How things changed in the space of a few weeks.

It was compelling to just sit and relax a bit, do nothing for a while. There was a quiet sound in the background that I had only now noticed. It sounded like a small water fountain splashing and wind chimes. I found a small footstool and sat on it.

What if I didn't find Lyt?

It was an excellent question. I only knew where he was going up to this point. If this was the right world. It might be the other, and that would take longer to reach but perhaps this was it. I was near a resolution though.

So if I found Lyt's world but not Lyt, how would I know? Perhaps it would be self-evident. The other dead worlds were sad places but I couldn't figure out truly if they were that way due to something they did or due to the Archivists. I just didn't have enough information.

I sat and thought in that most peaceful room, letting the ideas and worries flow through me like some placid, barely moving body of dark, cool water. My hands ached a little when I flexed them but it was okay. It was part of the moment.

After some long while I stood and inhaled deeply, the gentle odor of the flowers and the carpeting and the wood all like some fine, mellow tea for the soul. I was at peace. No matter what I found, it would be fine.

Turning and walking slowly and in thought, I left the home and went to the storage room.

Nyos was there, sitting cross-legged on the floor and with the look of the djinn. It struck me that no matter what form she took, she was beautiful. I scarcely wished to disturb what mental musings she might be forming.

She spoke as the moment came.

"You will find Lyt's home world. I am certain of that."

"Yes. I will. But I don't know what else we might find."

She looked up at me from her lotus position. "Michael." It was a soft word.

I knelt down beside her and placed a hand on the floor. "Yes, Nyos."

"I am worried. I cannot say why. I have a sense of something coming, something terrible." She shook her head slowly. "Be careful my love."

I felt something too. You can't say what when you're in the situation, but it's like some moments in your life have a crystal clarity to them, and you *know* that something important is happening right then. You know that some juncture has been reached and you must choose what happens next. That this single frozen moment is very important to what comes next. I've had that feeling maybe three times in my life, and something was coming now, almost tangible.

She spoke again.

"Love me always, Michael?"

My heart warmed.

I took her in my arms and held her closely on that hard, cold deck floor.

"Oh, Nyos. Always, without end. I will love you always. If you had never brought one single material thing to me, you will have brought me your love and that, to me, is the most wonderful thing that I have ever had in my life. You are my dream and nothing else matters to me."

I think that then, and only then, I saw a tiny tear in the corner of her eye. She was radiantly beautiful, so much so that I felt almost faint. We stood together and walked slowly to our home, and in that peaceful room with the lights darkened to little more than a whisper, we made love more tenderly than we ever had.

We lay in the dim, soft lighting in each others arms and all I could speak was "oh, Nyos, my dream." It came as a soft breath, barely more. But what emerged from my lips was something changed, something that escaped me from some place within. What I said was "Oneiros."

<hr />

I dozed lightly in that mild exhaustion and glow, completely at peace at last. We lay there until a soft chime sounded. I had some foresight in my rather manic activities to program an alert when we could make the final transit. My chest thumped hard. It was now; we were going to see exactly what had happened here. Lyt's home world was before us.

I roused quickly, kissed Nyos lightly on her softly glowing golden shoulder. She appeared to be sleeping; that was something new. Perhaps her other half was quiet for the moment, her power and ability in idle. Would she dream?

I left her for a moment, thinking that she had little experience with sleep. Perhaps it was best to let her experience it, to be at peace for a little while with no troubles. The thought of rousing her seemed out of place. Let the goddess sleep; let the djinn be at rest.

So I dressed quietly and went to the control room. We were in no hurry now; my concern was that this was the proper place and that Lyt would have left something for me.

I scanned for frequencies as a matter of habit. I knew what should show up and they did. They were logged and noted. Now it was time to set for a transit to Lyt's world and see, at last, what happened on that day so many years ago.

We transited.

It was hot, hotter than hell. The Roundhouse emerged into the sky of Lyt's planet, and it hit me that I had never once asked him the basic and obvious question. What was the name of his planet? Did that offend him in some way? Did it strike him as odd? Or was it simply a "human" thing?

I could not believe what I found. It was too fantastic, too unreal. I brought the Roundhouse down slowly and extended the landing legs, made contact with the surface and stared.

It was perfectly silent for about one minute.

My long coat was in place, my boots were on, I had my blazer and its loaded pockets. In disbelief I walked to the front ramp and brought the floater to the door.

I looked down at the round Persian rug that my dearest had placed there, and I thought of how she should be here to see this. This was incredible. Instead I let her rest.

The door opened and the floater rose marginally, just enough to clear the deck. A wave of hot, dry oven air hit me. It was breathable, yes. The sun was intensely bright, a very homey yellow sun like our own. What families had played beneath it and what lives had been lived and ended here?

In the presence of only a faint deep hum from the floater I advanced slowly to the surface. A constant hot wind blew from the east, a small amount of dust moving along on the gray, pebbled surface of shiny ceramic. One single, flat, mind-numbing piece of ceramic stretched from one horizon to the other, of such absolute flatness that it could not register in the mind fully.

The entire planet was like a billiard ball, a sealed and glazed surface. "Oh, my god."

I dropped the floater to the quizzical surface and stepped slowly and cautiously onto the hard plain. Kneeling to it and exhaling hard at once, I touched it lightly and felt the radiating heat from the sun above. It was simply baking the ground and its heat and light being absorbed, giving no life, making no clouds, driving no thoughts in the minds of any living thing.

There was nothing left. Lyt's world had been Archived.

I felt a rising gorge. This was the beginning of something beyond terror. Some force had *eaten* everything on a world, *this* world, reformed it and left only this. I felt that if I had tested, I would have found no insect, no cell, no virus.

Rising from the unforgiving and now dead surface, I turned to the ship and looked at it, feeling that it had become a target for this force, this thing that had been here and might even now be seeing us and wanting to do this to us as well.

Nyos walked slowly down the ramp and stopped, looked with incredulity at the dry, parched sky and the inviolate surface. She took two steps more quickly, then paused before stepping off the ramp. She bent low and reached to touch the ceramic as I had. I was starting to sweat through my clothing.

Her hand stopped on the surface and wiped it lightly. Then she shoved her hand at the ground. Her expression changed to astonishment.

"I can't... I can't penetrate it. This is impossible."

She stepped completely onto the surface and it looked as if she tried to swim on it. The ceramic stuff responded by glowing bursts of orange and yellowish where she lay. The light faded.

She stood slowly. "This world has been Archived." Something in her expression seemed to crumple. "Archived."

Her face set, she rose into the air and swept off in a twinkling. I heard a thunderclap as she left. I took the floater back inside and parked it. This was far beyond anything I had imagined. How could you fight this?

I looked all around the sky and saw no clouds, no dust, nothing. One thing eventually caught my sight but it was subtle. There was a very faint halo of rainbow around the sun. Some sort of tiny crystals of ice or dust were refracting the sunlight a bit.

Nyos reappeared from over the horizon, dropped in front of me and held out her hand. I presented my palm without thought.

From her clenched hand she spilled a fine grit of particles, each prismatic and dark. What was this?

She looked stunned. "We need to go."

"Okay. Let's do that."

We got back on the ship and closed the door. In moments I raised the

Roundhouse from that pale, grayish smooth wasteland and surveyed it. Nothing. No bumps, no shadows, no high or low spots.

"We need to go. Now." She was insistent.

"Okay." I transited.

"Please take us home. Go."

I found the shortest path to Earth and programmed the computer to handle it. It would take some time. My hand was still clutching the grit she had given me. It made sense to take it to the workshop and have a look at it.

Nyos wrapped her arms around herself and walked without grace, almost thumping, to the cabin. I wondered what she had on her mind. Something really alarming.

She needed to work it through. I needed to see what she had brought me.

A microscope showed that the dark granules were immensely complex. Each was a whole machine or computer or something else. These were nanostructures or made with nanotech, I didn't really know the difference or the meaning of it.

I showed them to the robots. They didn't know what they were. I checked the computers and I found an answer. They were little spy devices. Could we read them into the computer and see what they did or what they were for?

I went to my storage room of technical treasures and went through boxes, cylinders, and folded things until I located something, a nanodevice interface. This was it.

The computer read the instructions and figured out how to talk to it. I placed one of the granules in the thimble that came with the interface and the computer showed a new file. This was the same format that Lyt had used when we accessed his spy data from Kyochotz, before Farlin Dola had blown himself to bits. I opened it.

Lyt's image appeared.

"Michael, I know that you are resourceful enough to get this far. If you have then there are some things I must say. First, do not under any circumstance attempt to find me or follow me. You have no idea what you are doing.

"Second, this world was indeed Archived. So you can tell that the other dead tech worlds were killed by something else, perhaps even themselves.

But the Archivists have a very specific method and result, as you have now seen.

"Third, ask yourself some questions. How is it that you-" At this point the playback turned into floating boxes of random colors and the sound went to bursts of tones and white noise. Then it resumed.

"-will never see me again. Don't follow me, my friend. Good bye."

I read it a few times, trying to get past the garbage point, where the message was junk. The other nanospies yielded the same results. I had no luck figuring out what he was trying to say. But I had found it. I located his home world and found his message.

There was really no way to tell how old the message was, but I knew that he had only a small number of steps that he had taken, and that I could probably recreate them and figure out how he got here.

That would let me know which worlds he had stepped on and potentially when he arrived here. Maybe when he had to leave and possibly where he might have gone. I might still find him.

I had to go back to Earth. Nyos wanted to do that for some reason. She was upset, and I had not seen her that way before. Something here had affected her, made her very unhappy. She was up against some enemy that she couldn't fight.

I called on the kitchen robot to fix some dinner. Salmon, steamed vegetables and buttered biscuits sounded good. Not too fancy but a good meal.

She stayed in the cabin for some time. I was disconnected and unable to get any one idea in mind. The food started to smell good and that filled the hallways near the center of the ship.

I walked around the perimeter and stopped in front of Lyt's old cabin. It was dark and a sad reminder of the brief time we had and the things that he showed me. There was no point in hanging around there. I would want to retrieve Boron rather than let him spend his days waiting for the wizard who would never return. To that end I started the ship following a course that would take us back to the proper place where his floating workshop waited.

We spent a couple of days routing through various fast worlds and stepping-stone worlds, coming eventually to a transit that would take us to the very first desert world transit point where Boron waited patiently.

I was becoming worried about Nyos' retreat. She didn't say much and she sat for long times just meditating and looking troubled. I let her be. These clearly were matters that I had no knowledge of. There would be little help that I could give her. When she wanted my presence, she would come to me.

Lyt had been trying to tell me something. It was very strange that each and every one of the nanodevices had exactly the same break in the data. It told me that they had all been recorded from a flawed original message. Was he in such a hurry that he couldn't check them first?

Nyos had been insistent that we leave. She was scared for the first time. Something more powerful, something that she couldn't control must have been the reason. She had tried to sweep her hand into the crust of the Archived world without success. Her lack of success worried her.

We transited to a world that was so Earthlike that we stopped and landed. I spent a couple of hours flying over its surface and looking at the local forests and mountains. There were large mammals that grazed in herds like elk and others that were much larger still. They looked like plated armadillo things with clubbed tails and bizarre horns on their noses. An elephant would have been put to shame.

I didn't get too close to the ground after I saw the carnivores. I closed the ramp on the Roundhouse and had it lifted to twenty meters where it stayed for the rest of the visit.

These things were monsters and a couple of them could take down the giant rhino-dillo things without too much trouble. They were like cats but had some of the aspects of bears. Huge curving fangs made a memory click into place and I knew that these were equivalent to saber toothed tigers of the ancient past on Earth.

The area was tropical and didn't have any signs of technology or development. Animals everywhere, plants and trees in abundance. The forests were most interesting and were just loaded with monkeys or lemurs. Their calls and howls were the greatest source of noise.

I spent three more hours looking and taking pictures. After that, I felt an emptiness that couldn't be resolved. I wanted something, and my chest ached for some reason. I began to breathe a little faster. Each breath was shallow and somehow uncontrolled. "Oh, Nyos."

There was a soft rush of light and she appeared before me, hands together and bowed slightly.

"You have called Oneiros. I am here." She looked upward and relaxed her stance. "Oh, Michael, my love." She sounded sad.

"You said Oneiros. Why?"

"When you came to the Well, the source of my people, my name was taken from your mind imperfectly. I am Oneiros, one who crafts dreams."

I shuddered slightly. In my mind I saw the pale radiance of blue white light and hundreds of tubes with alien corpses in them. That soft voice that came from my computer returned to me and made my hair stand on end.

"This is... disturbing. But yes, now that you say it, I understand." I admit that there was a hint of panic behind my feelings then. But Nyos was good and loving, not the somnolent bringer of death. I would have to resolve this mentally. I could be aware of the nature of things and deal with it.

"We need to talk and figure things out. Let's do that."

"As you wish."

We returned to the Roundhouse with her snuggled against me, her head on my shoulder. There was a different scent of perfume from her now, a touch of musk and frankincense. It raised feelings in me that were in jarring contrast to the thing I had found out.

"Lyt's world. What happened?"

Her head shook back and forth slowly.

"Well, how can they make something that you can't move through? Was it some super-hard material or something?"

"No. You could have broken it yourself. It was much worse."

She looked up at me with fear. "I was unable to control my abilities. Something prevented me from being able to do things. Like a switch being turned off. I cannot find any physical reason for this; there were no strange energies or forces present. I know. I can feel all the forces of matter and energy. They are like the lifeblood of my senses."

Her grip faltered a little. "I feel the strength of the quarks and the field of the electrons. I *am* all those things together, and controlled. But then and there, somehow..."

That scared me, that she was scared.

"Then and there, something prevented me from acting in certain ways.

I have thought long about this and I have concluded that if such a force did not exist outside of me and apart from me, it must be from within. Something in me prevented me from acting. Something I do not know and cannot control."

I was stunned. "How. I mean. Well, there are two parts to you and one is human as you said. The other is something more powerful. What does it want?"

"I am being driven, it would seem. Compelled to do some things. This is very strange and dangerous. I only wanted you to have…"

She actually took a deep breath. I had never seen her breathe before. Her exhalation was slower and controlled. "…to have a wonderful adventure and an exciting life. To be fulfilled and happy. To have your dreams made real."

She had a look of dawning comprehension. "My purpose was to be what you needed, and to put you in control of your life. Your surroundings. Why?"

That sounded good, not bad. Why did it make me feel something dark and dreadful was moving massively behind the scenes?

"Oneiros, I love you always. Eternally. You aren't this force of control; you are a loving and feeling person." I was calling her by her true name, I realized. With it she became more at attention, more focused on me. There was some power within the sound of it.

She heard it. "You have been having a wonderful adventure. That was what my purpose came to be. What it always was. I see it now." She looked taller and more exotic. Something was changing in her look and stance. Her eyes were red-orange and radiant.

"And your love and care have shaped me and moderated me, made me what I am. Without that I would have been nothing more than a mechanism of base fulfillment.

"Michael, love of my existence, we must go back to Earth and resolve this."

Yes. There was a reasonable way to end this. I just wanted to spend my life with her, traveling the worlds and seeing the universe. To live for the rest of my days with the one person I cared for more than anything else. We could see this through.

Clarity descended once more on me. Things seemed sharper, more crystalline. I felt that I could see where it was all going. Yes.

I had a mission in mind and it would be done. She would help me, and then we would be free of this adventure thing.

We transited out over the first and oldest base site where it all started out, in the beginning. Lyt's workshop was there and waiting. I landed the ship on the place of its genesis and walked over the scrunching sands toward the wooden building that waited in the afternoon sun.

Boron was inside, passive. "Hey! I'm back!"

The robot acknowledged me. "I have done as you asked. Lyt has not returned."

I sighed. "He won't. He has gone to do other things. A shame, I miss him a lot."

What to do?

"Boron, I have a new program for you. You are to return to your home world. In six months you are to transit to Boro. Pay no attention to anything you see or encounter on the trip. Do not interact with anyone on Earth, do not stay on any longer than it takes to transit through. I will program a set of transits that you can use to get there.

"Once there, you help with the search for survivors and you tell your planet and its robots or whatever people might be there. Tell them what you saw and what happened here. I know it isn't much but I have a file for you to download. Share it with them, tell them everything. Try to keep them safe."

I uploaded the contents of my computer to Boron's systems. "That should be sufficient."

I walked through the quiet shop, spotted a thin shaft of sunlight coming through the roof. It would need repair.

"Fix the roof, keep this place in good working condition. It is your home for the next few months. You will need it to work properly. I may visit you, but your purpose will remain the same. Thank you for everything."

It took only moments to step back from the workshop, survey the scene, and know that I would not see this again.

I boarded the ship and thought about what had to happen next. Nyos—no, that was not her name. But in my heart it was her, Nyos was the one

I thought of. This new Oneiros was something more and less. But still my wife.

Oneiros had something very important to her that she had to do here. Perhaps it might help to mount some sort of defense against the peril that was hanging over us. If anyone could do something, she could.

So we transited to Earth, the Roundhouse a slow and beautiful disc floating over the late afternoon world. I turned on the light bars just for the sheer fun of it. It was the fulfillment of a fantasy, to drift over the landscape in a giant silvery disc while onlookers below stood in awe.

I set a course that took us slowly to the east, where the road trailed around like a meandering river. Low mountains and foothills spread before us and the scenery became rougher. Oneiros came to me and we watched the landscape pass below us like an emperor and his queen, and for that time she was like the woman I first knew. She was content to be at my side and to hold her head against my shoulder.

"Michael, I can tell you about my people. I have that knowledge now, so that you can learn something of them."

At last some concrete information. "Excellent. And we should probably transit over so we don't panic anyone else. At least nobody is shooting at us. Apparently the word is out." Some good seemed to have come from the incidents of the conflict.

I had a plan in mind, now that the fighting and spying was probably over. "Let's go to the island. Maybe we can do what I planned now, set things up and get started."

She smiled that wonderful, happy smile I knew. Nyos!

The Roundhouse accelerated to its top speed and we were moving along over hill and valley, our shadow long and reaching to the east. The sun was finally tiring and sinking to the horizon. We would be there in hours.

In our home there was a large and comfortable den. It was a place with pillows and pads in abundance, low tables with ornaments and trinkets of all descriptions. I had not spent any time in it; things were far too busy most hours.

She and I went to the den and made ourselves comfortable.

"Billions of years ago, before the sun and Earth were formed, when this galaxy was young, there were three races that each found that the universe was going to live for a limited time. They were not neighbors in space but had found resonant travel and met each other under peaceful conditions.

"The three races formed a powerful alliance and worked together, traveling the worlds and spreading through the universe. They could travel to other worlds in any solar system they encountered and so they could travel with resonance to all parts of the universe. They mapped and charted, studied and shared.

"It was clear to them that one day this would all end. There were few races older than them and they would sometimes find them and some meetings would result in conflict but others would resolve peacefully. They had the sense of adventure and excitement and lived to see what the universe could offer.

"Once they understood the true nature of the problem, they struggled with finding a means to end it. There had to be a solution. They needed more time to gather all the facts and to find a solution to the end of all things. This became their objective.

"The collection of races called themselves the Zhin Arr.

She paused in the telling, and with a motion a small pitcher and cup materialized. They were ornate and works of art that should have been in a museum. She poured some dark liquid into the cup and gave it to me.

"Thank you, dear."

I settled into a large beanbag pillow and took off my shoes and socks. This was getting to be good. "Go on."

"The issue was that each and every living soul had a different set of experiences and viewpoints. If all such viewpoints were brought together and given a very long time to think and consider, somewhere within it all the solution might emerge. To that end they created a method of recording all the thoughts and feelings of a person and putting them into a pool, a collective of ideas and science. Given time, they felt, they would know how to stop the universe from ending or to make a new universe that could support them all."

"It sounds really ambitious. Did it work?"

"In degrees, yes. One problem was that they needed a place to put this knowledge that would be secure, never lost. They became aware of a method of doing this.

"Old stars, those that have burned out and sometimes exploded, form all the time. These neutron stars are made of very dense, very durable matter. The Zhin Arr created nanodevices that could infect a neutron star and reorder its matter into an extremely dense and powerful computing medium. You would call this material computronium.

"In short, they could turn a star into a living computer of such power and density that it could support the images of minds, allowing them to create a simulation of the universe in such detail and fidelity that it could be used to perform the experiments needed without destroying the universe itself.

"They created many such dense star simulations, and they built within themselves a fine network that recorded their experiences and thoughts. Each and every member of the Zhin Arr was infused with nanodevices that created within their bodies a second nervous system that was unfelt and unsensed, and it stored their feelings and minds and personalities."

A strange feeling went through me. "That... must be how you find me no matter where I am, and how you can hear me call you. I've been *networked*. And my computer always updates my travels..."

She nodded at that thought.

"On their deaths, those recordings would be played into the simulation world and they would be recreated to think and operate a million times faster than the real world. Over the ages, trillions upon trillions of minds were loaded into the stars, and for safety from natural disaster and other forces, those stars were moved into the haloes of the galaxies.

"The ability to control all the forces of nature was at their disposal, but most of those beings within the computronium worlds were not scientists or teachers but average people. Their lives were effectively endless and they desired more than simple existence. Entertaining themselves became very important and so they created worlds of adventure.

"Those entering the simulation worlds, which became more real to the people within, would contribute their experiences and help to give new excitement and depth to those inside. It became a world of dreams, where anything was possible."

It was fascinating and chilling at the same time.

"So your people travel the universe and look for excitement and adventure. Then they bring it back to their worlds and share it with everyone there." I turned more fully to her.

"You've always been interested in my adventures, in seeing that I have a good time. That excites you. That's why."

She nodded briefly.

"So now I get it. You've wanted things to go the right way for me so I could have unusual experiences and do unusual things. So your people are saving the universe but they need something to fight the boredom of living billions of years without end. It makes sense now."

She looked at the floor and said in a tiny voice, "yes."

"Well. Well, that's not so bad. I mean, it's been fun, great. If what I'm doing helps some ancient race to fight off boredom while saving the universe, then everything's fine. I can't have a problem with it."

Her face rose a little and she gave me a look of softness. "I've become more powerful yet also sometimes limited. I cannot say what might happen next. It's all beyond my short experience."

"Hey, this is the real world, not the dream world. Anything can happen. The difference between reality and fiction is that fiction has to make sense."

Her face lifted completely to mine and seemed to light up. "Yes. Yes, it does. Anything can happen in the real world. And we are here, making two lives what they can be."

That was all it took to put me at ease. It made sense and the pieces fit in place. I had stumbled into adventure but it was for a purpose. We could make this work, travel the worlds in grand style and see things that nobody had before. Study the dead worlds, see gorges and waterfalls, maybe even hunt dinosaurs. It was all good.

And through it all, we might be able to save the world from the Archivists, to circumvent whatever they had in mind. Maybe I could set up a factory to make resonators and give them to people so they could spread to other worlds. They would have needs, and it would be a monstrously huge effort. But I could see it, it was possible.

That was what I should be doing on the island, making a resonator factory. Open the universe to humanity and just show them, don't argue or fight. A simple course, one that would be sensible and understandable.

I could do this. I set a course to the east-southeast and we raced toward the island through the night. She and I comforted each other and discussed what we would do next. We spent some time sorting through the treasures in the storage room, making outrageous plans, and just having the most enjoyment we could. This was what life was about.

In the late hours I tired and finally rested. We showered and I scrubbed her and we laughed with simple joy. She prepared the bed and lit candles, made the room so inviting that I anticipated simply resting.

Oneiros drew soft sheets over me as I lay. I heard the wind chimes in some distant place as she caressed my cheeks and kissed my forehead. She was humming again, the soft, entrancing melody of dreams.

I looked up once more before I slept and saw her as if in a haze, the most alluring and wondrous face I could imagine. This vision of her was soft and golden and wrapped in mystery. Peace descended and I slept.

We approached the island's location in this parallel world, and everything was right with my life for once. My sleep had been a wonder. Everything was outlined and sharp now; the world making its sense of permanence and solidity very evident.

We transited over the island and saw that the landing zone was clear. No ships or aircraft could be seen. Oneiros looked at the distant sky and said, "It is safe." We landed.

The island was a wonder. Grass had been planted and trees lined the landscape. The robots had been hard at work and there were buildings and roads completed. I surveyed it all and saw that it was good.

She and I walked slowly around the place, a transformed jewel, and I felt, I *knew* that this was going to work. I had a chance.

The morning sun was sharp and warm and the humidity was beginning to build. It was a sultry day by mid morning, with overcast coming in thickening waves. The lighting was soft and nearly shadowless and the trees tossed slightly in small, fitful breezes.

"We need to put some buildings here, something where we can start manufacturing. This would be close enough to the marina for some heavy equipment and we have a road here now, that makes everything so much easier."

There was a power plant not far from the potential business area. I had ordered that all the power be broadcast, not wired. Each building had a small antenna dish for Internet access on its roof, and I was amazed again at how much had been achieved in the few shorts days since we had left, leaving only remotely sent instructions to the robots and to the bank to cover their needs.

This was an inspiration. With each new sight I was energized and felt the growing hope. At least I had the sense that I was accomplishing something, not simply playing tourist and sniping at enemies.

We planned to get some people here to focus on the upcoming task and to explain what we had in mind to help fight this threat. We might want to bring some recovered hardware here to share with a few people that I felt might be able to study and learn from it. Every bit of knowledge would be one more tool in our arsenal.

At last I had what I felt was most needed. The plan was clear and it would be set in motion immediately.

CHAPTER 19

I t took a couple of days to get everything in shape. The island had been landscaped and cleaned and new buildings were being built on the sites near the marina. A landing strip was laid out not far from it and noise barriers constructed to keep the disturbances to a minimum.

We set up a large arena for a meeting, complete with tables of food and drink. Officials from all over the world were invited and I paid their airfare so they could get here, if they traveled on standard airlines. We arranged a short shuttle flight from the closest airport on the mainland and brought them in by the planeload.

I had a presentation to make and this was the way to do it. And, we had no opposition. Everything went perfectly.

The moment came and I was nervous, but somehow it made little difference. I had been sure to screen everyone for weapons of course. Anything of metal or even ceramic was suspect. Large plastic items were also not permitted. It went without saying that things can always go wrong. I had to be certain that nothing of the sort would happen now.

There was a large stage area lined with tall, thin hemlocks at the end of the arena. The people had had their fill of food and drink and were now hearing the call that had been issued. A huge video wall was behind the stage and shielded from the direct glare of the sun. It wouldn't do to have the video go unseen.

The people began to file into the seating area and the noise decreased somewhat as they sat. The video display was dark.

The presentation was simple. I went for effect and had Oneiros appear on the main stage in a fiery whirl. I don't know how she does it but it is truly impressive. She faced the crowd which had aahed at the appearance and placing her palms together, she executed a bow to them.

The video wall began to show some of the scenes from our travels. Panoramas of the dead technical worlds, scenes of jungles and deserts, remote seas with large swimming beasts; all were presented as we had recorded them.

She began to speak to the crowd.

"This is the most important message you will ever hear. I have been directed to share with you the nature of our campaign and to show you some of the worlds we have seen. What you will hear may determine the course of this planet's history, depending on how you choose to act.

"I present to you Michael Winston. He will explain what this is about."

I transited in above the stage on the floater. It lowered gracefully to the stage floor and I stepped from it to face the throng. My wife faced me and bowed deeply, making me a little more nervous. That made no sense but that's how it was.

"I am here to warn you of a threat to our world, and to recruit your help in fighting it. There is a faction known as the Archivists. They come to technical worlds and they destroy them. Our Earth is reaching a stage where they will be drawn here and eradicate all life, all structures, every work of man. There will be nothing left of this world when they leave, and we must work together to prevent the end of the human race.

"We have little time. There is a plan to help us save at least some part of our world, and perhaps all of it. But I cannot do this alone."

The images changed to Lyt's world, the barren gray place we had visited only briefly.

"This is what happens when the Archivists are done with a planet. I need you all to join together and find a way to prevent this from happening here. And it will."

I spread my arms. "Let me show you what I can offer."

Something kicked me in the chest. I fell backwards in response, struck the stage which was oddly soft and warm.

A short wooden rod stuck out of my jacket with black plastic fletching at its end.

There was a growing noise from the crowd. Oneiros stood looking at me, her mouth wide. She was turning in slow motion, everything was slow. She took the sight in and her head snapped back toward the crowd, singled out somebody. She had never screamed before, but that must be what the sound was.

There was a terrible thundering and a lightning strike erupted from her into the crowd. The flash was too brilliant to bear and it hurt my eyes, which seemed to be intent on sliding away towards the sky. Why was the ground crooked?

Faintly I heard screams from people, lots of screaming. Lightning was striking again and again, and I smelled ashes and burned meat. After a long, long time I felt a cool hand on my face. She was there, and I smiled at her. "My love," I whispered with what strength I had.

Her face was like marble, her expression shifted from anger to passive. "Finest of men, your adventure is done." A droplet of something fell on my skin, like warm rain.

A deeper voice spoke from somewhere. "IT IS DONE."

She stood and began to expand, to grow. She must have been three meters, six, ten. Her skin grew in brilliance and she seemed to transform into a pinnacle of lightning and glass. The honey color was replaced by a terrible violet radiance. I felt a shudder in the ground. A wind was picking up, cold and implacable.

I was cold and numb now, only seeing what my eyes were directed at. She would fix this, she could do anything. And she loved me.

Her arms stretched out and white fire began to grow from her. The noise was fading and everything became more quiet than I could imagine.

She began to transform things, and with an unstoppable expanding ring of cold, violet flame, Oneiros Archived the Earth.

It's odd, I woke in a soft, white place lying on a bed of fine linen. The curious eggshell look was here, soft and rounded walls and the ceiling that gave a soft, almost beneficent light. A faint smell of flowers was here.

My hand went to my chest. I was wearing some thin garment and I wondered if it was a medical gown. But no, that made no sense. I ran my fingers over the breastbone and wondered.

The skin was smooth and flawless. I sat up with care, hoping not to damage any possible stitches or other work that might have been done. I felt perfect. Better than perfect.

Standing, my feet met the smooth, rubbery floor. I began to walk toward the wall ahead, retracing my path of a couple of weeks before. What was I doing here? Did Nyos bring me? What happened on the island?

I felt a mild sense of confusion then, but it passed as I approached the wall and found the faint hexagons on the floor. I stopped and sat then, waiting to see if anything would happen.

Time passed and eventually I grew tired of waiting. I reached my fingertips out and touched the soft, nearly liquid material and felt its clinging, malleable form. I withdrew my hand and watched as the fluid flowed and moved a little.

The form began to grow as I expected, but this was a little different from before. It was sleek and different; beautiful without a doubt but not human at all.

When its eyes opened, it looked at me passively and said, "Welcome to you, Michael."

"Where am I?"

"This place is inside a star, far above a galaxy in the deepness of space."

From what I knew of stars, that seemed unlikely. But if this were the computronium simulation world, then it meant a lot of things. Nyos' people had made this.

"Where is Nyos?"

"Oneiros. She will be with you soon. She is out in the universe."

That statement was telling.

"I have prepared a place for you. Come with me."

Well, that sounded simple enough.

She (and I was sure now that this creature was a she) led me to the wall and a doorway opened in it. It led to the interior of our cabin, which should have been berthed on the Roundhouse. It looked far more inviting than this pale place so I stepped through to it.

The creature looked at me, then spoke softly.

"You have had a wonderful adventure. Take some time here. There is no threat, no danger. All is provided for you, anything you need or want. Learn to live here and your love will be with you soon. Be happy."

The creature retreated and as she did, the opening seemed to shrink until it simply closed like an iris. There was no path back to the white place.

I felt the cloth of the hangings, tested the water faucet. The tank was full, the power cell running. I looked in the refrigerator and it was stocked as normal. Everything but everything was exactly as it should be.

My cursory examination was done and a trip outside was the only thing left. The door opened as it should when I grasped the white ceramic knob with the complex red Chinese knots patterned on it.

Stepping slowly to the fine, grassy field I found that the cabin was on a small hill. The long grass rippled in the gentle breeze and I could smell spring in the air. The few steps from the cabin showed me a small lake just a few tens of meters away. This was the sort of ideal place I would have chosen to park the cabin, given a choice.

Surrounding the lake was a stretch of trees, mostly pine and some others mixed in for variety. I watched a fluttering leaf fall and loop as it strove toward the ground. Birds were calling somewhere.

What was this place? I had no idea what had happened. Wasn't I hurt or something? But this was a good place and my love would be with me soon.

It took a little while for me to find out exactly where I was and what had happened. I took it well, I think. I didn't scream or rave or punch anyone. But the people here are so nice, so perfect. I was in the simulation of course, but the biggest surprise was that *these* were the Archivists. This was the Archive. All the things around me were illusion, no more real than the patterns of binary in a computer chip, with no more substance than the passing figment in a dreamer's mind.

But think. The universe itself is just patterns, just atoms arranged a certain way. What is real? When we have an idea, we may work to make it become solid and real, but it came from that dreamlike space in our minds. It is easy to make our thoughts and intentions real. We do it every waking moment.

So what truly is the nature of reality?

I have traveled here now for many years, lived with my love and had a wonderful time. Some people here choose to create worlds that they can deal with, and to blank portions of their memory so that it is novel, something unknown and exciting. At the end of their simulation run, they awake and have a new lifetime of experiences to look back on and share.

It's all in our minds.

So think about this. It's all data, no more. As you go through your existence, you encounter problems and victories. You find solutions to things and you live with the boredom or excitement of your life. As you are living in that crappy corner apartment in a run down building, washing the dishes after a cheap meal of box macaroni and tuna, you have the unknown ahead of you. Tomorrow could be different and at *any time* almost anything can happen. Life is like that.

So I have my life ahead of me and I have somebody to share it with. That makes it so much more valuable. It's what we share that amplifies us, not diminishes us. Remember that. You have billions of years to deal with the consequences.

Because after all, it's just a dream.